Jake heard the crunch of a twig breaking and flinched at the unexpected noise, then cursed himself for flinching. He could already tell that the sound had been made by nothing but footsteps.

Turning, he squinted beneath the brim of his black Stetson and tried to make out who was coming toward him. A small woman with long, wavy blond hair. She wasn't on the barn staff; that he knew. He angled toward her more fully.

And then, very slowly, recognition began to slide over him. The hair on his arms rose.

It couldn't be her. Not after all this time. And yet the rational part of his brain understood that it could be. He knew she'd moved back to Holley. His mom had been nagging him to see her ever since, but he'd wanted no part of that, no part of her.

Yet here she was.

He went to stone, inside and out. Only his heart kept moving, knocking inside his chest, hard and sure. He didn't want her to look at him.

He was ugly. And she was beautiful.

Praise for *A Love Like Ours*

"Filled with genuine emotion and overflowing with positive examples of faith, the story captures the imagination while warming the heart."—*Publishers Weekly* starred review

"This is the third title in Wade's series about the Porter brothers and perhaps the most relatable. . . . Lyndie perseveres and keeps riding and loving Jake in this inspirational tale about how someone who is severely broken can become whole again."—*Booklist*

Praise for Becky Wade

"Inspirational-fiction fans can jump into the Porter world at any point and enjoy Wade's tales of heart and spirit."—*Booklist*

"Becky Wade creates characters readers will love."—**Lisa Wingate**, national bestselling author of *Blue Moon Bay* and *Dandelion Summer*

"I love finding new authors, and Becky Wade is definitely one to watch. Her debut novel offers romance, laughter, and poignancy. The perfect combination for a night out with you and your book."—**Deeanne Gist**, bestselling author of *A Bride Most Begrudging* and *Love on the Line*

Books by Becky Wade

My Stubborn Heart

THE PORTER FAMILY NOVELS

Undeniably Yours
Meant to Be Mine
A Love Like Ours
Her One and Only

A BRADFORD SISTERS ROMANCE

True to You

A LOVE LIKE OURS

BECKY WADE

BETHANYHOUSE

a division of Baker Publishing Group
Minneapolis, Minnesota

© 2015 by Rebecca Wade

Published by Bethany House Publishers
11400 Hampshire Avenue South
Bloomington, Minnesota 55438
www.bethanyhouse.com

Bethany House Publishers is a division of
Baker Publishing Group, Grand Rapids, Michigan

Printed in the United States of America

ISBN 978-0-7642-3056-1

Library of Congress Cataloging-in-Publication Data for the original edi-
tion is on file at the Library of Congress, Washington, DC.

Scripture quotations are from the Holy Bible, New International Ver-
sion®. NIV®. Copyright © 1973, 1978, 1984, 2011 by Biblica, Inc.™
Used by permission of Zondervan. All rights reserved worldwide.
www.zondervan.com

This is a work of fiction. Names, characters, incidents, and dialogues
are products of the author's imagination and are not to be construed
as real. Any resemblance to actual events or persons, living or dead, is
entirely coincidental.

Cover design by Jennifer Parker
Cover photography by Mike Habermann Photography, LLC

17   18   19   20   21   22   23   7   6   5   4   3   2   1

For Linda Kruger, my literary agent

You're an amazing supporter of my work, my ally
in business, and the one I count on to give me wise
feedback on each and every novel. Thank you!
I'm very fortunate to have you on my team and
even more fortunate to have you as my friend.

Special thanks to Kari, Aaron, Lily, and Claire
for sharing your family's story with me. Your
family inspired Lyndie's family. And your story
inspired me personally. God bless you.

PROLOGUE

Twelve-year-old Jake Porter never felt a hundred percent right unless Lyndie James was beside him.

She was his sidekick. Or maybe he was hers. She was the one with the flair and the imagination. He was the one with the even temper and the sense.

They were a pair.

Jake stood at the edge of the pond, watching Lyndie try to skip a stone. Without bouncing even once, her rock dropped straight into the afternoon sunshine sparkling on the top of the water. Another dud. Her fifth dud in a row.

"Well, shoot," Lyndie muttered. Standing halfway up to her knees in the pond, she bent over to look for another rock.

"Hold still. I'll get one for you." He didn't want her cutting her foot on a piece of glass or a sharp stone. Jake put his boots on just about as soon as he got up in the mornings. But Lyndie only wore shoes when her mom made her. He sort of wished her mom made her more often.

He handed her the two smoothest, flattest rocks he could find. Lyndie was ten. For a girl who could do almost anything else, she was getting kind of old not to be able to skip a stone.

Jake's brother Ty approached them. "Still can't skip one, Lyndie?" He grabbed a rock and showed her how to use her wrist. "Like this. See?"

Jake frowned at his brother, irritated. Ty was only fifteen months older than Jake, but he acted like he knew everything. It annoyed Jake, sometimes, to be the youngest of the three Porter brothers. He was only older than his sister, Dru, which didn't even count. She was just two years old.

Ty sent his rock flying and it bounced off the water four times, leaving circles. Ty had always loved for people to watch him do stuff, so he picked up another rock and did it all over again. "See that?"

"Lyndie doesn't need your help." Jake had already shown her how to skip a rock lots of times. "She just needs practice."

Ty looked at Lyndie and lifted one eyebrow. "I skipped one twenty times once."

Lyndie's eyes rounded.

Anger shot though Jake. "No, you didn't. The most I've ever seen you do is six."

"That one time, at the Millers' house?"

"No."

Ty shrugged and pushed sweat off his forehead with his wrist. "I'm getting hot."

Now that the spring weather had turned warm, the Porter brothers and Lyndie spent their weekends riding horses, exploring, and seeing what kind of orneriness they could get themselves into when their parents weren't paying attention.

"I'm going to jump in," Ty said.

"You're not supposed to," Jake warned.

"Who said?"

"Dad."

"Nah. I don't remember that."

Ty definitely remembered. Their dad had told them more than once that they weren't supposed to swim in the pond without permission or without an adult around.

Jake looked toward their older brother Bo, who was sitting against the trunk of a nearby tree reading a book about horses. Bo was sixteen. Their mom had made him come along to keep an eye on the rest of them.

Jake cleared his throat. When Bo lifted his head at the sound, Jake pointed in Ty's direction. Ty had already started climbing the hill that curved around the side of the pond.

Bo rose in one smooth motion, his book dropping to the side. "What are you doing?"

"I'm going swimming." Ty pulled off his T-shirt.

Bo started toward him. "No you're not."

Jake gave Lyndie a small smile. Tattling on Ty made having Ty for a brother a lot more fun.

Lyndie smiled at him in answer, her brown eyes dancing. A few pieces of long, white-blond hair blew in front of her face. She reached back, grabbed all of her wavy, windblown hair, and brought it over one shoulder. She wore a shirt with a faded picture of a dog on the front and jeans she'd cut off herself to make shorts. Both of her thin knees had Band-Aids on them.

"Ty!" Bo broke into a run. "Don't you jump in."

Ty yanked free his boots. "Of course I'm gonna jump in, Bo. Rolling in or crawling in would take too long."

Bo didn't have a chance of making it to Ty in time to stop him. Jake reached for Lyndie's hand and led her carefully from the water.

Two seconds later, Ty did a running cannonball off the hill. He hit the surface with a loud *ker-splash*.

Bo groaned and stuck his hands on his hips.

Ty came up smiling and laughing. He whooped and used both hands to send water high into the air.

One edge of Lyndie's lips tipped upward. "*Now* how am I supposed to learn to skip rocks?"

"You could go ahead and skip them right into his head," Jake suggested.

Lyndie laughed.

The sound made Jake's heart turn big and warm.

Bo and Ty started arguing about whether Ty should get out of the water now or later. Lyndie watched them with her arms crossed and Jake watched Lyndie.

He'd known her always. Their moms were best friends. Lyndie had a younger sister named Mollie with cerebral palsy, and since Mollie couldn't play with Lyndie, Lyndie spent a lot of time at their house playing with them. Playing with *him* was a better way to put it.

He'd heard Lyndie's mom say that Lyndie trailed along behind the Porter boys. But Jake had never let her trail. He'd always stayed beside her. And he'd never minded.

He had friends at school his own age, but he didn't feel the same way about them that he did about Lyndie. He was a normal kid, but Lyndie? Lyndie was more than that. She could draw amazing pictures. She loved

animals even more than he did. She was the bravest girl
in Holley, Texas. And she had a really good imagination.
Almost every day, she talked him into going on made-up
adventures with her.

She was his favorite person.

"Did you hear that, Jake?" She stilled and turned one
ear up.

"What?"

She looked hard into the area beneath a group of
trees. "It sounds like chirping. Like a . . . a little bird."

Together, they moved toward the sound. Off to one
side, a shrub shook, and beneath it, a black cat paused
to watch them. It had something in its mouth. Before
Jake could take a step in its direction, it dashed off like
a streak of black chalk.

Lyndie followed the chirping and located a baby chick
covered in fluffy gray and yellow feathers. A swipe of
blood marked its chest.

"Oh no," Lyndie whispered, kneeling beside it. "Hi,
little one. Okay. Don't be worried. Did the cat get your
nest? Hi."

Jake dropped onto his knees. The chick's mother had
made a ground nest of mud, grass, and sticks but the
chick had spilled out of it onto the dirt. If the rest of
the chick's family had been here earlier, they were all
gone now.

Lyndie and Jake lived outdoors more than they lived
in. They both knew they ought to leave a baby bird alone.
This baby looked weak and injured, though, and Jake
already knew what Lyndie was going to want to do. For
years the two of them had been able to communicate
without words, like two halves of a circle.

"He's hurt," she said.

"Yeah."

"I'm going to pick him up and take him to the house. If I don't, that cat will come back for him."

"What are you going to do with him once you get him home?"

"Mollie will help him feel better."

Jake didn't see how.

"And then my mom will take him to the wildlife center," she said.

"You think your mom will take *another* animal to the center?" This wasn't even close to Lyndie's first rescue.

"She will when she sees him." She scooped the chick into her palm. "Oh, little guy. Don't worry. I've got you." Then she pulled up the bottom of her T-shirt and used it like a hammock to carry the chick. She ran toward the horses, her legs moving fast.

Lyndie had more ideas than anyone he'd ever met. Some of them were pretty close to crazy, but when she got an idea in her head, she also got real determined about that idea. He'd learned that arguing with her was a waste of time. Keeping his mouth shut and helping her however he could worked better.

"Hey!" Bo called to them before they'd mounted up. Jake and Lyndie waited for him to draw near. "I can't leave yet, Jake. I have to stay with Ty until I can get him out of the water."

Jake glanced at the pond. Ty was doing the back-stroke.

"I found a baby chick," Lyndie said. Because Bo was twice her size, she had to tilt her head way back to speak to him. "I need to take him to my sister and my mom."

"You can't go by yourself," Bo answered.

Lyndie's attention moved to Jake. He saw loyalty and confidence in her face. "Jake will go with me."

"I'll go with her," Jake confirmed. Of course he would.

Bo eyed them.

Next to their dad, Jake respected Bo the most. Everyone said he and Bo were a lot alike, both of them calm and responsible.

"Please, Bo," Lyndie said.

"Okay, fine. Take her straight back to the house and keep her safe. All right, Jake?"

"All right."

Jake cupped his palms. Like they'd done a thousand times, Lyndie placed her foot in his hands and he lifted her onto her horse's back. He swung into his own saddle and they set off at a trot. Lyndie held the hem of her shirt protectively in one hand.

When the trees cleared and pasture opened, Lyndie's horse moved into a gallop. Jake increased his own horse's speed, riding close behind her and slightly to the side.

Lyndie's pale hair spread behind her like ribbons. Her face sharpened with concentration as she leaned forward over the mare's back. Her bare feet balanced on the stirrups. He'd never seen anything else on earth like Lyndie riding a horse. She guided the animals with willpower more than with her legs and the reins.

His dad called Lyndie a natural and that's exactly how she looked, like God had made her to ride horses, like she wasn't afraid even though her horse was racing toward home as fast as it could go.

Jake never could believe it, how such a small girl could

make a horse run so fast. It impressed him. It worried him, too.

Keep her safe, all right, Jake?

That was his job, to keep her safe. And that's what he would do.

She was his favorite person.

The chick lived.

But shortly afterward, Lyndie's family moved across the country and took her away from Texas, from the Porters, and from Jake. The Porters went on about their lives. All the Porters that is, except Jake, who missed Lyndie terribly.

Her departure from his life broke their circle of friendship into two pieces and left Jake with only half.

Lyndie would return one day.

And when she did, Jake would be the wounded one in need of rescue.

CHAPTER
ONE

It had been twenty years since Lyndie James had seen Jake Porter. Twenty years! The bulk of her life. By all accounts, Jake should not matter so much to her still. Her memories of him should not have remained so clear. But he did. And they had. And now she was about to see him again, face-to-face. After twenty years.

Lyndie steered her Jeep around a curve in the road that offered a beautiful view of Whispering Creek Ranch's Thoroughbred farm.

The towering gates and the security guard at the ranch's front entrance had been wildly impressive. The lodge-style mansion she'd glimpsed, jaw dropping. But the horsewoman within her appreciated this vista most of all.

Low green hills framed a picturesque redbrick structure. Behind it, white fences marked off paddocks and pastures that enclosed horses of varying hues.

It was mid-March, a time of year in Texas that could mean tank top weather just as easily as sweater weather.

Today classified as a sweater day, complete with low and moody gray clouds and tossing wind.

The scene made her fingers itch for her paintbrush. If only she could somehow capture the rare pale green of that tree up ahead. Such a bright, almost yellow-tinted green. The color of spring's first leaves . . .

Whoops. She straightened the car's trajectory before running herself off the road.

The guard had given her a map of the horse farm, which she'd clamped against the steering wheel with her thumbs. He'd told her to pass by this first barn, right? She double-checked the route he'd marked. Right. She continued along the paved road.

Jake's older brother Bo managed Whispering Creek Horses. Bo had told her that she'd find Jake at the barn that stabled the racehorses in training. Bo was the one who'd encouraged her to pursue the job opening on Jake's staff and the one who'd asked the guard to let her in.

Jake didn't know she was coming.

Which didn't seem, suddenly, like the best plan in the world. *Hi, Jake. I haven't seen you in twenty years. Do you remember me? No? Can I have a job exercising your Thoroughbreds, please? I'd really, really like a job.*

She'd purposely arrived here at the ranch late in the morning, knowing that by this hour Jake would have finished working out his Thoroughbreds. And she'd purposely come unannounced, because Bo had assured her that was her best strategy. Though he hadn't said why, she feared she knew. If she or Bo had given Jake an opportunity to prevent her visit, he'd have taken it.

The thought made her emotions twist, stupidly.

Jake.

Lyndie still recalled her last morning in Holley, Texas. She and Jake had been two kids shell-shocked with grief. Their sadness had been too deep for tears, even. In the final moments before she'd gotten into her parents' car, they'd simply stood facing each other, saying what could not be said.

Afterward, she'd cried into her pillow at bedtime for weeks. She'd pleaded to God through prayers. She'd written letters to Jake in her kid handwriting on lined notebook paper. For months, he'd written back. Then her letters and his replies had grown more scarce. She was positively certain, though, that she'd been the one to write last.

She'd followed every detail of his career as a Thoroughbred racehorse trainer. One might even say that she'd followed it a mite obsessively. Lyndie knew all there was to know about his professional success and little about his personal life, except what she could glean from the occasional updates passed from Jake's mom to her mom and the Porter family Christmas card photo.

Every year since her parents had moved the family to Southern California, the Porters' annual photo would arrive and her gaze would go straight to Jake. The dark-haired, hazel-eyed twelve-year-old boy had become a star football player as a teenager, then a Marine, then an aloof adult with a scar across one side of his face. Through her mom, she knew that Jake had received the scar in Iraq, when the Humvee he'd been traveling in had been struck by an IED.

Every December she'd stared at that family photo as if she had the power to divine the state of Jake's soul based on a 4x8 glossy from Walmart. She didn't.

Since she'd returned to Texas, Jake's family had been warning her that the state of Jake's soul ranged, due to the Post-Traumatic Stress Disorder he struggled against, somewhere between merely dark to downright terrifying.

Her Jeep crested a rise and the training barn popped into view. It looked as though she was about to have the opportunity to judge the state of Jake's soul for herself, a fact that made her stomach tighten with nerves.

The training barn looked like a twin of the first barn. Redbrick, white trim, a gabled metal roof. Blue pansies brightened the base of the building, and a few horses peered at her through the top halves of open Dutch doors. First class, all the way, which pleased her. Jake, her old friend, worked in a very charming setting.

She slid her Jeep into a parking place. The rearview mirror informed her that the makeup she'd put on earlier still looked okay. The hair was a different story. Uncontainable, as usual. She made her way toward the barn.

Ordinarily, she was not the anxious type. Then again, she didn't usually come face-to-face with someone who mattered after two decades of separation. She had a sentimental streak as wide as her independent streak, and the former was entirely to blame for the fluttery feeling in her chest.

Trust God with it, Lyndie. He's got this.

She let herself inside the building's shed row. A middle-aged male groom stepped from a stall holding a rake. "Good afternoon." He smiled at her kindly.

"Good afternoon. I'm looking for Jake Porter."

"Sure." He propped his rake against the wall and wiped his palms on his jeans while scanning the row. "He was here just a second ago. He must have gone outside to one of the paddocks or the pasture. I'd try that direction, there." He motioned toward the doors at the far end of the row. "Would you like for me to walk you out?"

"No, thank you. I'll find him." This meeting would be difficult enough without witnesses.

Both Lyndie and her mother had been wanting to move back to Texas for years. But her father's steady and reliable job had kept her parents—and thus her younger sister, Mollie, and herself—in California.

Mollie required a great deal of care. From earliest memory, Lyndie had understood that Mollie needed her and that her parents needed her help with Mollie. Lyndie had never, and would never—for as long as Mollie lived—roam far from her sister.

When Lyndie's dad's company had transferred him to Texas a month ago, the entire James family had made the long-awaited cross-country move back to Lone Star soil. Lyndie had assumed she'd see Jake shortly after their arrival and had been bracing mentally and emotionally for the meeting ever since.

Her parents and Mollie had settled into a house, and Lyndie had moved into an apartment. The other Porters had swung by. No Jake. When Nancy had invited the James family over for Sunday lunch three weeks ago, Jake's three siblings had been there. No Jake. When the Jameses had shared Sunday lunch with the Porters again two days ago, still no Jake. It had become clear to Lyndie that Jake was either a hermit, did not eat food, or was making an effort to avoid her.

His rejection stung, and she would've been content to let another few weeks go by before breaking the ice between them. But when Bo had informed her this past

Sunday that a job on Jake's staff had come open, her timetable for ice-breaking had changed.

She no longer lived in Altadena, California. There, she could drive to Santa Anita in twenty minutes and Hollywood Park in forty. Horse trainers were as common as in-line skaters. In Holley, Texas, Whispering Creek Horses was the only game in town. And Jake the only trainer. If she wanted a position as an exercise rider, which she definitely *did*, then she knew she needed to nab the job before Jake gave it to someone else.

She pushed open the door at the far end of the barn.

She'd come to Whispering Creek Ranch to see the very best friend of her childhood, at long last.

And she'd come for the job.

Jake turned up the collar of his brown corduroy hunting jacket, then rested his forearms on the top rail of the wooden fence that enclosed the thirty-acre pasture. His careful attention catalogued numerous things about the colt within, only a handful of them visual. Call it horse sense. Or instinct. Jake understood things about these animals that most people didn't.

A few days ago he'd decided to back off training this particular colt, Desert Willow, and give him more time to recover fully from his arthroscopic knee surgery. Willow liked to complain about his sore knee, which meant Jake needed to freshen him longer before Willow would be ready to resume training. Five more days maybe—

Jake heard the crunch of a twig breaking and flinched at the unexpected noise, then cursed himself for flinching. He could already tell that the sound had been made by nothing but footsteps.

Turning, he squinted beneath the brim of his black Stetson and tried to make out who was coming toward him. A small woman with long, wavy blond hair. She wasn't on the barn staff; that he knew. He angled toward her more fully.

And then, very slowly, recognition began to slide over him. The hair on his arms rose.

It couldn't be her. Not after all this time. And yet the rational part of his brain understood that it could be. He knew she'd moved back to Holley. His mom had been nagging him to see her ever since, but he'd wanted no part of that, no part of her.

Yet here she was.

He went to stone, inside and out. Only his heart kept moving, knocking inside his chest, hard and sure. He didn't want her to look at him.

He was ugly. And she was beautiful.

He'd already lived the life and died the death of the boy she'd known. She wouldn't recognize him now, same as he no longer recognized himself.

She wore jeans tucked into black riding boots. A white shirt under a pale green sweater that hung open down to her hips. Big hoop earrings. Her scarf, which had a lot of green, pink, white, and gray on it, didn't have ends. It just rested in a loop around her neck.

She no longer looked like a Texan. She looked like a Californian to him now.

She came to a stop a few feet away and stuck her hands into the back pockets of her jeans.

He couldn't speak, and she had the grace not to say

anything trite. She only took him in, her head tilted slightly, a half smile on her face, softness in her gaze.

He hadn't felt any emotion forcefully since his accident. Yet the sight of her caused bitterness to blaze through him, true and clean. *You left me behind,* he wanted to accuse. *You. Left. Me.*

It surprised him, the anger turning in his gut like a blade. She'd been a kid back then. Her father had gotten a better job in California, and so they'd moved. It hadn't been Lyndie's fault. But that's not what he was feeling, standing here all these years later. He was feeling a betrayal so strong it nearly took his breath.

"Jake," she said at last, her smile growing.

He dipped his chin. "Lyndie."

"Had you heard that my family moved back?"

"I had." Another pause opened. He felt no obligation to fill it. He'd grown used to uncomfortable silence.

Her features were even and delicate, unmistakably *her*, yet different, too. She couldn't be taller than five foot four. He'd looked down at her when she was ten, but he towered over her now.

Her skin held a light West Coast tan. She still had freckles across her nose, so faint Jake almost couldn't make them out. Her brown eyes were as perceptive as they'd once been, and her hair hadn't changed except in color. It had gone from shades of pale blond to shades of dark blond.

She looked confident and fresh and happy, and he wished like the devil she hadn't come.

"It's great to see you again," she said. "We were pretty good friends once."

"That was a long time ago."

"It was."

However long it had been, it felt like three times that to Jake.

"I heard about what happened to you in Iraq. I'm sorry."

He braced. She'd always been direct. Nonetheless, he hadn't thought she'd mention Iraq. Everyone who knew him knew that he refused to talk about the war, much less think about it. But she didn't know him, did she? She hadn't been around to know anything about him for decades.

"I've been following your career as a trainer," she said. "Congratulations on everything you've accomplished."

"Thank you."

"I can imagine all the work you must have put in."

"Can you?" He didn't see how she could imagine anything about him.

She lifted her eyebrows at his rough tone, not with hurt, only with curiosity. "I have a decent idea of what it's taken to achieve all that you have." Strands of hair lifted away from her temple, carried by wind. She caught them and dashed them behind one ear. "I've been exercising horses since I was sixteen for Southern California trainers."

"California trainers wouldn't know a Thoroughbred from a donkey."

She paused for a half second, then laughed. "Zenyatta was a California horse."

"Born in Kentucky."

"Trained by a Californian."

"Who was born in Kansas."

"California Chrome was born in California," she pointed out.

"Trained by someone born in New York."

Her lips set in an amused line. "I suppose you think only Texan Thoroughbreds and trainers have merit."

"Everything's better in Texas."

"I thought the saying was 'Everything's *bigger* in Texas.'"

"That too."

She crossed her arms loosely. "Be careful, or I might think you have a sense of humor."

"I wouldn't want that."

"No," she answered cheerfully. "I can see that you wouldn't."

He remembered how much he'd enjoyed making her laugh when they were kids. Now, it physically hurt him to see her smile. It reminded him of all he'd lost. "If you'll excuse me, I need to get back to work."

She considered him for a moment. "Sure. I don't want to keep you. I came out today because Bo told me that you have an opening for an exercise rider."

He frowned, vicious words filling his mind.

"If you're willing to give me an opportunity, I'd really like a chance at the position."

His heart set to striking again, like a hammer against a rock. "I don't think that's a good idea."

She didn't step back or break their eye contact. "Why not?"

Since they'd started talking, she'd stirred more hostility in him than he'd experienced in years. He couldn't do this daily. He couldn't be around her for hours at a time, the way he was with his riders.

She reached back with one hand, grabbed and twisted her hair and brought it over her shoulder. The move jarred him because she'd pulled her hair forward just that way when she was young. "Jake?"

"We knew each other when we were kids and our moms are friends," he stated.

"And?"

"It's not enough. I don't hire riders for either of those reasons."

She tipped her chin up. "I don't expect you to hire me for those reasons. I'd like for you to hire me because I'm qualified. I've built a solid résumé. I'll email it to you."

He didn't give a rip about her résumé.

"Bo told me that there's a training track here on the property."

"There is."

"May I come out one morning this week so that you can see how I ride?"

He didn't want her anywhere near his track. "There's no point." Which was true. "I already have someone else in mind for the position." Which was a lie.

"Please?"

What was the matter with him? What was it about her that made him want to help her, the same way he'd wanted to help her at the age of twelve? "I'll think about it. Like I said, I have someone else in mind."

"All right." She studied him, then walked backward a few steps. "I'll see you later."

He held himself still as she turned.

"Oh." After just a few paces, she swung back toward him. Her hair hadn't stayed over her shoulder. It never had when she was a kid, either. "Your colt?" She motioned to Desert Willow. "He had knee surgery, yes?"

Jake inclined his head.

"What are you thinking? Maybe five more days to recover?"

He furrowed his brow. How had she been able to diagnose a horse she'd hardly glanced at? "Something like that."

Her lips curved. "Bye, Jake."

Well, Lyndie thought as she walked back to her car, *that did not go well.* And through no fault of her own. Tall, Dark, and Brooding was not a very friendly person. Not at all.

As soon as she'd come face-to-face with Jake, the worry she'd been feeling had drained away. She'd been too fascinated by him, too busy trying to comprehend that the friend of her childhood had become the tall stranger with the cutting gaze.

Jake was huge. Well over six feet. Of the three Porter brothers, he had the leanest build. He looked like a man who pushed himself hard at the gym. And perhaps indulged himself too little. He was made of muscle, without an inch of softness anywhere. Least of all, his face.

Those eyes! Lyndie blew out her breath. His gorgeous hazel eyes were downright haunted. Tortured, even. Beneath his black Stetson, their green-brown color had all but glowed. He had a straight nose, lips both masculine and beautiful, and a hard, serious jawline that led to a square chin. All of which added up to a face that was almost hard-to-believe handsome, like something she

might give to a fairy-tale prince in one of her picture
books. A perfect face, except for the scar. Flat and pale,
his scar carved the skin from the side of his nose across
his cheek.

Despite it all—the scar and his eyes and his size and
his curt demeanor—he hadn't succeeded at intimidating
her. Well, not much, anyway. She'd spent her whole life
living with the fear that her sister might die. She wasn't
easily intimidated.

Her strides lengthened as she passed by the paddocks
on her way to the parking lot. One crystallizing emotion
had risen within her during her conversation with Jake:
determination.

Lyndie had never been able to stand in the presence
of suffering without experiencing an almost unbearable
inner compulsion to fix it. In some cases, like Mollie's
case, she could do nothing. But she sensed that she could
do something for Jake.

She just didn't know what it was yet. *God? He's a tall
order. You know that, right?*

Lyndie tugged her phone from her back pocket and
dialed. "Bo?"

"Hi, Lyndie. Did you find Jake?"

"I did, and he told me that he has someone else in
mind for the position."

"Figures. He's stubborn."

"Very stubborn. I asked him if I could at least come
out to the track and ride. He said he didn't see the point."

"Hmm." A brief pause. "He's not the only one who
can invite people out to the track. When would you like
to come?"

"Thursday morning? That'll give him two days to simmer down."

Bo chuckled. "Little chance of him simmering down, but Thursday's good. I'll meet you there at seven o'clock."

"I don't want you to go to any trouble."

"Are you kidding? I wouldn't miss this for the world."

"Thanks, Bo."

She wanted a job exercising Jake's horses, and she was going to go after exactly that. For her sake, and for the sake of whatever God might call her to do for Jake. She owed help to the boy she'd known. She hadn't forgotten just how kind that boy had been to her. Or just how much she'd loved him.

CHAPTER
TWO

S o? How did your meeting with Jake go yesterday?"
Amber Richardson, Lyndie's downstairs neighbor
and new friend, planted her elbows on the island that
divided Amber's kitchen from her living room.

"Badly. In fact, *badly* might be too hopeful a word."
Lyndie added a generous squeeze of chocolate to the two
steaming mugs of coffee sitting on the counter in front
of her. After her conversation with Jake, she'd thought
about him the rest of the day, gone to bed praying over
him, woken up to the memory of his face, then passed
most of today obsessing about him.

"He's difficult to talk to." Amber swept a strand of
shiny brown hair away from her face. Her royal blue
scrubs matched the color of her eyes. "I'm sure you did
better with him than I ever have. He makes me nervous,
and I end up babbling to fill the silence. I take it he didn't
offer you the job?"

"No, but I'm not going to let that stop me."

Amber let out an admiring whistle. "Good for you."

"I'm hoping to ride for him tomorrow morning and convince him to hire me."

"You're a much braver woman than I am."

"How long have you known Jake?"

"Ever since I moved to Holley."

Lyndie dosed the two mugs with flavored creamer, then got busy adding huge caps of whipped cream to the coffee and to a kid-sized cup of hot chocolate.

Amber had shown up at Lyndie's rented U-Haul the day Lyndie had moved in. The pretty brunette had picked up a cardboard box and managed to win over Lyndie and Lyndie's parents somewhere between the sidewalk and the top of the staircase that led to Lyndie's unit.

Since then, Lyndie and Amber had spent time visiting whenever they were out in the yard together—Lyndie with her dogs and Amber with her son. Lyndie had brought Amber one of her souped-up coffees during just such a visit, and a tradition had been established. Since Amber got off work early every Wednesday and since Lyndie worked from her home office on the children's books she wrote and illustrated, they'd recently started meeting for "hump day" afternoon coffee dates.

Amber moved next to Lyndie and shook peppermint sprinkles onto their drinks. "It's hard to believe because of the way time has flown, but Jayden and I lived at Whispering Creek for four years. I told you, right, about how Bo's wife, Meg, turned the mansion at Whispering Creek into a temporary home for single-parent families?"

"Right."

"Jayden and I were her first two clients. Is *clients* the right word?" She gave a small shake of her head. "Customers? Guests? Charity cases? That's really what we were. Charity cases." She whisked out a little tray and set the drinks, some napkins, and a plastic container of store-bought chocolate chip cookies onto it. "Meg's so generous. She's like a saint in my eyes, you know? If anyone deserves to be a mother, it's her."

"I talked with her both times I went over to the Porters' for lunch. She seems wonderful."

"She is. Did you know that she and Bo have been struggling with infertility?"

"My mom mentioned it to me."

"They've been trying for a baby for two and a half years. Meg had a miscarriage six months ago."

"I hadn't heard that part." Sympathy pricked Lyndie. "I'm so sorry."

"When and if Meg and Bo finally have a baby, I'll be the happiest person, next to them, in all of Holley. Meg's awesome. I was able to get my degree and a job with Dr. Dean because of her."

Amber worked as a nurse for Holley's beloved family doctor. Even Lyndie had been a patient of Dr. Dean's back in the day.

"Jayden and I just left Whispering Creek three months ago." Amber motioned to the living room. "If this place looks like a starter apartment, that's because it *is* a starter apartment."

"In that case, it's a great starter."

"I agree." Amber carried the tray to the kitchen table.

Their fabulous old brick building had once housed Holley's Candy Shoppe. It was situated in the Victorian section of town, just a half a block from the historic town square. Amber rented out the first floor, which had once functioned as the kitchen and candy store. Lyndie rented out the second floor, originally the owner's family dwelling.

Despite that Amber's apartment did resemble a starter—it was on the bare side and the mismatched furniture all bore the stamp of hand-me-downs—Lyndie liked Amber's half. The apartment reflected its tenant's personality: genuine, casual, unpretentious.

The bay windows that surrounded the table framed a view of Amber's five-year-old son sailing back and forth on a swing suspended from a tree branch. The roomy one-acre lot, almost all of it behind the house, doubled as Jayden's personal amusement park.

Amber leaned out the back door. "Jayden! Your hot chocolate's ready."

In response, he jumped off the swing when it reached its forward-most point, launching himself into the air. Amazingly, he managed to land on his feet without breaking his shin bones in half. The scent of cool, crisp afternoon air followed him indoors.

"Hi, Jayden."

"Hi, Ms. James." He gave Lyndie a high five before they settled around the table. Despite the day's cool temperature, his face had flushed from exercise and the light brown hair at his temples looked sweaty.

"Are you having a good day?" Lyndie asked.

"Yes, ma'am."

She suspected that Jayden used *ma'am* and *sir* on everyone because he knew he needed something endearing to help counteract his mischievous streak and boundless energy. Jayden was a tornado in 5T clothing. A lovable tornado with missing top front teeth and hair that stuck up adorably in the front, thanks to the styling gel Amber used on it in the mornings.

"Did you bring your dogs?" he asked.

"They're upstairs today."

"What's your cat's name again?"

"Mrs. Mapleton. She's taking a nap on my windowsill."

"She's always taking a nap."

"That's very true."

Amber lifted her mug. "Thank you, Dr. Dean, for closing your office at three on Wednesdays."

"Thank *you* for inviting me to join you for coffee," Lyndie said to Amber.

"Thank *you* for bringing the coffee and all the fixin's."

Jayden pushed up the sleeves of his sweatshirt. "Can we drink now?"

"Have I told you guys yet today that I love my job?" Amber asked.

"Yes, Mom."

"Okay, drink."

They took sips that caused them all to sit back and lick whipped cream from their upper lips. The hot milky coffee slid down Lyndie's throat, warming her.

Jayden aimed a white-topped grin in Lyndie's direction. "Have you been doing any drawings?"

"I'm still trying to sketch and develop ideas for the story I told you about."

"The fairy one?"

"Right, the fairy one."

Jayden pulled a disgusted face and began listing all the reasons why he liked superheroes better than fairies.

Lyndie had launched Starring Me Productions, her line of children's books, five years ago to supplement her income as a rider. From the beginning, her central idea had been to make each book customizable.

Parents could put their child's name into the story, but not only that. Because of Mollie, she'd made sure that parents could also choose fonts and sizes to make reading easier for kids with learning differences, as well as a variety of formats for kids with special needs. So far, Lyndie offered ten different picture books on Starring Me's website, featuring everything from pirates to firemen, princesses to mermaids.

Clients all across the country had been emailing her and sending her Facebook messages asking if and when she planned to add a book about fairies to her collection. The people had spoken, and the (little female) people wanted fairies. She planned to have a fairy book available in time for the Christmas shopping season. Since each book took between four and six months to create, she needed to get busy.

Except, for the first time ever, she'd been having a world of difficulty hitting on an inspiration that gave her that necessary flash of excitement. Which had begun to worry her.

Today, with Tall, Dark, and Brooding on her mind, her artistic efforts had totally bombed. Reason number five hundred why it was advisable to have oneself for a boss: Even when you hadn't earned it, you could still treat yourself to a coffee break.

"Have you settled on a plot that you like yet?" Amber asked. "For the fairy book?"

"No. I still haven't figured it out." She lifted her shoulders.

"Beat a person hard," Jayden said, "who, uh, gives up."

Amber broke into laughter. "No, honey. The quote is, 'It's hard to beat a person who never gives up.' Babe Ruth."

"That's a relief." Lyndie sipped her coffee. "I wasn't really looking forward to a hard beating."

Jayden finished the last bite of his cookie and sprang from his seat. His attention, which never remained long on any subject, had been captured by two squirrels bounding across the backyard.

"Honey, here." Amber reached a napkin across the table toward his face. "Let me just wipe your mouth—"

Too late. Jayden had already dashed outside.

"Remember to shut the door," Amber called half-heartedly.

The two women watched Jayden chase the squirrels until they darted up a tree. He peered after the squirrels for a few seconds, then planted his stomach on the swing's seat and used his tennis shoes to push himself in circles, twisting the rope arms of the swing around and around.

"So." Amber regarded Lyndie with gentle interest. She was the sort of person, unlike Lyndie, who could wear gray nail polish, turquoise eye shadow, lots of mascara, and make it all look good. "Let's bring this conversation back around to Jake Porter. I still haven't heard the full scoop."

"What else would you like to know?"

"Was he anything like you remember him being as a kid?"

"Yes and no." Lyndie wrapped both hands around her mug. "Some things about his face were so familiar it was uncanny."

"Like?"

"The way his mouth moves when he talks, the color of his eyes. The whole time we were talking, I was trying to reconcile my memories of him with who he is now."

"What was his personality like back then?"

"He never was a huge talker. He was sensible, way more sensible than I was. Patient and trustworthy. Calm."

"Calmness is a nice quality, isn't it? Not really Jayden's strength." Amber tipped her head toward the boy who'd raised his arms and legs and was spinning wildly as the swing unwound. "What about Jake's scar?" Amber asked. "Were you able to adjust to that okay? I've seen people look away from him when they're talking to him because they're either uncomfortable with it or they're trying to pretend not to notice it."

"The scar didn't bother me. My sister has cerebral palsy, so I guess I'm used to physical stuff that's not so pretty."

Amber nudged the cookies toward Lyndie. They each took one.

"I think Jake's handsome." Amber held her cookie suspended. "They say around town that before his accident he was the best-looking of all the Porter brothers, which is saying something." She took a bite. "They're all gorgeous. If Jake didn't scare the tar out of me, I'd date him."

"Has Jake dated anyone since his accident?"

"No one. Sort of like me. I haven't gone out with anyone in years. I've been thinking lately that it might be time for me to get back out there and go on some dates."

Amber was three or four inches taller than Lyndie, with the sort of curvy figure men salivated over. Her straight brown hair had been expertly cut in a blunt line at her shoulders. It always looked professionally blown-out even though Lyndie knew Amber did it herself. "You're beautiful, Amber. You won't have any difficulty finding men to date if that's what you want to do."

"What?" Amber pulled her head back, genuinely surprised. "You're the beautiful one, Lyndie."

"No!"

"Have you looked in a mirror lately?"

"I'm short and my hair's flyaway crazy."

"Your hair's flyaway pretty." Amber gave Lyndie a look that brooked no arguments. "The problem isn't with you or me. The problem we'll face is with the male dating pool around here."

Amber's use of *we'll* in the sentence struck Lyndie with unease.

"Have you been to church and to Deep in the Heart, the country-western place?" Amber asked.

"I've been to both."

"Then you've seen the selection of available men in this county. I daydream about finding someone cute and Christian. But I already know that if I decide to put myself out there, I'll need to widen my net. I'm a single mother, and I have access to the medical secrets of just about every man in this town. Those are two big strikes against me." She leaned back in her chair and smiled. "If we *are* able to find a good bachelor somewhere, whoever he is, he's going to want you, Lyndie."

"He's going to want *you*, Amber. I'm not the dating type, anyway." Lyndie finished her cookie and brushed the crumbs from her hands. The flavors of chocolate and sugar lingered in her mouth.

Amber angled her head. "Not the dating type?"

"This hair's really annoying me." Lyndie swept her hair into a topknot, extracted a pen from her purse, and speared it through her bun to keep it in place.

"Still waiting," Amber said, "for you to explain why you're not the dating type."

"I've never been that interested in dating," Lyndie admitted. "I've been focused on my riding and my illustrating ever since I can remember."

"And?" Amber prompted, unimpressed.

"I'm really close to my family. They need me."

"And?"

"I'm comfortable around people. I'm enjoying hanging out with you right now, for instance—"

"Thank you."

"—but I'm an introvert at heart. I like being on my own, just me and my animals and my paintbrushes."

"I'm not buying it. Don't you ever miss having a man in your life?"

"Occasionally." Lyndie had lonely days. She had moments, lying in her bed unable to sleep, when she pined for someone to love who'd love her in return. But for the most part, she'd learned to roll with her bouts of sadness.

"Do you want to get married one day?" Amber asked.

"Sure. I just don't know whether a husband is in God's plan for me or not."

"Are you easily attracted to guys you meet?"

"No." In fact, it was unusual for any man to stir her. She got asked out now and then, sometimes said yes, and even more rarely felt sparks. Even when she did feel sparks, though, they started dwindling by the fourth or fifth date. She was always relieved when she convinced the guys to move on.

"Have you had many boyfriends?"

"No. You?"

"My story's the opposite of yours." Amber pulled the cookie box in front of her and closed its plastic lid. "I was a serial dater. You know that girl in middle school and high school who had one boyfriend after another?"

Lyndie nodded. Girls who dated anything with a pulse baffled her.

"That was me. In the end it left me heartbroken and penniless and the unwed mother of a baby whose father's a sociopath."

"A sociopath?"

"I wish it weren't true, but it is. He's in prison now." They both glanced toward Jayden. His football had lodged between some branches. Repeatedly, he threw his soccer ball toward it, trying to free it. Amber's fingers moved around the perimeter of the cookie box, crimping it closed. "When Meg took us in, I knew I'd been given a second chance I didn't deserve. I got myself right with God, and I swore off men. With my lousy track record, I knew that even one attractive guy could mess up my priorities."

"But now you've accomplished your goals."

"Yes. I'm twenty-seven and I'm wondering if I trust myself enough to start dating again. I think I do. I think I'm ready."

Twenty-seven, Mollie's age. Vibrant, healthy Amber couldn't have been more different from her sister. "Then go for it," Lyndie said.

"If I do this, we're *both* going to go for it. I'm not

going to let my eligible upstairs neighbor sit at home with her paintbrushes on Friday and Saturday nights." Amber grinned. "I wish you could see the horrified expression on your face right now. It's comical."

"I'm happy sitting at home with my paintbrushes."

"You're not afraid of Jake Porter. You're not afraid of racing Thoroughbred horses. You're brave, remember?"

"Not about the singles scene. It's my weakness." Lyndie would rather be unattached than deal with the singles scene, as her unmarried-and-thirty status proved.

Amber leaned her forearms against the table, her focus on Lyndie. "How about we make an agreement? In the next three months, we'll each go on three dates."

"With whom?"

"That'll take some figuring out. But we can do it. We'll help each other find guys to go out with. Just three dates, Lyndie. It'll be good for both of us."

"Can all three dates be with the same man, or do they have to be with different men?"

"Are you kidding? The same man would be great. Frankly, it'll be a miracle if either of us can find a man in the next three months that we want to go on three dates with."

Lyndie had come today for coffee and friendship, not to be roped into awkward blind dates with people half as appealing as her Cavalier King Charles spaniels.

"Think of it!" Amber said. "This will give us a reason to get dressed up—to wear high heels!"

"I'm not sold." She'd never understood why women made such a huge fuss over men.

"Fine. I can see I'm going to need to bribe you." Amber considered for a moment. "If at any point in the future you need someone to take care of your animals for you, I'll do it."

Lyndie sat up straighter. When Mollie went into the hospital next—it was a *when* not an *if*, unfortunately—she'd need help with her pets, and she hated putting them in a kennel. "I'd so appreciate that—"

"Not so fast, Miss Illustrator Lady. First you have to agree to three dates." Amber extended a hand so Lyndie could shake on it.

Lyndie eyed the hand, then her friend, whose expression held the glint of challenge. "You're not as sweet as I thought you were," Lyndie accused.

Amber released a huff of laughter. "I'm very sweet. It's just that I've lived long enough to gain some street smarts, that's all."

"I have a feeling," Lyndie said as she shook Amber's hand, "I'm going to regret this."

CHAPTER
THREE

Early morning mist and darkness shrouded the training track at Whispering Creek Horses. Lyndie took a seat in the viewing stand, the metal bleacher hard, cold, and faintly ridged beneath her.

Like everything connected to Whispering Creek Horses, the track before her looked top of the line. It had been equipped with an irrigation system, starting gate, and modern lighting. Two riders were already out, one jogging a horse, the other working his mount at a gallop.

Below her and to the side, Jake stood against the inside rail just next to the track's entrance. When he finished talking with one of his hand-walkers, he turned in her direction and sent her a burning glare.

It was so scathing that she almost laughed. How had he known she was here? She could have sworn she'd taken her seat silently.

He went back to ignoring her.

She studied Jake's profile, wishing she knew more about what had happened to him in Iraq and how it had affected him. She didn't know for sure the extent of his physical injuries. Did he have other scars? Lingering aches?

He wore the same brown hunting jacket and black Stetson he'd worn the day before yesterday. His face remained as unsmiling as it had been then. He didn't appear to share a friendly rapport with his employees, precisely. Yet from what Lyndie could tell, they fully respected him. One of his riders pulled up, listened attentively to Jake's instruction, then set off at a trot. Lyndie's veteran gaze tracked them.

Because of her cross-country move, it had been more than a month since she'd been on a horse. Too long. She never felt more like herself than she did on horseback.

Growing up, she hadn't spent her weekends the way other girls her age spent theirs—playing soccer or swimming or attending birthday parties. During California's racing season, she'd spent her Saturdays and Sundays sitting beside her dad at the nearby horse tracks. During the off-season, she'd passed her free time either drawing horses or sprawled on the living room floor watching them race on TV.

As soon as she'd been old enough, she'd started volunteering at the stables of local trainers. She'd mucked stalls, walked horses, run errands. By sixteen, she'd earned herself her first job as an exercise rider. Throughout college and the years since, many things had changed, but her riding never had.

For her, it was therapy. Riding worked her muscles while quieting the noise in her brain to a single focus: the horse. Whenever she finished a morning of exercising

Thoroughbreds, she felt the way she did after a Pilates class—both energized and relaxed. Mentally reset.

She'd miss her horse therapy if she only did art. And if she only rode horses, she'd miss her creative outlet. Doing both was her way of straddling the best of both worlds. Not to mention, her income from her books plus her income from riding paid the bills.

Today she'd taken an optimistic approach and dressed in what she typically wore to exercise horses: leggings, boots, and a knit top under a lightweight jacket. Her helmet and vest waited in her Jeep if needed.

The sleek and muscular bodies of the horses became clearer as they emerged from the mist, their manes and tails tossing dramatically. Then Lyndie's view of them obscured again as they journeyed away. The sight, so full of mystery and beauty, caused Lyndie's imagination to stir.

She'd already done one book on horses and cowboys and a separate one on a kingdom full of pink and purple ponies. But the fairy-loving girls probably wouldn't mind the inclusion of a horse—no, a *unicorn*—in their book. A fairy and a unicorn could set off together on some sort of quest. . . .

So far, finding her way with her fairy story had been like bumping around in an empty, pitch-black room. But suddenly ideas were shifting through her mind in a kaleidoscope of bright, fresh patterns.

"Good morning."

Lyndie glanced up to see Bo approaching. "Good morning."

Kindness radiated from his gray eyes, marked at the outer corners by laugh lines. Bo had a way of making a person feel comfortable in his presence. He was dressed similarly to Jake, but wore no hat. Though both brothers had dark hair, Bo shaved his close to his skull.

"Has Jake seen you here yet?" he asked.

"Yes. He didn't look too happy about it."

"Interesting." Bo took her measure, half-smiling. "I remember how you and Jake were as kids."

"So do I."

"If we can convince him to hire you, I think you'll be good for him."

"I'd like to be," she answered honestly.

"Then let me see what I can do. C'mon." He led her from the stand to a position along the outside of the rail near where Jake stood. "Hey," Bo said to Jake.

"Hey."

"I'd like to see Lyndie ride. Is that okay with you?"

Bo might be the horse farm manager, but Lyndie knew that as trainer, this track fell under Jake's domain. The employees and these wildly valuable Thoroughbreds were his to command.

Jake looked across his shoulder and met her gaze, his eyebrows drawn down beneath the brim of his hat.

She returned his stare levelly, powerfully cognizant of the difference in their heights. He'd probably forgotten that her small stature and pleasant expression hid a backbone of iron. *Say yes*, she willed him. *Give me a chance, Tall, Dark, and Brooding. Say yes.*

He said nothing. His attention returned to the track.

She peeked at Bo.

Bo appeared unruffled by Jake's gruffness. Entertained, even. He beckoned to a hand-walker. "Juan?"

The man approached.

"Can you bring out one of the horses?"

Juan nodded. "Which one, sir?"

"Jake?" Bo asked.

Still, Jake hesitated. Still!

Lyndie caught herself biting her lip.

"Let's get her up on one of the horses," Bo prodded. "It's the least we can do for Mom's best friend's
daughter. Right?"

Jake exhaled roughly, his breath fogging the cold air.
"Gold Tide," he told Juan.

Lyndie could only assume Gold Tide was the name
of a horse. Victory rang through her. "I'll get my gear."
She took off before Jake could change his mind. All the
way to her Jeep and back, she couldn't quit grinning.

She'd donned her protective vest and secured the chin
strap of her helmet by the time Juan met her at the mouth
of the track with Gold Tide. The black filly stood calmly,
her nostrils flaring to catch the morning's scents.

Jake checked the Thoroughbred's girth strap, then
cupped his hands to offer Lyndie a leg up. With a powerful
sense of déjà vu, Lyndie set her foot in his hold and swung
into the saddle.

"Take her as easy as you can," Jake said. "She'll take
a big hold of the bit. Keep her to an easy gallop."

"Will do." Excitement and an indisputable sense of
rightness, of homecoming, twined within Lyndie as she
and Gold Tide set off together.

Jake wasn't sure what to do to his brother. Shooting
him with a shotgun would be faster but strangling him
with his bare hands would be more satisfying. "What do

you think you're doing?" he growled, his attention riveted on Lyndie as the mist did its best to steal her from view.

"I'm helping you," Bo answered.

"You're definitely not helping me."

"I think I am. You just don't know it yet."

Bo, who usually knew what he was talking about, had no idea what he was talking about. Help him? His brother was dead wrong if he thought bringing Lyndie here would or could help him in any way.

Jake had been telling himself to be glad that he'd gotten his first visit with her out of the way. Since their families were linked, he'd known he'd see her from time to time. Their first meeting should have made him better able to handle future meetings.

It had gone the other way. Her unexpected presence this morning upset him just as much as her first appearance, if not more. Maybe because she'd broken into his private training session uninvited. Maybe because he'd been unable to get her out of his head since Tuesday.

It was ridiculous. Lyndie James had rarely entered his mind in recent years. It was only when something made him remember the first twelve years of his life that he thought of her.

He'd see a lake and recall that she'd been the one to hand him the knotted rope the first time he'd swung out over Lake Holley and jumped off. Dru would talk about shooting, and he'd remember the time he'd shot a bull's-eye at their homemade slingshot target, and that Lyndie had been the one who'd clapped. An acquaintance of his would sprain a wrist, and Jake would recall the time he'd fallen out of a tree and broken his arm. On that day, he'd landed on his back, and Lyndie's face had been the first to block out the sun above him.

And *none* of that explained why she had the power to rattle him now. He was a thirty-two-year-old war vet. He hadn't seen her in a long time and should feel toward her like he would a stranger. He wanted to feel that way about her. It made him mad that instead, her nearness slammed him with a confusing mix of resentment and protectiveness.

Bo came inside the track to lean against the rail next to Jake, casually hitching a boot heel against a rung. "Well?"

"I still want to strangle you."

Bo had the bad taste to chuckle.

Jake had selected Gold Tide for Lyndie because he could depend on the filly to obediently do what Lyndie asked. Even so, worry circled through him so powerfully that he had to set his jaw against it. Exercise riders and jockeys were injured and killed every year when they fell on their necks, took a spill and were trampled, or got hung up in a stirrup and dragged.

As she galloped past, he noted every detail of her posture and balance. All these years later, her light hair still curled and snapped behind her. She still moved with a horse intuitively, which for some stupid reason caused his chest to ache. Her experience was evident in her form. She rode safely, expertly following the instructions he'd given her.

"The suspense is killing me," Bo said.

"I can hope."

"What do you think of her?"

"She's good," Jake admitted.

"Did you know she's been exercising Mark Osten's horses at Santa Anita for years?"

"No." Osten had an excellent nationwide reputation.

"I gave him a call yesterday. He couldn't say enough good things about her. He told me that she's hardworking and reliable. He trusted her with horses he wouldn't trust to other riders. She exercised Unhindered for him."

Unhindered, a young horse full of raw power, had won multiple stakes races. Jake would never want to put Lyndie on an animal as headstrong as Unhindered.

"She'd be a great hire for us," Bo stated.

Jake narrowed his eyes. Lyndie had only been riding his horse for ten minutes and already she had him anxious for her well-being and furious with himself because of it. Ninety percent of him wanted her to leave. The other ten percent had gone rebel. That part wanted her to stay, which scared him even more than the prospect of her taking a spill off Gold Tide. "I'm not interested in hiring her."

"Why?"

"Too much history there."

"Make new history. It's time." Bo stepped forward, bringing them shoulder to shoulder as they both continued to watch Lyndie. "She tried to jockey for a few years, back when she was twenty-three, twenty-four. She couldn't get enough trainers to take a chance on her and had to give it up. Osten told me that if he'd known then what he knows about her now, he'd have put her on his horses."

Jake grunted. "Don't you have work to do, Bo?"

His brother laughed. "Nothing more important than this. You and I both know that good exercise riders are hard to find around here. She's better than good. She's the best prospect you've got."

Jake held his tongue.

"It almost seems to me like God arranged the timing just right," Bo said.

"Or that I'm the brunt of a bad joke." Most of his staff had been with him for the full eight years that he'd been training for Whispering Creek. He rarely had available openings for exercise riders.

"Why don't you just commit to take her on for the season at Lone Star?" Bo suggested.

Resistance sharpened inside Jake.

"Lyndie can start now and continue working for you when we move our horses to Lone Star's barn in April," Bo said. "When Lone Star's season wraps in early July, she won't go with you to New York for the summer because it would mean leaving her family. You'll only be taking her on for a total of four months."

Every spring Jake ran a contingent of horses at Lone Star Park's track, located forty-five minutes from Holley, as well as a contingent in Florida under the care of an assistant trainer. When summer came, Jake took some of his horses to New York to race. In the fall, Kentucky. But Lyndie, who needed to remain close to her sister, would be limited to Texas.

"The season at Lone Star Park is fixin' to start." Bo said. "If you don't hire her, one of the trainers there will snap her up. We treat our horses better than they do, Jake. When our horses get to Lone Star, they're ready. Another trainer might put her up on a horse who's not."

How did Bo know what to say to push a knife into the softest parts of him? He didn't want Lyndie working for him, but he wanted her working for another trainer ten times less.

Four months.

His work had been his sanity for a long time. It was all he did. Training Thoroughbreds to run to their full potential, his only goal. If Lyndie could assist with that goal, could he bring himself to deal with her for four months?

How much damage could four months do?

⌒

"I'm here," Lyndie called as she let herself into her parents' house.

"I'm reading to Mollie." Her mother's voice drifted to her from the hallway that housed the bedrooms.

"Be there in a sec." Lyndie entered the living room. "Hi, Grandpa." She gave the old man's shoulder a squeeze. "How are you today?"

Awkward with affection, he patted her hand indecisively. "All right, I guess. In other words, doing my best."

Her father's father was one of a rare breed: an eighty-five-year-old male who'd outlived his wife. When he'd become a widower two years ago, there had been no discussion about him living independently. Grandma had spoiled Grandpa Harold. Asking him to cook, clean, buy groceries, or iron for himself at this point would have been akin to throwing a babe into the woods.

Lyndie's parents had taken him in, bringing their number of adult dependents to two.

"The Golf Channel keeps running commercials," he stated. "That's all I've seen today. Ads."

Grandpa spent approximately twelve hours a day watching the Golf Channel. When Lyndie's dad arrived home from work in the evenings, the programming switched to Thoroughbred racing and whatever sport happened to be on ESPN. The two of them, who looked like older and younger versions of football coach Jimmy Johnson, sat side by side in a matched set of blue-and-green plaid recliners. Both preferred to wear khakis—Grandpa's far more high-waisted—shiny golf shirts, and gold wedding rings.

Whenever Lyndie's mom forced Grandpa Harold to get out of the house and go to the senior center or take a walk, Grandpa grumbled the entire time.

"If I could figure out how to use this fool control remote," he said, "I'd change the channel."

"The remote control?"

He gestured toward it with disgust.

Lyndie picked it up. "What channel would you like?"

"I guess the O Network will have to do."

Lyndie cocked her head. Talking to Grandpa Harold was a bit like decoding a riddle. "Oprah's channel?"

He reared back, staring at her like she'd offended him. Oops. She'd flunked the riddle.

"Goodness, no, girl. The *entertainment* channel. Oprah? Oprah's not entertaining."

"E! Entertainment Television?"

"That's what I said."

Lyndie found E! for him. *The Soup* was on. She stayed beside him for a few minutes because there were only two ways to commune with Grandpa: watch TV with him or bring him food on a tray.

Beyond the TV, a triangular-shaped wall of windows overlooked a grove of live oaks. The two-story A-frame home her parents had purchased had been built in the '80s on a ten-acre wooded lot by a Dallas family in want of a weekend getaway. Because of Mollie's medical expenses, money had always been in scarce supply for Lyndie's mom and dad. But thanks to the value of homes in Southern California, when her parents had sold their house in Altadena, they'd been able to afford this place, plus put the excess toward a chunk of hospital debts.

"Knickerbockers," Grandpa said.

"Hmm?" Another riddle to solve.

"The Knicks, in other words, the basketball team from New York? That's what they used to be called. The Knickerbockers. You know what I mean?"

"Umm . . ."

"Go on back now and say hello to your sister."

Lyndie placed the remote at his side, then made a pit stop in the kitchen to wash her hands. Germs were Mollie's enemy.

When she entered her sister's room, Karen James lowered the book she'd been reading aloud, one of the Forsythia Castle series. "Hi, honey." She was propped up against a burst of pillows, Mollie next to her.

"Hi, Mom." Lyndie gave her a quick hug.

"We just read the part where Princess Adelaide and her army of giants defeat the goblins," Karen said.

"Awesome." Lyndie went around the queen-sized bed to sit on its far side. She took hold of her sister's hand. "I'm here, Mollie." Mollie turned her head toward Lyndie. "Wouldn't it be cool if the two of us had an army? We could wear golden suits of armor and draw swords made out of crystal."

Mollie listened attentively, her eyebrows raised. Lyndie continued talking so that Mollie could process her nearness.

A tragedy at birth had resulted in cerebral palsy so severe that it had left Mollie blind and nonverbal. She had very little control of her muscles and was the victim of numerous daily multi-focal seizures. To simply get through a day, Mollie required breathing treatments, tube feedings, and a percussion vest to shake her lungs because of her chronic lung disease.

Despite all that, at this very moment, Lyndie could read a smile in her sister's eyes. Mollie's eyes were her main window of communication, and the gentle sweetness there caused a lump to form in Lyndie's throat. She continued speaking through it.

The James family considered it a miracle that Mollie had lived to her current age of twenty-seven. God had somehow sustained her frail body. The only thing Lyndie knew for sure was that He'd used their mother, in part, to do it. Karen's dogged love and optimism had refused to let Mollie go and likewise refused to let her husband or Lyndie fracture under the strain of Mollie's condition. It hadn't come without cost to herself.

At some point during her latter high school years, Lyndie had begun to recognize that her mother needed a degree of mothering. If Lyndie didn't keep an eye on her mom, her mom had a tendency to run herself into the ground. When that happened, then the whole family would begin to come undone. Thus, Lyndie did almost all the grocery shopping for her parents' household and the scrub-the-sinks type cleaning. Her mom managed the rest, except for cooking, which she'd given up for good one famous day in 1997. Since that day, the Jameses had gotten by on sandwiches, frozen meals, or soup at dinnertime.

"Do you remember how old you were when I read the Forsythia Castle series to you?" Karen asked. "Fourth grade?"

"Yep, fourth. You also read the Sugar Spun books to me and the Raven's Flight series."

"That's right!"

"It's all your fault that I ended up painting things like knights and dragons." Lyndie stretched out on the bed, sticking two throw pillows under her shoulder and facing her mom with Mollie between them. "None of my art will ever hang in museums, you realize."

"Stop stalling. Did Jake Porter hire you?" Her mom had a cute new haircut working. Long, wispy blond bangs melded into a style cut short over her ears and in the back. She peered at Lyndie above her pink-rimmed reading glasses. At fifty-six, her skin had lost its tightness, but nothing would ever change her beautiful bone structure or the brightness in her brown eyes. "I'm trying to be subtle, but I can't wait any longer."

Lyndie smiled. "He hired me."

"Yes!" Mom levered herself upward and jabbed a fist toward the ceiling.

Mollie had picked up on the excitement in the air and began to turn her head from side to side.

"Lyndie got a job, Mols! She's going to exercise horses for Jake and Whispering Creek Horses." Karen beamed at Lyndie. "Tell me what happened."

Lyndie detailed the morning's events. "When I finished the set, he simply told me that if I'd like the job for the season at Lone Star, then I could have it."

"And you thanked him and said you'd definitely take it."

"And he said he'd see me Monday morning."

Mom half-leaned over Mollie to press a kiss to Lyndie's forehead. "Such good news. Congratulations, honey."

"Thank you."

"I knew he'd hire you."

"I didn't. When he offered me the job, it looked like it physically pained him to do it. Which maybe it did."

Karen laughed. Her mom might not have found it so hilarious if she'd been there to witness Jake's glower.

"He might not know it yet," Karen said, "but you'll be good for him."

"Funny. That's the same thing Bo said."

"I'm glad he gave you the job. God is good."

"He is." *God is good* had become their family mantra. During their happiest moments they used it, like now, in celebration. God is good! But they used it in their worst times, too, when the faith required to believe those three words felt like hanging off the ledge of a tall building by their fingertips. God *is* good, they'd reassured each other on the many occasions when Mollie had hovered near death.

Lyndie gestured to the discarded book. "Had you finished your chapter?"

"We have a couple pages left."

Mom found her place and resumed reading. Lyndie snuggled up next to Mollie. All three of the women on the bed were small-framed. Not one taller than five four. Mollie wore cotton jammies and socks. Karen wore her usual at-home outfit: silky-looking sweatpants and a colorful Nike sweatshirt. She'd painted her toenails lavender.

The words of the Forsythia Castle saga wound and dipped through the air. The sound of her mother's voice cast the same spell of comfort over Lyndie that it always had.

Karen James was the sort of person you met and five minutes later trusted with your life's story. She'd been an elementary school teacher at one time, but for the past twenty years she'd been a part-time Christian counselor. Some people had jobs that fit them poorly. Not so Lyndie's mom. Her blend of calmness, self-deprecating humor, vulnerability, listening skills, and enthusiasm worked like a balm on everyone—friends and clients alike.

In fact . . . her mother would no doubt have a positive influence on Jake Porter. Really positive. As would Mollie. The notion sent down roots. If humanly possible, Lyndie needed to figure out a way to get Tall, Dark, and Brooding here.

Beyond the room's cheerful yellow walls, two bird feeders hung suspended from a branch. Mollie couldn't see the bookcase that contained her medicines and equipment. Nor could she see the cozy lamps, the drapes, or even the birds beyond her window. But Lyndie and her mom believed that Mollie enjoyed the warmth of the sunlight pouring in and the chirping sound of the birds. And so, in Mollie's difficult existence, there had always been sunlight and birds and a mother, father, and sister who loved her.

CHAPTER

Four

Jake's attention swept the interior of the tent. A group of Marines were playing dominos in one corner, others were looking through magazines, napping, writing.

"Panzetti," Jake said. The dark-eyed, dark-haired corporal from New Jersey was his junior in rank and experience, but not by much. They'd been on two previous tours together.

Rob Panzetti made his way to where Jake stood, near the flaps that served as the tent's doorway. "Where we headed?" He grinned. "Night club?"

"That's on the schedule for tomorrow."

"In that case, how 'bout we go to a golf course? I'm good with a golf club, man. You should see me hit a drive."

Everybody in the squad knew that half the things that came out of Panzetti's mouth were bull. What was true about Rob: He was always in a great mood, and he loved his wife and two kids. "Fine. We'll go golfing."

"I bet you're terrible. Everybody knows cowboys can't golf."

"Cowboys do everything well."

Panzetti laughed, fist-bumping Jake's arm.

Jake's attention caught on Justin Scott. The twenty-one-year-old African American out of Atlanta had stretched out on his sleeping bag, his head and shoulders propped up by gear. He was reading a thick, dusty book about psychology. "Scott."

Scott responded as quickly as Panzetti had, stashing his book and approaching. Jake had come to count on Scott's quiet and dependable personality.

"Get Barnes." Jake moved his chin in the direction of the eighteen-year-old.

The men in Jake's squad called Dan Barnes "Boots" because he was on his first tour. Boots had stuffed earbuds in his ears. His head bobbed to music only he could hear, and his fingertips tapped against his thigh. Scott nudged Barnes' shoulder, and the kid quickly pulled out the earbuds and hurried over. "Sergeant Porter." Barnes' childhood in Corsicana had left him with a Texas accent just as unmistakable as Jake's.

"Stash your iPod," Jake had to remind him.

"Yes, sir."

The kid was green. At times nosy, at times eager, at times worried. Jake had been keeping a close watch on him and would continue to.

"You three will be riding with me." He raised his voice, so the rest of the guys could hear. "Time for patrol."

The Marines immediately went into motion. By the time they'd readied themselves to leave camp, they each *carried nearly a hundred pounds of gear and ammunition.*

"We're going golfing, boys," Panzetti announced to Jake's squad of eight as they strode from the tent. "Afterward, I'm going to try to talk the sergeant into lunch at a real nice place. China and crystal and all that. Except maybe for you, Boots. I'm not sure you'll clean up good enough."

Jake didn't need to tell his Marines that they wouldn't be playing nine holes or eating off china today. They all knew they were headed into the brown Iraqi landscape.

"I'm looking forward to having one of those little cart girls come around and offer me an ice-cold beer." Panzetti's eyes glittered with humor.

They passed the chow hall, a couple of shower trailers, and rows of blue portable toilets. Their desert boots kicked fine brown dust into afternoon heat that felt near to a hundred degrees. Thanks to a childhood in Texas, Jake recognized a hundred when he saw it.

Jake led the others toward a line of HMMWVs, commonly known as Humvees. They were the Marines' workhorses. They served on every part of the battlefield as command centers, troop transporters, weapons towers, even ambulances.

"I call shotgun," Panzetti said.

"Shotgun's mine," Jake replied, as Panzetti well knew. As vehicle commander, Jake rode in the front passenger seat. Scott had been trained as a machine gunner, so he'd take the turret that rose from the center of the roof. Panzetti always drove. Boots climbed into the back.

Jake positioned his M249 squad automatic weapon between his legs and shut his door, which was like shut-

ting himself into a metal box. Except less roomy. Scott, in the turret, sat in an elevated position. His calves and boots jutted down between Jake and Panzetti.

The window on Jake's right framed an image of camp as Panzetti steered them down the gravel road. This afternoon, their convoy included four Humvees, all of which fell in behind them.

They approached a berm strung with concertina wire marking the camp's boundary. Inside a wooden guard tower, two Marines halted their progress and called CLC for permission to let the convoy exit. That done, they waved them forward.

An unmistakable sense of anticipation shifted through Jake, same as always when he left the base. The feeling reminded him, every time, that he was where he belonged, where God had called him to be. He was setting out to do what he'd been born to do.

His father and grandfather had raised him on Marine Corps stories. They'd brought him up to be a Marine, the way that some parents brought kids up to be Longhorns or Aggies. In Texas, even babies wore the orange of UT or the maroon of A&M. Not Jake. He'd had Marine Corps posters in his room. For Halloween, he'd covered his face in camo. He'd read books about Marines. Watched movies about them. When he'd closed his eyes at night, he'd dreamt about them.

As he'd grown into his teenage years, his skill at football had made him quarterback of his high school team and his skill with horses had gained him recognition throughout the southern states. Still, his plan to pursue a career in the Marines had never wavered.

As it turned out, the path he'd chosen for himself

in childhood suited him. He liked everything about it:
the challenge, the structure, even the danger. The Corps
had given him a chance to serve his country, and it had
shown him something important: his own capability.

He'd been in the service for six years and had steadily
been promoted. He planned to do this job over the long
haul. He could see himself as an old guy, sitting behind
a desk at Pendleton.

The dirt road snaked into land marked with rocks and
scrubby vegetation. Jake had grown familiar with this
stretch, as they all had. He combed the scene, hunting
for anything off or wrong, no matter how small. His
main mission today, and every day in Iraq, was to get
his squad home safely.

In the far distance, he could make out two Bedouin
men wearing checked head scarves and long white robes.
The waves of heat rising from the earth distorted their
image—

Jake heard himself scream as he jutted to a sitting
position in bed. The scream hadn't been vocal. It had
torn into the gray space between nightmare and waking.
Silent. Maybe worse for its silence.

His chest panted in and out, his breath choppy and
gasping. Sweat trickled down his face and his bare chest.

Frantically, he tried to use the familiar surroundings
of his bedroom to anchor him. The light he always left
on in his bathroom fell across plain white walls. A chair.
The bowl on his dresser where he kept his change. He
carefully avoided looking at the drawer he never opened.

He was home. In Holley. He hadn't set foot in Iraq in
eight years. *This* was what was real. *This* was the present.

He pressed his palms into the bed on either side of

him and hunched over. His fingers curled in, squeezing up handfuls of sheet and blanket.

He remained in that position for tortuous minutes, minutes that made him curse himself and doubt his sanity. Minutes filled with guilt so crushing his lungs could hardly draw breath.

Jake gritted his teeth, struggling to bear up under it. This time might be the time he came apart mentally. If that happened, he knew he might never be put back together, which only filled him with more dread—

A memory flashed through his mind of a blond woman walking toward him at Whispering Creek. He grasped at the image, like a drowning man would a rope. She'd worn a pale green sweater and a scarf. She'd had compassion in her face, and knowledge of him. She was his oldest friend, the one he'd protected when he'd still been capable of protecting. Her petite body held strength in its graceful curves. Her brown eyes were beautiful to him.

"I heard about what happened to you in Iraq," she'd said. *"I'm sorry."*

The memory of her fought against the darkness in his mind, and gradually, the sharpest edge of misery began to pull away.

Jake pushed from the bed and turned on his shower. While he waited for the water to get hot, he planted a palm against the shower door to steady his shuddering body.

His watch read 4:02 a.m., a small mercy. He knew from experience that he couldn't fall back to sleep after a nightmare. Had it been 12:02, he'd have had many more hours of sleeplessness ahead of him.

He stepped into the stall and hot spray beat against the back of his neck and upper shoulders.

Another memory of Lyndie, this time of her galloping Gold Tide, tried to slip into his thoughts. He blocked it, refusing to think about her any more than necessary.

He had only two goals where Lyndie was concerned: to interact with her as little as possible and to keep her safe.

Whispering Creek Horses took every precaution with their exercise riders. In the past, a few had sustained minor injuries but none had been seriously hurt. There was no reason to worry about Lyndie.

He should be more concerned about himself. He couldn't afford to let a pretty blonde mess with his head.

Except, she didn't mess with your head just now, did she, Jake? Thinking of her helped you.

He cranked off the shower. After pulling on shorts and sneakers, he entered the room in his loft he'd filled with workout equipment. A rowing machine, treadmill, ropes, barbells, a chin-up bar, and weight-lifting benches waited for him. The back-breaking regimen he put himself through every day helped him believe that he still had some small control over his body. Over his life.

After he'd worked out, he'd feel better. Maybe.

He blew out an angry breath.

He'd work out. And then he'd feel better.

He couldn't afford to let a pretty blonde mess with his head.

In the pre-dawn darkness on Monday, Lyndie let herself into the training barn for her first day of work and found Jake waiting for her. He wore his black hat and jeans with a simple gray waffle-knit shirt, pushed up at the wrists to reveal muscular forearms.

It jarred her, yet again, that the boy she'd known had become this hard-bodied, closed-hearted man. No trace of boyishness remained. "Good morning."

"Good morning."

"Are you here to show me the ropes?"

He dipped his chin, a mannerism she'd noticed he often used in lieu of speaking. He took her first to the bulletin board, where he explained he'd daily post his plans for the five horses she'd be riding each morning. Then he spent time familiarizing her with the tack room and educating her about the barn's organizational system. Lyndie listened carefully, committing his words to memory.

They made slow progress down the shed row, stopping often so that Jake could introduce Lyndie to the barn foreman, grooms, and hand-walkers, as well as the horses in training.

She spotted evidence of orderliness everywhere. The barn and the horses were kept rigorously clean. Pails hung neatly outside each stall's doorway. Fresh hay and oats scented the air. No music or TV played. Rather, the atmosphere had a calm and industrious quality to it.

Each time they reached a stall containing one of the horses Lyndie would be exercising, Jake talked at length about the horse in question. He catalogued the animal's breeding, faults and strengths, racing history. The whole time he spoke, his attentive gaze centered on the horse under discussion.

Since there was little hope he'd glance her way during

these monologues, she occasionally watched him out of the corners of her eyes. Everything about him riveted her interest: his voice, the faint mesquite and spice scent that clung to his shirt, his size and leashed power. Most of all, she was fascinated, *utterly fascinated*, by the fact that she could still sense a bond between them. As if by the silken thread of a spiderweb, the two of them were somehow connected.

"This is the last horse of the five you'll be riding." Jake crossed to a stall that overlooked the barn's front yard and the road.

So far, he'd assigned her to two fillies and two colts. Each of the four had been lovely. They possessed excellent conformation, and she'd been able to read their fitness in their musculature. As she caught sight of her final horse, though, her gait stuttered.

He stood tall, at least sixteen hands. His coat gleamed dapple grey, darkening down his legs. His mane and tail fell in unbroken waterfalls of white.

"This is Silver Leaf." Jake propped a shoulder against the opening that led to the horse's enclosure.

Silver Leaf swung his head in Lyndie's direction and regarded her placidly.

Something about the animal, something wordless—an indefinable X factor—caused Lyndie's arms to pebble with goose bumps. She had met and ridden many, many good racehorses. Some of them had been stakes winners, even. But this horse . . .

My goodness. She rested her palms on top of the stall's half-door. This horse had a magical quality about him that called to the dreamer in her and made her heart beat faster. "What's his story?"

"He's five years old now."

A stallion, then. Too old to be called a colt. "Did he begin his racing career at two?" Most horses did.

"He's a unique situation. He was immature at two."

"So you started racing him at three?"

"I tried to campaign him at three and at four without success. I pulled him both times."

Lyndie wrinkled her brow and slanted a look up at Jake.

"He has all the hallmarks I look for in a horse," he said. "He was born at Whispering Creek, and his breeding represents the best of what Bo and I have been trying to do. He's sound. His immune system is solid."

"But?"

"He won't run." For a man filled with shadows, Jake's hazel eyes regarded her with unusual brightness. "During a race, he gallops at the back, and no one can make him go faster than he wants to."

Lyndie studied Silver Leaf. Barns all across America housed Thoroughbreds that couldn't or wouldn't run. Even if a horse had been purchased for hundreds of thousands of dollars, if he or she lacked the ingredient Lyndie thought of as *heart*, then that horse would never achieve glory on the track. A horse had to have the will to win.

"When he was young, Bo and I believed he was full of promise."

"I can see why." Silver Leaf ambled over to them and lowered his regal neck just enough so that Lyndie could rest her palm on his forehead. She stayed that way for long moments, joined to the horse through touch.

"By now, I would have retired any other horse who'd run as poorly as he has," Jake stated.

"Why didn't you retire him?"

"I wasn't willing to give up on him after his three-year-old season. There was something about him that appealed to me."

"What about after his four-year-old season?"

"I'd have retired him if it hadn't been for Meg."

Lyndie waited for him to elaborate.

"Meg shares everything she has with Bo," he said. "But, technically, she owns this whole place. The ranch, the barns, all the horses."

"I'm guessing she's a great owner to work for."

"She is. In all the years I've worked for her, she's only come to me with one request about a horse. She asked me not to give up on Silver Leaf."

The stallion stepped back a few paces and peered at them as if he knew they were discussing him. "Meg loves Silver Leaf," Lyndie guessed.

"Yes. Silver Leaf was a yearling when her father died. He was her father's favorite."

"I see. So Silver Leaf links Meg to her father."

Jake nodded.

"But he won't run."

"No. Meg still hopes, or still wants to hope, that he has potential. But it's my job to be practical."

Lyndie found herself wanting to hope in Silver Leaf's potential, too.

"I told Meg," Jake continued, "that I'd put him back into training and give him two more races. This is his last chance."

Lyndie's life with Mollie had cultivated in her a tender

heart. She'd always been sensitive to those who were weighed down with difficulty, like Jake. Or who were considered a disappointment, like Silver Leaf. "Oh," she whispered.

"Oh what?"

"Nothing." But her *oh* moment had not been nothing. She could see, suddenly, that the trainer and his horse were tied together. If she could improve the outlook for one, she just might be able to improve the outlook for the other. "I'll do everything I can," she promised, "for Silver Leaf."

The horse's dark eyes measured her.

Jake and Bo were excellent horsemen who'd carved out successful careers for themselves in the world of Thoroughbred racing. If the secret to Silver Leaf's refusal to run were easy to diagnose, the brothers would have done so. "Once I've finished riding for the day, is it okay with you if I hang around and spend some time with Silver Leaf?"

A frown line appeared between his brows. People found her odd at times. She was an artist, after all. "If you want to."

"I want to." In order to unlock Silver Leaf's mystery, she'd need to take a crash course on the statuesque gray stallion. She'd start the best way she knew, with observation.

Silver Leaf behaved as if he had more royal blood coursing through his veins than Prince William himself. The big and beautiful Thoroughbred treated Lyndie the way a king would treat a guest who'd come to call. That is, formally and politely.

When she mounted up in the mornings, he stood completely still, his neck arched in an elegant line. He never danced nervously beneath her or showed signs of skittishness. In fact, when other horses on the track or in the shed row exhibited that sort of behavior, Silver looked down upon them with disdain. He allowed Lyndie to lead him through his exercise regimen with indulgent good humor, as if, could he have spoken, he'd have said, *Certainly, Ms. James. I acquiesce to gallop.*

His behavior would tempt anyone to believe that he possessed the right sort of disposition to handle the excitement of the racetrack. Which only made the oddity of his failure as a racehorse more perplexing.

On Saturday, the final day of her first work week, Lyndie cooled Silver by jogging him around the training track. As usual, Jake stood just inside the rail, arms crossed. A handful of other riders worked their mounts around the oval while she rode. It shouldn't be, then, that Jake's gaze never seemed to leave her. Yet, as far as she could tell, it didn't leave her. Ever. Every single time Lyndie cut a glance at him while she was riding, for six mornings in a row, his attention had been focused on her. Day after day, horse after horse. She could only guess that he watched her constantly because she was new and he didn't want her making a mistake with one of his horses.

She peeked at him as she passed by. And yes. There it was again, his attention locked on her. His gaze met hers with the force of a laser.

In response, something hot pinged in her stomach. He slid from view. This type of reaction to Jake had been sneaking up on Lyndie over the past couple of days. The pings and pangs were part physical magnetism, part awareness. Rare and delicious sensations for Lyndie. Also bemusing. It seemed that the girl who was not easily attracted to men had developed a small, uninvited attraction to one particular man.

Tall, Dark, and Brooding? Great choice, Lyndie. He's your boss. He's so solemnly in control of himself that he has no softness left. He doesn't allow himself vulnerabilities. And nor, lest you forget, does he seem to like you in any way.

She didn't know whether to blame the pings and pangs on the fragile connection that remained between the two of them or on the fact that Jake was . . . well . . . gorgeous.

He was. It really couldn't be disputed. He was gorgeous in a ruthless, commanding, scarred pirate type of way. If you liked that sort of thing.

Her lips curled into a rueful smile. She hadn't liked that sort of thing in the past. But surprisingly, she wasn't immune.

How long had it been since she'd experienced a stirring of desire for anyone? Ages. A couple of years at least. It was fun and harmless to . . . *tingle* . . . over someone again. It wasn't as if Jake was in danger of returning her feelings. Or as if this altered her intentions toward him.

She was determined to help him and his horse. The kind of help she had in mind for Jake had nothing to do with Valentine's Day emotions and everything to do with God's power to redeem.

Once she'd finished Silver's cooldown, she brought the horse to a stop near the track's rail. Jake held himself with the sort of stillness that might have been identified as contentment in another man. In him, it reverberated with edgy tension. His face looked drawn with tiredness today, his scar stark. He angled a look at her from beneath his Stetson.

"He's running well." Lyndie smiled and tucked back a wayward wisp of hair.

"Yes."

You're a real chatterbox, aren't you, Jake? "What a beautiful morning. I'm loving the sunshine. It's like California weather." Crisp and bright.

"That'll do for today."

"Okay." Conversational skills were not Jake's strong point. She walked Silver in the direction of the barn.

Every chance she got, she'd been trying to engage Jake in simple conversation. He'd not yet been receptive. Apparently, he did not much enjoy communicating with his fellow human beings. Horses, yes. Humans, no.

Silver's groom, Zoe, waited for them beside the path. Zoe had clothed her lanky six-foot frame in her usual work wardrobe of skinny jeans and a fraternity event T-shirt. Her lime green Hunter rain boots sported floral fleece liners that folded over the tops. With her super long and thin legs and arms, the twenty-two-year-old would never pass for a textbook sort of pretty. As it happened, Zoe possessed something far more winning: immediate likability.

Zoe gave Lyndie her customary salute, took gentle hold of the reins, and guided Silver into the barn. As usual, Zoe had pulled her blazing red hair into a braid that ended mid-back. "Were you trying to talk to Mr. Porter again?"

"Yep."

Zoe's eyes danced against her porcelain skin. "I'm impressed."

"Why don't *you* talk to him more? You like to chat with people."

"Sure, I do. But Mr. Porter doesn't. I answer when he asks me questions and approach him when I have an issue to discuss. That's about it. I mean, I'm filled with respect for him and all. But he's intimidating!"

"Well, I'm going to keep talking to him. It's good practice for . . . life. Don't you think?"

"I do think. If I ever work my way up to assistant trainer around here, Mr. Porter will have to put up with a lot more of my talking." She grinned. "I'm not sure he'd like that. He'll probably never promote me."

"He could always send you to his Florida barn. He wouldn't be able to hear your talking from there."

Zoe laughed, a young and lighthearted sound.

They'd reached the tack room. Lyndie hopped off and went to work unfastening the saddle while Zoe switched Silver's reins out for a halter and lead shank. "Mr. Porter wants me to walk him for twenty minutes. Are you going to join me for his bath today?"

"See you there." Since Monday, Lyndie had spent an extra few hours each day with Silver.

Lyndie finished cleaning the morning's tack, grabbed a granola bar from the warm room, then met Zoe. The horses' bathing station had been set up outside a far corner of the barn. A water spigot connected to a wall-mounted hose that looked like a showerhead on a three-foot-long pole. Two buckets held brushes and supplies. The third waited empty, for use during baths.

Lyndie took hold of Silver's halter and worked on her granola bar. Zoe rubbed the soft oval curry brush into Silver's back, concentrating on the sweaty area where the saddle had rested.

Zoe was a girl after Lyndie's own heart. Over the past days, Lyndie had learned that they'd both been horse-crazy youngsters. Both had started volunteering for Thoroughbred trainers as teens. Both had ended up working for Jake.

At the moment, Whispering Creek Horses employed both Zoe and her brother, Zach. The siblings worked in the early mornings and lived at home so that they could afford to take college courses in the afternoons and evenings.

"Did you know that I used to want your job when I was younger?" Zoe asked.

"You did?"

"Yeah. But since I'm not one hundred and fourteen pounds and five four, that didn't really pan out for me."

"Exercise riding only panned out for me because my father's medium-sized and my mom's tiny."

"I wish I had a medium-sized dad and tiny mom. Instead, thanks to my parents, I was six feet tall by the seventh grade."

Lyndie winced. "Oh no."

"Oh yes." Zoe switched to a dandy brush that resembled the end of a long broom. Expertly, she moved it in short, fast strokes across Silver's body. "I was taller than my middle school teachers, even. I was probably the tallest person in the whole building. I started walking around like this"—she curved her back into a C shape and hunched her shoulders—"hoping nobody would notice. It wasn't that great for my self-esteem. Horses saved me."

Lyndie understood. Animals had helped her through numerous rough patches. "Did you have any horses of your own?"

"Our family only had one old mare. Her name was Sweetie, and she was in her twenties. I'd talk to her and take care of her and ride her every day. A few times a week at least, I'd have a little sobbing fit on her neck, and she'd make me feel better. I'm guessing you know what I'm talking about." Zoe raised one copper-colored eyebrow hopefully.

"I know exactly what you're talking about."

"You see? This is why I like you. I can tell you stuff and you get me."

Lyndie tossed the granola bar wrapper in the trash. "I love your height."

"I don't. You know how hard it is to find tall guys to date?"

"You'd make a great character in one of my picture books, Zoe."

"Seriously? That'd be awesome."

An image took shape in her mind. A willowy fairy who had a way with unicorns. She'd draw Zoe with pale skin, green boots, and long, fiery hair. She'd put her in a backdrop similar to the one that stretched away from them now. Land broken only by wooden fences. Baby wildflowers sprouting in patches. Shades of color ranging from olive to emerald.

This past week, her enthusiasm for her fairy story had been growing each day as she sketched and brainstormed ideas. At last! Whispering Creek had been feeding her imagination the way kids with handfuls of bread feed ducks. When she reached her apartment later today, she'd test out a drawing of a Zoe-inspired fairy.

Zoe turned on the water, waited for it to warm, then aimed the spray at Silver's hooves.

The horse submitted to the ritual of the bath like a monarch accustomed to being cleaned by his servants. So far he'd tossed his head a few times and stepped from foot to foot. Otherwise, he'd barely moved except to prick his ears and listen to Zoe talk. "Aren't you a beautiful boy?" Zoe murmured to the stallion. "Such a dream horse."

"Okay," Lyndie said. "So we've talked all week long about Silver's history." Zoe had been Silver's groom ever since he'd arrived at the training barn.

"Yep."

"And we've covered all there is to cover about his personality."

"Pretty much." Zoe tugged on a bath mitt and started shampooing Silver's coat.

"Why do you think he hasn't had success on the track? What's your best guess?"

Zoe's motion paused as she looked across at Lyndie. "I don't know." She shrugged a thin shoulder. "He's had the same opportunities that Mr. Porter's best runners have had. I'm sorry, Lyndie. I wish I could help you more."

"It's okay."

"I know we're here to prepare racehorses. But he seems pretty perfect to me just the way he is. Are you a perfect boy?" she asked the horse. "You are, aren't you?" She turned her face up, and Silver answered by placing his head next to hers and exhaling a sigh against the place where her neck met her shoulder. Zoe gave his damp neck a few delighted pats. "It could be that he's meant to spend his life over at the barn where Zach works, giving trail rides and making everyone who lives at Whispering Creek's big house happy. If he goes, though, I'll cry buckets. I'd have to . . ."

She didn't finish her thought. In fact, Zoe often left ideas hanging. And Lyndie never could resist supplying endings. Would Zoe have to . . . go to the beach? Fly to Vermont to make maple syrup? Drive to an auction to buy herself a new gray stallion?

Once Zoe completed Silver's bath, the two women escorted him to his stall. As they approached, Blackberry, Silver's next-door neighbor, stuck her head into the row and whinnied in welcome. Silver returned the greeting.

Zoe offered Silver water and fed him exactly what Jake had specified. When Zoe moved on to care for another of the horses under her charge, Lyndie stayed. As she'd been doing all week, she let herself inside the enclosure with Silver and sat on the straw, leaning her back against the wall.

Was Silver meant for a life as a trail horse, as Zoe had just mentioned and Jake had come to believe? Or could it be that racing greatness lived within him still, and someone simply needed to find the key that would unlock it?

If so, there were no horse psychotherapists or mind readers on staff. The "someone" that needed to find the key to unlock Silver Leaf's greatness . . . was her.

She'd spent a good deal of time already observing this horse. But unfortunately for her—and maybe for the horse and definitely for Jake—she'd drawn no closer to unraveling his mystery.

CHAPTER
FIVE

Amber had the *will* to go on a date—but not the *way*. She needed reinforcements.

Thus, on Monday Amber let herself into Cream or Sugar, her most favorite bakery on all of God's green earth. She'd come in search of dating advice. It didn't hurt that the bakery also offered addictive desserts.

Dr. Dean's office was located in a corporate building that sat three plots away from Holley's town square. To save money, Amber typically brought her lunch from home and ate in the small kitchenette at the rear of the office. A few times a week, though, she gobbled down her boring food just so that she'd have time to walk to Cream or Sugar and treat herself to something fattening before the end of her lunch break.

Like all the storefronts on the square, the bakery faced inward toward the central courthouse. The words *Cream or Sugar* scrolled across its picture window in cursive.

"Hi, Amber." Celia Porter, the bakery's owner, greeted

her with a smile. Celia had a petite build, curly brown hair, delicate features, and wicked baking skills.

"Hi, Celia. How's it going?"

"It's going well." Celia bent down to the Pack'n Play behind the counter and pulled a fussing baby into her arms. "It would be better, however, if I could convince Hudson here that he likes to sit and play with his toys."

"Aww!" Amber went into her usual crooning fit over the baby. "He looks so cute today, Celia."

"Thank you."

Six-month-old Hudson had blond peach fuzz for hair, a face worthy of a Gerber jar, and shining blue eyes. Celia had dressed him in a soft and miniature pair of jeans and a T-shirt that read, *Keep Calm and Give Me to Mom.*

Since Hudson's birth, Celia had cut back on her hours at the bakery. Amber still saw her often, though, because Celia tended to work during the hours when Amber stopped by—the middle stretch of each weekday.

Now that his mother had picked him up, Hudson looked as self-satisfied as could be. The twinkle in his eye assured Amber that Ty Porter's son had come out of the womb every bit as confident and mischievous as his father.

Amber peered into the display case. "What're my choices today?"

"All the usual plus iced sugar cookies in the shape of shamrocks for St. Patrick's Day, a flourless chocolate cake, and oatmeal and apricot cookies."

"Just kill me now, Celia. I'd die happy."

Thanks to four years of friendship with Meg Porter, Amber had come to know the entire Porter family. Bo and Jake, of course. But also their sister, Dru, only twenty-two and recently back from serving in the Marines. And their brother Ty, a former professional bull rider. Ty had reconfirmed his wedding vows to Celia about a year and a half ago in a big, happy ceremony. In addition to baby Hudson, Ty and Celia had a six-and-a-half-year-old daughter named Addie.

Amber ordered the cake, a shamrock cookie to take home for Jayden, and a cup of coffee. Celia rang her up while balancing the baby on her hip.

"I was hoping to talk to your uncle," Amber said. "Do you think he'll be coming by?" Danny, Celia's surfer dude uncle, rarely missed his daily twelve-thirty latte.

"He should be here any minute."

Amber lowered onto one of the padded barstools that cozied up to the countertop. "I'm planning to ask him for dating advice."

Celia threw her an amused look as she used a triangular spatula to serve a slice of cake. "He'll enjoy that."

"I need his input. Have you met Lyndie James?"

"I have. Her family joined us for a few of the Porter family lunches."

"She's my upstairs neighbor at the Old Candy Shoppe."

"How lucky is that? Lyndie will make a great neighbor for you, just like you will for her." Celia settled the cake and an antique china cup full of coffee in front of Amber.

"Lyndie and I have agreed that we're each going to go out on three dates over the next three months."

"Interesting."

Amber pretty much felt that if someone *did* kill her while she had this bite of flourless chocolate cake in her mouth, she *would* die happy. She made herself chew and swallow slowly so that she could enjoy it longer.

A group of lady friends entered the shop, and Celia went to wait on them. Amber watched little Hudson wrap his hand trustingly into the collar of his mom's shirt.

Hudson always reminded Amber of Jayden as a baby. Unfortunately, her memories of Jayden at that age were always chased with regret. She'd been young and immature and alone when she'd had Jayden. The first eighteen months of his life had been a nightmare.

When other girls her age had been enjoying their senior years in college, she'd been struggling to earn enough money to feed Jayden and to keep them from getting evicted from their apartment. Whenever she thought about those days now, she did so with a heavy heart, wishing she could have given Jayden a better beginning.

The lady friends had situated themselves at a table, so Celia returned to stand on the other side of the counter from Amber.

"This cake is delicious," Amber informed her.

"Thank you."

It reminded Amber of a Charles M. Schulz quote: *All you need is love. But a little chocolate now and then doesn't hurt.*

"Tell me more about the dating thing," Celia said.

"Basically, Lyndie and I need help. I'm not sure how to find men for us to go out with."

"Hmm . . . Let me think who I might know." Celia held the baby out, grinned at him, then brought him close to kiss him under his chin. He giggled. "How many eligible single men do we know, Hudson?" She brought him back out, then in again. "Oh." Celia lifted her head and stared at Amber. "I just thought of someone."

"For me or for Lyndie?"

"For you, I'm thinking."

Amber set down her fork. "Who?"

"Will McGrath. Have you met him?"

"Nope."

"He's older than you are. What's your upper age limit?"

"Um, I don't know. Maybe thirty-seven? Ten years older than me?"

Celia clicked her tongue, thinking. "I'm not sure, but he may be a few years past thirty-seven."

"Is he even somewhat good-looking?"

"He's a fireman. Actually, he's a *captain* in the fire department. He's tall and ruggedly handsome."

"Suddenly I'm not so concerned about his age."

Ty Porter rounded the corner from the kitchen into the bakery. "Who is my wife calling tall and ruggedly handsome?"

"Will McGrath," Celia said.

A blush rose up Amber's neck. Ty Porter was so crazy good-looking that he always made her self-conscious. Like the sun, she found it hard to look directly at him.

Ty exchanged greetings with Amber, then faced his wife and son. Baby Hudson squealed with happiness and stretched both arms toward his father, who scooped him against his chest. "Will's not taller or more handsome than I am, sweet one." He gave Celia his most irresistible smile. Oh, the flash of white teeth. The dimples!

"He's twice as tall and handsome as you, showboat."

Ty lifted an eyebrow. "He's twice as tall?"

"*Twice.*"

"Whatever you say." He tugged Celia close to kiss her temple. "Did you hear that, Amber? I've learned the three magic words every husband needs to know in order to have a happy marriage: Whatever. You. Say."

Amber laughed. Ty was so famously wild about Celia that he'd bought this bakery for her, then gutted the second floor and built "his and hers" offices for the two of them just so that he could be close to her.

"Ty," Amber said, working herself up to speak a full sentence to him, "Jeannie had an appointment with Dr. Dean last week. She raved about the great job you've done with her mom's financial portfolio." Ty's investing smarts had become a point of pride for the whole town.

"Shoot, Amber. I'm not sure you should believe Jeannie. I wouldn't know a financial portfolio from a modeling portfolio."

"He's so falsely humble," Celia said to Amber, laughter in her voice, "that he's actually vain."

Just then, Cream or Sugar's front door sailed open, admitting Celia's Uncle Danny. "What's up?" He raised a hand to everyone in the place and several of the bakery's faithful greeted him in return. Grizzled, tan, and pushing the age of sixty, Danny was beloved by everyone in Holley, Texas.

"Huddie Potuddie!" Danny said to the baby, leaning over the counter to offer his fist. "You cool?"

Ty encouraged Hudson's fingers to close into a ball, then helped him return Danny's fist bump. "He's cool," Ty supplied.

"I'm glad you're here," Celia said to Danny. "Amber was hoping to ask you for some dating advice."

"Sweet." Danny took the stool two down from Amber's and turned his full attention on her. "I'd be happy to help you out, Amber."

"Let me get you some cake, Danny," Celia said, "then Ty and I will leave you two to talk."

"Good," Ty told Celia, "because I have something I want to ask you about in the, um, pantry."

It sounded to Amber like Ty wanted to kiss Celia in the pantry. But then it had been years since she'd spoken in code to anyone about kissing, so maybe not.

Ty disappeared with the baby. Celia brought Danny cake and a latte.

"Just so you know, Celia, I'm definitely interested in the fireman," Amber said, wanting to make herself clear before Celia dashed off.

"Will comes in once a week or so for coffee and the occasional donut right after he drops his girls off at school."

"He has daughters?"

"Two. They're in high school. Is that a deal breaker?"

He was a tall and ruggedly handsome fireman. "No."

"Next time he comes in, I'll text you." She nudged a notepad in Amber's direction. "Jot down your number."

Amber scribbled it across the page. "I'll do my best to get here when I hear from you."

"Perfect. It'll seem to Will like a happy coincidence. I'll introduce you two, and once he leaves you can tell me what you think."

"I have pantry questions!" Ty called from the kitchen.

Celia winked at them and headed back.

Over cake, Amber explained to Danny about the three-date goal she and Lyndie had set for themselves.

Danny listened, nodding as seriously as a United Nations peace negotiator. As always, he'd dressed in the surfer wear of board shorts and flip-flops. Today, he'd topped them with a faded In-N-Out Burger T-shirt.

"I think it's great, what you girls are doing," he said. "It's always good to work the scene, you know? To inspire yourself to get out there on the market and meet new people. Had you heard that I have a girlfriend now? Oksana Shevchenko?"

"Yes, I'd heard." Holley operated on gossip the way cars operated on gas. "Congratulations."

"She's a widow with married kids. Not much of a surfer or a mountain biker, but really supportive, you know?"

"That's great."

"Just goes to show that there's someone for everyone, even in a small town."

"Hear, hear!" Amber raised her china cup, and he clinked his against it.

"Fellowship Church is having a meet-up event for young singles soon." He paused to sip his latte, then returned it to its saucer. "I think I read that there'd be dancing."

"I love to dance."

"Then be sure to go to the church's website and sign yourself and Lyndie up."

"Will do."

"I must still be a member of five different local dating groups. I'll let you know whenever I see a good mixer on the schedule."

"Thank you. I really appreciate the help."

"There's someone for everyone, Amber." His face crinkled into a smile.

For the first time in a long time, hope for her dating life began to push upward within Amber like a new flower making its way past the dirt. "There's someone for everyone."

Maybe, God willing, even for her.

⁂

The next afternoon Jake walked the row of the training barn, troubled. He'd been driving past the training barn just now, on his way to work with his yearlings, when he'd spotted Lyndie's Jeep parked out front. Irritation had caused him to pull his truck into the lot.

More than two hours had passed since she'd finished exercising his horses. She should be at her apartment by now, dry and warm. Instead she was still here, in a cold barn on a rainy day, so that she could spend more time with Silver Leaf.

Enough already. If she didn't have the sense to go home, then he was going to have to force her.

When she'd asked him if she could remain at the barn with Silver Leaf after work hours, he'd thought it would be a short-term thing. Instead, she'd proven her determination and stubbornness by sticking around every day for more than a week. March was about to turn into April, and still she spent hours sitting in Silver Leaf's stall.

It was bad enough that Jake had to watch her exercising his horses each morning. The whole time she was out on the track, worry clawed at him. And deep beneath the worry, anger.

Since he couldn't understand or explain the anger, even to himself, he focused on trying to talk himself out of the ridiculous worry. She was one of the most qualified riders he employed. His horses were all well-trained.

On the other hand, Thoroughbreds ran at speeds of

up to forty miles per hour. Just three months ago an exercise rider had been killed at Saratoga when he'd fallen and his foot had caught in a stirrup. The horse had dragged the rider, hitting him in the head and chest with his hooves. He couldn't escape his fear that what had happened at Saratoga could happen to Lyndie.

Jake stopped at Silver Leaf's stall. The horse had his head down, chewing hay. It took Jake a moment to spot Lyndie's small form in the dim space. She sat to one side, her back against the wall, her knees drawn up and her arms wrapped around them. She must have heard him coming because she was already gazing up at him. Her lips tipped into a gentle smile.

For a long moment Jake stared at her. Foolish woman, sitting in a horse stall for hours every day. Even more frustrating, looking at him as if she liked him and trusted him. Looking at him as if she believed he was worthy of her friendship and trust. Raw pain gathered in his chest. "I saw your car," he said.

"I'm still trying to get to know Silver Leaf. I'm learning a lot, but I don't yet understand him."

"I never said that I expected you to make him into a runner." The words came out more harshly than he'd planned. "I don't think anyone can."

"I think that I can." She spoke quietly but with confidence. "I hope that I can."

"I hired you to exercise him and that's it."

"I know."

"Go home, Lyndie. It's too cold for you here." A front had moved through late this morning. The rain had grown stronger since he'd let himself into the barn, drumming now against the roof.

"I'm all right." She motioned to the light blue vest she had on over a long-sleeved shirt and her riding leggings.

Was she trying to point out that she'd dressed warmly enough? He wasn't buying. Her hands looked pale and cold to him.

"I'm just going to stay with him a little longer, Jake." She'd put her hair into some sort of bun on top of her head. "If that's okay with you."

He should order her to leave like he'd planned. To do so was certainly within his rights. But for reasons he didn't understand, he found it hard to say no to her when she looked at him like that.

He went to the warm room and made her a cup of coffee using the Keurig. He hadn't wanted to know things about Lyndie, but he'd nonetheless learned a great deal since they'd started working together.

He'd learned that she liked coffee. He knew that her cheeks turned pink when she rode. He'd memorized the exact shade of her pale brown eyes, like the color of Jack Daniels. It took physical strength to do the job she did, and he knew that she had that strength. He'd learned that short strands of her hair always came free of her ponytail. He knew that an angel charm dangled from her riding hat. He knew that she worked hard and didn't complain.

From the cupboard, he pulled free a throw blanket stored there. Meg's doing. As he made his way back to her, Blackberry leaned out her doorway and Silver Leaf leaned out his. The neighboring horses touched noses in greeting.

Jake handed Lyndie the cup of steaming coffee.

Her expression softened with pleased surprise. "Thank you."

Her profile created a perfect line, so sheer and sweet that hunger filled him.

Hunger? *No.* But it was hunger. The realization sent fear slicing into him. He wasn't right or whole. Not good enough for her or anyone. Caring about Lyndie, wanting her, could only cause him misery.

Without grace, he opened the blanket and dropped it onto her knees. "I'm going to give you thirty more minutes." He needed to get out of here and away from her. "That's it."

"Thirty more minutes," she agreed.

His boots pounded the floor as he strode toward the exit. He'd made a mistake, hiring her. It would be better for them both if she went to work for one of the trainers at Lone Star.

"Thanks again," she called after him.

He didn't respond. He desperately needed to make it outside so the rain could wash over him and carry away the longing he'd begun to feel for her.

CHAPTER
SIX

"Jake brought me coffee and a blanket today." Lyndie steered Mollie's chair along the gravel pathway that wound through the woods behind her parents' house. "He brought it with a ferocious scowl, mind you. Really ferocious. I'm glad you didn't see it, Mols, because it would have scared the pants off of you. Still. It was nice of him. And it might indicate that I'm making progress. Then again, it might not."

A beginner would probably find it uncomfortable to speak to someone who never spoke back. Lyndie, though, had had a lifetime of practice.

She'd arrived at her parents' house earlier with a trunk full of groceries. Mom was working at her counseling job today, which meant that no one had badgered Grandpa Harold into an outing. Lyndie had found him, Mollie's day nurse, and Mollie sitting in the living room while the Golf Channel played.

As soon as the rain clouds had slipped eastward and the sun had fought free of the gloom, Lyndie had taken

Mollie for a walk. Her sister couldn't see the water-logged leaves and ground, but she could enjoy the sunshine and the breeze. Plus, Mollie had to be craving a break from golf.

"Jake's a mystery to me." Her memory replayed the moment when he'd walked into the stall with a cup in one hand and a blanket in the other. He'd brought her coffee! He'd covered her with a blanket! Which had to mean he didn't *entirely* dislike her. And yet he'd been as gruff as usual about it. So maybe he did entirely dislike her. "I don't know what's going on in his head. He's closed off and guarded, so I'm not sure how much he still struggles with PTSD. I'd like for him to open up to me, but I have no idea how to convince him to do that." The walkway took them around a long, graceful curve. "I wish I could bring him here because I know you could help him. I'll work on it."

Lyndie had first noticed Mollie's healing magic when she'd been eight and Mollie five. Their dog had been so sick that he couldn't eat, walk, or lift his head. The vets had done their best, but even they had begun to give up hope.

Lyndie had adored that dog. He'd been her first pet. Her parents had purchased him for her after a bout of pneumonia had forced Mollie and their mom to be life-flighted away from the vacation cabin they'd rented for a week one summer.

The situation had traumatized Lyndie. She'd been terrified that Mollie might die and dismayed to have her mother snatched from her. For the next six months, she hadn't spoken. She'd trailed around after Jake wordlessly. At home and at school, she'd gone silently through the motions. A therapist had recommended that her parents give her a dog, and the dog had proven to be far better medicine than anything else they could have chosen. Gradually, her voice had come back to her.

Later, when her dog had been so ill, Lyndie had carried him to Mollie, crying brokenly the whole way, and laid the dog between them on Mollie's bed. Lyndie could still remember praying over that dog, her fingers buried in his soft fur.

Not two hours later, her dog had padded to his dish and eaten his food. Two days after that, he'd been as good as new. Ever since, no one had been able to convince Lyndie that Mollie didn't have a secret superpower.

A lot of *nevers* marked Mollie's life. She'd never walk or speak. She'd never experience a healthy body. She'd never see the faces of her family or the sun setting over an ocean or the cross. She'd never attain any worldly achievement. But Lyndie was certain that God had looked down, had compassion on Mollie, and blessed her with one special ability.

The path led them to a view of a tiny valley ripe with ferns. The trees above formed a ceiling of branches, and the earth below smelled dark and rich with the earlier rain. "Oh, this is pretty. Dad and Grandpa did a great job when they put down this pathway for you." She described the scene to Mollie, all the while picturing how she might re-create it with watercolors.

She envisioned a whole family of tiny people living beneath the ferns. They could have a village made out of twigs. One of those cute, old-fashioned waterwheels. A mansion of stones. The little boy who'd inherited the mansion could ride around on his trained earthworm—

ew. He could ride around on his trained bird, protecting the village from raccoons and humans and floods.

Lyndie typed her thoughts into her smartphone. She'd add it to the computer file that contained ideas for future books.

When they completed their walk, Lyndie steered Mollie's chair in the direction of the ramp her dad had added to the house's wraparound porch. She settled onto a step and pulled Mollie near so that their knees touched. Leaning forward, she tucked the blanket more snugly around Mollie's shoulders and straightened her knit cap. "I love the hat on you, sweetheart. It's purple. You look dashing."

Mollie responded with her version of a smile. Though her eyes didn't look in Lyndie's direction, they were alert and bright today.

"Very dashing." Lyndie kissed Mollie's hand, a hand that smelled sweetly of the peach soap their mom used when she bathed Mollie.

Lyndie pulled back and saw that Mollie had puckered her lips.

Poignant love welled within Lyndie.

It had not been all hearts and rainbows between the sisters since the day Mollie had healed Lyndie's dog. Nowadays, Lyndie wished that it had been, but in truth, growing up as Mollie's older sister had been rocky. In many ways, Lyndie had been an only child, except without the undivided attention. Mollie's needs had always been more urgent than Lyndie's and had required the bulk of her parents' energy.

Lyndie remembered phases during her childhood and adolescence when she hadn't wanted to give Mollie the token daily hug her mom required. Anxiety had eaten at Lyndie whenever Mollie had been admitted to the hospital. Resentment, too, because with every hospital stay, Mollie had taken their parents away. There had been days when Lyndie hadn't wanted to tube feed Mollie or care for her during a seizure or babysit her while their mom did dishes.

From the start, Karen had taught Lyndie that God had chosen her to be the older sister of a sister with challenges. By the time she'd reached her latter teenage years, that lesson had finally sunk deep. She hadn't been the best older sister that Mollie could have hoped for. But Mollie had been the best younger sister. For certain.

An hour later, Lyndie pulled up in front of her apartment, otherwise known as the Old Candy Shoppe. The front door had been painted dark chocolate and recessed directly in the middle of the rectangular facade of beige bricks. Big windows flanked the door on both sides and a mini metal awning divided the first floor from the second. Lyndie had lucked out because all of her upper-story windows were fabulously round-topped.

A stone path steered her around the side of the house, past climbing ivy. Instead of doing what she usually did, taking the exterior staircase to her door, she made her way into the backyard and knelt near the base of what had been a hollow stump. She and Jayden had made it into a miniature fairy house, with an upside-down red funnel for a roof, faux windows, and a door that swung outward, revealing the hole in the stump where his army figures and plastic dinosaurs could enter. Since calling it a fairy house had insulted Jayden's masculinity, they'd ended up christening it a hero house.

Lyndie took the baggie of black-eyed peas she'd swiped from her mom and dad's place and formed them into a curving walkway leading away from the door of the hero house. She lined both sides of the walkway with golf tees, also pilfered.

There. Now she needed to take her muse indoors and see if it would cooperate and transfer itself to art paper.

She climbed the sun-sprinkled stairway to the second story. The moment she opened her front door, Empress Felicity and Gentleman Tobias tumbled out, tails wagging.

Lyndie dropped to her haunches, grinning. "What good dogs! Aren't you little sweeties? Aren't you?" Overcome with joy, both tri-colored spaniels flopped onto their backs and presented their bellies for scratching. "Have you been behaving? You have? Why am I not surprised? If you were any more gorgeous you'd just disappear because God would take you straight to heaven."

She fed them both a treat. Oh, why not live a little? She fed them both a second treat, then threw their tennis balls deep into the yard. They pounded down the stairs, high on the weather, treats, and tennis balls.

Leaving the door open so the dogs could return at will, Lyndie crossed to the windowsill where her ragdoll cat lay snoozing. "How are you, Mrs. M?" She ran her palm down the length of the cat's spine.

Mrs. Mapleton blinked her stunning blue eyes, then tucked her nose under her paw and went right back to sleep.

Lyndie bent to pick up a few throw pillows that the

dogs must have kicked off the sofa. She'd left her apartment in good shape this morning, a blessing, since she didn't have much energy in reserve for cleaning.

The dreamy palette of soft beige and cream accented with sea glass blue that she'd chosen for her open-concept living area soothed her. She liked for her apartment to function as a neutral canvas, perhaps because her paintings and her imagination were always drenched in color—

Her cell phone rang.

She freed it from the pocket of her vest. Unknown number. "Hello?"

A beat of quiet. "Lyndie?" A solemn masculine voice. A voice she recognized.

Her heart did a funny little dip and stutter. "Hi, Jake." He was calling her? This was an unexpected first.

"I just wanted to make sure that you weren't still sitting in Silver Leaf's stall."

The pirate had called to check on her. He must not entirely dislike her. "No. I'm at home. I only stayed thirty minutes after you left, just like," *you ordered*, "we agreed. I'm super obedient by nature."

A slight pause. "Obedient?"

"By nature."

"I've known unbroken colts more obedient than you."

She laughed. He was almost, sort of, bantering with her! "All right. So maybe obedience isn't my strongest suit. In this case, though, I did exactly what you asked."

His end remained silent.

"In fact," she continued, "ever since I started working for you I've been following your instructions carefully."

"Which hasn't come naturally to you."

"I've changed since we were kids."

"Not that much," he stated.

He wasn't flattering her or flirting with her, yet warm pleasure seeped into her just the same. She could get used to this, to chatting with him on the phone.

More silence passed than was customary in normal phone conversations. She always kept a glass dish of fresh flowers on her antique farm table. Their scent drifted to her while she waited. Lilies and roses.

"Have you considered getting a job at Lone Star Park?" he asked abruptly.

All her enjoyment in the conversation rushed away.

"I think that you might be better suited to a position there, working for one of the other trainers," he said.

He was trying to—to *fire her*? Even though she'd given him no reason? "I don't want a job at the track, working for a different trainer." He hadn't called to check on her. He'd called to fire her. The realization pulsed through her like a painful electrical shock. "I want to stay on at Whispering Creek. I've only just gotten started."

No reply.

"You're the best trainer in the southwest." It was true. The jerk! The blind, insensitive villain! "I don't want to work for any of the trainers at Lone Star. I want to keep working for you."

Still no reply. It was like talking to a piece of lumber. Her heart started to race, her emotions to swirl. With effort, Lyndie fought to keep her voice calm and as detached as his. "Has my job performance been lacking in any way?"

"No."

"Then why would you want me to look for work elsewhere?"

"Like I said, I think another position might suit you better."

"No position will suit me better than this one, I'm positive of that. I'm happy with my job. I'd like to keep it." She gripped the phone hard and screwed her eyes shut, praying furiously while she waited.

"I'll see you at Whispering Creek tomorrow morning," he said, curt. Then *click*.

Lyndie pulled the phone in front of her face and growled at it. Disgusted, she threw it onto a chair and stormed toward the back of her apartment.

She'd counted on Bo to help her get her job at Whispering Creek. But ever since Jake had hired her, she'd counted on herself to keep her job. She'd done well for Jake. She'd exercised his horses as skillfully as they could be exercised. He himself had watched every second of it. He couldn't find fault with her job performance, and *still* he'd rather she leave. Which, frankly, insulted her professionally and hurt her feelings personally. She'd been working with Thoroughbreds for fourteen years. He'd only been working with them for eight. What did he know about what position would suit her best?

Except . . . except her sense of fairness wouldn't let her go quite that far. Even at twelve, Jake had been masterful with horses. He knew everything about Thoroughbreds.

He knew nothing about women.

Her apartment had two bedrooms. She sailed into the one she'd made into her studio and lowered onto her stool. Nope, couldn't bear to sit. Back on her feet, she crossed her arms and fumed, staring out the window at her dogs below.

His call had angered her, but it had also sharpened

her purpose. No matter what he thought of her or how often he tried to persuade her to leave, she was dead set on working for him.

Whether or not he felt the same tug of attraction toward her that she felt for him—which, clearly, he did not—she was going to do an excellent job for him. She hadn't done anything to benefit Silver Leaf or Jake yet, but she firmly believed that she could.

She could and she *would*.

Then why, despite the brave turn of her thoughts, were her eyes brimming with tears?

Lyndie spent the following Friday evening exactly the way she preferred to spend her Friday evenings: with a paintbrush in her hand.

The meet-up event at Fellowship Church that Amber had talked her into attending was still more than a week away, blessedly. Which meant that she had a few more days to carry on with her not-very-social life. She'd grown accustomed to a schedule that included her family, riding, art, and pets. She was familiar with those things and content, for the most part, with her undisturbed peace.

She'd changed out of her riding clothes and into even comfier stuff hours ago: yoga pants, slipper socks, and a lightweight burnout hoodie. She perched on her stool and used the tip of her brush to swirl pale pink watercolor paint along the top of a fairy's wing.

Yes, indeed. Undisturbed peace was wonderful! And would be even more so if Jake Porter would quit stealing into her thoughts.

It had been three days since he'd tried to fire her. Since

that time, he'd treated her the same way he'd treated her on her previous workday mornings. In return, she'd endeavored to treat him the same, too. He'd decided to let her keep her job, for the time being anyway, so she'd been polite and friendly to him. She'd tried to pull him into conversation just as often.

Inwardly, though, her feelings toward him had shifted. Before he'd tried to fire her, Lyndie's emotions for Jake had revolved around compassion. She'd felt about him the way she'd feel about an injured lion limping around, doing its best to soldier on. This week, though, the lion had proven that he had teeth. And ever since, she'd been stewing in a peculiar mix of frustration, empathy, hurt, and cautiousness.

If her libido would quit noticing the lion's handsomeness, then all the rest would be a lot easier to manage.

Drawing back, she tilted her head to study her painting. She'd been praying for Jake twice as often as she had before his phone call to her. Again and again, she'd asked God to intervene in Jake's life. She kept telling God that she was ready to do whatever He might call her to do on Jake's behalf. She just needed Him to show her what that looked like.

She dropped the brush into water, picked up a pen, and added a bit more thickness to a unicorn's tail. After capping her pen, she jabbed it into her bun and left it there. She almost always twisted her hair into a topknot while painting. It got the unruly strands out of her way and made a serviceable pen and pencil holder.

The watercolor paper mounted on her easel revealed a scene she'd drawn first in ink. A majestic gray unicorn inspired by Silver dominated the drawing's center. Just beside and behind him stood a smaller chestnut unicorn inspired by Blackberry. A short fairy with wavy blond hair that tumbled all the way to her thighs gazed up at the unicorns fondly, her hands interlaced behind her back. Zoe, in fairy form, hovered in the air in front of the unicorns, her knees bent and feet crossed, her smile broad, her hand outstretched to the animals.

Mrs. Mapleton rubbed against Lyndie's ankle. Gentleman Tobias let out a shuddering snore from his spot on the chair in the corner, Empress Felicity asleep beside him. Both spaniels had, as usual, ignored the perfectly good doggie pillow Lyndie had placed on the floor for them.

Music helped Lyndie's creativity, and she always chose tunes that matched the mood of the piece she was working on. Sometimes happy, sometimes dramatic or adventurous. At the moment, a track that sounded mystical and contemplative played.

As Lyndie considered her painting, she leafed through the potential plots she'd come up with for these four characters. She wanted to write a book about friendship and bravery and kindness—

She gasped softly as an epiphany expanded inside her.

Slowly, she brought her hands up to her cheeks. She looked in turn at each of the characters she'd painted, her pulse skittering excitedly.

She . . .

She may have just stumbled upon Silver Leaf's secret.

CHAPTER
SEVEN

The moment Lyndie finished riding and cleaning tack the next morning, she went in search of Jake. She found him inside one of the training barn's two-and-a-half-acre paddocks, working a black filly on a lunge line.

She knew exactly when he'd registered her approach because his big shoulders hunched beneath his charcoal sweater. Resting her forearms on the fence, she watched him bring the filly from a walk to a jog and back out again. If a horse was beginning to experience leg problems, the transition between the two could reveal the issue first. To a trainer, anyway, who had the experience to spot tiny breaks in form.

Once he'd let the filly come to a rest, he glanced at Lyndie, his expression inscrutable. "What do you think?"

"I think she looks fine. What do you think?"

"I agree." He unclipped the line from the horse's halter. "I thought I saw something this morning, but I'm not seeing it now. She looks good to me." He approached the fence, rolling the line. He'd worn his hat earlier but at some point had abandoned both it and his jacket.

She wasn't used to seeing him without his Stetson. Sunlight glimmered in his dark hair and illuminated the world-weariness in his eyes. Faint lines marked his forehead above straight brows. Without the hat he seemed less protected, since he could do nothing to shadow the scar that crossed his face and ended at the clean, hard angle of his jaw. "Is there something I can do for you?"

His fierce beauty tangled her thoughts for a second. *You'd do best to be careful, Lyndie. This lion has teeth.* "An idea came to me last night. About Silver Leaf."

He waited for her to explain.

"He should have been named Casanova," Lyndie said.

"Casanova?"

"Because I think he's a lady's man." She smiled, excited about her theory.

"I don't understand." He let himself out of the paddock.

She stepped away from the fence and faced him. "His groom, Zoe, is female. Blackberry, the only horse in the barn he seems to have a deep connection to, is female. And now his exercise rider is female." The sight of it on paper last night, a male horse surrounded by females, had jogged the idea free. It made perfect sense to her.

Jake was staring at her, though, like it made zero sense to him. His body language told her she'd stepped too far over onto the imaginative side of things.

Her hunch about Silver was just that—a hunch. But sometimes in life and in horse racing, the future could turn on the knife's edge of a hunch. "When you moved

Silver Leaf from Whispering Creek to the racetrack in
the past, did Zoe go with him?" she asked.

"No. Some employees stay here with the horses in
training, some go to Florida, and the rest come to Lone
Star Park with me. Zoe's always stayed here."

"What about the exercise riders Silver's had at the
track? Male or female?"

"Male."

"His jockey?"

"Male."

It wasn't surprising. Though women had made deep
inroads into the world of Thoroughbred racing, the majority of grooms, foremen, exercise riders, jockeys, and
trainers were still men.

"You think Silver Leaf will run better for a woman
than a man," Jake said.

"The short answer is yes."

"I've never heard of a horse like that."

"Me either. But you and I both know that each horse
is unique." Many of the great Thoroughbreds possessed
one-of-a-kind foibles. "I suspect that Silver Leaf prefers
the ladies."

The sound of a whinny carried past them on a rush of
wind that smelled like cut grass and possibilities. Heavy
awareness pulled between them, almost tangibly.

"You really haven't changed much," he stated.

He was referencing all the crazy schemes she'd chased
as a girl and repeating one of the things he'd said during
their ill-fated phone conversation. "And?" She placed
her hands on her hips and purposely kept her tone and
expression light. "Are you going to try to foist me off on
another trainer again today?"

"Foist? Is that a word?"

"It's a word. Are you? Going to try to foist me off?"

"No."

"Good."

"Not yet, anyway. It's only ten thirty in the morning. I still have time."

Had he just made a little . . . joke?

He started off in the direction of the barn.

Lyndie fell into step beside him. She could clearly sense the mass of his body next to hers—the weight of him, his size, the solidity and power in his muscles.

It came back to her forcefully, how many times they'd walked just like this as children, next to each other. Day after day. Year after year. She'd always hurried along beside him, chattering about their next adventure. She'd convinced him once that it was up to the two of them to find the Dunham family's lost cat. Another time, she'd insisted that they ride their bikes to the tire swing hanging from the old pecan tree to make sure that trolls hadn't taken up residence.

Jake had always listened to her respectfully, had always done his best to support her strange plans. The simple pleasure of walking next to him again the way she once had caused a lump of tenderness to form in her throat.

"What's the long answer?" he asked, staring straight ahead. "You've told me the short answer. I want to know the long."

She drew in a big breath, trying to think where to start. "Silver Leaf strikes me as a regal horse. There are horses who work their way up and take on a regal air once they've won a lot of races. In Silver Leaf's case, it seems that he was born regal. If he's treated that way first, he may respond by winning races."

His chiseled features hardened with skepticism.

"He's dignified," she said. "He treats everyone politely."

"He's well behaved."

"But I've only seen him display what I'd classify as true affection to Blackberry and to Zoe. Zoe told me she's been his groom ever since he came into training."

"Yes."

"He loves her." Love was love, rare and wonderful in all its forms. "What about Blackberry? How long has she been stabled beside Silver Leaf?"

"More than two years. But Blackberry's not running the way she used to. She's had a solid career. I'm about to send her to the brood mare barn."

"Is there any chance she can come with us when we move the horses to Lone Star Park? We can give her the stall next to Silver's, and she can be his lead pony." As lead pony, Blackberry would escort Silver to the starting gate before his races.

He frowned.

"We move Silver and some of the other horses to the track next week, yes?"

"Yes."

"We'll need to bring Blackberry and Zoe when we go."

"Is that all?" he asked dryly.

"No. We'll need to bring the rest of Silver Leaf's home comforts. His favorite kind of hay, his blankets, et cetera."

"Lyndie. You'd be better off with a different—"

"I will not be better off with a different trainer. I'm staying."

He stopped and turned toward her. They'd neared the entrance of the barn.

"I don't think Silver Leaf gives away his loyalty easily." She drew herself up and strove to sound rational in an effort to temper her outlandish suggestions. "With Silver, it has to be earned."

"He's given me his loyalty."

"I don't think so. He's merely polite to you the way he is to everyone."

He pulled back his head, insulted. "I was there the night he was born."

"No offense, but to Silver Leaf you're the guy that stands at the rail. You're not the one that bathes him and feeds him and talks to him constantly the way Zoe does. Also, you're male. You can't motivate him to run."

His hazel eyes blazed with such ferocity that she couldn't help but laugh. "Don't feel bad, Jake. He's not loyal to me yet, either, and I've spent days with him in his stall. I'm hoping to get there with him, but I'm not there yet."

He crossed his arms over his muscular chest, the lunge line dangling from one hand.

"Your horse thrives on familiarity and routine," she continued. "I'm guessing that he'll never be a good traveler, so we're going to have to compensate by keeping all the things he cares about around him when we move him to the track. And we're going to have to surround him with females."

"Which jockey am I supposed to use?"

Me, she wanted to say. The fledgling hope had just begun to take shape in her mind. She wanted to jockey Silver. If she told Jake about that now, however, on top of all her other odd requests, she knew she'd push him over the edge. "A female jockey."

"I use Hank Stephens."

"Hank's an excellent jockey. And he can keep on riding all your other runners. But he's no good for Silver Leaf."

The door to the barn bolted open. At the sudden noise, Jake threw an arm in front of her instinctively, as if to protect her.

One of the grooms exited, nodding to them with a slightly confused expression.

Lyndie looked up at Jake. Their eyes met for a brief, scorching instant before his face went blank. He stepped quickly away from her. At his side, his free hand curled, then flexed.

She wished she could ask him about Iraq. But the trauma that had changed him was also the trauma that separated them. She could all but see him wrapping his isolation around himself like a cloak.

"Your ideas about Silver Leaf?" he asked.

"Yes?"

He presented her with his back and stalked away. "I'll think about them."

※

"Will?"

Will McGrath looked up from where he sat at his usual table at Cream or Sugar. Celia Porter, the bakery's owner, stood nearby alongside a pretty brunette.

He rose to his feet.

"I'd like you to meet Amber Richardson," Celia said. "Amber, this is Will McGrath."

He extended his hand and Amber shook it. "Nice to meet you," he said.

"It's nice to meet you, too." Amber's big blue eyes were surrounded by the longest, darkest lashes he'd ever seen.

The link of their hands broke, and they straightened apart.

"Amber lives in the Old Candy Shoppe building," Celia told him. "She mentioned to me the other day that she might like to have a deck put in at some point. I was just telling her that you build decks on the days when you're not working for the fire department."

"Right." He pulled his wallet from his back pocket and handed Amber one of his cards. "I'd be happy to come by and give you an estimate any time."

"Great. Thank you."

"More coffee, Will?" Celia asked.

"I'd like that."

"Sit, sit," Celia waved Amber to the table next to his. "I'll bring coffee to you both." They settled into chairs. Their side-by-side tables kept them in easy speaking distance. Since Will had already given her his card, he wasn't sure what else to talk to her about. It was eight thirty on a Monday morning, and while Amber was attractive and seemed nice enough, he'd been enjoying the peace and quiet of sitting by himself. Small talk had never been his strong suit.

"I want one of these, Mom." A young boy turned in Amber's direction, his finger pushed against the glass display case, pointing at the chocolate glazed donuts.

"When Mrs. Porter comes back," Amber answered, "ask her nicely if you may have a chocolate glazed."

"With sprinkles."

"Fine."

"Is this your son?" Will asked. She looked too young to have a child this kid's age.

"Yes, this is Jayden. He's five and a half. Jayden, this is Mr. McGrath."

"Hello, sir."

"Hi."

Celia hurried over with a coffee pot, then made a return trip with a chocolate glazed donut with sprinkles for Jayden and a slice of banana nut bread for Amber. Jayden took a seat beside his mom, swinging his legs and drinking milk through a straw from a little carton.

Amber caught Will's eye, her expression friendly. "So tell me about some of the decks you've been working on lately."

He did so. And before he knew it she steered the conversation to his work with the fire department and mutual Holley friends.

She was surprisingly easy to talk to. Outgoing. With a smile that lit up the whole room.

"What kind of work do you do?" he asked.

He found it hard to look away from her as she told him about her job as a nurse for Dr. Dean. There was something very interesting about her, something warm and genuine. And that smile . . . I mean, it *really* lit up the room. On the other hand, he didn't want to look at her too long because she might think he was a creepy old man and get the wrong idea.

Good grief. Self-conscious, he stared at the watch his daughters had given him for a few seconds before looking back up. Next to Amber, he felt every one of his forty years.

Amber had to be at least a decade younger than he was, and he'd guess that she'd had Jayden in her very early twenties. His ex-wife, Michelle, had been twenty-one when their oldest daughter, Madison, had been born. He'd been twenty-four at the time. Michelle had split at age twenty-five to go and experience all that life has to offer twenty-five-year-old women who aren't wives and mothers. She'd left him with a four-year-old and a two-year-old.

Had the early baby plan worked out better for Amber than it had for him? He wondered whether Jayden's father had stuck around, whether Amber was still in love with him and happy. She wasn't wearing a wedding ring, but she might be married. Not all married women wore rings every minute of every day.

Jayden pushed to his feet, clearly bored out of his skull by the adult conversation. "Mom?" he broke in. "Is it time to go?"

"Don't interrupt me, Jayden," she said patiently. "If you have something to say put your arm here"—she laid his hand on her forearm—"and I'll know you want to tell me something."

"Yes, ma'am."

"So anyway," she said to Will, "I—"

"I want to tell you that *I'm ready to go*," Jayden said urgently.

"—I really enjoy working at the doctor's office," Amber continued as she stood and pushed in her chair. "Maybe one day soon I'll be able to afford a deck."

Will stood, too.

"I have to head out so that I can get Jayden to daycare and make it to work on time."

"Sure."

Jayden began to tug on Amber's forearm.

"It was nice meeting you, Will."

"Likewise."

"Have a good day." She tossed their trash before Jayden pulled her through the door and they disappeared.

Will stood there, staring at the place where she'd been. He regretted his grumpy reaction when he'd first realized that he needed to make conversation with her. He'd forgotten how nice it could be to visit with someone, without any goal to it other than that—to visit. Maybe he wasn't totally lousy at small talk, after all. Or maybe Amber was just really good at it.

The guys at the station teased him about his sorry dating life, with good reason. He pulled his keys free as he made his way outdoors to his aging Chevy Tahoe.

Since Michelle left, it had pretty much taken all he had in the way of time, attention, and money to raise his girls. Whenever he'd made an effort to go out with someone, he'd been aware the whole time of how dull he was. He was a father whose faith was important to him. He didn't want to party, go to clubs, get drunk, or sleep with people just for the heck of it. The non-Christian women he'd taken out had wanted at least one of those things; the Christian ones had wanted to marry him immediately, which had scared him twice as much.

He was rusty at relationships. Even so, if Amber had been older and unmarried, he'd have been tempted to ask her out.

He rubbed the side of his forehead, trying to understand what had just happened to him. He'd come to Cream or Sugar for coffee. But those blue eyes and that smile of Amber's had dazed him a little, had made him think about things—like dating—that he hadn't thought about in years.

≈V

"Will's handsome, Lyndie. He has dark blond hair and gray-blue eyes, the kind that tip down at the outside corners. You know? Bedroom eyes?"

"I sincerely like bedroom eyes," Lyndie put forward.

"Me too. Will's eyes make him look a little bit sad or vulnerable or something."

Amber had texted Lyndie earlier in the day, requesting a coffee meeting, despite that it was Monday and their usually scheduled coffee meetings occurred on Wednesdays. Lovely warm breezes stirred the late afternoon air, so they'd taken Amber's kitchen chairs onto the small flagstone back patio of the Old Candy Shoppe. Jayden had his buddy Bryce over for a playdate. The two were sprawled on their stomachs in front of the hero house, playing with plastic army men.

"I'm guessing that Will's age didn't bother you?" Lyndie asked.

"No. I mean, if he's forty, he's like Ewan McGregor at forty." Amber went on to compliment Will's manners, his fitness, his height, and his professions of fire department captain and deck builder.

Lyndie sipped from her mug. The whipped cream registered first, followed by a decadent slide of hot, milky coffee flavored with chocolate.

A tiny dollop of cream stuck to the corner of Amber's lip when she lowered her own mug.

"You have a little whipped cream . . ." Lyndie indicated the spot.

Amber used one of the leftover Valentine's Day napkins she'd brought out to wipe away the cream. "Thank you. We've officially become good friends, Lyndie, if you're willing to tell me I have food on my face."

"Officially. You can count on me to be extra quick about telling you should you ever have food on your face in front of Will."

"I'm not sure if I'll see him again." Amber sighed. "I'm cautiously interested, but I'm not sure if he feels the same. And even if he does, I don't know when we'll cross paths."

"Well, let's think about this practically." Lyndie watched Empress Felicity and Gentleman Tobias plop onto the grass next to Jayden and his friend. The dogs' mouths hung open in identical doggie grins. "First things first: Does Will know that you're single? Before this can go anywhere, he'll need to know that about you."

"I don't wear a wedding ring."

"That doesn't necessarily mean you're single. Plus, you had Jayden with you."

"Which makes me look like a married mom."

"Right."

"But"—Amber shifted to face Lyndie more fully, her shiny dark hair swishing around her shoulders—"I *think* I was giving off available signals. I can't be sure. It's been a long time since I've put myself out there. I may have lost my touch."

"I don't think you've lost your touch. But let me just

say that men don't always respond to subtle signals. My mom will stand in front of the TV sometimes with her hands on her hips and my dad and grandfather will go right on watching their show as if she wasn't even there."

A muted *oof* came from the backyard. Then a few grunts.

Amber and Lyndie looked to the boys, who'd kicked off an impromptu wrestling session. "Is that . . . okay?" Lyndie asked.

Amber waved a hand. "It's fine. Jayden and Bryce spend half their playdates wrestling. So. What do you think my next step should be?"

The situation seemed upside-down. The person clearly more skilled at dating was asking the novice for advice on men. Lyndie did not have good credentials in this area. The man she was attracted to seemed eager to shove her into the arms of another employer. "Could you ask Celia to mention to Will that you're single? I bet she could drop it into conversation without being obvious."

"I bet she could."

"And I'm sure she'd be happy to continue sending you texts when he visits Cream or Sugar. If you show up at the bakery again when he's there, it will seem to him like a coincidence."

"True."

"What about inviting him over to give you an estimate on a deck?"

"I don't have the funds for a deck, but I suppose I could tell him that the deck is in my long-term plan and keep to myself the fact that my long-term plan is to marry him." Amber shot Lyndie a glance full of humor.

"I have no idea why I'm helping you. I'll be very sad if

you go on all three of your dates with this fireman while I'm stuck having to eat dinner with guys that are into anime or World of Warcraft and haven't seen sunlight in months."

Amber laughed. "Remember that we're going to the Christian singles meet-up at Fellowship Church Saturday night. You have it on your calendar, right?"

"Mmm-hmm."

"That'll count as one date for each of us."

Maybe Amber would forget about the meet-up or lose enthusiasm for it between now and Saturday. Saturday was five days away. Amber might still forget. It really was possible Amber would lose enthusiasm.

But even as Lyndie told herself these feeble lies, weight settled upon her. There would be no escaping the meet-up. She'd given up all chance of that the moment she'd caved at the promise of dog-sitting and vowed to attempt three dates in three months. There would be no escape.

Across town, Jake and Bo were meeting, as they often did, in the warm room of the yearling barn to discuss their horses. "So." Bo leaned back slightly in his chair. "Have you decided what you're going to do about Silver Leaf? Are you going to give Lyndie's theory a try?"

At the mention of Lyndie's name, Jake's senses rushed to life. For pity's sake. Could he have a conversation with his brother without having Lyndie pushed to the center of his thoughts? He'd like to go five minutes, *just five minutes*, without thinking about her. "First of all, I think she's probably wrong." A horse ran for the person sitting

on his back, male or female. They didn't discriminate
by gender.

"You said 'probably wrong.'"

Jake tightened one edge of his lips. "There's a chance
she's right."

"You're going to test her theory."

"I'm leaning that way. It won't cost me anything extra,
just the time it'll take to get Blackberry ready as a lead
pony."

Bo nodded.

"You approve," Jake stated, because he could tell that
Bo did.

"A last-ditch effort is all we have left with Silver Leaf.
We have nothing to lose by trying out Lyndie's ideas."

The sound of nickering drew Jake's attention to the
window. Outdoors, a yearling ran along the paddock
rail, throwing his head.

He'd told Lyndie . . . he'd tried to tell her. No one
could help Silver Leaf, just like no one could help him.
She'd said, *"I think that I can."* She'd looked at him,
calm and confident. *"I hope that I can."*

Hope.

Jake's hope had been stripped from him long ago.
He'd forgotten what it felt like to hope. It felt lousy, to
be honest. It felt like disappointment waiting to happen.

He hadn't given Lyndie permission to make him hope
that she could make his Silver Leaf run. And yet she'd
managed to blow onto the ashes of his hope and coax
one tiny red ember to life.

CHAPTER
EIGHT

The next day Silver Leaf arrived at Lone Star Park like P. Diddy might arrive at a night club. That is to say, in luxury and surrounded by an all-female entourage.

Lyndie stood outside the barn that Whispering Creek Horses had rented on Lone Star's back stretch. Holding up a hand to shade her eyes, she watched Silver's trailer pull to a stop. She still couldn't fully believe that Jake had decided to support her Casanova philosophy.

When Jake had informed her that he'd chosen to move forward with her ideas about Silver, he'd done so in a very no-nonsense way. He hadn't become her accomplice. Rather, he'd opted to tolerate her plans while continuing to treat Silver Leaf in the manner in which he treated all of his horses, with care and strikingly keen observation.

Zoe jumped down from the cab of the truck and came around to begin the process of unloading. "Have you seen any tall men since you've been here at the track?" Zoe asked, slanting hopeful looks in both directions.

"Not yet."

"Well, bummer." Zoe led Blackberry down the trailer's ramp, handed her lead to Lyndie, then headed back into the trailer. "The trip over was . . ."

Bumpy? Lyndie wondered. Well air-conditioned? Enchanted by a sorcerer's spell?

Zoe reemerged with Silver. "Look at this, perfect boy. We're here. And you did so well on the ride over. Aren't you a star? Yes, you are. You're a star." Then, to Lyndie, as they started toward the barn with the horses, "Isn't this great? A new place. Races coming up soon. The possibility of meeting tall men."

They guided the horses past a motorized walking ring into the quiet calm of the barn. Lone Star Park nestled in Grand Prairie, a suburb located between Dallas and Fort Worth. It boasted a mile-long racetrack and a collection of backstretch barns that could house up to a thousand horses.

Less cushy than their barn at Whispering Creek, the barn at Lone Star had been painted green on the outside, use-scarred ivory on the inside. Loamy dirt blanketed the shed row.

For the duration of the three-month-long season, Zoe, two other grooms, all Jake's exercise riders, their barn foreman, their night man, and two hand-walkers had relocated here. Some of those employees had decided to rent nearby rooms made available by the track. Others, like Lyndie and Zoe, had opted to commute forty-five minutes each way from Holley.

"Right in here, Silver." Zoe flicked the Post-it Note that had been stuck to the front of Silver's stall, then led him in. "Isn't this nice? Look, Lyndie brought down your own hay, and it's waiting right here. You have fresh bedding and your very own water pail from home."

Lyndie and Zoe settled both horses into their side-by-side stalls, then hand-fed them apple slices as a house-warming gift.

At the sound of a muted conversation, Lyndie swung her gaze to the far end of the barn. Jake came around the corner, flanked by his foreman and a groom. He stood half a head taller than the other men, who were listening attentively as he spoke. He'd turned up the collar of his hunting jacket, and from what she could see beneath his hat, it didn't appear that he'd shaved this morning. His five o'clock shadow lent him an even more disreputable pirate air than usual.

If you liked that sort of thing.

Jake's attention fixed on Lyndie. He continued forward without acknowledging her in any way other than his eye contact. Even so, her body responded with another of those wonderful hot pangs deep in her midsection.

She glanced back in Silver's direction. *He doesn't like you, Lyndie. Enough with the physical reactions to him. He'd be happier if you were working in another trainer's barn.*

When Jake reached them, he asked his two companions to continue to the barn's office and wait for him there.

"Hello, Mr. Porter," Zoe said.

"Zoe. Everything go smoothly on the drive over?"

"Sure did."

He took his time observing Lyndie and Zoe with their apple slices and Silver Leaf, surrounded by his horse luxuries. She knew he thought her far-fetched for treating his five-year-old stallion who'd yet to win a single race as if he were a multimillion-dollar Breeders' Cup champion.

Jake braced a hand on the entrance to Silver's stall. "How are you finding the customer service so far?" he asked Silver Leaf, irony tinting his voice.

Lyndie chuckled. "The customer service agrees with him."

Zoe's eyes rounded as if she couldn't believe she'd just heard Jake say something mildly humorous.

"Show these ladies that you like me, Silver Leaf. This one here"—Jake tilted his head in Lyndie's direction—"thinks you're only being polite."

Silver nibbled on a few strands of hay.

"Huh," Lyndie said. "Not very convincing."

Jake gave her a look both challenging and condescending. "Neither is your theory." Then he pushed away from the stall and continued in the direction of the barn office.

"You told Mr. Porter that Silver Leaf doesn't like him?" Zoe whispered.

"Yep."

"*Why?*"

"Because I think it's true."

"Oh my gosh! What'll be next? Flying pigs?"

"No. But we just might see a dapple grey stallion run. If we're very, very lucky."

"I'm praying over it." Zoe stroked Silver's neck. "Hear that? I'm praying over it." Two more pats, then, "I need to go check on my other horses. What're you up to?"

"I'm going to stay here with him for a bit."

"Catch ya later."

Lyndie lowered into her usual seated position against the inner side wall of Silver's stall. New barn. Same position. For long minutes she observed the horse and accustomed herself to the sounds of Lone Star Park.

Blackberry and Silver whinnied back and forth to each other a few times. Once, Silver stuck his head out of his doorway and reached toward Blackberry. The female horse responded by stretching toward Silver. Their noses touched briefly in their customary sign of affection.

Lyndie saw no outward signs of agitation in Silver Leaf. But, of course, that was part of the difficulty. He hid his displeasure.

When she readied to leave, she rose quietly. Silver Leaf studied her. She stared back at him, trying to communicate her affection and acceptance of him without motion or words.

After a time, he nudged his face into her hair, cataloguing her scent. Then he rested his head where her neck met her shoulder, just as she'd seen him do with Zoe, and gave a sigh.

Lyndie's heart soared. Silver was letting her know that he liked and accepted her, too. She'd finally gained his trust! Moisture gathered on her lashes, warbling her vision.

All her life, Lyndie had harbored a deep love of animals. They were God's creatures, innocent, full of loyalty. Many poured out their lives in service to their owners. Whether or not Silver ever won a race, he had intrinsic value, just like every other horse in this barn. Just like her pets at home. How lucky was she that she got to do this job? "I'll do my best for you," she promised.

Jake's training regimen had made Silver Leaf into an

athlete built to sprint with breathtaking speed. She could see the evidence of Silver's conditioning in his physique. What she didn't know: whether the horse would decide to put his potential into practice.

"Will you do your best for me?"

Silver Leaf would answer Lyndie's question three days later.

Aware that his horse needed time to adjust to his new environment, Jake had Lyndie take Silver through easy workouts the first two mornings after arriving at Lone Star. On the third morning, a Friday, less than two weeks before Silver Leaf was scheduled to race, the moment of truth arrived.

Jake wanted to see him run.

Nervousness squeezed long fingers around Lyndie's chest as she sat aboard Silver near the outer rail of Lone Star's track. She'd already warmed up the horse. No time remained to stall or pray. Today's events would either render her theories about Silver valid or debunk them completely.

She ran her hand along the reins, feeling the nub of the leather. Dawn had recently crescendoed over the horizon, christening the horses and exercise riders on the track with rosy light. The clouds this morning, high and distant, looked like the clouds in a kid's drawing, flat at the bottom and puffing into gentle mounds on top.

Jake approached, two mounted riders in his wake.

"I want to give Silver Leaf a hard work in company," Jake told the three of them, Lyndie included. The other two riders, both male, sat astride the best three-year-olds Jake had.

He'd already informed her of his plans privately. He hoped to spur Silver's competitive juices by giving him challenging competition. If, by chance, the situation did motivate Silver to run, the other horses would then serve as a measuring stick. They'd let Jake know whether Silver possessed any real speed.

"Build them to a gallop," Jake instructed, "then open it up around the far corner and go for a half mile." His gaze flicked to Lyndie's.

She gave a nod, trying to look more confident than she felt. Suddenly this whole idea of hers seemed a little harebrained and unfounded, even to her. Like Jake, she'd never actually heard of any other horse that had a Casanova complex.

"Good?" he asked her. Beneath his hat, unflinching seriousness shone in his eyes. Brackets marked either side of his mouth.

"Good." She was doing this. This was happening. Wrenching away her attention, Lyndie turned Silver, and the trio of riders set off. Carefully, safely, they increased their speed.

This is your last chance at this, Silver. Okay? You're fit and ready. If you're going to be great, you have to show him now. I believe that you're great. Now you have to believe it. You have to have the heart of a champion.

It's important. For Jake, it's important—

That was too much. Unfair. She couldn't tie all her hopes for Jake's welfare to this horse who had no connection to Iraq and the Marines and PTSD. Silver had

had nothing to do with the scar that marked Jake's face and the worse scars that ran through his psyche.

As they started into the turn, the other riders began to let their horses' speed unfurl. Lyndie gave Silver the freedom to do the same. She rode in the classic jockey's body line; her boots resting in their high stirrups, her knees bent so that her lower legs and upper legs formed a ninety-degree angle.

The other two horses started to pull away. Silver tracked them with his gaze, his ears flicking forward and backward. She gently nudged her heels into his sides, encouraging him. "Run," she whispered.

He merely galloped. The other horses lengthened their lead. One of the riders shot a glance over his shoulder at her.

Lyndie's spirits sank. "Silver Leaf, come on. Run!"

His pace remained the same. She'd been wrong. Her wild idea hadn't panned out. This horse was exactly what his past had proven him to be.

And yet, her stubborn streak refused to give up. She could *feel* the ability in him. He could run like the wind, her intuition was positive of it. "Please," she urged. Leaning into him, she did her best to propel him forward with the force of her will. *"Run!"*

And suddenly . . .

He answered.

Silver's legs stretched out in longer and longer strides, his hooves biting into the dirt in a quickening cadence as he began to devour the ground. He was coordination personified, astonishingly smooth and fluid.

"Yes!" Lyndie moved her hands in tandem with his

rhythm so that he could sprint faster. They melded into a seamless unit, fully in sync.

They closed in on the other two Thoroughbreds. The track zipped toward them and flew beneath. Silver shifted into yet another gear, moving even faster in an effort to catch and best the other two. He had heart. She'd known it! He had *heart*.

His raw power sent chills coursing over Lyndie's skin. She'd ridden a lot of fast horses, but this kind of pace was as rare as diamonds. What's more, she could sense that he had additional strength in reserve. If she asked him to give more, he'd be able.

They came even with the other two, filling the wide opening between them. Silver would have surged ahead, except that they'd reached a half of a mile and all three riders eased their horses' speed.

They flashed by Jake at a gallop. He was standing upright, as if he'd pushed away from leaning against the rail when Silver Leaf had begun to make his move. His hands hung at his sides, one clutching a stopwatch. Unguarded surprise stamped his expression.

Lyndie laughed with pure joy. *Silver Leaf!* Silver Leaf had just run for her as he'd never run for anyone. She was female, and she'd earned his trust—so when she'd asked him, he'd run. And what a run! As they slowed, she whooped and tilted her face upward to heaven, where all good gifts originated. *Thank you, God!* Exhilaration surged through her limbs.

She cooled Silver, then steered him to Jake. Now that he'd had time to recover, Jake had regained his usual tight control over himself. Except that a slight curve—almost a smile?—lifted one side of his lips.

That small, subdued curve turned her emotions into a river of honey. Much too strong a response to such a mild stimulus. It's just that . . . She'd done it. She'd solved Silver's mystery, and she couldn't have been prouder or gladder. *For you, Jake,* she wanted to say with a grand "Ta-da!" motion of her arms. *I hereby present to you a racehorse.*

Jake took hold of Silver's bridle. He looked at the horse as if he couldn't quite believe what he'd just witnessed, shaking his head slowly.

Jake was perhaps a man too unaccustomed to miracles.

Silver Leaf held his neck at a kingly angle and stood with still and patient hauteur. It was if he were saying to Jake, *Why so surprised? Of course I'm fast, plebeian.*

Jake turned his attention to Lyndie. "Silver Leaf is a lady's man."

"Yes." She beamed. It took effort to restrain herself from dismounting and wrapping him in a celebratory hug. "Not only can he run, but he had more in the tank when I pulled him up. Did you see how he was increasing his speed there at the end?"

"I saw."

"You did a good job training him and preparing him, Jake."

"None of my training made any difference before you came."

Lyndie gave a small shrug. "I wanted to help. If I did, I'm happy." In fact, she'd desperately wanted to help. Maybe even more desperately since Jake had encouraged her to look for work elsewhere. It meant a lot to

her to know that she'd proven both his horse's merit
and her own.

"Good work, Lyndie."

"Good work, Jake."

A hundred unspoken words charged the air. She got
lost in his hazel gaze. She swallowed with effort, feeling
her pulse stitching faster and faster.

"Mr. Porter?" Another of Jake's riders neared.

Jake stepped away from Silver. Lyndie's contact with
him was severed, and his face returned to stone once
more.

***

For the remainder of the day, Jake replayed the memory of Lyndie and Silver Leaf together, racing toward
him down the stretch. He'd been standing in his usual
position, suffering through the same gut-twisting worry
he experienced whenever he put Lyndie on a horse. And
then he'd seen them do . . . *that*.

Silver Leaf had moved with the sort of smooth and
terrific stride that Jake's dreams were made of. And Lyndie had looked like she'd become a part of the horse. She
was small, but she was made of fine muscle, excellent
instincts, and innate timing.

He set aside the foil container that held what remained
of his take-out dinner. Basketball filled the big-screen TV
in his living room. He hadn't been paying attention to
the picture or registering the noise, however. He couldn't
see or hear anything except Silver Leaf's run.

Leaning back on his leather sofa, he stuck his hands
behind his head and peered at his loft's white ceiling,
marked regularly with recessed lights.

He had worked Silver Leaf in the round pen as a yearling. He'd developed him over countless dark and cold early morning practice sessions. He'd raced him at the track repeatedly. Never had he seen the horse run like that. Or anything even close to that.

It had almost seemed supernatural to him, what he'd seen today. He'd clocked Silver Leaf at a time so fast that it opened up a world of possibilities and more than fulfilled the hope for Silver Leaf that Lyndie had stirred within him.

He'd trained strong horses before, but Silver Leaf just might be the one that he and Bo and Meg had been waiting for. A champion. If so, Silver Leaf would put Whispering Creek Horses on the center of the map.

And he knew who was responsible.

When they were kids he'd seen Lyndie gallop every single one of the horses they'd had on their property. He could remember what she'd looked like, and it was very much what she'd looked like this morning. There was a freedom about her when she ran a horse, as if she'd been made to ride headlong into the wind.

The sight of her on Silver Leaf today had struck him deep, like a whip uncovering skin and muscle. The beauty of her—

He brought his hands around to cover his face. His fingertips dug into his scalp.

He knew that it wasn't Zoe or Blackberry who'd transformed Silver Leaf. It was Lyndie. Something about her made a person want to offer her their best. That's what Jake had seen Silver Leaf do today.

The horse had run.

The horse had run *for her*.

Amber turned out to be both the best and the worst singles function escort. Best because she was outgoing, friendly, and knew almost everyone. Worst because she was so popular that other people kept sweeping her away.

Amber had just been drawn deep into conversation with a pair of brunettes, so Lyndie moved to the dessert table. She went to work straightening the platters of cookies and brownies as if the world depended on her ability to organize baked goods.

Will McGrath, the fireman Amber was interested in, wasn't present tonight at Fellowship Church's meet-up event. Nor was Jake, of course. In this environment, Jake would have been as out of place as a hardened fighter jet surrounded by tricycles.

Because of the mild weather, the organizers had decided to host the event in the large central courtyard of the church. The festivities had begun with a welcome desk and stick-on name tags followed by a catered buffet dinner washed down with iced tea or watery lemonade. The red-and-white gingham tablecloths gave the atmosphere a bright and cheerful air, as did the strings of white lights swagging the perimeter of the space. Overhead, dark ribbons of clouds decorated a sky of dusky purple.

What a sky! Lyndie nibbled a peanut butter cookie and tried to commit the palette of colors to memory. She'd love to draw a dragon against just such a sky—

"Lyndie!"

Lyndie looked toward the voice, relieved to see Silver Leaf's groom, Zoe, crossing toward her. The long-limbed redhead had her hair down tonight and her outfit—a multicolored top with jeans and yellow flats—couldn't have been cuter.

"You look darling." Lyndie gave her a quick hug.

"So do you! I'm not used to seeing you in anything except riding gear. Is that a shirtdress?"

"Yep." Lyndie smoothed the front of the garment. Amber had pronounced her first attempt at an outfit too casual and had then talked her into wearing this belted shirtdress over brown leggings and high-heeled boots. Amber had also made her wear her hair down and badgered her into pink lip gloss. "Have you been here the whole time?" she asked Zoe.

"Yes. You?"

"Yes, but I haven't been looking around much for the last few minutes. I didn't want to accidentally make eye contact with anyone."

Zoe laughed and selected a brownie. "You're afraid to make eye contact with people?"

"We all have our kryptonite. Singles functions are mine."

Amber's friends, both male and female, had surrounded Lyndie with conversation during the dinner portion of the evening. Every one of them had been above and beyond kind and welcoming to her. The meet-up had impressed Lyndie with its fastidious organization and light tone, and she supposed that this type of venue suited the vast majority of the women here.

Just not her.

Her issue with tonight's meet-up was completely attributable to her own internal flaw: She struggled with singles events because of the way they made her feel. This evening's outing ought to have made her feel festive. Instead, dressing up and smiling her way through it had made her feel like a one-pound package of ground beef that had started to brown because all the shoppers had left it sitting on the shelf.

See? Her internal flaw. She was not ground beef, and if she felt that way it was because she'd made herself feel that way. No one else had.

"Who did you come with?" Zoe asked.

"My neighbor Amber. I promised her I'd go on three dates in the next three months. What about you?"

"I'm here in search of men over the height of six feet two. Have you seen any of those?"

"A few."

"Thank goodness. I think I . . ." Zoe's sentence hung as she set about choosing another brownie.

How might Zoe have completed her thought? I think I . . . only like brownies shaped like trapezoids? I think

I . . . might consider setting up a roadside watermelon stand?

Lyndie's vision snagged on the activity in the center of the courtyard. "Why are they taking away the tables?"

Zoe's lips quirked. "You don't know? Prepare yourself for more kryptonite."

A blonde stepped onto a raised dais and tapped a microphone a few times. "Good evening, everyone! Thank you for coming. I hope you're having a nice time. I thought I'd offer a word of prayer, and then we'll get started."

Started? Lyndie had thought they were ending.

"Lord," the blonde prayed, "thank you for the fellowship we've enjoyed tonight. Thank you for the food we just ate and for the hands that prepared it. And bless the square dancing. Amen!"

Square dancing?

Lyndie aimed a questioning glare toward Amber.

It'll be fun, Amber mouthed to her, looking unrepentant.

"I bribed her." Zoe motioned toward the blonde with the microphone. "We're going to do two rounds of square dancing. I've no idea how she's going to pair us up for the first round. But for the second round I gave her a box of Godiva to make sure that she pairs us by height."

This was sounding worse and worse.

"I'm so tired of you short girls stealing all the tall guys. God *obviously* sent the tall men to earth specifically for the tall women." Zoe tilted back her head to tip the last of the brownie crumbs into her mouth.

"I haven't stolen any tall guys from you."

Zoe's eyes sparkled. "Not yet."

"To mix us up—" The sound system gave an electronic shriek. "I'm going to ask you to find a dancing partner for the first set whose first name starts with the same initial as your first name. You've got five minutes. Go!"

Lyndie wasn't afraid to race a Thoroughbred, but the notion of trick-or-treating for a square dancing partner whose name started with *L* cowed her.

Zoe groaned. "What chance do I have of finding a tall man in this group whose name starts with *Z*?"

"There are more women here than men. I'll hang back with you and then maybe we can dance together."

Amber came over, laughing. She linked elbows with Lyndie on one side, Zoe on the other, and tugged them both into the fray.

"Actually, Amber," Lyndie interjected, "I think Zoe and I might dance with each other—"

Amber was quickly scooped up by a cute guy named Andy.

"Zoe, hurry, let's go hide in the bathroom—"

"Hey." A twenty-something man with chin-length blond hair parted down the middle stepped in front of them and checked Lyndie's name tag. "I'm Luke."

She was busted! Her plan for a bathroom escape deflated. "I'm Lyndie."

"Looks like we both have *L* names. Would you like to square dance with me?" Despite the Sir Lancelot haircut, Luke was actually kind of appealing, in clothes that looked like they'd come from Banana Republic and a pair of beige Vans.

"You two dance together," Zoe insisted. "I see my friend Vera. There's no way she'll find anyone with a name that starts with *V,* so I'll dance with her." Zoe gave Lyndie's forearm a squeeze and took off.

"Are you new in town?" Luke asked.

She told him that she was and, when he asked, explained her dual professions of exercise rider and author/illustrator.

While she was speaking, Luke startled her by jerking his head back and making a honking noise, the sort of honking noise that people with sinus congestion make when trying to pull the snot back up their noses. Now that Lyndie was getting a better look at him, she noted that his eyes were red and watery, his face somewhat gaunt and pale.

"What do you do?" Lyndie asked.

Another honk. "I work for an allergy doctor."

Not a very effective one, apparently.

"It looks like they're about ready to start," he said.

An Orville Redenbacher look-alike took over the dais and microphone. He introduced himself as their square dance caller. His assistant moved through the crowd, grouping everyone into squares of four couples.

"They're putting us in groups of eight." Luke released a trio of sneezes.

Lyndie hunched away from him slightly.

"They don't have a real band," Luke commented. "Just a CD and a sound system."

Lyndie began to suspect that the bulk of Luke's conversation centered around pointing out the obvious.

The caller taught them a few square dancing basics: the promenade, the star, the do-si-do. Luke obligingly took hold of Lyndie's hands and squired her through the moves. The others in their square—an M couple, a C couple, and a J couple—likewise lurched into action.

"I'm a good bit taller than you are," Luke offered.

"Yes."

"You're wearing a dress."

"I am."

They paused. A twangy country tune began to play.

"Music's on," Luke observed, then honked again.

Lyndie experienced an actual, physical ache of longing for the solitude of her apartment, her animals, her art, and her hair in a topknot.

Everyone in their square did their best to sashay around according to the caller's instructions. Some of them were bad at dancing and the rest were hideous. Once, they messed up so royally that they could do nothing but stop and laugh.

"We messed up," Luke informed them all.

Lyndie burst into fresh laughter.

Luke sneezed.

When the set finally finished, Lyndie and Luke stepped apart.

"That was cool." He scratched the back of his head.

One thing she knew: Luke was not the man for her. She didn't relish the idea of going through life with a commentator. *There's a dog, Lyndie. You're driving thirty-five, Lyndie. You're awake, Lyndie.*

"Would you like to go out sometime?"

His interest in her was all the fault of Amber's pink lip gloss, of that she was certain.

"Just for fun," he added. "With a group of friends."

"Sure, maybe."

He handed her his phone. "Here's my phone," he pointed out.

Luke was a nice person. Lyndie had no desire to hurt his feelings so she entered her details.

The blond event organizer resumed control of the mic. "Before we begin the second set, I'd like all the men to line up on one side of the courtyard, and I'd like the ladies to line up on the other. Tallest on this side, please, going right on down." She did a stairstep motion with her hand.

Lyndie contemplated renewing her earlier strategy and hiding in the bathroom.

Amber rushed over. "Isn't this fun?"

"Uh . . ."

"I love to dance."

"I'm never wearing this lip gloss again."

Amber eyed her knowingly, amusement edging her mouth. "The men like it, don't they? I'm not surprised." She tugged Lyndie down the row of women. "Look, Lyndie, I think you belong right here." She inserted Lyndie between two women, comparing their relative heights. "Yep! I'll see you after the set."

Once they'd all found their places, the men's line and the women's line moved toward one another. Lyndie's counterpart stood at approximately five feet seven. He had the face and body of an accountant but the soul of a punk-rocker, because beneath his black T-shirt and black jeans, his arms and neck were covered in tattoos. Holes as big as nickels marked his earlobes. Small, scholarly glasses perched on a round head crowned by tidily cut mouse brown hair.

"I'm Teddy." He spoke in a quiet, thoughtful voice.

"I'm Lyndie."

"I've taken a purity pledge," he said. "I thought you should know."

"Oh." Lyndie was all for purity. But so far she and

Teddy had done nothing but exchange names. No one's purity seemed to be in jeopardy.

"I've vowed to keep myself morally clean so that when I make a covenant of marriage one day, I can do so with a clear conscience."

"That's great."

He nodded, utterly serious. "I'd like to hold hands with my wife for the very first time on our wedding night."

"I see."

"I'm not sure I should be dancing."

"It sounds like you shouldn't be, honestly, since you and I will have to hold hands in order to square dance."

"It's all right."

"No, we probably shouldn't—"

"It's fine. If you and I get married, we can look back on this night and laugh."

Or cry.

"For this set," their caller informed them, "we have a surprise for ya'll. We're going to be dancing to pop tunes! The kind of music you young people like." "Who Let the Dogs Out" burst from the speakers. "I bet you didn't think we could square dance to this type of music, did you? Well, we most certainly can. We'll dance the steps we've already learned. Except, this time, be sure to pause whenever the barking comes on, cup your hands around your mouth like so, and shout out, 'Ruff, ruff, ruff-ruff-ruff!'"

Lyndie no longer felt like a browning package of ground beef. No, her beef had, at this point, turned quite black.

A distance away, she caught sight of Zoe looking completely self-satisfied with the very tall businessman she'd landed. At the other end of the courtyard, Zoe's friend Vera wore a woebegone expression. Vera had a unique first initial and was also the shortest female, which meant she hadn't scored a male partner for either set. Had Lyndie been able to donate Teddy to Vera's cause, similar to the way you could donate Girl Scout cookies to the troops, she would have done so.

Teddy took her hands in his soft palms, and they started in on "Who Let the Dogs Out." After which, they square danced to "U Can't Touch This" and the Macarena.

When the dancing came to an end, Teddy peered at her. "Can I have your number? I'd like to call you sometime."

Blasted lip gloss!

"So?" Amber asked, when they'd shut themselves in Lyndie's Jeep and were on their way back to the Candy Shoppe. "How did your evening go?"

"I met a lot of wonderful people, and I gave my phone number to two men who I really hope never call me."

"These men are single, Lyndie."

"Yes."

"And Christian."

"Yes."

"Then maybe something could develop over time—"

"I don't think so, Amber."

"Well, God is full of surprises." Amber grinned, clearly high on the excitement of an evening that hadn't included Hot Wheels or superhero figurines. "That's one date down."

"I think I may have to beg off the other two. I have a lot of work to do—"

"Don't even try, Lyndie. One date down. Two to go."

"What are you doing here, man?" Bo came to a stop in the doorway of Jake's first-floor office, located in Whispering Creek's lodge-style mansion.

Jake swiveled his desk chair from his computer toward his brother. "Working."

"Have you noticed that it's Sunday afternoon?" Bo motioned to the windows and the party Meg had going on the lawn for all the families that lived in the mansion. Lots of people and balloons. "Why don't you come outside and join us?"

"Thanks, but I'm good."

"Would it fly if I ordered you, as your boss, to take the day off?"

"It wouldn't fly."

"That's what I thought." Sighing, Bo took a seat in one of the chairs across from Jake's desk. He picked up a binder clip and turned it end over end. "Did you hear about Lyndie and Amber's night out last night?"

Bo's question drew Jake's full attention. "No."

"Amber told Meg that the two of them went to a singles function at Fellowship Church."

A murderous emotion surged to life inside Jake. A singles function? Lyndie was trying to pick up men?

"They square danced while they were there, apparently." Bo tilted his head, studying Jake with interest. "Why are you staring at me like you want to kill me?"

"What kind of man goes to a square dance to meet women?"

"Men that are luckier in love than you are. Lyndie and Amber have agreed to three dates each over the next few months. The square dancing was the first."

The tension within Jake mounted.

"This is just the beginning," Bo said. "They still have two more dates to go."

Ever since Jake returned from Iraq, his mental state had kept him disconnected from people. He'd been living behind a shield that had protected him from emotions and from relationships he couldn't handle. He hadn't liked nor hated the shield. It had just . . . been.

Lyndie, though. What was it about her? Her sense of humor, her determination, her kindness? Lyndie had somehow broken down his shield. And now that he found himself without it, he wanted it back.

But it was too late for that now, he feared.

Some horrible part of him had gone soft over her.

No, he told himself. He couldn't care about her. He refused to. His head wasn't right. He didn't know a lot of things, but he knew that he was too messed up for a relationship.

He'd employ Lyndie until the end of Lone Star's season, and then she'd leave and things would return to normal and everything would be fine.

CHAPTER
TEN

Sometimes, when disaster comes for you, it comes quickly.

On Monday morning, Lyndie cantered Desert Willow past the grandstands at Lone Star. As always, numerous other Thoroughbreds, each traveling at a different speed, populated the track. All the trainers had just a four-hour window in which to exercise their horses.

The gunmetal sky hung low, effectively muting the colors of the trees and buildings that surrounded the oval. Though the morning had remained dry, strong gusts of wind buffeted Lyndie, stinging her cheeks with cold. Just a few more laps and she'd be done with Willow, her final mount of the morning. There'd be coffee and probably a box of donuts waiting back at the barn.

Lyndie gained on a colt ahead of her and to the inside. Just as she was about to draw past, the colt spooked and veered toward them. Willow reacted instantaneously, swerving to avoid the other horse. Lyndie's center of gravity jerked to the side and before she could regain her balance, the colt wheeled into Willow, bumping them farther off course.

The reins slipped through her hands. Sky and earth carouseled as she fell.

Jake shouldered away from his foreman, who'd been talking to him. Throwing down his clipboard and stopwatch, he started running. *No!* Fear leapt within him as he watched Lyndie land hard on her side in the dirt. He flinched against the impact as if he'd been the one who'd fallen. Viciously, he wished it had been him. He ran harder.

He watched Lyndie's body curl inward as if in pain a split second before he saw the rider galloping toward her. Time spun out, slowing. Lyndie lay in the rider's path, and Jake could see that the rider had no distance left to steer his mount away from her. With horrible certainty Jake knew what would happen—was happening—and could do nothing. He was too far away to stop it, to save her.

His hand shot out, reaching. "No!" he yelled as the horse ran over the top of her. Cold terror flooded him.

He sprinted, then skidded to his knees beside her. She was conscious, wheezing for air.

"Lyndie," he choked.

She turned her gaze to him, her brown eyes wide, and gripped his hand.

He wanted to ask her where she was hurt, but he couldn't speak. His battle-trained gaze combed her form. He used his free hand to search her limbs for broken bones, blood.

She was going to die, he knew it. He'd watched the

horse go over her, and he hadn't been able to stop it. He'd known the dangers, been aware every day that this could happen to her. But he'd let her ride, she'd been injured, and it was his fault. And now nothing would ever be the same.

The pitiful sound of her struggling for breath tore at his heart. He couldn't stand it. He jerked his head up, looking for help—

The track's outrider had gone after Desert Willow. The ambulance that always waited nearby eased onto the track and made its way in their direction.

"I'm . . ." Lyndie rasped. She squeezed his hand urgently. "Jake."

He looked into her face.

"I'm . . . fine."

He couldn't answer. Water filled his eyes. His heartbeat thudded, painful. The last of the resentments he'd been harboring toward her burned clean away in the face of his panic.

"Wind . . ." She gasped. "Knocked . . . out of . . . me."

Her reassurance did not comfort him. He'd seen the horse run over her. Eying his watch, he began to count her respirations per minute.

The ambulance parked and its doors sprang open. "Hurry," Jake growled, furious that it was taking them so long. Her breaths were slowing and becoming smoother.

Lyndie attempted to sit.

He stilled her with a scorching glance. "Don't move until they say you can."

Two EMTs, a man and woman, ran over and knelt beside her. They began by asking her questions and gently unzipping her protective vest.

"I'm okay." While still weak, Lyndie's voice sounded firmer than it had moments ago. Her hand remained in his, holding tightly. "I just had the wind knocked out of me when I fell. That's all."

"A horse ran over her," Jake told them.

"Is that right?" the woman asked Lyndie.

"Yes. I mean, I think so. When I saw the horse coming I closed my eyes and braced. May I sit up?"

"If nothing's hurting, then yes."

Jake let go of her hand so that he could support her behind her shoulders and ease her onto her bent elbows.

"Where did the horse hit you, ma'am?"

"He didn't."

"Lyndie," Jake threatened.

"He didn't." Slowly, she looked to either side of her. "Look." She pointed to a gouge in the ground a few inches from her shoulder. "Here." She found another fresh imprint near where her feet had been. "And here."

The male EMT whistled under his breath. "That was a close call."

"Yes," Lyndie agreed. "Very."

Jake bit down on his back teeth to keep from speaking. He didn't see how the horse could have missed her.

The female EMT listened to her heart with a stethoscope. Lyndie tugged off first one glove with her teeth, then the other. She handed them to Jake, and he pushed them into his jacket's pocket. Once she'd released the chin strap, she pulled her helmet free. A small gold angel charm dangled from the knob on the helmet's top.

She showed it to the male EMT. "This isn't the first time I've had someone watching over me."

"Not your first close call, huh?"

Wind pushed across them. "No."

"I'm a believing man, myself." The EMT smiled at Lyndie.

Jake wanted to rip his face off. He had no idea why anyone was smiling.

"Do you think you can walk over to the ambulance?" the female EMT asked Lyndie. "If not, we can bring a stretcher."

"I think—"

"No stretcher," Jake said flatly. "I'll carry her."

"Jake . . ."

"Sir, we can get the stretcher—"

"I'll carry her," he insisted, commanding their silence. As carefully as he could, he collected her in his arms. She inhaled with surprise as he gathered her against his chest. With a surge he pushed to standing, then moved toward the ambulance.

"You like me," she said slowly, with a mixture of accusation and wonder. "You had me pretty convinced that you didn't. But you do. You like me."

"You're in shock."

"Maybe." She locked her elbow over his shoulder. Her hand came to rest against the back of his neck. Then, lightly, her fingers sifted through his hair.

He spared a look down at her and saw that she'd focused her attention on her fingers, as if intent on testing out the new sensation of touching him.

He shouldn't let her touch him. . . . Worry had his thoughts going five different ways, none of them straight. But he knew she shouldn't be touching him.

She was, though. And it was the sweetest physical

contact he'd experienced in years. His traitor body responded to it.

"Wow," she said quietly, almost to herself. "You're stronger than expected. You're making this look easy—"

"This *is* easy."

"But you didn't have to carry me. Really." Her fingers continued to play over the cords of his neck, between the short strands of his hair.

What was she saying? He couldn't concentrate. . . . Had the horse truly missed her when it had galloped over her? What was the likelihood of that?

"I'm feeling better now," she said. "I could've walked."

"I don't want you walking. I want the EMTs to do their job and take you to the hospital."

"*What?* No. I don't need to go to the hospital. I'm—"

"You could have a concussion. You might not correctly remember what just happened, but I remember it exactly. That horse ran over the top of you, Lyndie. You might have internal injuries—"

"I might. But I don't. Jake?"

"Lyndie. Let them do their job." He set her down on the back stoop of the ambulance.

She grabbed both of his hands and tugged until he lowered onto his heels in front of her.

"Please believe me." She searched his face, while gripping his hands. He could feel her warmth and strength. "Your face is white, and I'm actually worried that they need to check *your* blood pressure. I don't want to make a bigger spectacle than I already have. I really am fine."

He felt like his chest was caving in. She was going to talk these worthless EMTs into letting her walk away. "If they recommend a visit to the hospital, you're going."

"I don't need—"

"If they recommend it, you're going."

The EMTs did more testing. Jake waited at the open back doors of the ambulance like a protective watchdog, his arms crossed over his chest. He'd been on numerous tours with the Marines. He was no stranger to triage, and he knew his way around injuries. When the EMTs finished, they informed Lyndie that they didn't think a trip to the hospital was necessary.

"I want her seen by a doctor," Jake stated.

"It's up to you," the female EMT said to Lyndie. "It wouldn't be a bad idea to see your doctor. Just to rule out a concussion."

Lyndie slid a look in his direction. He scowled at her.

Her brows lowered and she mumbled something wry that sounded like "tall, dark, and brooding."

"Excuse me?"

"I'll have Zoe take me to see Dr. Dean in Holley," Lyndie said.

Both EMTs turned their faces in his direction, waiting.

He could see by the stubborn angle of her chin that she'd made her best offer. "Fine." He helped her from the ambulance.

His heart still hadn't settled into a regular rhythm. His brain kept replaying her fall, sending fresh spikes of anxiety through him each time.

The helplessness he'd felt when he'd seen the other horse closing on Lyndie had brought back the helplessness that had branded into him eight years ago. He'd never, *never* wanted to feel that helpless again.

He'd definitely never wanted to feel that helpless where

Lyndie was concerned. Lyndie, the girl he'd spent his childhood protecting.

What was he doing, getting himself all worked up over her like this?

For the first time, Jake noticed the outrider standing a short distance away with Desert Willow and Jake's barn foreman. Activity on the track had been suspended and wouldn't resume until they'd all cleared the area.

"Do you want the ambulance to take you back to the barn?" he asked Lyndie.

"No, I'll ride Willow back."

Figured. He spoke briefly to the outrider, then gave Lyndie a leg up onto Willow. "Hand-walk her back to the barn," he instructed his foreman.

"You're not coming?" Lyndie asked.

"No." Without looking at her, he turned and strode toward his usual position at the rail.

For a full hour he stood, unmoving, his hat shading his eyes, his shoulders hunched, his hands buried deep in his pockets. The cold sank into his bones, and he let it come. Horses and riders moved past while the wind hissed around and inside of him.

CHAPTER ELEVEN

Later that night, Lyndie's phone chimed to signal an incoming text.

Ah. From Luke, her square dancing partner who'd been fond of noting the obvious. *It's Monday*, he wrote.

She waited for him to venture more, but nothing came. *Yes*, she typed back.

Can't find anything good on TV. Want to grab dinner?

Thanks for the offer, but I fell this morning at work so I'm going to stay in and take it easy tonight.

You okay?

I'm okay.

All right. I'm signing off now.

Lyndie set her phone facedown on her art desk. After the square dancing meet-up, she had a renewed appreciation for girl's night in. Never more so than tonight, after her spill this morning, her visit to Dr. Dean, and the ensuing fuss made over her by her mom, dad, Zoe, and Amber. It was seven thirty, and she'd only gotten rid of the last of them half an hour ago.

She positioned herself on her stool in her studio, her hair in a topknot. She had her pen in her hand, two different studio lamps lit, and her pets jockeying for the prized position of foot warmer.

And now, finally, she had time and solitude to marvel over what she'd been wanting to marvel over all day. Namely, the fact that Jake did not entirely dislike her. No, no. His behavior today at the track had proven it. He liked her at least a little, and the truth of it made her heart melt and turned her thoughts into hopeful, unwarranted mush.

When he'd come running over to where she'd been lying in the dirt of the track, he'd looked stricken. He'd taken her hand and tested her arms and legs for broken bones. At one point she thought she'd seen his eyes go shiny. With tears? Lord above! Could Jake Porter's eyes have glistened with tears? Over her?!

If she hadn't just fallen off one horse and been run over by another, she'd have been able to remember everything Jake had done and said in more minute detail. As it was, the pain of her spill had fuzzed her memory slightly.

He'd carried her. That part, she recalled perfectly. The rugged power of his arms and chest had enclosed her. Warmth and his mesquite-and-spice scent had seeped into her through his jacket. She'd wanted to turn her face into his shoulder and pass out from ecstasy.

Since that would have been uncouth, she'd dared to run a few fingertips into the dark hair at his nape instead. She'd intended to be so subtle about it that he wouldn't notice. But she was pretty sure he'd noticed.

Maybe she *had* been slightly in shock. She'd said,

"You like me" to Jake—her employer, let's not forget—
and combed her fingers through his hair.

Twenty minutes later, Lyndie was dabbing her tini-
est paintbrush into the cake of purple watercolor paint
when a knock sounded on her front door.

Pray, let it not be Luke.

She padded to the door wearing the outfit she'd changed
into after her shower. An ancient pair of jeans, her favorite
hoodie, and pastel-striped slipper socks.

She pulled open the door and found Jake on her landing, almost as if her thoughts had called him into being.

Surprise momentarily froze Lyndie. Not so her Cava-
liers. They fell over themselves jumping up on him and
trying to impress him with their excitement.

He wore no cowboy hat. He was holding a package of
something in one hand. The blazing yellows and sulky
oranges of sunset framed his imposing silhouette. And
she was *still* having trouble adjusting to the reality of
him on her porch. Especially after everything that had
gone down between them this morning.

"May I come in?"

She started. "Yes! Sorry. Of course."

"Were you expecting someone else?"

"When I heard the knock I was thinking that it might
be my mom, delivering me ice cream from Braums," she
fibbed.

"I can go to Braums and get you something, if you
want."

"Having you visit is enough." She stepped back. "Come
in." When he made no immediate move, she pulled on
the sleeve of his jacket, drew him over the threshold, and
shut the door behind them. Touching him may not have

been the wisest move. His arm had hardened noticeably beneath her grip.

"Dogs! Down." She pressed them both into sitting positions. "Stay." The moment she brought her attention back to Jake, they jumped up on his jeans again. "Stay!" Then, to him, "Sorry. They love everyone. This jumping thing is their only flaw."

He gave each dog a quick scratch under its chin. "What're their names?"

"This one is Empress Felicity and this one is Gentleman Tobias."

He quirked a dark brow. "What kinds of names are those for dogs?"

"Charming and creative ones." She pointed down the hallway. "There's Mrs. Mapleton." Her ragdoll cat gave them a bored frown, then disappeared into the studio.

Jake was here! "Um . . . Would you like to sit down?"

"I . . . can't stay long," he said stiffly. "I just wanted to come by and . . ." He exhaled. His mouth set in a solemn line. "Are you okay?"

Tenderness formed an almost painful knot in her chest. Surly Jake Porter had cared enough to come and check on her in person. "I'm fine."

"These are for you." He extended the package, a bag of Reese's Peanut Butter Cups.

She took them, fighting back a sudden urge to cry over them. She'd been a Reese's Peanut Butter Cup fanatic as a kid. He'd always given her all the ones he'd collected on Halloween. Looking back, she couldn't remember why she'd let him do that. She should have insisted he keep them to enjoy.

"Do you still like them?" he asked.

"Some things"—she lifted her gaze to his—"don't change." The dogs' tails thumped the floor. "Thank you for bringing these." A handsome man delivering chocolate to your door? Nationally recognized cure-all. "Sit down and have some with me. I'll take your coat."

He hesitated. She held out her hands for his jacket, and he finally shrugged out of it, revealing a baseball-style T-shirt. The torso of the shirt was white, the sleeves navy. It was well worn-in, like all the times through the washer and dryer had softened it.

He looked big and untrusting and sexy. Physical awareness turned within her, delectable heat.

She hung his jacket over one of her dining room chairs, catching the same campfire scent that had enveloped her when he'd, oh yes, *carried her in his arms* and she'd accused him of liking her and then petted his neck. "I'm in the mood for some coffee with these peanut butter cups. Is decaf okay?"

He nodded, and she went to work scooping the expensive blend she considered well worth the cost into her coffeemaker.

It wouldn't do to read too much into the fact that he'd carried her this morning. His actions may not have had anything to do with her and him. Them. His past in Iraq may have ingrained a sense of responsibility into him that had made him react that way. It could be he'd have done the same for any of his riders.

She set three Reese's on the bar in front of one of the rustic wooden stools, near where he stood. She remained on the kitchen side of the space.

He didn't immediately take the bait and sit.

Honestly, he was more skittish than the squirrels she

and her mom had tried to entice onto their porch with chopped nuts when she'd been little.

C'mon, squirrel. C'mon. Sit yourself down.

He lowered onto the stool and rested one boot on a rung. He left his other leg outstretched, ostensibly in case he decided to bolt.

She unwrapped a peanut butter cup.

"You're not going to wait for the coffee?" he asked.

"Goodness, no. Are you?"

"Yes."

"Rule follower." She took a bite. The taste, creamy peanuts and milky chocolate, took her back in time.

"What did Dr. Dean say?"

She held the half-eaten cup to the side. "He didn't see any signs of concussion. Certainly no evidence of anything more serious. I'm simply supposed to call him if I start having symptoms."

He frowned.

She didn't want to paint too rosy a picture and make him suspicious. "The only thing I'm dealing with now is a little soreness." She finished her Reese's. Circles of chocolate remained on her thumb and pointer finger. She didn't want to stick her fingers in her mouth in front of him, so she wiped them off on a dish towel.

"You're completely fine?" he prodded.

How was she going to resist falling for this man? "Yes."

"Lyndie?"

"I'm completely fine."

His posture relaxed slightly. The sight of his apparent relief made her glad she'd downplayed it. The *little soreness* she'd copped to was an understatement. Immediately following the accident, adrenaline had mostly covered her pain. As the day had worn on, the hip, ribs, and shoulder she'd fallen on had begun to ache. Bluish bruises had risen beneath her skin down that half of her body, and she'd been taking ibuprofen every four hours.

Jake didn't need to know that, though. If he even suspected, he wouldn't let her ride. "I'll be at work in the morning."

He regarded her doubtfully.

"All five of my horses have races coming up."

"The other riders can cover for you."

"I want to work. I'll be there in the morning."

The coffeemaker stopped gurgling, and she filled two cream-colored mugs. He took his black. She didn't.

"I'm sorry you saw me take that spill today." She savored her first sip of coffee. "It must have been pretty bad to watch."

"Yes." His blunt, strong fingers toyed with his mug's handle.

"Do you think I could have done anything to avoid the collision?"

"No."

"You responded really quickly, and you seemed to know what you were doing. I remember you looking at your watch. Were you monitoring my pulse?"

"Respirations."

Huh. My word, he was gorgeous. Jake, the third son and the one who'd once been, and in her opinion still was, the most handsome Porter brother. The implacable lips. The blatant scar. The seriousness chiseled into his features by hard experience. Formidable. Yet after the events of the morning, she saw something ever-so-slightly vulnerable in him, too.

She fervently wished she had on the shirtdress and the lip gloss she'd worn square dancing. Instead, Jake had shown up on her doorstep when she was wearing a hoodie. A snug hoodie, but still. *Where was Amber's lip gloss when she could actually use it?*

Jake hadn't sipped his coffee or touched his Reese's, so she leaned across and opened one of his squares, presenting the peanut butter cup to him on her palm. "Eat."

He peeled off the paper cup, tipped his head back, and popped the whole thing in. His mouth curled sheepishly as he chewed.

Lyndie went to work on her second Reese's, enjoying watching him eat his more than she enjoyed her own. He was huge and muscled, but a shade too hard and lean. If she had her way, she'd make sure that he ate more in general, and more dessert in particular.

He tried his coffee. "I still can't figure out how that horse didn't trample you."

She angled her head. "Can't you?"

"No."

"I meant what I said to the EMT. I don't believe it was luck or coincidence that caused that horse to miss me. What are the chances that his hooves would fall so close and not leave a scratch on me?"

"Slim."

"Exactly." Downstairs, she could hear the quiet sound of Jayden's muffled voice singing. The rich smell of coffee tinted the air. "God's the one who's behind the miracles." She leaned the ball of one foot into the ankle of the other.

Jake's face didn't change.

"Do you still have the faith you had when you were younger?" She already knew the answer. She asked the question because it gave her an opportunity to raise a difficult subject.

"No."

"Why?"

Long seconds dragged by. "I can't . . . Just . . . No."

"God's still in the business of doing miracles, small and big. For me. For you."

His forehead knit.

"The miracle of Silver Leaf running the other day? That one was for you."

"Silver Leaf ran for you, Lyndie."

"Not for me. I think that God empowered him with the ability to run . . . for your sake."

"Why would God do that?"

"Because it's one of the only avenues of communication He has left with you. You've shut Him out, but I think He wanted to show you that He hasn't shut you out."

With athletic grace, Jake pushed off the stool. He went to one of her living room windows and peered out at the dark backyard.

She'd troubled him. Having a conversation with Jake was like walking through a field pitted with land mines. Much of what she wanted to say to him was guaranteed to trouble him. If they were going to have a relationship that was anything more than extremely superficial—and she very much hoped they were—then she was going to have to step on a few land mines.

Did she dare step on another land mine tonight and ask him for the chance to jockey Silver Leaf? She wanted to. The words waited, hovering. She kept them back because they were too important to risk speaking at the wrong time. She'd just taken a fall off one of his horses. Now was not the best time to convince him of her jockeying prowess or press him further on the issue of God. Right now, he needed her to lighten the tone.

"Here." She crossed to him, handed him his coffee mug, and considered the view beyond her window. "We all love the big backyard. Especially Jayden. You already know that Jayden and Amber live downstairs?"

"Yeah."

"I moved in two months ago. I'll give you a tour. It should take all of thirty seconds." Carrying her own mug, she pointed to a few of the pieces in the living room and told him where she'd acquired them. She stopped to brag on the merits of her pride and joy, the antique farm table in her dining area. Then she took him down the hall. She merely waved in the direction of her bedroom and bathroom. A single girl never wanted a man to look too closely at those areas unless she'd had time to stage them properly.

"This is my studio." Her desk ran along one wall before bending and traveling beneath the wall that held the room's large window. She'd hung all kinds of art above her desk, creating a charming hodge-podge of inspiration and color. Some of the pieces she'd framed with scrolly antique frames. Some, she'd covered with minimalist glass. Two of the pieces were ringed with birch wreaths.

Jake examined everything, including the collection of picture books she herself had written and illustrated. They stood in a row beneath the window. "These are yours?" he asked.

"Yes."

He set down his mug with extra care, as if worried that he might spill coffee on her work. Then he picked up the boy's book that featured a knight with his helmet askew on the front cover. "Did you go to art school?"

"I got a degree in fine art from the Art Center College of Design. It was close to where we lived in California." She lifted a shoulder. "I didn't want to leave Mollie."

He opened to the middle, studied one illustration, then flipped to the next page. "How do you do this?"

"Once I have an idea for a story, I write it out in long-hand in a notebook." She showed him her current spiral-bound notebook, a big one, beautifully bound with fanciful flowers. "Then I do the ink drawings at my desk. When I get a drawing how I want it, I move the paper to this easel and watercolor it in."

"Where do you sell the books?"

"From my website. My company's called Starring Me Productions because all the books can be customized with a child's name. Parents can also choose formats that suit kids who have special needs."

"What kind of formats?"

"For example, the dyslexie font seems to make reading easier for kids with dyslexia. Parents can specify that they want that font when they order the book."

Carefully, he flipped another page. "Do you manage the website yourself?"

"I took a few courses, so I'm not a stranger to website management and design, but the answer's no. The complexity of my site is above my pay grade." She smiled. "I hired a tech guy to host and update the site for me."

"And once a parent orders a book online? What happens then?"

"The order goes straight to a printer I contract with, and he prints and ships."

"Can I read this one?" he asked.

He wanted to read one of her books? The idea hit her in a sentimental spot and simultaneously made her nervous. What if he thought it was junk? She hadn't exactly written them for the target audience of thirty-two-year-old war vets. "Sure."

"While I'm at it . . ." He picked up two more of her books and took a seat in the room's chair, a well-loved pale blue velour number. Privately, she thought of the chair as her Throne of Dreams because she often sat in it to read. That was TMI, though. No doubt he thought her oddly whimsical already.

She clicked on the floor lamp beside the chair. Buttery light fell across him and the overstuffed bookcase behind where he sat.

"Were you working when I knocked?" He motioned with his chin toward the piece on her easel.

"I was, but I can work anytime."

"Don't let me keep you."

She gave him a questioning look.

"Go back to work."

"Okay." Because, yes! She was accustomed to having a man that made her heart wring sitting on the Throne of Dreams behind her while she painted.

She lifted her paintbrush and started back to work on autopilot. Her hand did what it wanted while her brain focused solely on praying. *Lord, he's here. He's here and it has to be a good sign. Move in his life, God. Rescue him from his darkness and reveal to him the unimaginable depth of your love for him, of your mighty grace.*

I believe, God, in your power to redeem. And not just
your power to redeem, but your power to redeem Jake.

————

He set the books on the tiny round side table and studied Lyndie. Delicately, she swirled color over the paper
on the easel, making one of the fairy's dresses purple.

She had an imagination he couldn't fathom. She named
her animals ridiculous names. She had soft and girly non-
sense music playing.

And against his wishes, she fascinated him.

Lyndie was talented and unique. He'd never met anyone like her. He didn't think there *was* anyone like her.

No matter how often he tried to will himself or talk
himself out of it, he couldn't stop wanting to shield
her from hurt, from reality. He'd learned the hard way,
though, that he didn't have that power. Her fall today
proved it. Foolish emotion expanded around his heart.

She reached for a pen and added more definition to
the hill rising in the distance behind the fairy. How did
she do that? Make paper come to life with ink? Finished
with the pen, she capped it and stuck it into the bun on
top her head.

He couldn't stop staring at her. It felt like a gift, to
be able to sit behind her like this, and simply watch her.

Without warning, one of her dogs jumped onto his
lap. He jerked reflexively.

Lyndie swiveled. "I'm sorry. I can get him down."

"No." He wished he had better control over his reactions to sudden noises and motion. The dog's bulgy,
liquid dark eyes were looking at him like he'd hung the
moon. "He's fine."

Lyndie turned back to her easel. Her dog grunted and

settled across Jake's lap, resting his chin on the chair's arm.

Awkwardly, trying not to disturb the animal, Jake balanced one of the picture books on top of Lyndie's dog. He read every page, taking his time. Then he read the next. And the next.

They were incredibly good. Both the stories and the very detailed feminine drawings.

When her dog started to snore, Jake set the final book aside and combed his fingers into the dog's fur. Heat traveled up into his hand. He gazed at Lyndie as she painted, beyond grateful that today's fall hadn't injured her. *She's safe*, he reassured himself.

The stillness, the music, and her nearness caused him to feel the weight of his exhaustion. He rested the back of his head on the chair and let his eyes sink closed. A minute or so later, he felt more than heard Lyndie glance at him. He didn't need to open his eyes to confirm it. If they'd been in a pitch-black room together and she'd looked at him, he'd have been able to feel it.

He cracked one eye open and found her staring at him.

"I thought you were asleep," she said.

"I am asleep."

She laughed, a soft and tempting sound.

And suddenly, he had to go. He wanted desperately to stay, just a little while longer. But he couldn't be here, in this place, with her. It was calm here. She was innocent and beautiful and perfect.

He was not. He didn't want his mess or his mental illness or his past anywhere near her. He wanted to protect her from a lot of things, but most of all from himself.

He helped the dog off of him and went to the front part of the apartment. Lyndie followed.

He found his jacket and pushed his arms into it.

"You're welcome to stay longer. You can rest with your eyes closed in my chair anytime."

"I have to go." He paused, studying the flecks of caramel in her intelligent brown eyes. "Your books are great."

She didn't answer for a moment, then her cheeks turned pink with pleasure. "Thank you."

A piece of curling blond hair had come loose. She swept it behind her ear. His attention traced down to her chin. Then up to her lips. His hunger for her intensified, demanding. More than sanity or sense, he wanted to kiss her.

His body—his body had become hard to control when he was near her. Which made him furious. "You really are fine?" he asked. He'd been sick with worry and regret all day long. "After the spill?"

"Yes," she assured him.

"What can I do? I mean it." The three words came out sharp-edged. "I want to do something for you."

"Because you feel responsible for the fall? It wasn't your fault. If anyone's, it was mine."

"What can I do?"

She looked as if she was going to wave it off and tell him she didn't need anything. But then she pulled herself up and seemed to think better of it. "Actually . . . Now that you mention it, I can think of two things that you can do for me."

CHAPTER

TWELVE

T his is where I was imagining the deck," Amber said to Will the following afternoon. She indicated the little flagstone patio at the back of the Candy Shoppe.

"Okay." He took in the site.

This was very bad of her! Very bad, because, of course, Amber had no intention of hiring him to build her a deck. Not unless she won the lottery, that is. She shouldn't have stooped to calling him and asking for an estimate. But she'd seen him now three different mornings at Cream or Sugar. Each time, Celia had secretly texted Amber to alert her to Will's appearance at the bakery. And each time, she and Will had enjoyed great conversations spiced with plenty of chemistry. The more she learned about him, the more she liked him.

Amber hadn't wanted to wait for Will's next donut craving before seeing him again. So she'd called him and asked for an estimate.

"What kind of deck were you thinking of?"

"Maybe an L-shaped deck?" God have mercy, she'd

given this some thought. She walked out a few paces, indicating how she wanted her not-going-to-happen deck aligned. "That way, I could put a table and chairs in this area and a grill over on the short side?"

Will pulled out a tape measure and extended it from the back wall of the Candy Shoppe. His jeans fit him perfectly, and his T-shirt advertised a fireman's chili cook-off for charity. The fact that she could still see fold marks in the cotton of his T-shirt gave her a fluttery sentimental feeling toward him—she supposed because those fold marks had come from his own efforts at laundry, not his wife's.

"Is this about right?" He stopped several yards from the house, holding the tape against the ground.

"Yep." *You're about right.* She slid her hands into the pockets of her cutest pair of capris.

He set a rock in the spot and continued measuring off the perimeter of the deck, asking her along the way for her input and opinion.

It gave her a giddy feeling, to have Will here. Genuinely good guys with killer bedroom eyes were hard to find.

He finally zipped his tape measure inward and stepped beside her. "How about I work up an estimate and email it to you in the next day or two?"

"That'd be great. I'd love to have a deck out here, I'm just not sure when I'll be able to swing it financially."

"I understand." He gave her a crooked half smile that made her nerves sizzle.

"Thanks for coming today. You've proved that you do exist outside of Cream or Sugar. Until now, I wasn't sure."

His smile grew. "I wasn't sure you existed outside of there, either."

"Well, I do."

"Where's Jayden today?"

"He's up at Whispering Creek, gardening with their landscaper." *So you see, Will, this is a perfect time to ask me to join you for an early dinner if you wanted.* Since their last conversation at Cream or Sugar, Amber had been hoping that he'd ask her out on a date. Dinner, however, might be aiming a little too high. So far, he hadn't even invited her out for a cookie.

"I remember those days," Will was saying, "when the girls were small and one or both of them would be out of the house for a few hours. It felt like a vacation."

"Exactly."

"And then I'd feel guilty for being relieved, since I was already away from them every third day." He scratched the side of his head. "I don't know why I felt guilty. That was dumb."

"It might just be a single-parent thing. Or maybe it's just a parent thing. I constantly feel guilty about putting Jayden in daycare. Did you use daycare for your girls?"

"My mom lives in town. For the last twelve years she's taken care of them when I've been at the station."

"That's wonderful."

"I don't know how I would have done it without her help. She comes to my house and stays in the guest bedroom on the nights I'm gone so that the girls don't have to mess up their routine."

"Is your father still around?"

"No, he died when I was in college." Sadness flickered in his face. "I think that's part of the reason why my mom's been so involved in Madison and Taylor's lives. She would've been lonely without them. Do you have family nearby?"

Old hurt stung her. "No. They live in West Texas, and I haven't spoken with them in years."

He regarded her with concerned kindness.

"I keep telling myself I should go and see them and . . . fix things." Her laugh fell flat. "I'm a little bit afraid, I guess."

"You seem brave to me."

"I don't rush into burning buildings."

"You have your own kind of bravery."

"Winston Churchill once said, 'Success is not final, failure is not fatal: it is the courage to continue that counts.' It seems like you and I have both faced some hard things and had the courage to continue." A heated pause, full of what felt like mutual attraction, opened between them. She remained silent, because at this particular moment, she worried that failure with Will might actually prove fatal.

"I better go." He checked his watch. "I have to take Taylor to softball practice."

"Sure."

"See you soon." He looked back as he walked along the path that led to the front of the building. "I'll email you the bid."

"Thanks!" She waved.

When he'd disappeared from view, Amber wrapped her arms around herself and turned, looking out into the budding spring captured by their tree-filled lot.

In her younger days, she'd had one boyfriend after another. What she'd realized, since giving her life to Christ four years ago, was that everything she thought she'd known about romance wasn't actually about romance. She had no knowledge of real romance at all. She had a bucketload of knowledge about sexual attraction.

There'd been a time when she'd been able to put her hand on a man's arm, lean into him, and get him to ask her out just that simply. She'd been able to proposition men with her eyes. She'd worn low-cut shirts and high-cut shorts.

All of that had made her a great success at snagging boyfriends. They'd come as easily to her as a ball bouncing into her hands. What she'd never been able to do?

Keep them.

Not a single one of her boyfriends had lasted past a year. Even the primary man in her life, her father, had let her go. At eighteen, restless and full of stupid confidence, she'd fought with her dad and then left her hometown on a Greyhound bus. Three years and three boyfriends after that, she'd hit bottom: alone, broke, and pregnant.

Until Meg had taken her in and until she'd met the God of unconditional love, she'd never thought she was worth much. Back then, her little books full of famous quotes had given her the only imitation of intelligence she'd been able to scrape together.

For the past four years, she'd taken classes and studied, held down a part-time job, and spent every free second mothering Jayden. Knowing that men spelled disaster for her, she'd stayed away from them. The whole time she'd been learning and relearning how to accept God's forgiveness. Even harder and more gradually, she'd begun to find her worth in God's view of her.

Amber made her way to the hero house that Lyndie

and Jayden had made from a hollow tree stump. They'd added more to it since Amber had seen it last. A home-made ladder of twigs led to one of the windows. A doll-house chair sat out front as well as two flower pots the size of thimbles. The flower pots even had green shoots growing from them.

Unexpectedly charmed, Amber stooped to blow dirt speckles off the upside-down funnel roof. She picked a few leaves off the pathway and uprooted a weed.

It could be that her dream of one day marrying was like this imaginary house. Sweet to look at. But wholly, entirely empty.

She'd given herself permission to date again now that she'd reached a point of financial independence for herself and Jayden. And in Will, she'd even found someone she'd like to date. But Amber wasn't sure how this new person she'd become should communicate her interest to Will, and she wasn't sure whether Will had any interest in her.

Will McGrath had integrity. Her own intuition and everything she'd learned about him assured her of it. Perhaps, even after all her years of trying to better her-self, he could tell that she was white trash and not good enough for him. He knew for certain, of course, that she was no virgin.

She set into motion, walking along the fence that marked the yard's boundary. Will himself hadn't had a perfect past. But she couldn't really compare his his-tory to hers. The consensus around town was that his divorce had been the fault of his wife, who'd been self-centered and unready to settle down. According to Am-ber's friends' opinions, Will had done nothing wrong.

See? Different. Because she'd done a thousand things wrong.

Amber really liked Will, and it was awful how horribly tempted she was to slip back into her old, familiar ways in hopes of making him like her in return. She had confidence in those ways. She could try putting her hand on his arm, leaning into him, and propositioning him with her eyes—

"Amber. Quit thinking like that." She continued to walk, working through the kinks in her heart, watching her flip-flops crush the grass. She had a strong relationship with the Lord. So how come her old way of thinking about men wanted to creep into her new life?

Experience had taught her that her old way of thinking didn't work. If you gave a man your body for free, then it cost him nothing to discard you when he was done.

God, help me remember that you bought me for a price, she prayed. *If I'm uncertain, then I don't need to rush to do anything except trust in you. You've given me a second chance, and I don't need to look to anyone or anything else to determine my value.* She was a daughter of the King, even with her scratched-up past. She wasn't just poor Amber Richardson from the wrong side of Sanderson, Texas, anymore. And she refused to exchange the future she wanted for the man she wanted right now.

***

Jake had looked forward to counter-insurgency ops more than he was looking forward to this.

Last night, when Jake had visited Lyndie at her apartment, he'd insisted that she tell him what he could do for her. She had. Now he was stuck and had no one to blame but himself.

He'd arrived at Lyndie's parents' place a few minutes before two o'clock, which was when he and Lyndie had agreed to meet. He'd parked his truck in the driveway and stood leaning against its side, his boots crossed at the ankle, trees shading both him and the house.

Of all the things in the world Lyndie could have asked of him, she'd asked for two things that were hard for him to give.

First, she'd asked if she could tag along with him for an hour or so each day after she finished her riding responsibilities. She'd said, with such an innocent expression that he didn't know whether to believe her or not, that she'd shadowed other trainers she'd worked for. She claimed that she'd learned a lot by studying their different training methods and styles of operations management.

So, great. He'd be dealing with more of what he already couldn't handle: nearness to Lyndie.

Second, she'd asked him to come with her to visit Mollie, which was the request he was about to fill.

Mollie. He remembered her as a small child who'd lain in bed or been wheeled around in a special wheelchair. Whenever his mom or Lyndie had wanted him to talk to her, he'd done so out of politeness. He'd always been uncomfortable around Mollie as a kid. She'd made him feel sad.

He'd aged, but he didn't expect that twenty years were going to make this visit between him and Mollie any less awkward.

Jake pulled off his Stetson, set it inside the truck's cab, then ran his fingers through his hair a few times.

Lyndie had arrived at work and ridden for him today just like she always did, despite her fall. She'd hidden her pain from him very well. Which only concerned him more, because his sixth sense told him that she *was* hurting. She just wasn't showing it to him.

The whole time he'd watched her exercise his horses he'd dressed himself down for hiring her in the first place. Her riding had made him miserable with worry before; now it literally caused his heart to pound, his muscles to lock against waves of anxiety.

Lyndie's Jeep rounded the bend in the long driveway. He let out a slow breath.

She parked and approached. "Have you been waiting long?"

"No."

"Good, I'm glad."

Her hair was down, six shades of blond, and incredibly pretty. She wore shorts, a roomy black and white top with zigzags on it, and earrings so long they almost touched her shoulders. He didn't think he'd ever get used to her beauty. It hit him fresh every time he saw her.

She opened her passenger-side door, revealing reusable grocery sacks. Before she could lift any of them, Jake looped two around each hand.

"Thank you."

"What's all this?"

She led him onto the deck that surrounded the house. "My mom doesn't cook or grocery shop. Since I don't want any of the people living here to starve, I supply food." She held the front door for him, and he passed

through into a house that smelled faintly of dryer soft-
ener. "Jake and I are here," Lyndie called.

"Your mother will be right back." The voice had come
from the living room. "She went to go get more scrapbooking supplies."

Jake set the sacks in the kitchen, then followed Lyndie into a living room that ended in a bank of windows
overlooking more trees.

"Hey, Grandpa."

"Hello." Lyndie's grandpa sat in one of two recliners
that directly faced the TV. He tilted his head up to look
at them, his attention immediately focusing on Jake.

"I'd like you to meet Jake Porter. Jake, this is Harold
James, my grandfather."

"Nice to meet you, sir."

"You're the horse trainer?"

"Yes, sir."

"Mike and I follow your racehorses—in other words,
your Thoroughbreds. They've done very well." Harold
wore a yellow golf shirt and high-waisted pants. He had
a head full of pale gray hair and a stare so intense his eyes
squinted. "You've got a pretty good scar over there." He
tapped a bony finger against his own cheek.

"Grandpa," Lyndie scolded.

"I think," Harold said to Lyndie, "he's noticed his
scar."

Jake could still remember the despair in his gut the
first time they'd let him see himself after the initial surgery to stitch together his cheek. He'd looked into the
mirror and tried to make himself believe that the man
with the angry, jagged scar was him.

"Jake served with the Marines in Afghanistan and Iraq," Lyndie said.

"You were a Marine, eh?"

"Yes, sir."

"So was I. Korea. Once a Marine . . ." He waited for Jake to complete the saying, his brows lifted.

"Always a Marine," Jake finished.

"Good man." Harold faced the TV as an episode of *The Big Break* returned from commercial. Jake and Lyndie moved off.

"Iwo Jima!" Harold barked.

Lyndie paused. "What was that, Grandpa?"

"Iwo Jima. The Marines. Do you know what I mean?"

She shot Jake a pleading look.

"Yes." Jake raised his voice so Harold could hear. "The Marines were at Iwo Jima."

"Iwo Jima?" she asked under her breath.

"World War Two battle against the Japanese."

"He's always asking me if I know what he means. I almost never do."

They both washed their hands with soap that smelled like a pine tree before continuing down the home's central hallway to a yellow-painted bedroom.

"Hi, Eve," Lyndie said.

"Good to see you, sweetie." A heavyset African-American woman rose from the pink chair next to the bed. "I'll take my break and give ya'll some privacy."

"Thanks. Jake, this is Eve, Mollie's day nurse."

He nodded at the woman. In response, she smiled at him as she passed from the room.

Lyndie went to the small figure lying in the bed. "How's your day been, Mols? You look good." She sat on the edge of the mattress and smoothed back a section of Mollie's hair.

Jake hesitated two steps inside the room, feeling like he didn't belong. He was only good with horses. He wasn't good with people who spoke back, much less those who couldn't.

Lyndie pulled gently on the sleeve of his brown sweater until she'd brought him to stand beside where she sat. She kept a light hold on his wrist; it held him prisoner more surely than iron could have. Her touch made him aware of just how long he'd been alone. It made him feel the weight of just how much he wanted her.

"I brought someone with me today," she told Mollie. "This is Jake Porter."

Thank God Mollie was blind and couldn't see him the way that Harold had. His face would have terrified her.

The woman on the bed wore a green T-shirt that said *Home Is Where the Heart Is*. Her thin arms folded across her chest. A blanket covered the rest of her. Mollie looked a lot like Lyndie and at the same time completely unlike her. She had wavy, dark blond hair pulled back into a short ponytail and facial features similar to Lyndie's. But Mollie's body contained none of the purpose and vitality that was so much a part of Lyndie. Her face was slack, her mouth half-open. Her wide and staring gaze aimed downward and to the side.

"We knew Jake a long time ago"—Lyndie gave his wrist a squeeze—"when we were kids. He's a trainer, which means he teaches horses to be great runners." Her words fell off, and he knew she wanted him to say something.

"Hi, Mollie."

Lyndie gave him a glance full of gratitude, as if he hadn't just fallen ridiculously short. Honestly, he couldn't handle her thankfulness when he was so rotten at this. He was a fake. A man afraid of a person who was as gentle as any person could be.

He didn't want to stay. This small, airless room left him nowhere to hide.

Lyndie released him and started telling Mollie about their day and the horses he had in training. Jake strode to the room's window, staring hard at the bird that took to the air at his approach.

He'd seen vicious things during war. Bloated bodies in the street. Innocent civilians shot. Children killed. His own men torn apart and dying. Why, then, did it trouble him to see Mollie? She was harmless—

Except she wasn't.

She was the opposite of harmless because she made him feel. She put him in touch with his own sorrow. And his sorrow was a scary thing, black and deep.

Lyndie's voice stilled. Then, "Do you want to take a seat, Jake?"

She indicated a wooden chair next to a dresser topped with a TV. He lowered into the chair, propping an elbow against the dresser's side and bending the fingers of that arm into his hair.

"When I come over I usually read to Mollie out of her devotional." Two books waited on the low shelves next to the bed. One had a castle on the front. Lyndie picked up the other. "Would that be okay with you?"

He nodded.

She read a few verses from the Bible, then some application about finding peace in this difficult world. He

watched her with burning eyes, watched her as if his
breath would stop if he didn't.

"You've shut God out," Lyndie had said to him last
night, *"but I think He wanted to show you that He
hasn't shut you out."* The stories his parents had told him
about God when he'd been a kid seemed like naïve fairy
tales to him now. A God who could listen to everyone's
prayers at once? Who lived in a place in the sky called
heaven behind pearly gates? Angels? A baby born out of
a virgin? Really? A God who cared about and protected
those who trusted Him?

If so, where had that God been back when Jake had
trusted Him? When Jake's men had been killed? Where
had He been when soldiers and civilians were dying in
Iraq and Afghanistan? Why would He have given Mollie
the body she'd been given?

It wasn't that Jake had shut God out like Lyndie
thought. That implied that he'd shut out someone he
believed in. It was more that he didn't believe in God
anymore. Foolishly optimistic or weak or imaginative
people clung to the idea of God so they'd have something to hope in.

The sounds of doors closing and voices drifted to him
from the front of the house. Moments later, Lyndie's
mom, Karen, hurried into the room wearing a brightly
colored sweatsuit and pink glasses. She spotted him at
once, a grin filling her face. "Jake!"

No sooner had he risen to his feet than she wrapped
her arms around him.

He stood inside her embrace, stiff with shock over the
fact that she was hugging him. She'd seemed tall to him
when he was a kid, but she was so short that she hardly

reached his shoulder. When she stepped back, she kept a hold of his upper arms. "It's good to see you again."

"Thank you."

She finally released him and went to give forehead kisses to each of her daughters.

"Now that you're here," Lyndie said to Karen, "I'm going to go unpack groceries and put in more time with Grandpa."

"Sure."

Lyndie met his gaze before abandoning him to her mother and sister.

He returned to his seat, and Karen pulled the pink chair a few feet closer to him. She settled into it and took one of Mollie's hands in hers. "It's been a long time, Jake. Too long. You were a child the last time I saw you."

Looking at her now, he could remember things he'd forgotten. The other parents in Holley had insisted on being called *ma'am* or *sir*, but she'd asked all the kids to call her Karen. She'd fixed him tuna fish sandwiches with the crusts cut off, sliced into triangles. Her prettiness had made him shy.

"I'm glad for the chance to tell you, Jake, how much we appreciate you giving Lyndie a job. She loves exercising your horses, as you probably know."

He dipped his chin.

"She's been telling me about Silver Leaf. Mike and I are planning to drive out to Lone Star for his first race. Do you think he has a chance of success?"

"I make it a habit not to predict what my horses will do. Whenever I think I know, they do the opposite."

"That's how life is, isn't it? Full of surprises good and bad." She played with Mollie's fingers.

"Do you mind me asking what that machine does?" Jake pointed to a black electronic box with two red number readings on its front. It rested on the shelves that also held the books, paper towels, and some medical supplies.

"Not a bit. That's an oximeter. It measures Mollie's oxygen and her pulse."

"If there's a problem, it alerts you?"

"It does. Though, between Eve, Lyndie, Mike, and me, we usually know if Mollie's having issues before the machine does. We're pretty in tune with her after all these years."

Birdsong and the sound of Mollie's soft breathing filled the space. He watched Mollie, saw her open and close her mouth slightly.

"She's very peaceful unless she's in pain," Karen said.

Mollie, in pain. Just the thought caused Jake's heart to take on weight, like a hundred-pound rock gathering mass. In what kind of screwed-up world should a person who'd done nothing wrong be forced to suffer pain? "I can't remember if anyone ever told me what caused Mollie's cerebral palsy. Was there a cause?" As he transferred his concentration from Mollie to Karen, he realized he'd probably just offended Karen with his question.

"I like it when people ask me about Mollie. Every single time they do, God gives me a ministry opportunity through her." Looking completely unoffended, she bent to unlace her tennis shoes.

A ministry opportunity? He'd just had to listen to a devotional reading. He had no interest in being the focus of Karen's ministry opportunity. The flight instinct he'd been battling ever since he'd entered Mollie's room intensified.

He forced himself to remain in his chair. It could be that he'd made too much of a habit of avoiding people and situations and reminders that upset him. He'd stay for a few more minutes so that he could find out what had happened to Mollie. Lyndie's life had been wound together with Mollie's for as long as he could remember. What affected Mollie affected Lyndie and every other member of the James family.

Karen folded her knees to the side and tucked her feet onto the pink chair. "When I was expecting Mollie, we were living at our old house in Holley. Do you remember it?"

"Yes."

"Lyndie was three at the time, and the biggest worry I had in life was what color I was going to paint the nursery." She shook her head, as if she hardly knew her old self. "And then I went into labor. There were complications. They couldn't get Mollie free of the birth canal, so my obstetrician used forceps. In doing so, he ended up fracturing Mollie's skull in three places."

The muscles along Jake's jawline flexed and hardened.

Karen threaded her fingers through Mollie's. "We went into the hospital thinking we'd be coming home with a healthy little newborn, and instead our whole lives were turned upside-down in a day."

He understood. His own life had been changed forever in one fast twist of time. "Would she have been completely healthy if the doctor hadn't fractured her skull?"

"The medical tests showed that she would have had some issues. But nothing nearly as severe as this."

"I see."

"The first few years after Mollie's birth were miserable

for me. I was furious at God. We sued the obstetrician,
so I had to deal with a trial on top of everything else. I
struggled with depression." Uncensored honesty shone
from her brown eyes, eyes that reminded him of Lyndie.
"Mollie was in the hospital six to eight times every year.
She needed major surgeries, a body cast. Our financial
situation almost dragged us under. Mike and I nearly
divorced. Our reality wasn't what I'd wanted"—emotion
began to clog her voice—"for Lyndie or me or Mike or
Mollie." Tears glittered on her eyelashes.

Why had he asked her about this? "I—"

"Don't worry, it's just in my nature to be sentimental." She gave a quiet chuckle and dashed a finger under
her eyes. "I really am glad for the chance to talk to you
about this."

He struggled to imagine how hard life had been for
Karen and Mike, but his brain reeled even more at the
thought of Lyndie. She'd been very young back then,
and caught in the middle of a storm.

"Things were awful," Karen said. "And then your
mom, your sweet mom, whom you know I love dearly?"

"Yes."

"She made me go to Bible study with her. For weeks
I hated it. It didn't matter. She came every Thursday
morning and drove me to that Bible study. The study
ended with a worship concert in Dallas that your mom
and I went to together. As soon as the music started
that night, I began to cry. I cried all the way through it."

He didn't understand the joy in her expression. "That
was a good thing?"

"For me, yes. Those tears marked the beginning of

my renewed trust in God. My whole life was no longer consumed with what might have been."

That hit dangerously close to where he lived. *What might have been.*

"Instead," she continued, "I began working through my anger and grief. I moved forward with what was. We went on the wait list for this wonderful thing called the Medically Dependent Children's Program. For the five years until that came through, I was Mollie's main nurse. She and I slept together every night. Didn't we, Mols?" She smiled at Mollie. "Do you remember?"

Mollie arched her face toward her mother's voice.

"Once MDCP came to the rescue," Karen told him, "I started taking classes for a degree in counseling. It was like therapy for me, to work with people." Karen lifted Mollie's hand and kissed it. "God is good." She looked right into his eyes. "'His love endures forever.' Second Chronicles 7:3. Do you know that one?"

"No."

"What I've been discovering is that it's not so much that God provides the medicine that heals. Rather, He *is* the medicine."

Silence fell over the three of them.

"I best be going." Jake started to move.

"Not so fast, mister." She waved him back into his seat. "I've talked about myself twice as long as I should have, and I haven't heard anything about you." She re-settled her pink glasses. "You've been through hardship, too."

"Yes." Karen had been handed a tragedy and had dealt with it courageously. He'd been handed one, and he'd withdrawn from life.

"An IED explosion took the lives of three of your men and caused your injuries." She said it with confident ease, as if she were saying to him that the day was sunny.

He lowered his brows. No one talked to him about the IED. They'd tried to, at the beginning, and he'd told them all to go to hell.

"What happened when you came home from the war?"

What happened? He'd been granted the one thing he'd wanted most—a return to his family and Holley, Texas—only to discover he didn't want it after all. He'd been surrounded by friendly, concerned people who had no idea what he'd gone through or what war was. He'd missed his squad the way a person missed a leg that had been amputated. He hadn't wanted to be around anyone, yet he'd been out of practice at living alone.

Those early months back home had been so bad for him, his mental chaos so powerful that he'd wanted to go back to the desert, the adrenaline he'd never feel again, and the life he'd known. "I don't want to talk about it." He spoke low, his voice scratchy. His pulse made a thrumming noise in his ears.

"Did you go to the VA for treatment?" She asked the question calmly, as if he hadn't spoken. "Once you were home?"

"Yes."

"And they diagnosed you with PTSD?"

It still had the power to strip him naked and humiliate him, the acronym PTSD. He'd hoped the doctors would tell him he had anything else, a terminal sickness, even. PTSD had a stigma. It meant he was non-hacker.

He didn't answer. Didn't need to. Karen knew the answer. "Did they prescribe antidepressants?"

Silence.

"I'm guessing they did. You didn't take them?"

Inwardly he swore. He eyed the distance to the door. It was none of her business what he'd been prescribed or whether he'd taken the pills.

"Do you go to therapy?" She tipped her head. "No? Therapy can help. You know, I treat a few vets with PTSD. Would you consider coming and seeing me at the church where I work?"

"I'm sorry, no." He pushed to his feet.

"If you won't come to my office, then you have to come back here and talk to me and Mollie again." She, too, stood. "Do you remember how Lyndie has always believed that Mollie has a healing effect on animals and people?" she asked.

Now that she'd jogged his memory, he nodded. "I do remember." And now he understood why, when he'd asked Lyndie what he could do for her, she'd told him he could visit her sister. Lyndie hoped to heal him. Like one of her injured chicks or birds.

"Well." Karen smiled. "It could be that Lyndie's right."

Dark disbelief shifted through him. It insulted him, the realization that Lyndie viewed him the way she would a cat with a broken leg. He was a successful trainer with an impressive stable, numerous employees, and the respect of people from New York to California. He made a great deal of money. He took part in the lives of his family. He drove his body to the height of its capability for physical strength.

But she'd known—of course she'd known, just like everyone else knew—that he was wrecked inside. So the woman with the tender heart had decided to help him.

She didn't recognize what he recognized about himself. Over the past eight years, his mental and physical scars had driven themselves too deep, had grown too hard.

He could not be cured.

⟨⟩

"There is no cure for PTSD." Karen opened a bag of chips that Lyndie had just bought from the store, then tipped them in Lyndie's direction.

Lyndie helped herself to a handful and studied her mom. Once Jake had gone, the two of them had relocated to the patio table on the deck with the chips and icy cans of grapefruit-flavored sparkling water.

"No cure," Lyndie said. "Really?" It went against her nature. Resignation came harder to her than passionate belief in something, no matter how far-fetched that something might be.

"Jake can't un-see the things he's seen or un-experience the things he's experienced."

"But he can move past them."

"He can learn to live with them," Karen corrected, scooping chips into her cupped palm. "He can improve, he can use coping strategies. The degree of recovery is as individual as the person. There are Vietnam vets still struggling with post-traumatic stress."

"What are the symptoms?"

"The classic symptoms are rage, nightmares, substance abuse. Let's see . . . survivor's guilt, hyper-vigilance, insomnia, emotional numbness. Have you seen evidence of any of those in Jake?"

"The emotional numbness? I haven't noticed any of

the rest—wait. He flinches sometimes at sudden sounds. Is that hyper-vigilant?"

Karen nodded. "No evidence of substance abuse?"

"No." She nibbled on a chip, tasting the crisp tang of salt.

"It's good that he's kept himself from addictions. They only complicate everything else."

Lyndie selected another bent and crinkled chip. "I'm assuming that people who suffer from PTSD abuse substances because they're trying to escape from their thoughts?"

"And feelings. When these guys are at war, they're exposed to horrible things. They stuff them down and either pretend they never happened or that they don't care that they happened, simply so they can continue doing their jobs. There's not much room for regret or grief when you're a serviceman on a tour of duty."

"I understand."

"Eventually, though, they have to deal with what happened to them. Because it *did* happen, and it's still there. It was only stuffed down."

Lyndie swept the crumbs from her palms, then set her grapefruit water on her lap, cradling it with both hands. Mom and Dad's neighbor must be going at it again with his smoker, because the scent of roasting meat tipped the breeze. Sun spiced the nearby trees, their leaves riffling sweetly.

There was joy and peace to experience in this life. She didn't want Jake to be stripped of joy and peace because he'd volunteered to serve his country.

When he'd asked her what he could do for her last night, Lyndie had seized her opportunity. She'd asked

him to visit Mollie, and she'd asked to spend time with
him each day trackside, something she planned to put
into practice tomorrow. "Did you ask him to meet you at
the church so that you could counsel him?" Lyndie asked.

"I did. He said no."

She wrinkled her nose. Tall, Dark, and *Brooding*.
"He's stubborn."

"Since he won't come to the church, I told him that
he needs to come back here, to visit Mollie and me."

"I'll do my best to get him back here."

"Easter's just four days away. Since we've been invited
to lunch at Meg and Bo's, I'll probably have a chance to
talk to him again there. Those eyes . . ."

"I know," Lyndie said, with heartfelt understanding.
A bleak and unholy light inhabited Jake's eyes. It was
more than enough to cause an old lady to have a heart
attack, a young girl to run from him in fear, and a thirty-
year-old with a dreamer's heart to want to love him so
much and so relentlessly that he'd have no choice but
to come back to life.

CHAPTER

THIRTEEN

The dirt road snaked into land marked with rocks and scrubby vegetation. Jake had grown familiar with this stretch, as they all had. He combed the scene, hunting for anything off or wrong, no matter how small. His main mission today, and every day in Iraq, was to get his squad home safely.

In the far distance, he could make out two Bedouin men wearing checked head scarves and long white robes. The waves of heat rising from the earth distorted their image.

A few hungry-looking dogs ran past the Humvee as they slowed to enter the town of flat-topped houses nearest the base. Men squatted outdoors, some drinking tea, others smoking. Irrigation canals bordered the street. A couple of kids hurried toward their vehicle, shouting, "Mister!" in accented English, holding out their hands in hopes of candy.

Jake's fellow Marines waved to the kids but didn't

stop. They were headed farther into the desert this af-
ternoon, to the next village. The buildings fell away.

Rob Panzetti elbowed Justin Scott's shins. "What were
you reading back there at camp?"

"The Principles of Psychology," Scott answered from
his elevated position in the machine gun turret.

"It looked old," Panzetti said.

"It was written in 1890."

"What?" Dan Barnes, the one they called Boots, leaned
in from the backseat. "1890? What can a book that old
have to do with anything nowadays?" They went over
a hole and the teenager's helmet slipped down in front.

"Tighten your helmet," Jake instructed.

"It has plenty to do with today," Scott answered
calmly. "I'm going to get a degree in psychology when
I get home."

"What about you, Boots?" Panzetti spared a quick
glance at the kid. "What are you going to do when you
grow up?"

"Well, I ain't gonna get a degree in psychology. I'm
glad to be done with school." His Texas accent reminded
Jake of Sonic and barbecued brisket. "What I wanna do
when I get home is marry my girlfriend. I might go to
work for her dad someday."

A lot of the guys had girlfriends back home. Some
of them had a hard time thinking about anything else
and worried all the time about receiving a Dear John
letter in the mail. It had always amused Jake, seeing how
soft his highly trained Marines could act over women—

A flash of white cut into Jake's vision. Their vehicle
went airborne, ripping apart. Roaring noise.

Unstoppable power threw Jake through the air. He

wheeled his arms and legs, trying to get himself upright. Before he could, he landed with a bone-jarring crush in a ravine.

He wheezed and bent his arms into his body. Instinctively, he rolled toward the dirt in reaction to the agony in his ribs. His cheek throbbed and pain cut into his thigh and his side.

My God. What . . . What had happened? His ears were ringing. He could hear nothing except that ringing and the frantic panting of his own breath. They'd been driving. . . .

He squinted at the sky and saw smoke rising from flames.

An explosion. They must have been in an explosion.

His men. He pushed himself to his knees, then staggered upright. His men. Where were his men? He ran with limping, uneven strides.

Through a cloud of smoke and dust, he saw the remains of his vehicle tilted into a crater. The front had been blasted away, and the rest lay black and smoldering. Flesh and blood splattered the scene.

A daisy chain of IEDs must have detonated, because he could see evidence of more explosions in a line stretching back along the road. The other vehicles in the convoy had maintained proper distance, so the next one had been damaged, but not badly. Marines were pouring out, moving in his direction.

Oh, God. He scanned the view for Panzetti, Scott, or Boots. No sign of them.

He neared the vehicle, lifting his arm to shield his mouth and nose. It only made it worse. He glanced down *at his sleeve and saw that it was covered in dirt and streaked with black. All of him was.*

Through the flames, he could finally make out what had been the backseat. And Boots . . . Dan Barnes was still there. Metal had bent around him, trapping him. If he hadn't been killed instantly, the fire had done it right after.

"No," Jake rasped, wanting to look away but unable to. Boots was an eighteen-year-old kid. He'd been Jake's to protect. Sickening fury and confusion and despair circled within Jake. It should have been him dead and burned. Not the kid.

He stumbled back. "Panzetti!" he screamed, but he could barely hear his own hoarse voice.

Two of the Marines in his squad ran in his direction. "Make sure someone's called Medical," he yelled to them.

They hesitated, nodded, and turned back to follow his order. Jake ran down the road, his attention cutting left and right, searching. He couldn't breathe right through the liquid in his lungs. He continued to run. Saw nothing.

Where were Panzetti and Scott?

Jake bolted upright in bed with a gasp.

The inside of his bedroom surrounded him. Dim and quiet. Far less real to him than the moments he'd just been living inside his nightmare. Fighting for breath, he screwed shut his eyes to avoid the sight of his bottom corner dresser drawer.

Unlike the kind of nightmares other people had, he couldn't tell himself his wasn't real. How bitterly he wished it wasn't real. His soul would burn in hell because it *was* real. It had happened.

But it's not happening now, he told himself. *That was years ago. You're in Holley.*

His breathing grew even more shallow. Panic tightened his throat.

He saw her then, sitting on her stool in her studio. She was clean and sweet and so pretty he almost couldn't bear it. She had her hair up. Her dog was snoring on his lap. And she was painting innocent things that had no darkness in them at all.

Slowly, the mess of Jake's mind began to steady.

"Are you planning to stand there in silence the whole time?" Jake asked Lyndie later that morning.

"I was under the impression that you didn't like conversation." She'd finished exercising her horses and arrived at Jake's position near Lone Star's track ten minutes prior. He'd agreed to let her shadow him for a short period each day, and she intended to make him follow through. She wasn't sure, though, of his preferences. Not wanting to disturb him, she'd been standing quietly to the side and a little behind him.

Below his black Stetson, he looked at her out of the corners of his eyes. He appeared to be somewhat . . . entertained by her. "I like conversation more than I like you standing there watching me without saying anything."

"Duly noted." She moved up, directly next to him. "As it happens, I like conversation more than standing there watching you, too."

He angled his chin toward Firewheel, one of his young colts. "Look." Firewheel had spooked at something. It took the horse a moment to regain himself and settle back into his stride. "He's not learning as quickly as he should."

"And he seems to spook at the same things over and over."

"That bush he just passed must look like a mountain lion to him," Jake said dryly. "It bothers him day after day."

"Maybe Firewheel has an imagination like mine. To me that bush looks like a hunched-over dragon."

One edge of his lips ticked up. "You'd make a bad racehorse."

She laughed. After her fall, things between her and Jake had softened in some hard-to-define but integral way. Praise God! His extreme reserve had cracked. He trusted her enough now to talk with her, to show up at her apartment unannounced, to visit Mollie. They were, perhaps, becoming friends for the second time in their lives. It hadn't been easy to get to this point with him. That she'd managed it, that he'd let her, was a present more valuable than gold.

Surreptitiously, she skimmed a peek down the firm, uncompromising line of his profile. The sight reminded her once again of a scarred pirate, surveying his domain. If you liked that sort of thing.

She—the girl who didn't lose her head over men—did. Like it.

"If you were Firewheel's trainer, what would you do to help him?" Jake asked.

"Is this a test? You already know what you're going to do about Firewheel, right? You're testing me to see if I come up with the same answer."

"Maybe."

For certain. "If I were Firewheel's trainer, I'd put blinkers on him." The nylon hood with cups for the eyes limited a horse's vision to what was in front of him. In the case of Firewheel, the blinkers would likely calm him. "That's what you're going to do, isn't it?"

"Nah."

"What?" she asked, incredulous. "Of course it is."

A span of quiet passed. "Of course it is."

Lyndie grinned with self-satisfaction. "Mmm-hmm. I passed the test."

"I wouldn't get too bigheaded over it. The teenager who sells ice cream in the clubhouse would know to try blinkers on Firewheel."

"Then give me a harder test."

He looked at her then, a look of mixed caution and admiration. As if he both wanted and didn't want to find her charming.

She returned his level regard. Something real and enticing passed between them.

"Did I tell you that I liked conversation?" he asked.

"Yes."

"I changed my mind." The words were gruff, but there was a tiny shade of teasing in his expression that blunted them slightly.

"Too late." So, Jake wasn't very good at friendship yet. Still, he was trying. His stilted, unpracticed efforts at it warmed her far more than effusive affection from another person ever could have.

One of his riders brought his mount to a halt in front of Jake. "Hold up for a second," Jake instructed him, then knelt near the filly's front hooves. Jake ran his hand down the delicate bones of the filly's leg, his strong fingers amazingly gentle and articulate.

Lyndie watched, swallowing back tenderness. Did he know just how much his treatment of his horses communicated about him? It revealed to Lyndie his deep kindness. Unfailing fairness and compassion. Intelligence. Dedication. He worked through the weekends and watched over his recuperating horses vigilantly.

You could tell a lot about a man by the way he treated animals, and Jake treated the animals under his care as finely as any animals could be treated.

If you liked that sort of thing.

Lyndie was returning Willow to the barn at Lone Star the next morning when she spotted Jake. He stood outside Silver Leaf's stall with a short, dark-haired woman next to him.

Lyndie came to an abrupt halt. She needed to return Willow to his groom, yet all of a sudden she couldn't get her feet to move because, with a plummeting sense of disappointment, she recognized the woman next to Jake.

Elizabeth Alvarez had been a jockey at Santa Anita during the years when Lyndie had been striving to make a go of her own jockey career. At that time, they'd been the only two female jockeys at the track and so had shared a tiny, makeshift room off to the side of the main dressing room.

To be female in a male-dominated field had been a struggle for them both. They'd had a difficult time convincing trainers to trust them with their best horses. Which became a downward spiral, because unless you had a shot with the best horses, you couldn't win, and if you couldn't win, trainers didn't want to put you on their best horses.

Her grip on Willow's reins tightened as she watched Jake incline his head to listen to Elizabeth. It appeared that Jake had decided to stick with her "lady's man" strategy for Silver Leaf. He was going to try a female jockey on him. But judging by the riding clothes Elizabeth had on, the female jockey wasn't going to be Lyndie.

Why had she waited so long to ask Jake if she could ride Silver in his opening race? She'd wanted the perfect moment, but her bide-my-time strategy had failed her.

Willow's groom approached, and Lyndie released the bay colt into his care. Heartsick, she made her way toward Jake and Elizabeth.

When Jake looked over and saw her, a jolt of awareness and power traveled through their eye contact.

Elizabeth acknowledged her with a reserved inclining of her head. "Hello, Lyndie."

"Good to see you again, Elizabeth."

"You two know each other?"

"We both worked at Santa Anita," Elizabeth answered.

"I've thought of you several times since I've been here at Lone Star," Lyndie said to her. "I remembered that you'd started coming to Texas in the spring."

"This'll be my fourth season here. As soon as Lone Star closes, I head to California. Are you going to the West Coast this summer?"

"No, I'm here full time now. My sister . . ."

"That's right." Elizabeth's face took on that down-tipping look people always gave Lyndie when she mentioned Mollie.

"Elizabeth is going to breeze Silver Leaf," Jake stated.

Even though Lyndie had expected as much, the words still wrenched her. A *breeze* gave a horse an opportunity to stretch out in a run, not an all-out sprint, but fast enough to feel the breeze in his face, thus the term. In the days leading up to a race, a breeze could reveal much to a trainer about a horse's mental and physical readiness. After today, Jake would likely gentle Silver's training regimen in order to conserve the best of the horse's energy for when it mattered.

"He's a good-looking horse." Elizabeth stepped to the stall's opening, her hands entwined at the small of her back, her gleaming black hair caught in a low ponytail.

Lyndie shifted so that she could see into the stall and for the first time noticed Zoe kneeling within. By the looks of it, the tall redhead had nearly finished wrapping the stallion's rear legs.

Misgivings swamped Lyndie. *Swamped* her. The whole situation felt wrong. She didn't know whether that was because putting Elizabeth on Silver was actually, intrinsically wrong or because of the envy twisting inside her. She had no right to say anything against Jake's decision to let Elizabeth breeze Silver. Jake trained Silver Leaf; Lyndie did not.

Elizabeth had been jockeying for seven or eight years straight now. She might only be two years older in age than Lyndie, but Elizabeth far surpassed her in race experience. On paper, Elizabeth was obviously the better choice.

Zoe led Silver out and saddled him. Elizabeth donned her riding helmet, then Jake gave her a leg up into the saddle. "I'll walk to the track behind you," he said.

Elizabeth set off.

Zoe shot Lyndie an urgent look and did a double head tilt toward Jake. It seemed that Zoe didn't want Elizabeth jockeying Silver, either.

"If it's all right with you, Jake, I'll join you," Lyndie said. Silver would have been the final of her horses to exercise. Since Elizabeth was riding him instead, Lyndie had completed her work.

"All right." Jake started walking.

Your enthusiasm overwhelms! Hurriedly, she shucked off her protective vest and pulled a pale pink sweater over her white tank. She caught up with Jake outside the barn.

Ahead, Elizabeth sat atop Silver, completely relaxed.

Lyndie wrestled against jealousy she didn't want to feel. *Elizabeth has never been anything but professional toward you, Lyndie. Remember?*

She and Elizabeth had once shared the camaraderie of two outsiders banded together. They'd stuck up for each other, treated each other with respect, and encouraged one another through losses and setbacks. However, there had always, always, been a thread of competitiveness between them, too.

Because they'd been the only two female jockeys at Santa Anita, the racing faithful had naturally compared them. As good as Lyndie had believed she'd had the potential to be, the stats had continually favored Elizabeth.

Elizabeth was a blunt, no-nonsense, tremendously driven person, and her intense work ethic had paid off. Lyndie had been driven, too. But she'd been needed at home to help with Mollie. She hadn't been free to put in the same number of hours as Elizabeth.

During her jockeying days, Lyndie had begged God

month after month for a trainer—just one—to give her a chance on a great horse—just one. That trainer and that horse had never come, but nonetheless, she'd poured every spare minute, plus all her hope and energy, into jockeying for two whole years. Eventually, though, unable to make ends meet, Lyndie had let go of jockeying and the tall dreams she'd built for herself around it. It had not been an easy decision. She'd grown up imagining herself riding in the Kentucky Derby.

Elizabeth had continued jockeying. She'd toughed it out through seasons of low pay, danger, and adversities. Over time, she'd carved out a modest career for herself. She'd never ridden a big horse, the kind of Thoroughbred that the racing community called a World Beater. But Lyndie kept atop of things enough to know that Elizabeth had finished last year's season at Lone Star near the middle of the jockey rankings, making her the best of the female jocks the track had to offer.

So. Why, knowing what she did of Elizabeth and her journey, didn't she have the grace to hand over Silver to her with blessings? Goodwill? Instead, miserable protectiveness, like that of a mother for her baby, engulfed her. She'd put in so much time with Silver. She loved the horses she exercised. For goodness' sake, she loved all animals. But there was something about Silver. That indefinable magic. *She'd* been the one to comprehend his inner workings. *She'd* been the one to make him run.

She and Jake, walking side by side, had covered most of the distance to the track in silence. Only fifty or so yards to go. *Lord, should I say something?*

No discernible answer. She definitely didn't want to ruin her fragile, hard-won camaraderie with Jake. Then again, she'd known she'd *have* to step on land mines with him occasionally. "Elizabeth's very good."

Jake made a sound low in his throat.

"She's experienced. She has great instincts."

"Why do I think you're about to tell me not to put her aboard Silver Leaf for his opening race?"

"Because that's exactly what I'm about to tell you."

Without looking at her, Jake frowned. "I thought you'd be pleased. She's female."

"But she's not me."

He came instantly to a stop. He surveyed her face as if searching it for answers. "No. She's not you."

Lyndie straightened to her full height. "I want to ride Silver Leaf in his opening race."

Charged quiet. "What?" he whispered.

"I want to be Silver Leaf's jockey. Please."

"No."

"I jockeyed for two years. I've kept my license current. I won't ask to ride any of the other horses, but I'd really appreciate the chance to ride Silver Leaf."

"You're very good at what you do. But the answer's no." He turned and stalked toward the track, shutting her out.

She stayed abreast of him. "I realized that I wanted to race him a while ago. I've simply been waiting for the chance to talk to you about it."

"It's not going to happen, Lyndie."

"Why?"

"It's too dangerous."

"But it's not too dangerous for Elizabeth?"

"No. It's not."

Betrayal stung her. "I'm as capable as she is."

He didn't answer.

Surely he wasn't holding her spill against her? He himself had said that there'd been nothing she could have done differently the morning she'd fallen. . . .

Maybe her spill wasn't at the root of his reluctance. His experiences in Iraq and the wounds he'd sustained there had likely made him more susceptible to worry, both justified and unjustified. "There are certainly risks involved in jockeying," she said carefully. "But they're calculated risks. I've been riding for years and I've had a few injuries, but they've all been minor."

"We both know that doesn't mean you won't be seriously injured the next time."

"I'd like to be the one who makes the call about whether jockeying Silver Leaf is safe enough for me to take on. It's my neck."

"I'm Silver Leaf's trainer. I make the call about jockeys." His tone held the ring of finality.

Lyndie saw that two of Jake's other horses stood ready, both with their jockeys instead of their exercise riders astride. It appeared that Jake was going to breeze Silver in company, using the same method he'd employed with her a few days prior.

"I'm worried," she said, "that putting Elizabeth on Silver Leaf this morning is going to set him back." Stupid tears pricked the back of her throat. She *would not* cry over this. She was an adult, a professional.

"I disagree."

"You've paired him with a female, but that's only part of the equation. He has to know and trust his rider before he'll race for her." She couldn't be sure of this, of course. It could be that now that they'd unearthed

Silver's potential and he'd had a taste of competition, that he'd race for anyone.

"Silver Leaf can get to know and trust Elizabeth," Jake said.

"I spent hours a day with him for two weeks straight before he began to trust me. His first race is in seven days."

"My decision stands, Lyndie."

She bit the inside of her bottom lip to keep herself from arguing. He'd agreed to let her join him at the rail each day, and he'd asked her opinion on his horses a couple of times. But she was painfully aware that those things in no way gave her permission to dictate to him what he should do about his racers.

They reached the trio of jockeys, and Jake issued curt instructions to each. The horses moved off.

Anxiety knotted Lyndie's stomach. Just yesterday they'd stood at this very spot talking easily. Her hopes for them and for the future had lifted. Today, this.

Jake raised his stopwatch, punching it the moment the horses began their breeze. Two of the three horses surged forward. Silver Leaf lagged, which wasn't out of character. He preferred to let the others dash ahead, assess them, and then unleash his own power.

But this time, he didn't.

He unleashed none of his own power. The tall dapple grey stallion galloped along exactly as he'd infamously done in all his prior seasons, slow and imperturbable. The other two horses swept far, then farther, in front of him.

Elizabeth had breezed countless horses. Her technique couldn't be faulted. But to Silver, Elizabeth was a pleasant stranger. She had not earned her way into his inner royal court and so for her, he would not exert himself.

Lyndie's hunched shoulders eased, and she took a deep breath of relief. It was terrible of her, but she couldn't help feeling glad. Silver's refusal to run for Elizabeth meant that she still had a shot at convincing Jake to give her an opportunity to ride him.

Jake said nothing and gave nothing away with his body language, yet she could sense his deep frustration. As the seconds dragged, his control over himself seemed to ratchet tighter and tighter.

If she said anything to him now, she feared he'd shut her down hard. She'd wait and approach him about jockeying Silver Leaf when he wasn't so defensive.

Between now and then, she'd pray.

Exercise was supposed to be healthy. But Jake knew that if anyone could see him now they'd think he'd driven off the road marked healthy and straight into a ditch called crazy.

It was one o'clock in the morning. Jake continued lifting his body to the chin-up bar in his loft's workout room. Again, then again and again, as if his life depended on it.

Crazy. There was a word.

For years now, it had taken all he had to hold himself together. Since Lyndie had returned to his life, his grip had begun to slip.

His breath rushing from him, he dropped to the ground, then staggered a step before leaning his shoulder into the wall for support. His muscles were rubber. Air sawed in and out of his lungs.

He hadn't been able to sleep, so he'd done what he'd always done when he couldn't sleep: He'd come here. First, he'd run on his treadmill. Unable to outrun his thoughts, he'd begun weight-lifting more than an hour ago.

He should call it a night. Shower. Try to act like someone who wasn't crazy and attempt sleep.

Jake's legs weren't feeling so steady, so he laid out on a weight bench. His lungs continued to drag for breath. He stacked his hands on his forehead palms-up and glared at the line where the room's ceiling met the wall.

Why couldn't one thing have gone his way? Silver Leaf should have run for Elizabeth this past morning. Everything he knew about horses, all his experience, told him he'd prepared Silver Leaf for his upcoming race. He and Lyndie had brought him to just the right condition at just the right time. The horse had been cleaning up his feed, passing his veterinary tests, impressing Jake on the track. He should have run today.

"You've paired him with a female, but that's only part of the equation," Lyndie had said. *"He has to know and trust his rider before he'll race for her."* No part of him wanted to believe that, then or now. Racehorses didn't discriminate. They'd run for any good rider. Calvin Borel had ridden Mine That Bird, a horse he'd never raced before, to victory in the 2009 Derby. Ten other examples sprang to Jake's mind of horses who'd won big in similar circumstances.

An experienced jockey accounted for maybe ten percent of a horse's success at the track. Only ten. So why hadn't his horse performed for Elizabeth today the way he'd seen him perform for Lyndie?

Curse him, he knew why.

Lyndie was Silver Leaf's motivation. He'd seen their poetry with his own eyes. He hadn't thought there were any wonders left in this world, but Lyndie and Silver Leaf together? They were one.

The fact that Lyndie had been unhurt the other morning after a horse had galloped over her? That was another. Unexplainable. Illogical.

Is it? a voice within asked.

He shoved the thought aside. All day, frustration and confusion had been dogging him over the issue of who would jockey Silver Leaf. He'd never once considered putting Lyndie on him in a race. She'd retired from racing long ago. She was only an exercise rider. She was—

He didn't want to understand all the things she was to him.

He liked Elizabeth Alvarez fine. He could put her on his racehorse and sleep at night. But the idea of putting Lyndie on Silver Leaf in a contested race made his heart turn to rock. All those horses jostling for position, the great speed. Her spill at practice had been bad enough. Much worse could happen to her in a race.

How could he risk Lyndie? She painted pictures of fairies, for goodness' sake.

He couldn't—he just couldn't lose anyone else he was responsible for. He'd lost people already, and it had nearly killed him.

He groaned and pushed the heels of his hands against his eyes. How could he *not* risk Lyndie when she was the only one who could give Silver Leaf a chance of success?

He and Bo had been the ones to decide on the pairing between Silver Leaf's dam and sire. When Silver Leaf had been a half-grown colt, Jake had carried carrots for him in his pockets and fed them to him by hand. He'd trained him himself in the round pen as a yearling. His sister-in-law, Meg, loved Silver Leaf.

How could he justify not giving Lyndie a chance to ride him?

He couldn't.

How could he stand to let her ride him?

He couldn't.

CHAPTER
FOURTEEN

D anny!" Amber approached Cream or Sugar's counter, pleased to see that Celia's Uncle Danny occupied his usual barstool.

"Amber!"

She'd hurried through her lunch at work so that she'd have time to seek more of Danny's dating advice. As much as she'd been hoping that Will would ask her out, he still hadn't. And Lyndie certainly wasn't making any progress in the dating department. So it fell to Amber to rustle up more outings for the both of them.

"What's up, girl?" Danny asked. "Everything cool?"

She settled onto a stool. "Everything's going fine with work and with Jayden, but things haven't really improved on the dating front."

He nodded with understanding. Holley's very own California surfer dude had made an orange Hurley shirt into a tank top by cutting off the neck and arms. A tan at least five decades deep covered his upper body and face. "It takes time."

Ty Porter approached on the other side of the counter wearing jeans and a T-shirt, both fabulously worn-in. "Hi, Amber."

Feminine fascination short-circuited her brain. She had to grope around inside her head to remember what to reply. Turns out, he'd said "Hi, Amber," so she only needed to say, "Hey, Ty."

"What can I get you?"

"Coffee with cream and . . . since it's Friday, did Celia do her TGIF cupcake?"

"Yes, ma'am."

"One, please. And an Easter Egg sugar cookie to take home to Jayden."

"You got it." He moved off.

"How did the singles event at Fellowship Church turn out?" Danny asked.

"I had a great time. I met several new people."

"What about Lyndie?"

"To be honest with you, I'm a little worried about Lyndie's dating skills. As beautiful as she is, I mean"— she shrugged—"I'd classify her as *really* beautiful—she's not very outgoing around men. I'm not sure if she's just out of practice or what."

"I've heard she's an artist."

"She is."

"Cool. Wow, very cool. Maybe you're just picking up on Lyndie's creative mojo, you know? Artists can groove on another plane."

Huh?

Ty placed a teacup filled with steaming coffee before her as well as a tiny cream pitcher. He retrieved her cup-cake, flicking a dish towel over his shoulder as he brought it to her. There could be no more welcome sight in the life of a single woman than that of a hunk with a dish towel over his shoulder bringing you a cupcake.

"Celia and Hudson aren't here today?" Amber centered her gaze on Ty's forehead, since she had a hard time looking into the handsomeness of his face.

"They're at a playdate with a few other moms and babies. Here's the Easter cookie for Jayden." He set a small white sack within her reach.

"Thank you."

"Sure thing." Ty went to wait on an elderly man with a cane.

"You know . . ." Danny's attention took a vacation before returning to her. "I'm remembering a mixer that one of the local groups has coming up. It's for thirty-fives and under. It's modeled after a *gokon*."

"A what?"

"The Japanese, you know. Very zen people. They're doing some sweet things with group blind dating. At a gokon everyone brings a friend or two with them."

"Sounds interesting." Amber gently peeled the wrapper off her TGIF cupcake. Celia spiked the vanilla cake batter with dark chocolate chips. Top that with peanut butter frosting decorated with chocolate shavings, toffee, and a drizzle of butterscotch and there you had it—a true celebration of Friday.

"They're having the gokon at a Japanese restaurant in Allen." Danny took a bite of his chocolate chip cookie, then dabbed his mouth with his napkin. "Do you want me to email you the link?"

"I'd like that. Thank you." Incredible, how good this cupcake was.

"I'm guessing nothing's happened yet between you and the fireman?"

"He gave me a bid for a new deck."

"It's a start."

"If so, a very slow start. I really like the fireman." She smiled sadly. "But I don't think the feeling is mutual."

"He may yet come around."

"A girl can hope, Danny. Until then?"

"Yes?"

"I have this cupcake."

Most people could not be found at their workplaces on beautiful Saturday afternoons. But even before she'd spotted his truck in the lot, Lyndie had known where she'd find Jake.

She hopped down from her Jeep and made her way around the yearling barn at Whispering Creek.

Jake still hadn't said anything to her about jockeying Silver Leaf. More than two days had passed since Silver's failed breeze with Elizabeth, and less than a week remained before Silver's race. Fortunately, the stallion had run as fast as ever for Lyndie the past two mornings. Which meant his outing with Elizabeth hadn't set him back the way she'd feared it might. And which ought to mean that Lyndie had an advantage in scoring the role of Silver's jockey.

Yesterday morning, when she'd stood beside Jake after she'd finished riding, there had been plenty of breaks in the conversation, many quiet moments when he could have informed her that he'd decided to let her jockey

Silver Leaf in his upcoming race. But no. He'd remained silent on the topic, so she'd chosen to remain patient.

The past two nights she'd lain in bed and stared out the half circle of glass atop her bedroom window. White clouds had crept past an ebony sky while her mind concocted worrying scenarios about Silver Leaf and Elizabeth and a man who would not bend.

This morning she'd been determined that the time had come to discuss Silver. But when she'd finished her duties and walked out to meet Jake, he'd been gone. His foreman had been there in his stead and had informed her that Jake had been called away to meetings.

All day since, Lyndie had been trying to convince herself that it would be fine to wait until Monday to talk with him. She'd done a Pilates class, showered, run to the grocery store, hung with Mollie, then returned home to work on art. Contrary to the sketch she'd intended to draw, a dark and gloomy prince in a black tri-fold hat (a black Stetson would have been entirely too literal) and long cape had overtaken her paper. The blond fairy, the redheaded fairy, and the gray unicorn all stood in a line before the prince, timid and frowning, waiting to see what he would command.

Lyndie had pulled back from the sketch to examine it. Then and there, she'd hit her limit. She couldn't wait, timid and frowning, until Monday to see what Jake would decree. There was no such thing as the perfect time to broach a subject with him, something she'd already learned to her detriment. She'd decided to ask Jake in a civilized fashion whether he'd let her jockey Silver Leaf. The question might prove to be another land mine to their personal friendship, but it was within the bounds of their professional relationship, she felt quite sure. Right?

Right. It was.

Her riding boots had become such an extension of her when near horses that it felt novel to walk on Whispering Creek's soil in flip-flops. She hadn't wanted to look too sloppy or too dressy so had chosen jeans, a tangerine scoop-neck tee, and one of her brightly patterned infinity scarves.

Behind the barn, several horses grazed in the paddocks and pasture. She spotted one male figure, but even at a distance she could tell he wasn't Jake.

Lyndie let herself into the barn, her eyes adjusting as she made her way down the row, looking into each of the stalls. She exchanged hellos with two workers. Still no sight of Jake.

She reached the warm room and opened its door—

Jake's hazel stare clashed instantly with hers. He had a clipboard in his hand and was leaning on the room's central table, his weight supported by it. No black Stetson this afternoon.

She let herself into the room. Whispering Creek employees used the space for meetings, as a lunch spot, and as a storage area for equipment and horse medicines. It offered one big window, a sink, a mini-fridge. All kept exactly as neat and organized as the rest of Jake's barns. "Hey."

He regarded her with both alert intensity and wary warning. "Hey."

She extended the small peace offering she'd brought. A wrapped Reese's Peanut Butter Cup.

Gravely, he took it from her. After a brief hesitation,

he set both it and the clipboard aside. "Is everything okay?"

"Everything's fine."

"Is there something you need?"

"I drove out here to find you."

"Because?"

Here goes nothing. She'd learned it was best with him not to dance around the issue. "I was hoping to talk to you about Silver Leaf. I'd planned to ask you about him this morning, but when I went out to see you, you were gone."

"I had meetings."

"I heard." She pushed her fingers into the front pockets of her jeans. "Have you decided who'll be riding Silver Leaf in his race?"

"No. I haven't decided yet."

Just say I can do it already, Tall, Dark, and Brooding! "I'd really like the chance to ride him."

"I know you would."

He wore his gray knit shirt, the top three buttons open to reveal a downy white T-shirt beneath. His eyes looked bloodshot today and even more bleak than usual. He hadn't shaved. Strain etched across his forehead and into the faint lines at the corners of his eyes. His hair showed tracks from where he'd shoved his fingers through it, probably in frustration.

Lyndie had come here concerned about herself. But as she catalogued the details of his face, her concern shifted. "You're struggling." She spoke quietly, but with confidence. "You're not sleeping, are you?"

He scowled.

"Why aren't you sleeping?" PTSD? Anxiety? What?

"Nighttime hours are not my favorite hours. Look, if we're done here—"

"We're not done here."

"Go and enjoy your Saturday, Lyndie."

"Now that I'm getting a good look at you, I won't be able to go and enjoy my Saturday. I'll be too worried about you. What can I do to help?"

He turned instantly defensive. "Nothing."

Jake's poor face. His poor, ravaged face, both undeniably handsome and unbearably exhausted. As big and strong as he was physically, he was also wounded. He needed someone to care about him.

Following pure instinct, she stepped forward and reached up to place her hands on either side of his face.

"No," he rasped, trying to pull back.

"Shh," she replied, firm. She'd purposely placed her hands in the same position on both sides of his face, favoring neither the perfect side nor the scarred. His old injury felt the way it looked, thin and slightly stretched.

"Lyndie," he said brokenly. "Don't."

She didn't lose her courage. Her hands remained, holding his profile tilted down to hers so that she could read his face, so that there was no place for either of them to hide. "I want to help you if you'll let me," she said. "You're the best friend I ever had."

"I'm no longer that kid."

"No. You were a boy then and now you're a man. But you're still Jake Porter. I'd know this face anywhere."

"My face is unrecognizable."

"Not to me. Your face would be beautiful to me even if all the skin had melted away."

His hands came up, banding around her wrists. He

stopped short, though, of yanking down her arms. She could feel tremors going through him for the length of one breath, two.

Exquisite lightning twined back and forth between them. She'd been motivated to put her hands on him out of compassion and determination. But now that they were bound together in this intimate position, the wild strength of their attraction leapt to life. Her heart began to drum. "I want to help you," she said again.

He wrenched away and prowled to the window, anchoring a hand against its frame. His chest pumped in and out unevenly.

She could tell he was desperate for space, so she followed him only halfway to the window, giving him time to gather himself.

Jake needed someone to talk to, someone to listen to him and hug him and cry with him and pray for him. *Talk to me!* she wanted to shout. But—*still!*—he held his silence, hunkering down behind the walls he'd built to keep others out.

The faint sound of a clock ticking and of footsteps passing by the door melded with the throb of Lyndie's pulse. "I'm sorry that my family moved away all those years ago." She chose her words carefully, trying to find a pathway that would reach him. "And I'm very sorry that I didn't contact you after you came home from the war. I regret that I wasn't there for you when you needed a friend."

No response.

"But I'm here now, and I'm not going anywhere. Will you tell me why you aren't sleeping?"

A long pause, then he turned from the window to

face her, crossing his arms. "Responsibilities," he said, his voice level. "Worries."

It was a beginning. "Are these worries centered on things in the past or present?"

"Both."

"Do you want to talk about them with me?"

"No."

A verse rose in her mind. *For our struggle is not against flesh and blood, but against the rulers, against the authorities, against the powers of this dark world and against the spiritual forces of evil in the heavenly realms.* What must it be like for him? To struggle against this dark world and Post-Traumatic Stress Disorder without God's help?

Protectiveness gusted within her. The powers of this dark world could not have Jake. "What about the IED? Will you talk to me about that?"

"I just . . ." A muscle flexed in his cheek. "I can't."

"Can you tell me what physical injuries you sustained in the IED explosion?"

A gap of quiet. "A punctured lung. Broken ribs. Lacerations."

"Lacerations where?"

"My face, my leg, my side."

He was talking to her, trusting her with some of the details. "Did you consider returning to service once your injuries healed?"

He shook his head. "I received an honorable discharge."

"Do your old injuries still bother you?"

"The physical ones? No."

That the old mental injuries still bothered him greatly

went unsaid. "What have you found that helps you sleep?" she asked.

He looked at her pointedly, a vertical line grooving the skin between his eyebrows. "There's nothing that helps, Lyndie."

"There *is* one thing that can help, Jake."

"You going to preach God to me again?"

"God again. Would you consider coming to church with me?"

"No." He made his way to the far side of the table to gather his clipboard and the Reese's Peanut Butter Cup. He was closing the conversation and dismissing her.

"Well, if you change your mind . . . let me know. I meant what I said earlier. If there's anything I can do for you, I want to. If you ever decide you want to talk about stuff, I'm here."

He stood with his arms down, the clipboard and Reese's held against the outside of his thigh. Heat and tumult lit his eyes.

The table separated them as surely as a continent. It almost seemed that he'd put it there on purpose. A buffer between them, certainly. But also, perhaps, a protection. Could he be protecting himself from her? Her from him? "Will you consider going back to see my mom and Mollie? Please?"

For a few extended seconds, he studied her. "Fine."

"Really?" Her spirits brightened. "When?"

"Right now."

"I'll come with you—"

"I'd prefer to go alone."

His words hurt even as she told herself not to let them hurt. They'd made progress today. It was, for now, enough.

Jake's healing process would happen God's way, not her way.

"Go and enjoy your Saturday," he said. Then he shouldered through the door and was gone.

Lyndie remained alone in the middle of the small, endlessly empty room.

She touched my face, Jake thought over and over as he drove across town. *She touched my face.*

Why had she done that? She'd put her hands on him. She must not have any idea of the kind of chaos that set off inside him or how little control he had over himself.

Since the Marines, he'd lived a simple life. He'd ruthlessly avoided alcohol and drugs and sex, knowing that he wasn't strong enough to deal with any of them. It had been another lifetime when he'd last been touched by a woman he was attracted to.

But just now Lyndie—heaven help him, *Lyndie*—had touched his face. She'd stood so close he could feel her body heat and smell her soap, a scent so clean and clear it reminded him of a waterfall. Need had overwhelmed him.

Why couldn't she let him be? Why did she have to ask questions and say things he wished he could rewind and delete?

"I won't be able to go and enjoy my Saturday. I'll be too worried about you. I want to help you if you'll let me. You're the best friend I ever had. I'm sorry that my family moved away all those years ago. I'm here now, and I'm not going anywhere."

His hands were shaking. He gripped the steering wheel

harder and drove to Lyndie's parents' house. He hadn't agreed to this visit because Lyndie suggested it. He'd agreed because he needed to talk to Karen.

Still, it was probably a bad idea, he thought as he knocked on their front door, to show up here out of the blue. Not good manners.

Lyndie's dad answered the door. The older man's face immediately broke into a smile. "Jake Porter! It's Mike James." He shook Jake's hand with a strong grip and used his free hand to clap Jake's shoulder.

Mike looked exactly like Lyndie's Grandpa Harold, only thirty years younger. He stood a head shorter than Jake and was built like a bull. His thick brown hair had grayed at the sides.

In the living room, Jake could see Harold's feet resting on the extended part of his recliner. Mollie sat nearby in a specialized wheelchair. Horse racing filled the TV screen.

"We're watching the racing down at Gulfstream," Mike said. "Did you see that Ladd's Lady won the stakes race there yesterday?"

"I did."

"Good horse. Real good horse."

"Yes, sir."

"Please, come join us. Make yourself comfortable."

He hadn't come to watch horse racing with Mike, Harold, and Mollie. "I came by to speak with your wife. Is she at home?"

"She sure is. Right over here." Mike led him to the first room off the hallway. Instead of a regular door, it had two French doors full of glass. Mike pushed one open and leaned in. "Here's my girlfriend right here."

Karen rose to greet him. "Jake! Come in." She spoke like she'd been expecting him.

"Time's played a dirty trick on me," Mike said. "I'm getting older, but Karen looks prettier than the first day we met." He winked at his wife.

Karen smiled at Mike before turning her attention to Jake. "He's lying. Come over here and let me show you what I'm working on." She drew him to the big table that took up most of the room's space. A laptop rested on one corner of the surface. Pictures and papers and stacks of albums covered the rest. Late afternoon sunlight fell over everything, catching a few pieces of dust that hovered in the air. "Scrapbooking's my hobby."

"Karen's been scrapbooking for what," Mike asked, "ten years?"

"Maybe more now. Here we are." She turned an album so that Jake could see a picture of Lyndie wearing a dress and socks that came up to her knees and carrying a lunch box. "I've finally made it to Lyndie's first day of kindergarten."

Jake glanced at Mike, who sent him a look full of laughter. "She's making slow and steady progress. I'll be in the living room watching TV, babe, just so you'll know where to find me."

"I always know where to find you and your father, honey. You two never budge."

Mike chuckled and closed the glass doors behind him.

"Is it very bad of them to watch so much TV?" Karen asked Jake.

Did she actually expect an answer? "You're the therapist."

"True. I'm the therapist, and for your information,

I think it's very bad of them to watch so much TV."
She pushed her pink glasses up her nose. "But I allow
it because it's one of their greatest joys in life. And, if
you must know, it gives me a few hours to myself to
work on my books." She flipped through the nearest
album. "There was a picture of you, Jake, just a few
pages back. . . ." She pointed to a photo. "Here. Isn't
that darling?"

He looked to be about seven. He was holding a lead
rope attached to Rusty, one of the Porter family's old
horses. Lyndie stood next to him, a scrawny girl with a
tangled halo of pale hair. One of her knees was scraped.
She had a dirt streak on her cheek and the strap of her
sundress had come off a shoulder. She'd placed her tiny
hands on her hips and was smiling a mischievous smile.
The reliable-looking, brown-haired boy he'd been was
looking down at her, with a half smile on his mouth and
softness in his eyes.

The love he'd had for her then couldn't have been more
obvious. *"You're the best friend I ever had."* Memories
circled inside and around him. "She's why I came," he
finally said.

"Lyndie?"

He nodded.

"Have a seat." Karen offered him her leather desk
chair, then settled herself onto a stool positioned near
the laptop.

"Has Lyndie told you that she wants to be Silver Leaf's
jockey in his race on Thursday?" he asked.

"No. But I'm not the least surprised to hear that."

"You can't want her to ride Silver Leaf in a race, can
you?" Lyndie wouldn't see sense, but he hoped Karen

would. Jake wanted her to give him a reason to tell Lyndie she couldn't ride.

Karen took her time studying him. "It sounds to me like *you* don't want her to ride."

"No, I don't."

"Why?"

He frowned.

"Are you scared for her?" Karen asked.

"It's not safe."

"Lyndie has never had a soul that was bent toward safety."

He could hear the muted sounds of a commentator calling a race on TV. The picture of Lyndie with the scrape on her knee stared at him from the open page of the album.

"Do you remember what she was like when she was young?" Karen asked. "Always exploring. Or playing imaginary games or running off on rescue missions?"

"Yes."

"I'm ashamed to say that I probably didn't watch her as closely as I should have in those days. I trusted you, for one thing. For another, I was just so tired. Thanks to God's protection, she came through her childhood unscathed." She sighed and straightened the wrinkled blue polo shirt she had on over sweatpants. "When Lyndie was nineteen she fell off a horse and fractured her wrist. Did you know that she'd fractured her wrist?"

"No."

"It scared me, Jake. She'd broken her wrist, but I was very, very aware that it could have easily been her spine. In my heart of hearts, I didn't want her to work with horses anymore."

"Exactly."

"However, if I'd told her she couldn't go to the track, I knew she'd have rebelled. She's kind, but she's also strong-willed. If I'd said no, she'd have wanted to work with horses twice as much." She smiled a mother's smile, full of affection for her child. "I thought about it, and I prayed over it. I probably prayed over it for two weeks straight. What I finally realized was that I'd have to let her make her own choices." She looked at him with sympathy.

This was not what he'd come to hear.

"Mike and I haven't done it perfectly, but we've tried to teach Lyndie not to let fear govern her life. Does the idea of her as Silver Leaf's jockey worry me? A little. But her safety in a race is something I have no control over. I'll give it to God, and then I'll try to let it go."

"I do have control over it," Jake said.

"What's that?"

"Whether Lyndie can race."

"Do you think that Lyndie will give your horse the best chance of winning?"

"Yes."

"Then I recommend that you let Lyndie ride."

Could Karen really be that brave?

"After all we've been through with Mollie, we've learned that it's best to live in love and not fear. Mike and I trust God with our family's future, Jake."

Despair sank through him.

"It's not always easy. My greatest fear is dying before Mollie dies. If that happened, who would take care of her? She needs me." Tears gathered in her eyes.

He remembered that she'd gotten teary-eyed the last

time he'd visited, too. For pity's sake. Were therapists supposed to cry this much? "If something happened to you," Jake said, "Lyndie would take care of Mollie."

"But I want to take care of her. I'm her mother. So it's sort of a daily thing I have to work through, handing the situation over to God, trusting Him with it again and again."

He wasn't going to get what he'd come here for. Slowly, Jake pushed to his feet. "Thank you for talking with me. I'm sorry to have interrupted you—"

She wagged a finger at him. "Don't even try to leave yet."

"I have to go."

"Take a seat, if you please." She extended her hand palm up toward the chair he'd left.

They stood that way in heavy silence for a few moments before he lowered back into the chair.

"I told you my greatest fear. Now I want to know yours. . . . And you look as happy as a person about to face a firing squad. Am I really so intimidating?" She waited for him to answer.

"Yes."

Oddly, his answer made her laugh. She was a strange counselor, with her bare feet and her tearfulness and her messy scrapbooking desk. He did not feel comfortable here, with her. Yet he hadn't forgotten the bald, over-worked counselor he'd seen at the VA. He felt ten times more comfortable with Karen than he had with that guy.

"Your greatest fear?" she prodded.

Something happening to Lyndie. "I'd rather not say."

She looked at him as if able to read the answer on

his face. "Remember how I mentioned to you that I see a few clients with PTSD?"

"I remember."

"Each case is individual. A treatment plan that includes yoga and meditation might help one person."

If she thought he was going to try yoga, she was crazier than he was.

"Another might benefit from EMDR therapy. Another, prescription medications. Some do well within a support group of other vets. Some need a recovery program like AA. You catch my drift?"

"I do."

"There are just two things I've found that seem to help all my PTSD guys, across the board. Now, I'm just speaking about my personal experience, you understand. I don't have a huge number of patients with PTSD, so this observation isn't scientific."

He leveled a narrow stare on her.

"One." She held up a finger. "A renewed relationship with the Lord. I'm not a Christian counselor for nothing. I wouldn't do the counseling part unless I could do the Christian part, too. Whatever things you've done that you regret cannot be atoned for by anything in this world except the blood of Jesus Christ. Once you realize that, then you simply have to lay your regrets at the cross and accept His grace."

He had a lot of regrets. And it was certainly true that he'd learned that he, himself, had the ability to atone for none of them.

"Two." She held up a second finger. "Remembering."

Now he knew she was crazy.

She mounded her hands in her lap, calm and at ease.

The kind of calm and ease he'd give anything to experience, even for an hour.

"You see, the more you try to avoid your memories, the more power you try not to give them, the more power you end up handing them. The idea is to relive your worst memories. Second by second, over and over."

Jake said nothing.

"Does that make any sense to you?"

"Some."

The muffled sound of the TV cut away. Karen straightened, cocking her head. Then she hopped down from the stool. "Mollie's having a seizure. Excuse me." She hurried out, leaving the glass doors open.

Jake didn't want to see Mollie having a seizure. On the other hand, there might be something he could do to help, so he wasn't going to hide in the scrapbooking room like a pansy.

Mike passed Karen going the other way down the hall. "I'm getting her suction machine."

Jake followed Karen at a distance. She went to Mollie in her wheelchair and rested her hands on her head, gently rubbing. "I'm here, Mols. I'm here, my sweetheart."

Jake took in the situation with a sweeping glance, seeing it through the eyes of a man trained to be a sergeant of Marines. They'd already turned off the TV and killed the lights. "What can I do?"

"You can pull the curtains, if you wouldn't mind," Karen answered.

He did so.

Mollie continued to seize.

"Maybe you and Harold could step outside for some

fresh air?" Karen looked pointedly from Jake to Lyndie's grandpa.

The old man hadn't moved from his recliner. His hands gripped the armrests. He'd focused his attention on the carpet, the lines of his face tight. It must be difficult for this man—who'd fought in Korea and outlived his wife—to bear his granddaughter's suffering on top of his other griefs.

"Sir?" Jake extended a hand to him.

Harold took it.

"Dear God"—Karen continued massaging Mollie's scalp—"Please be with Mollie. Please ease her pain and help her to breathe. We invite you here, into this very room, to bring us peace. To rescue our girl."

Jake held back a section of the curtain and opened the sliding door for Harold. The two of them emptied onto the patio, where there was no sickness or prayer. Nothing but the tall trunks of trees and spreading branches for as far as Jake could see.

"Would you like to take a seat?" Jake asked.

"I believe I'll stand." Harold and Jake continued to the edge of the porch.

"How often does Mollie have seizures?" Jake leaned against the porch rail, setting his hands against it.

"Three times on a good day. Could be as many as fifteen on a bad day. Today's been a pretty good day." Harold took a deep breath, his frail chest lifting beneath his green golf shirt.

Jake wasn't one to fill silence with meaningless talk, so he just let it sit.

"Native Dancer," Harold said, out of nowhere. In the distance, birds chirped. "Do you know what I mean?"

"Do you mean the racehorse?"

"Excellent racehorse. One of the greats, in other words. I saw him race myself, you know. At, ah, Saratoga. He won all of his starts his first year. That must have been nineteen fifty . . ."

"Nineteen fifty-two."

"Yes. And how many starts?"

"Nine."

"That's right. Nine."

Karen opened the slider and sent Jake a grateful look. "Mollie's doing fine now."

"Good."

She ducked back inside.

"Native Dancer," Harold stated, "had more than twenty starts in his career, and he only came in second one time. At the ol' Kentucky Derby."

"That's right."

"I mention him because he was a gray horse. They called him the Gray Ghost of Sagamore because he was raised and trained at Sagamore Farm there in . . ."

"Maryland."

Plenty of intelligence shone from Harold's faded eyes. "Don't *you* have a gray stallion in your barn at Lone Star?"

"Yes, sir. I do."

"Might be you've got the next great gray champion."

Jake nodded, noncommittal.

"In order for a horse to become a champion, there's someone important who first needs to believe it can happen."

Jake waited.

"His trainer," Harold said, looking Jake right in the eyes.

⌘

Thirty minutes later, Lyndie's phone chimed to signal an incoming text. She set aside the canister of whipped cream she'd been using to crown her coffee. Since she'd failed at concentrating on her art after returning from Whispering Creek, she'd decided to concentrate instead on a mocha, heavy on the chocolate and whipped cream.

She checked her phone and saw that the text was from Jake.

If you're sure you want to jockey for Silver Leaf, he wrote, *I'll give you the chance.*

A stunned breath broke from her lips, followed by a wide grin. "Yes!" She peered at the words on the screen in astonishment and gratitude. Easter was tomorrow, and no one could have given her a better Easter gift.

A new text arrived. *Take time to think it over*, he typed.

I don't need time to think it over, she wrote back, her fingers flying.

I was afraid of that, he replied.

I'm sure, POSITIVELY sure, that I want to jockey for Silver Leaf.

CHAPTER

FIFTEEN

Lyndie sliced off a portion of the beautiful cake Celia had made for the Porter family Easter lunch. Vanilla cake with buttercream frosting. It sat on a serving table at the side of the room surrounded by clearly inferior dessert offerings like cherry pie and banana pudding. Goodness. The rich scent of the buttercream hung in a nimbus around the dessert, making Lyndie's mouth water.

She should try to bring this cake to life via a storybook. She could write about a girl who liked to bake? Who was . . . hmm . . . a baker of birthday cakes?

Lyndie lifted her cake plate with one hand and her coffee cup with the other and wove through the numerous tables toward her seat while mentally scrolling through possible story ideas.

The James family was celebrating Easter in high style this year thanks to the Porters, who'd insisted they join them for lunch. The Porter Sunday lunches Lyndie had attended in the past had been very casual affairs held at

Jake's parents' house. They'd involved paper plates, a barbecue grill, bags of chips, and an abundance of red meat.

For Easter, however, Meg and Bo were hosting the gathering of forty or so at their home, a home that managed to hit both luxurious and rustic notes. Their rambling one-story ranch house had been built from Texas stone. It featured stunning wood floors, comfortable seating arrangements, cozy fireplaces. Meg and Bo had situated the house on a hill on a corner of Whispering Creek Ranch far removed from the horse farm. An abundance of windows let in light and framed views of rippling Texas land.

Lyndie spotted her parents and Mollie sitting with Jake's parents at a table near an oil painting of wildflowers. They'd all recently finished a feast of ham and side dishes. Some guests were too unpleasantly stuffed to consider dessert yet. Some, like Lyndie, were merely pleasantly stuffed. Some were halfway to snoring.

Lyndie slid past someone's uncle and into her chair. Dru, Jake's younger sister, sat to her right. Ty sat to her left at the head of the table, Celia next to him, Amber next to Celia, and then Jake, followed by Porter family cousins. Their long rectangular table had been covered in a tablecloth so pale a pink that it almost looked like ivory, accented with floral arrangements of peonies, roses, and tulips. Tiny porcelain bunnies peeked out at Lyndie from hiding spots near the bases of the flower vases.

Ty held his baby son with one hand and used his other to help scoot in Lyndie's chair. "Bo just stopped at the table and told us we should congratulate you because you're going to be riding Silver Leaf in his race this week."

"Yes." She settled her coffee and cake onto the table. "I'm really excited about it."

Everyone congratulated her, which then kicked off a conversation about Lone Star Park, which led to chitchat about Lone Star's recent renovations.

Lyndie glanced at Jake. He gave her a subdued nod, both grave and yet—dare she hope—warm? Whatever it was, there in his eyes, it had the ability to make the space between them hum.

Thinking back on the exchange between them in the warm room yesterday, she was glad that she'd had the nerve to touch him and to say the things that she had. Jake could have no doubt now that she cared about him, that she wished to help, and that he could talk to her.

She watched Jake say something to Dru, then lift an eyebrow at Dru's response. It had been a joy to watch him interacting with his family over lunch. He was not an outgoing man. But here, with this group, he wasn't cold or withdrawn, either. Lyndie had been very aware, since he'd taken his seat at the table, of every word he'd spoken to his cousins, of his posture, of how much he'd eaten. Her attention kept returning to him the way a compass returns to north. Right now, for instance, she knew that he'd crossed his muscular arms over his chest, which had caused the fabric of his white dress shirt to tighten over his shoulders, that he'd rolled back the sleeves—

"Lyndie?"

She startled. "Hmm?" Celia, Ty, and Amber were all watching her. Since Amber hadn't maintained ties to her own family, Meg had pretty much adopted Amber and Jayden into hers.

"I was just telling Amber that I'd love to go to the track

on Thursday and cheer for you," Celia said to Lyndie. "Can I wear a big hat?"

"Sure."

"Any excuse to wear a big hat is a good excuse," Celia declared.

"I agree!" Amber said. "I'll find someone who actually owns a big hat and then I'll borrow it. I want to come, too."

"Can we all fit into Meg's owner's box at Lone Star?" Ty asked Jake.

"Yes. All of you and then some."

"If I can get the time off work," Dru said, "I'll come, too." The youngest Porter sibling, a full ten years younger than her brothers, was pretty much the most beautiful woman Lyndie had ever seen in her life. Lyndie's vague memories of a crying infant with a puff of dark hair had ill-prepared her for the adult version of Jake's sister.

At twenty-two, Dru had already attained the confidence and poise of a woman twenty years older. Long, straight brunette hair, so dark it was almost black, fell halfway down her back. Her sculpted features were almost icy in their sharp loveliness. And she had the same startling eye color as Ty. A clear turquoise blue so rare and bright it hardly seemed real.

"Are you nervous at all, Lyndie?" Amber asked. "About riding as a jockey again?

Lyndie carefully sectioned off a bite of cake. "No. Just really glad for the opportunity." No sane jockey raced Thoroughbreds without a degree of nervousness. But whatever amount of nervousness she felt was so fully eclipsed by eagerness that it wasn't worth talking about in front of Jake. "I didn't get many opportunities with horses of Silver Leaf's caliber back when I was riding. This feels like a second chance. A once-in-a-lifetime opportunity."

"I'm all for second chances." Ty gave Celia a crooked smile, then leaned back in his chair with his baby tummy-down on his broad chest. Little Hudson blinked heavy eyelids. "It took me more like four or five chances before I finally convinced you of my obvious desirability," he said to his wife.

"I'm still not convinced," Celia said wryly.

They all laughed, the sound causing the baby to jerk and raise his head. "Shh," Ty crooned, wrapping his big hand around Hudson's head and gently guiding it back down. "Your mother's just talking smack again. It's nothing I can't handle." Ty tugged Celia close and pressed a quick kiss to her lips.

Dru groaned. "I cannot believe that two of my brothers are this hog-tied over their wives. *My* brothers! They used to be so . . ."

"Normal?" Jake supplied.

"Lonely?" Celia offered.

"Available." Amber's voice held a note of regret.

"I was going to say," Dru continued, "that Bo and Ty used to have a drop of testosterone in their bodies. Especially you." She pointed at Ty.

"Speaking for myself," Ty drawled, "this body still has plenty of testosterone left."

"I can vouch for that," Celia said.

"It's embarrassing," Dru persisted. "All this mushiness. Isn't it, Jake?"

"Very."

"I don't like mushy." Dru had recently returned to

Texas after serving four years with the Marines. She'd immediately been hired by a private security firm in Dallas. According to Jake's mom, Nancy, Dru regularly traveled to pistol shooting competitions and was so skilled with a gun that she'd become Grand Champion Pistol Shooter of the Universe or whatever title they gave to the best female shooter alive.

It wasn't a stretch to imagine Dru with a pistol in her hand. Today she'd dressed in a tailored gray suit jacket, killer jeans, and wicked black high heels. Dru was a lynx. The rest of the women at their table were house cats in comparison.

"I like mushy." Amber raised her hand. "I'd definitely like someone to go mushy over. And so would Lyndie."

Um . . . Should she try to kick Amber under the table to stop this conversation before it began? A slicing motion across the throat might be too obvious.

"Didn't you two make an agreement to each go on three dates?" Ty asked. He adjusted Hudson, now fully asleep, his small hands fisted on either side of his face.

"Yes," Amber answered.

Lyndie could feel heat climbing up her neck into her face. She didn't dare look toward Jake.

"We've gone on one of our dates so far." Amber took a sip of her coffee. "Next weekend we'll go on the second one. It'll be a Japanese-style blind date called a gokon."

"Would anyone else like coffee or cake?" Lyndie asked, a trifle desperately.

"Nice try," Dru murmured.

"A go-what?" Ty appeared highly amused.

"A gokon." Amber answered. "Should be fun. Right, Lyndie?"

"Yep." Because the square dancing sure had been a bundle of delight.

"Why are you going on group dates instead of one-on-one dates?" Dru asked. Dru, who could probably force a man to his knees with date proposals just by looking him in the eyes.

"One-on-one dates would be great," Amber told Dru. "But since no one we want to date has asked us out yet, we're having to get creative."

Lyndie laid her palms on the tablecloth. "No one wants dessert or coffee? Really? What about you, Cousin Lennie? Cousin Starlene?"

"Lyndie received a lot of attention at our last group date," Amber continued. "Both of the guys she danced with have been asking her out ever since—"

"Excuse me." Jake rose from the table so suddenly he drew everyone's attention. Without a word, he exited the room in the direction of the back porch.

Dru watched Jake's retreat. "That was odd." Slowly, she swiveled around to peer at Lyndie, her brows pinched together. "Do you know why he stormed out?"

"No."

Entirely too much intelligence gleamed in the depths of Dru's eyes.

"As far as the dating scene goes," Celia said to Amber, "I still think Will McGrath is perfect for you. He's gorgeous."

"I'm sitting right here!" Ty protested.

"I noticed you there, showboat. You're gorgeous, too. Eat cake." She pressed his plate into his hands.

"Who's Will McGrath?" Dru asked.

"A local fireman," Lyndie answered. Had Jake left his family's Easter lunch?

"And who's he perfect for?" Dru wanted to know.

"Any single woman with a pulse," Celia replied. "But especially Amber here. I haven't given up, Amber. I'm going to find out when he's working this week, and then I'm going to have you deliver some baked goods to the fire station for me. What do you think?"

"Oh! I'd love to deliver baked goods to the fire station."

"Then consider it done."

"What about Lyndie?" Dru asked. "Who's perfect for her?"

Celia looked at Lyndie with speculation. "We're still working on it."

Jake had not left his family's Easter lunch. Lyndie knew this because after a covert, trying-to-look-casual search, she'd spotted him in a far corner of the backyard. He was sitting on one of the two Adirondack chairs positioned there, and he had Addie, Ty and Celia's six-year-old daughter, on his lap. One of Addie's hands rested trustingly on Jake's shoulder. She gestured with her other hand as she talked. Jake listened attentively, nodding now and then, giving Addie an uneven smile of fondness. Lyndie didn't know how the little girl was reacting, but that smile of his was thoroughly and completely captivating the big girl—herself.

Brutal events had toughened Jake, yes. But he still had the capacity for love and devotion.

Lyndie parked Mollie's wheelchair on the edge of the

enormous two-level flagstone terrace that spread out behind Meg and Bo's house. "What do you think, Mols? Can you feel the sun and the breeze? There are several children playing out here. Hear them?" She described the scene to her sister.

A short distance away, Meg had set up a kids' table. Big, plastic blow-up chicks sat in chairs at the head and foot. Earlier, when all the kids had been sitting and eating, they'd worn bunny ears. At the moment, about half the children were playing a rowdy game of tag on the manicured stretch of lawn and beyond, in the wooded areas that encircled the house. Not many—other than Jayden and a towheaded blond toddler—still wore their bunny ears.

Lyndie let the charm of the setting soak into her. Surely there could be no more perfect home to be raised in than this one, and no better parents to do it than Meg and Bo. She caught sight of Meg, speaking with two of the young mothers.

From all she'd heard, Meg and Bo were dealing with infertility by holding tightly to each other and trusting God in the way that Lyndie's family had learned to trust Him: as fully in the seasons of peace as in the seasons of doubt.

It must have been painful for Meg on some level, to put together such a wonderful Easter celebration for the kids included in the extended Porter family when she wanted children of her own.

Across the yard, Jake lifted Addie onto his shoulders. As they passed beneath trees, Addie reached up and tickled the leaves with her fingertips, giggling.

Meg parted from the women she'd been speaking to

and came toward Lyndie. She wore a pink-and-white
dress and silver heels that threw glints of light as she
made her way across the flagstones. Meg had blond hair
like Lyndie did, but Lyndie couldn't help but note that
Meg's hair was *much* better behaved.

"Did you get enough to eat?" Meg asked.

"More than enough. It was all delicious. Celia's vanilla cake . . ."

"I know. When no one was looking I sliced off about
a quarter and hid it in my pantry." Meg knelt in front of
Mollie and rested her hands on Mollie's knees. "Happy
Easter, Mollie. You look like you're doing really well,
which makes me happy." Meg slanted her attention to
Lyndie. "Is there anything I can get for her or for you?"

"No, thank you, though."

"Okay." Gently, Meg smoothed a wrinkle from the
light blanket that covered Mollie's legs. Meg was a sentimental person, innately considerate, with a heart big
enough to love anyone the Porter family brought into
their midst. "I'm so pleased to have you here at my house,
Mollie. Thank you for coming. I hope you'll visit again
soon, sweetie."

Lyndie's eyes misted. Her sister was her soft spot,
and kindness extended to Mollie always got to her. She
swept a lock of Mollie's hair back into the little Easter
headband she had on, then squeezed her sister's shoulder.

Meg rose to standing. "I'm glad I saw you two. I've
been wanting to talk with you since I heard that you're
going to ride Silver Leaf in his race this week."

"Yes. Is that all right with you?" Though Meg trusted
Bo and Jake to make decisions regarding the horse farm,
she was and always would be Silver Leaf's official owner.

"Better than good." She smiled reassuringly. "I first met Silver Leaf four years ago. I'm not much of a horse person, you know. Even these days, I don't often ride."

Lyndie nodded.

"It's sort of hard to explain, but . . . I fell in love with Silver Leaf the first time I saw him."

"I did, too, Meg."

"He has that effect on people."

"Yes," Lyndie agreed wholeheartedly.

"I've believed in Silver Leaf since that day. Bo and Jake have both tried to talk me into retiring him at different points along the way." She exhaled, watching the children scattered in her yard. It looked to Lyndie like the game of tag had devolved into a case of kids running around, shrieking for no reason.

"I've never disagreed with Bo or Jake on any other detail of the Thoroughbreds," Meg said. "But I put my foot down about Silver Leaf. I wanted him to have one last opportunity. I've been hoping, really hard, that he'll make the most of this chance."

"He just might. He has great potential."

"But we couldn't figure out how to tap in to it, until you. Bo's kept me updated, about the way that Silver Leaf's run for you in practice." Meg searched Lyndie's face. "Had you heard that Silver Leaf was my father's favorite horse?"

"Jake mentioned it to me."

"Silver Leaf was born here at the ranch, and my father watched him grow. Even then, as a colt, my father put a great deal of stock in Silver Leaf. He passed away when Silver Leaf was a yearling, so he never got to see him race."

"I'll do my very best with him on Thursday. For you and for your dad."

"I know you will." Meg reached out and gripped Lyndie's hand. "I'll be there to cheer you both on."

"Thank you."

"Whatever happens, it'll be a big day for me because thanks to you, I'll have the satisfaction of knowing that I did the best I could for my father's horse."

"And your horse, too, Meg."

"And yours, Lyndie. And Jake's and Bo's. He's *ours*."

Emotion clutched Lyndie so strongly, she almost didn't trust herself to speak.

Meg's words entwined her. *"I'll have the satisfaction of knowing that I did the best I could."* She yearned to be able to say the same. About the horse.

And about his trainer.

CHAPTER
SIXTEEN

At the sound of a woman's voice, Will lifted his head from the computer and the report he'd been typing.

Amber, he thought with dumb hope. It didn't even make sense. Amber, here, at his fire station in the middle of the day on a Tuesday? Even so, he left his office and headed in the direction of the bay. He'd been thinking about Amber a lot lately: when he was driving his girls to activities, grocery shopping, filling the dishwasher.

He rounded the corner and saw Amber standing near the engine with two of his guys, Ryan and Toby. It *was* her. For the first time on this overcast day, it was as if sunlight was pouring down, making him feel alive in ways he hadn't for the twelve years since Michelle had left him.

Over the past few weeks, Will had seen Amber several times. If he didn't know better, he'd say he was developing a crush on her. Man, how embarrassing. Could you call it a crush still when you were forty? He hadn't had a crush on anyone in a really long time.

Today she wore pale green scrubs. Her shiny brown hair had been pulled back with a little clip on one side in the front. She carried a rectangular tray holding two apple pies.

"Captain," Toby said, "this is Amber—"

"We know each other."

"Hi, Will."

"Hi." He smiled at her and pushed his hands into the pockets of his navy pants.

"She brought us pie." Ryan sent Will a look that said he was excited about more than the dessert.

"I see that."

"Celia had these left over," Amber explained. "When I went by Cream or Sugar just now, she asked me if I could bring them by. She wanted you guys to have them."

"Thank you." Seemed kind of strange to Will that Celia had two freshly baked pies left over at this time of day. It was only twelve thirty. "Will you take the pies into the kitchen for her, Toby?"

"Oh!" The younger of the firefighters had been too busy gawking at Amber to notice the heavy tray. "Sure. May I?"

Toby and Ryan were both good guys, single, the perfect age for Amber. So perfect that there was no way that Will was going to take the tray into the kitchen and leave her out here with them.

"Ryan, would you go tell the other guys that there's pie in the kitchen?"

Ryan went to do as he'd been asked, leaving Will alone with Amber.

"It's fun to see where you work," she said. "I don't think I've visited a fire station since I was"—she shrugged—"maybe ten?"

"Would you like a tour?"

"I'd love one, if it's not too much trouble."

He took her around the bay, kitchen, dining room, and living area. Pride filled him as he showed her his home away from home and answered her questions about his job.

Amber's combination of confidence and down-to-earth sweetness did him in every time. He felt slightly self-conscious around her. He liked her so much that he didn't want to look like an idiot in front of her.

Eventually, they returned to where they'd started, near the mouth of the open bay door. "Are you on your lunch break?" Will asked. It would have taken her more than twenty minutes to drive from downtown Holley to the station.

"Yeah. In fact, I probably better go so I can get back to work on time."

"When will you have lunch?"

"I always bring food from home. I'll eat it between patients this afternoon."

Guilt nicked him. "I'm sorry you spent your whole lunch break coming here."

"I'm not. I wanted to." She met his gaze. Her eyes were very blue, surrounded by those thick, dark lashes.

You're too old for her. You're too old, Will. That he knew it was true didn't stop him from regretting the truth of it. Where had his years gone? Why couldn't Amber have been older?

"See you later," she said.

"Yeah." He shook himself from his daze and stepped back. "Thanks for bringing the pie."

"You're welcome." She climbed into her car, waved, and drove away.

Frustrated, he scrubbed his hands down his face. He was a father of two teenage daughters. A captain. A man who'd spent only five years of his entire adult life married and who hadn't really wanted to care about anyone again after what loving Michelle had put him through.

"She likes you, boss." Ryan came to stand next to him, both of them looking outward at the cars passing by.

"She's too young for me," Will answered.

"Is that what she told you?"

"No."

"Then why don't you ask her if *she* thinks she's too young for you?"

Will wasn't sure whether Amber was just being friendly or whether she was attracted to him. He was rusty, but he thought it might be the latter. If so, then their age difference might not bother Amber. But it did bother him.

"Maybe she's just looking for someone who'd be good to her," Ryan said. "Who's responsible and trustworthy."

"You make me sound like the most boring guy alive."

"You are." Ryan's laugh softened his teasing.

"I'm sure she can find someone her own age who'd be good to her." He was trustworthy enough for Amber, yes. The old grandfather walking down the sidewalk with his cane and his terrier was probably trustworthy, too. Trustworthiness couldn't make either him or the grandfather right for Amber Richardson.

"She's a mother, you know." Ryan said. "As soon as she walked up she told Toby and me how much her son would enjoy seeing the trucks."

"Her son's five. My girls are sixteen and fourteen."

"So? All kinds of families can work."

Will frowned and Ryan chuckled.

"What's so funny?" Will asked.

"I'm just imagining how Madison and Taylor would react if you finally started dating someone seriously."

"They'd hate it."

"Well? You've spoiled them. Do you want them dating boys?"

"No way."

"Do you think your disapproval is going to stop *them*?"

Will eyed Ryan, who was proving himself too smart for his own good. "No." He'd already heard a rumor that Madison had a boyfriend. Just the idea had been keeping him up nights.

"Amber's pretty," Ryan said.

"I know."

"I'd date her in a minute."

"Ryan, even that flagpole over there could tell that you'd date Amber."

"She's too pretty for you to pass up, boss."

"I'm too old for her."

"Haven't you heard? Forty is the new thirty."

Will snorted. "That's not true."

"Age is just a number. Why are you looking at me like that?" Ryan fist-bumped his shoulder. "Age is just a number, boss."

⌇⌇

"Mom!" Jayden yelled. "Can you kick with me some more?"

Amber squinted at Jayden from where she and Lyndie were sitting on the grass next to the backyard hero house.

Jayden dribbled his soccer ball the length of the Candy Shoppe and back, Lyndie's dogs tumbling beside him. Amber had spent the day working. Then she'd picked up Jayden, hit the grocery store, and kicked the ball with her son for ten minutes after arriving home. Her apartment needed cleaning and dinner needed cooking. This bubble of time to talk to Lyndie and drink delicious coffee felt like a vacation.

The last thing in the world she wanted to do at this moment? Kick the soccer ball more than she already had.

"Not right now, honey," she called. "I'm taking a rest. Give me a few more minutes." She tucked her coffee mug against her chest and turned to watch Lyndie pat moss into the ground around Jayden's hero house. That done, Lyndie freed two adorable miniature trees from tiny pots and planted them beside the moss. "Is that a tire swing?"

Lyndie nodded. "I thought Jayden's action figures might like it." She'd fastened a black metal circle to a length of twine. Delicately, Lyndie hung it from the branch of one of the little trees.

"I'm amazed," Amber said, "by your creativity. I wish I had in my whole body the amount you have in your pinkie."

"Mom? Has it been a few minutes?"

"It's only been half of one minute," Amber called to him.

Jayden's shoulders sagged.

Amber sighed. "I'm an okay mom to Jayden," she whispered to Lyndie, "but I make a lousy father."

"You're a really good mom, Amber."

"But a father would probably enjoy kicking a ball."

Jayden left the soccer ball behind and picked up a stick. He launched a kicking attack against imaginary bad guys.

Her son had no dad and no siblings. Sometimes being Jayden's *only* person felt like a crushing weight. "I went to see Will at the fire station today."

Lyndie's face lifted at Amber's words. "What? Why didn't you tell me sooner?" Amber's upstairs neighbor looked like a "How to Do Effortless Beach Hair" page out of a magazine. Amber wished she could make Lyndie's artistic style, with the earrings and scarves and hair, work for her the way it worked for Lyndie.

"Because it's not good news. I brought him pies from Cream or Sugar. Pies! Plus, I think I stared at his lips for a full minute. He still didn't make a move."

"He was at work."

"He didn't have to kiss me. He simply could have asked me out." As if they could sense heartache from a mile away, which maybe they could, Lyndie's dogs ran over and tilted their heads to stare at her with sympathy. "Well, c'mon." She patted her lap and the one closest to her climbed on. The other lay next to Lyndie, resting his chin on the top of her flip-flop. "It's strange, Lyndie, because I really feel something between Will and me. It's strong, and I think it might be mutual."

"Maybe it is."

"Maybe it's not. I'm worried that my interest in him is blinding me to the fact that he's giving me I'm-not-into-you vibes. I'm also worried that I might not be successfully communicating I'm-into-you vibes to him."

Lyndie retrieved the coffee mug she'd set aside and took a sip. "What are you going to do?"

"*We're* going to a gokon this weekend."

"Maybe it would be best if we postponed our next date."

Amber had never met a single, thirty-year-old woman as reluctant to go on dates as Lyndie James. "You're not going to talk me out of it," Amber assured her.

"That's what I'm afraid of."

"We're going. And you're going to thank me afterward, because you'll probably be introduced to the love of your life."

Lyndie's expression turned skeptical. "One of my square dancing partners texted me again today."

"And?"

"He's not the love of my life."

Amber chuckled. "We're going to the gokon, Lyndie. We're going."

The next morning Lyndie stood next to Jake at Lone Star's track. The time she spent with him after she finished riding had become her favorite time of day. She looked forward to it and enjoyed it even more than coffee. Or Reese's.

"That's the laziest horse I have." Jake gestured to a black gelding cantering past. "'He hangs out more often than Mama's washing.' Are you too Californian to have heard that saying?"

"I'm a Texan, thank you very much. My parents are Texans, and I was born in Texas. *Texan* is stamped on my passport along with a picture of a football and little dangling state flags."

"Huh." He aimed an amused look down at her.

She could have accused him of having lived a good

portion of his life outside of Texas, but that would have brought difficult memories of Iraq and Afghanistan into the conversation.

They were both leaning into the rail. Jake had one boot planted on a slat, his black Stetson angled particularly low today. He looked big and bad and certain of himself.

"'Lazy as a bump on a log'?" Lyndie ventured. "Have you heard that one?"

He grunted. "Everyone's heard that one. You're going to have to do better to impress me."

She grumbled under her breath about hard-to-impress cowboys who thought they knew everything.

"What do you think of Mist Flower here?" The chestnut filly walked up to them with her exercise rider astride.

"I think that she still hasn't found her form after her bruised foot," Lyndie said.

Whenever Jake asked her for feedback on his horses, he weighed her words thoughtfully, in a manner that Lyndie found enormously flattering.

"One of the trainers I worked for used to treat bruised feet with bran mash poultice," she said.

"What year was that? 1982?"

Cheeky! "Some old-school ideas still have merit," Lyndie insisted. "He'd apply bran and cooked flaxseed mash to the sole and wrap it around the hoof with vetwrap to draw out soreness. I saw it work a few times."

Jake gave instructions to Mist Flower's rider and the two set off.

Lyndie earnestly wished that she had the power to heal wounded horses, wounded minds, and wounded bodies.

She'd repair both Mollie and Jake in a snap. While she was at it, she'd fix Mist Flower, too.

Lyndie stared at the distant line where the track's buildings met the sky, ideas cascading into her mind. What if she gave the blond fairy in her fairy story a magical healing . . . ring? Necklace? No, wand. With every sweep of her wand, the fairy would be able to fix what was broken.

The healing fairy could set out on a mission to fix the gloomy prince. To make things spicy, she'd need to overcome an obstacle or two along the way. Her wand could crack? Yes, and the fairy would have to find a way to repair the wand in order to repair the prince—

"You're a million miles away in your head, aren't you?" Jake asked. The humor in his eyes tempted her to believe that he really had come to like her, despite himself and despite her quirks.

"Yes," she confessed, "I was at least a million miles away."

"Dreaming about a story idea?"

"Yes." It seemed he could sense things about her, just like she could about him.

"What kind of a story idea?"

"Two unicorns and two fairies set out together to rescue a tall, dark, and brooding prince."

He let that sink in for a few moments. "The unicorns and fairies sound nice. The prince guy sounds like a bore."

Lyndie laughed. "He can be at times."

"Why don't they go rescue a lost kitten or something?"

"Because one of the fairies believes that the prince is wonderful underneath his gruff exterior. She's not interested in kittens. She's dead-set on the prince."

"Is rescuing him going to be worth it in the end?"

"Very much so."

They stared at each other as their words ebbed into silence. Heat and longing grew palpable. Lyndie's breath turned shallow. Was it possible that he—he might kiss her? Maybe?

He didn't. He turned back to face the track.

Foolish, errant wish. If he ever kissed her, which was quite a wild hypothetical, he would not do it at the track during working hours with so many witnesses present.

Her physical attraction to Jake had started out as entertaining and charming. Harmless. Like riding a bike down a country lane. But lately, both her physical reactions and her emotions toward him had grown large. They felt serious now and potentially harmful. Like riding that same bike down a steep and narrow mountain path strewn with rocks.

She'd long suspected that Silver Leaf's improvement would be intertwined with Jake's improvement. So far, Silver Leaf had accomplished much. Jake, too, had made strides. He was talking with her, after all. He'd seen her mother two times, and both times her mom had talked to him about PTSD. He hadn't called her lately to try to fire her.

Lyndie was not a person given to worry. Typically, she battled it only when Mollie had to be hospitalized. Recently, though, she'd begun to worry that she might be investing a bit *too* much of her heart in Jake.

She'd see a haunted expression come over his face when he didn't know she was looking, and she'd want to weep over what the war had done to him. Five minutes later, she'd watch him interact in genius fashion with one of his horses, and pride would pour through her because of what the war had *not* been able to do to him.

She'd gone her whole life without a heavy-duty, serious boyfriend. She'd been fine with that. In fact, it would be better for her to continue along that track than let herself fall wildly in love with Jake Porter. First, her mom had told her outright that Jake could not be cured. Second, his reclusive personality might make disastrous boyfriend material. Third, as far as she knew he hadn't dated anyone in years. He might not date or marry anyone, ever.

It would be best for her if she could hold the remainder of herself back.

What, then, did she want from Jake, exactly?

She adjusted her position, resting a forearm on the top of the rail.

She wanted Jake's trust. She dearly wanted him to let her into his world so that she could see the landscape there. Whatever the landscape, she thought she could accept it. It would be difficult for her to live with the fact that she couldn't change it. But she really did think she could accept it, and *him*. Just how he was. God had been teaching her during her lifetime with Mollie to trust Him with the things she couldn't alter or control. She'd had practice.

"Thinking about the unicorns again?" The tone of his low-pitched voice sent a delicious shiver between her shoulder blades.

"Actually, I was thinking about the prince."

When Jake's alarm clock sounded the morning of Silver Leaf's race, it did not wake him. He was already wide awake, lying on his back, frowning upward at his dark ceiling.

He fisted a hand and used it to punch off the alarm clock's noise. Then he groaned and brought his wrist up to cover his eyes.

How had he gotten to this place? How had he reached a day on his calendar when he'd be putting Lyndie James into a race on his Thoroughbred? Of all people, *Lyndie*. The last person he'd ever want to see injured.

It wasn't that some other trainer had hired her to ride. It was him. He was the one responsible. If she hurt herself today, he'd be the one to blame—he'd be the one he'd never be able to forgive.

He'd wrestled with insomnia all night, sick with worry. His stomach had churned so that he couldn't stand to think about eating or drinking. His chest ached with anxiety.

He'd been going over and over each of the decisions he'd made concerning her. They'd all seemed logical at the time. Hiring her. Following her recommendations about Silver Leaf. And yet since his choices had brought him to this point, clearly he'd made at least one bad choice along the way.

The odds were that nothing would happen today. She'd be fine just as she had been over all the years of her career—

No. None of his lousy reassurances to himself made a bit of difference. He'd lived too long to put stock in idiot reassurances.

For the first time in eight years, the events he'd face today filled him with just as much dread as one of his nightmares.

Today was the day Lyndie would race.

CHAPTER
SEVENTEEN

Today was the day she would race!

For at least this one sweet day, *she* was a jockey. It seemed to Lyndie that even God approved. He'd given her conditions ideal for racing. The track was dry, the temperature mild. The startlingly bright, fat clouds would do nothing to obscure anyone's visibility.

Excitement and nervousness fluttered within Lyndie like the beating of butterfly wings as she walked with the other jockeys to Lone Star's saddling paddock. Silver Leaf's race was the next race up.

Lyndie had her goggles positioned on her helmet, her hair pinned back in a neat bun at the base of her neck, her stick in her hand, her hopes in her throat.

All the jockeys wore white breeches and black riding boots. Beyond that, they varied widely because they'd each dressed in silks representing the owner of the horse they were about to ride. Lyndie wore the pale blue and brown of Whispering Creek Ranch. Her helmet cover and the body of her shirt shone a deep brown. Her sleeves, pale blue. A large white X had been sewn across the front and back of her shirt, the tips of the Xs meeting atop her shoulders.

She was doing this. Time had fallen through its hourglass, and she was about to run the horse of her heart. She desperately wanted to do well. For Silver Leaf, but for Jake most of all. *Don't think about it, Lyndie. You won't do anyone any favors by going sentimental right now with spectators watching.*

As always, a crowd of people jammed the rail overlooking the saddling paddock. Many were bettors, hoping to get a last-minute read on the horses. Some were tourists or those merely interested.

Lone Star housed their saddling paddock in a long building full of three-sided stalls. Each stall's open side faced outward so that the spectators could watch the proceedings.

The other jockeys branched off, allowing Lyndie her first view of Silver Leaf. Zoe stood at the horse's head, holding his lead. Jake had taken up a position near the back of the stall. A powerful *zing* went through Lyndie at the sight of him. In his black sweater and black Stetson, he melded into the band of shadow that fell across him. His features appeared pale and rigid.

"Look at you, Miss Jockey!" Zoe grinned and gave Lyndie a swift hug. "I'm excited for you."

"Thank you."

For the occasion, the redhead wore a pale blue shirt monogrammed in brown with *WCH* for Whispering Creek Horses. "Did you happen to see any cute tall guys back there in the jockeys' area?"

"Tall guys?" Lyndie asked. "In the jockeys' area?"

"I know there aren't any tall jockeys. But maybe the master of scales? Or a steward? Or . . ."

Someone on stilts? Lyndie wondered. A friendly neighborhood giant? "I didn't see any tall guys just now, but I'll keep my eyes open for you."

"Zoe," Jake said in a serious tone. He asked her to attend to final preparations, and Zoe went into action.

Lyndie needed a minute to compose herself before facing Jake, so she assessed Silver Leaf. The dapple grey Thoroughbred seemed alert and as unruffled as ever. He regarded Lyndie with his big liquid eyes, then lowered his neck and rested his muzzle on her shoulder. "What a good boy," Lyndie murmured. "You really should be the king of a small country, you know. You'd be good at it, and it's no less than you deserve." Affectionately, she patted his cheek.

When Silver stepped away to glance at Zoe's ministrations, Lyndie walked up to Jake.

Tall, Dark, and Brooding looked like a storm cloud. His arms were crossed over his chest, his defensive body language warning her to keep her distance.

"Did you study the racing form?" he asked.

"I did." She'd spent a great deal of time researching each of the other horses in the race, their style of running, past performances, trainers, jockeys.

"You're clear on our plan?"

"I'm clear." They'd already discussed it in detail. They both believed Silver Leaf to be a closer. Lyndie planned to patiently wait in the early going while he settled into his stride, then make a late move with a burst of speed.

"Are you sure you want to do this, Lyndie?"

For goodness' sake, she was just seconds from saddling up. "Yes. I'm sure."

"It's not too late to change your mind."

"I'm not going to change my mind."

"Because I'm willing to scratch Silver Leaf from the race."

Fear dove from Lyndie's breastbone into her stomach because she could see that he meant every syllable. "Jake, I can't express to you how much I want to do this. I'm positive that I want to ride. More than that, I'm grateful to you for giving me the chance—"

"No. No gratitude."

Lyndie set her lips, trying to understand where he was coming from. Did he regret tapping her as Silver's jockey? Did he wish he'd gone with Elizabeth instead?

He hadn't said so. He'd asked her if she was sure she wanted to do this. What would make him doubt her assurance? She'd given him no reason.

"Lyndie." Anguish smoldered in his eyes.

All at once, she understood what he'd really been saying to her. *He* was the one full of doubt about her riding. *He* was the one toying with the idea of changing his mind.

She didn't understand why he'd feel that way. Would he take her off Silver Leaf now? At the last moment? He couldn't. He could. But he wouldn't, surely. Please, God. Distress tried to creep in on her, but she blocked it. She'd need a cool head in order to ride Silver well. "I'm going to say a quick prayer. Okay?"

"No. I . . ."

She tipped her head and closed her eyes. "God, please be with Jake. This is hard on him, and he needs you. I pray that you'll cover him with your peace. Amen."

She glanced up and found him staring at her, a line

of consternation between his brows. She got the feeling he hadn't closed his eyes. "Aren't you going to pray for yourself?" he asked.

"I already prayed for Silver and me earlier. God has it taken care of."

"Don't you think you might want to put in another word?"

Finally, she could see in him a glimmer of the Jake she knew. It was going to be okay. He'd let her ride. More eye closing on her part. "God, please watch over and protect Silver Leaf and me. And thank you in advance, because I already believe that you'll do just that—"

"Jockeys up!" the paddock judge called.

"—Amen."

"*Lyndie*. It's not too late—"

"I'm not going to change my mind, Jake." It took some doing, after the scare he'd just delivered to her, but she managed to wink at him and smile. "You heard the man. Jockeys up."

Gravely, he bent. She put her boot into his hands, and he effortlessly gave her a leg up into the saddle. They held eye contact for a long moment—the jockey full of faith, the trainer without any.

"He's ready for this race, Lyndie," Zoe said from where she stood on the opposite side of Silver. "I think he's going to do great for you."

"I agree."

The horses started forward, led by their grooms. As Silver eased into a walk, Lyndie returned her attention to Jake for a final split second. Transposed in front of the man, she saw in her memory the brown-haired boy he'd been. Kind and careful.

She tugged her attention from him and willed herself not to look back. He'd be all right.

When they reached the track, they met up with Blackberry, who was serving as Silver's lead pony. Silver greeted the mare with a whinny, then the exercise rider astride Blackberry took over the job of leading Silver. Together, Silver, Blackberry, and their riders entered the post parade toward the starting gate.

Very little time remained before the race's start. Lyndie purposely set aside the confusing conversation she'd just had with Jake. She set aside, too, her awareness of the friends and family watching from the grandstands.

Lyndie brought down her goggles and focused on giving Silver the warm-up he needed. The other jockeys were doing the same. Just a few dozen yards away, she spotted the red and yellow stripes of Elizabeth Alvarez's silks. Elizabeth would be riding a solid speed horse in the race.

The two of them had shared a dressing room earlier, just like old times. Elizabeth had reacted with equanimity to Jake's decision to put Lyndie on Silver Leaf. The world of Thoroughbred horse racing was small. Smart, professional jockeys knew better than to burn bridges with trainers.

The starting gate had been pulled into position by a tractor. The gate crew swarmed around it, leading the horses into their slots one at a time. Silver Leaf went into position with his usual well-bred etiquette.

Once inside the tight enclosure, Lyndie took deep and measured breaths. She ran a final check of her equipment. She brought everything she'd studied about the other Thoroughbreds to the fore of her mind. She visualized how she hoped the race would go down.

The horses filed in. Almost all of them, now. The starter watched hawkishly, waiting for the right moment to hit the button that would release the magnets holding the doors closed.

She could feel the sturdy pressure of the stirrups against the soles of her boots, her vest beneath her shirt, the nub of the reins against the inside of her hand. Warmth radiated upward from Silver's flanks. She attuned herself to the suppressed energy of the big stallion. *We can do this, Silver Leaf. We can.*

The gates sprang open.

All ten horses lunged forward. Lyndie's world turned into hectic motion, jostling, mounting speed. Then space opened around her as the front runners rushed forward. Her ears filled with the thunder of hooves and the huff of horses' breath. Steadily, Silver built his pace.

More horses moved past them, putting them close to the rear of the pack. Lyndie checked her instinct to compel Silver into a faster gear. Instead, she rode him the way she'd been born to ride horses, in perfect synchronization with his movement and spirit. She let him run the way that he wanted to run. In response, Silver stretched his stride, comfortably within his abilities.

Maybe too comfortably. The horses competing for first widened the gap between themselves and Silver. Still, Lyndie waited.

As they entered the stretch turn, Lyndie at last urged Silver forward. Through her body's cues she invited him to fly. *Go, Silver Leaf! Go!*

He responded smoothly, opening into his sprint and

unharnessing the same breathtaking power he'd shown in practice. She could feel the depth of the surging energy he'd kept back.

She guided him out of the turn on the outside, passing a handful of horses in a sweep. Impossibly, he increased his speed even more.

A trio of horses rode almost side by side in front of them. When the Thoroughbred nearest the grandstand drifted out slightly, a hole opened, and Lyndie shot Silver through it.

Now it was only a matter of reeling in the two leaders. She could tell by their form that they were tiring. Silver seemed to have noticed their weakness, too. He pursued them fervently. Lyndie hunched low, moving her hands in rhythm, Silver's mane slapping against her helmet. She leveraged every ounce of her frame and every drop of her fortitude to drive him onward.

*　　　*　　　*

Jake stood in a deserted corner of the clubhouse, watching the race on a mounted TV.

His heart raced with panic as Lyndie came down the final furlong. Silver Leaf overtook the two leaders as if they were standing still. Lyndie darted looks behind her, but Jake could tell that no one in the field had the ability to answer Silver Leaf's closing speed.

Silver Leaf whipped past the wire. Immediately Lyndie sat up, releasing Silver Leaf from his sprint, letting him know they were done. Gradually, she slowed his pace.

His jockey had ridden perfectly. The horse he'd raised

had fulfilled his potential. And he felt like he was about to have a heart attack.

She's fine, he told himself. He jerked off his hat and tunneled a hand through his hair. *She's fine*. Yet his body had never had much interest in listening to his brain. It kept on with its stubborn terror. His muscles were trembling the way they did after a nightmare, and he couldn't catch a full breath.

The camera showed Lyndie raising a fist into the air, a huge smile on her face.

She's fine. Which didn't change the fact that he'd endangered her life today.

He leaned a shoulder into the concrete wall and concentrated on inhaling and exhaling through the exhaustion and worry that had hollowed him out.

In a couple of minutes, they'd be expecting him in the winner's circle. The pressure of needing to act a certain way for the benefit of others made everything worse. He didn't know if he could do it. He was in bad shape. He might not be able to leave this spot, here—leaning against the wall—for hours.

⌇

"We did it!" Lyndie said to Silver for maybe the third or fourth time, laughing with astonishment and patting his sweaty neck. "We did it. We won! Congratulations, Silver. What a great racehorse you are." The thrill of triumph gusted within her like a hurricane too large for her body to contain.

Zoe and one of Jake's hand-walkers rushed forward to meet them. "I knew it!" Zoe beamed. "That was so awesome, Lyndie. Way to go!"

"He was ready, just like you said."

Zoe hoisted the sponge that floated atop her bucket of water and ran it over Silver's head.

Lyndie looked around, reorienting herself with the world that existed beyond the track. The sky was still in its place. The grandstands. Faraway trees. There was one important landmark, however, that she couldn't locate. "Where's Jake?"

"I don't know. He should be here any minute." Zoe continued to attend to Silver, chattering to him excitedly all the while.

Silver Leaf hadn't just won his race, he'd crushed the competition. He'd soared. This had to be one of the top ten happiest moments in Lyndie's life, and she was beyond eager to share it with Jake.

In the winner's circle, a boisterous group greeted them with congratulations. Beneath a beautiful white hat, tears of joy ran down Meg's face. Bo hugged his wife, laughed, and handed her a tissue.

"You made me a hundred bucks!" Amber announced, holding her betting ticket in the air.

"You made me five hundred," Ty said.

Lyndie scanned the group. Celia, Dru, her own parents, and Grandpa Harold caught her eye and called out more well wishes. As did Nancy and John Porter, Jake's mom and dad. Had Silver Leaf won the Breeder's Cup, they could not have been more jubilant than they were over Silver's miracle run.

Lyndie bent toward Bo. "Where's Jake?"

He craned his neck to search through the crowd. "I don't know—ah, here he comes."

Lyndie straightened, finally catching sight of Jake

striding toward them. It didn't seem right that the man most responsible for Silver's success had arrived last. He accepted handshakes as stoically as always.

What he didn't do? Look up at her. She waited. Waited. Until he finally angled his attention in her direction. One burning half second passed between them, then he turned toward the photographer, who bustled everyone into position for a picture.

Lyndie dismounted as soon as the photo had been snapped. Silver needed to be cooled down thoroughly and taken to the testing barn. Lyndie needed to weigh herself and her gear again.

Meg wrapped her in a hug. "Thank you. This means a lot to me."

"You're very welcome." Lyndie hugged her back. "I'm so happy for you, Meg. Your faith in Silver Leaf paid off."

Meg stepped away, smiling through more tears. Bo swiveled his wife into his chest and kissed her soundly.

"Sheesh," Dru muttered.

Zoe led Silver away from the group. Jake and Lyndie followed, their families applauding as they passed.

They threaded their way through a throng of track employees on their way to the tunnel. One young man laughed at something his friend had said, then stumbled backward into Lyndie's path.

Jake's hand shot out, stopping the man before he could bump into her. "Watch it."

"Oh. Sorry about that. Wasn't paying attention."

Jake scowled so intensely that the poor guy swallowed nervously.

"It's all right," Lyndie reassured the young man as Jake steered her into the quiet and shade of the tunnel.

Lyndie stopped to talk to him, but he continued on as if he hadn't noticed.

She hurried to catch up, putting a hand on his arm to stay him.

Instantly, his steps halted.

They should both be overcome with elation, right? Instead, his eyes glowed like chips of ice in a face carved with tension.

"You don't look too happy." She slid her hand from his sleeve.

His shoulders were very wide, his height towering. "You rode a good race."

"Thank you. I didn't do much, as you could probably tell. Silver Leaf was outstanding."

"You did plenty."

The depth of her feelings for him rattled her. She *really* wanted him to be thrilled, like she was. Also, she wanted to hug him. Badly. "Congratulations, Jake."

He inclined his head. "Congratulations, Lyndie. I'll see you at work in the morning—"

"Wait," she blurted when he moved as if to leave.

"Yes?"

What are you going to do, Lyndie? Follow through on your desire to hug him? Throw your arms around him and kiss him? Tell him how you feel about him?

The hard look on his face convinced her not to try any of the above. She didn't want to be swept away by post-race excitement and do something that would end up setting their relationship back. "Never mind. I'll see you tomorrow."

He turned and stalked away.

EIGHTEEN

W elcome to tonight's gokon!" A plump brunette with a beautifully curly bob beamed at the long table of twelve.

Before sitting, the singles had been asked to enter a private room at the Hibachi-style restaurant, take off their shoes, and find their places on patterned pillows at a table so low to the ground that its dimensions would have better suited four-year-olds. The men lined one side, the women the other.

"This is fun," Amber whispered from the pillow next to Lyndie's. "Admit you're glad you came."

"I'm reserving judgment," Lyndie answered.

"The event tonight is inspired by the Japanese group-dating model," the brunette with the curly bob announced. "Each of you has come with a friend or two or three, which is great. So." She set her palms together. "How about we begin with an icebreaker?"

Lyndie hid a sigh. To her, icebreakers always felt painfully forced.

"Have ya'll ever played truth, truth, lie?" The brunette smiled wide. "Tell us two truths about yourself and one lie. The rest of us will try to guess which one's the lie. Okay?"

Everyone murmured uncomfortably while shooting bland smiles at the strangers sitting across from them in their stocking feet.

Lyndie had the last pillow on her end of the table. Lucky for her, the game would be kicking off at the other end. She peeked in that direction, her gaze accidentally intersecting with Luke, her former square dancing partner. When she'd first spotted him here at the Hibachi restaurant, she'd hoped for a coincidence. Alas, no. He'd signed up for the gokon.

He gave her a grin and launched into a trio of allergy sneezes.

A guy with a beard, a do-rag, and a Megadeth T-shirt received the first turn at truth, truth, lie. "I've done time," he stated. "I flunked my GED once. I like to bet on dog fights."

Two of these things were true?

A round of nervous laughter erupted from the table. A few people shifted their eyes from side to side, maybe charting exit routes.

Some of the attendees attempted to guess which was the lie.

"Remind me why I agreed to go on three dates in three months," Lyndie said to Amber, her voice hushed.

"Because I offered to care for your animals. Anyway, I think the jailbird down there is kind of cute in a really terrifying way."

"You don't."

"No, I don't. But remember, I'm wishing that I was on a date right at this moment with a fireman who has the prettiest blue-gray eyes I've ever seen. Instead of being grumpy about the gokon like you, I'm choosing to be positive."

"Which is the lie?" the brunette finally asked the jailbird.

"I didn't flunk my GED once," he said.

Chittery laughter from the brunette. "Of course you didn't!"

"I flunked it twice."

Silence fell.

Amber's shoulders slumped. "I may need a drink."

"The only thing we drink is coffee."

"Oh, right. Drat. I'm paying a babysitter for this."

When it came time for Luke to take his turn, he began by knuckling red and watery eyes. "My name's Luke. I have blond hair. It's the month of April."

"None of those are lies, dude," the guy sitting next to him pointed out. "It is April."

"One's a lie," Luke insisted.

"Do you dye your hair?" a timid girl the size of a dragon-fly ventured.

"Nope."

"You're not named . . . Luke?" Amber asked.

"No, I'm not. I go by Luke but it's not my first name. My first name is Alejandro."

"I'm looking at my watch, and fifteen minutes have gone by!" The brunette pushed to her feet and clapped. "Ladies, you can stay in your seats all evening. Gentle-men, you're going to move one seat to your right every fifteen minutes so that we can mingle. Say *sayonara* to your current seat and *konnichiwa* to your new one!"

Which meant Lyndie was going to lose the nice red-headed guy with the face full of cinnamon freckles who was currently sitting across from her.

"Okay, now let's continue with truth, truth, lie!" The brunette gestured to a pale and flushing woman with an ultra-short haircut. "Your turn."

Lyndie wanted her dogs, her apartment, and the fresh flower arrangement she'd brought home this afternoon. She missed Jake.

After Silver Leaf's win, for the past two mornings, she and Jake had picked right back up where they'd left off. Her, exercising his horses. Him, letting her hang out with him afterward.

Jake, Jake, Jake. Jake, who could set her heart racing with a glance. Jake, who was poetry with horses. Jake, whom she desperately wanted to see smile. He was difficult to comprehend and injured and shielded and dangerous. He was also the one who captivated her thoughts, who filled her with physical yearning, who'd made her care.

⁂

Jake pulled his truck to the curb across from Lyndie's apartment. At this hour, the houses in her neighborhood sat either completely dark or almost completely. Nothing moved on her street except blades of grass and tree branches. He kept his engine idling and checked his watch. Eleven forty-five.

He and Bo had been present at a foaling tonight, and he was on his way home. He'd driven by Lyndie's because . . .

He glanced at her apartment, then out his front windshield. He didn't know why he'd come. He wasn't going to stay and he definitely wasn't going to knock on her door. He'd driven by, he supposed, just to make sure that she was all right. And to try to get his head straight.

Because Amber had told Meg, and Meg had told Bo, and Bo had told him, he knew that Lyndie had gone out earlier tonight on that group date everybody had been talking about on Easter.

He'd been telling himself that if Lyndie had met somebody tonight, someone who was happy and solid and who'd love her like she deserved, then that would be the best thing for her. Which meant he should be okay with it.

Yet just the thought of her dating someone else filled him with so much misery and jealousy that he couldn't stand himself. He bumped the back of his head against the seat.

He wanted what was best for Lyndie. But he also wanted her for himself. That was his torture.

Lately, he'd begun to wish that he could show her how he felt about her, trust her with his fears, or explain about the things he'd seen overseas. He wouldn't let himself, though, because he didn't want his problems anywhere near her.

Already, Lyndie was too brave and forgiving—

"Good evening."

He flinched at the sound.

Lyndie had called the words softly from across the street. In the dim light, she smiled at him.

He cursed under his breath. She'd caught him. How could he explain why he was sitting outside her house alone in the dark? He couldn't.

Lyndie hugged her long sweater around her body and made her way to his truck. Under the sweater, she wore a white T-shirt, dark leggings, and a pair of fuzzy socks stuck into slippers. The wind lifted pieces of her beautiful, wavy hair.

She stopped on the other side of his door. "I looked out my kitchen window just now and saw you."

Unlike his face, hers was perfect. She had smooth skin, a few freckles, clear eyes full of optimism.

"What brings you to the neighborhood, Jake?" Humor played over her lips. "Are you staking out a house for the FBI? Stargazing?"

When he didn't answer, she tilted her head, letting him know that she was prepared to wait for an answer.

"I wanted to make sure you were okay," he said. "That's all."

She blinked once. "Really?"

Jake nodded.

"That's so kind of—"

"I'd better be going." He reached for the gear shift—

"Step out of the truck."

"Excuse me?"

"You're not leaving."

He aimed a disbelieving look at her. "It's late and—"

"Step out of the truck, Jake." Lyndie regarded him with endless determination. "Please."

He looked away from her because he was worried she'd see his hunger for her in his eyes. He curled his fingers into his palms to stop himself from climbing from the truck and reaching for her.

Helpless devotion. Hopeless love.

He should go. Right at this moment, he should go. If he stayed, he was downright scared of what he might do, of what he might reveal.

Lyndie watched him, full of concern that he'd ignore her request and drive away . . . that she might never break down his barriers . . . that he might spend the rest of his life running away from her.

He'd been hurt physically and mentally, and she understood. However, she was done with giving him space because giving him space had not helped him.

She'd been meant to see Jake out her window, she just knew it. Unable to settle her mind, she'd been lying in bed praying about him for the past twenty minutes. She'd padded into her kitchen for a midnight snack and— boom—caught sight of him sitting alone in his truck in this unrelenting darkness.

He still hadn't moved.

Please, Lord, she begged as she opened the truck's door.

Jake shot her an inscrutable look, and her spirits tumbled. She'd lost him. He was about to pull the door closed and drive away.

Instead, he turned off the engine. He stepped down from the cab and pushed his keys into a front pocket of his beat-up jeans.

Oh my. Her brazen demand that he exit the truck had actually worked. Now she had a big, surly cowboy standing in front of her. Beneath his navy shirt, the powerful muscles of his upper body had tensed. He wore his size and a cynical frown like shields.

She ignored all that and took a step toward him. He stepped immediately back. His truck gave him little room to retreat. Courage and fear swarmed so furiously in her brain that she couldn't find a coherent thought. She supposed she should be worried about wrecking the friendship they'd built. She was, a little.

Still, she followed instinct and took another step toward him. He stepped back again, which brought him up against the bulk of his truck.

Nowhere left to hide, Jake.

She placed her palm on his chest. Just like that.

His eyes glowed feverish in the moonlight. She could feel the warmth of his skin beneath her hand. The fast rhythm of his heart matched the rapid beat of her own.

Wind gusted, ruffling his dark hair. His ragged breathing filled the silence. He was painfully desirable to her, with his scars and his fractured soul. He was Jake. "I want to kiss you," she whispered.

His upper body went rigid, as if preparing for another IED explosion that would do them both irreparable damage.

She placed her other palm on his chest and tugged him down to her as she rose onto her tiptoes. Slowly, she neared, pausing just an inch away from his profile. Their forceful chemistry overtook her, and the scent of mesquite wrapped around her the instant before she set her lips to his.

His mouth was warm, smooth. Also . . . unresponsive.

She pulled away the distance of a trembling inhale and dug her fingers into his shirt. *Kiss me*, she wanted to demand. *I adore you, and I want you to adore me*.

Still nothing from him except stricken stillness.

Lyndie leaned into Jake again, this time kissing the edge of his lips with a caress as light as the whisper of silk. *Kiss me back. I'd do anything in the world for you. Kiss me back.*

Nothing. She gave him a long, torturous moment to respond.

When he didn't, her soul shriveled. She lowered onto her heels. Her hands dropped to her sides, and she stepped away. She'd held his face in her hands that day at the ranch. Just now, she'd kissed him. And both times, nothing.

He was like a statue. And though she wanted to be good for him, he wouldn't let her be good for him. She wished she could say something to lighten the moment, but if she tried, he'd know she was lying. This moment of crushing disappointment couldn't be lightened.

She swung away from him and walked two paces toward her house—

His fingers banded around her wrist, stopping her. Unfounded hope leapt into her breast as he turned her to face him in the middle of the deserted street.

Jake lifted the wrist he'd grasped, then bent his head and kissed the heart of her palm. Wonder and thankfulness brought tears to the rims of her lashes. She willed the moisture away, wanting nothing to interfere with her vision of this, of him. He lowered their hands but didn't let go. His fingers interlaced with hers.

For the first time, the mask he wore had gone. She could see in the devastated honesty of his face that he cared about her. "I . . ." He looked to be fighting an internal war with himself. "You shouldn't have kissed me," he said at last.

She gave him a small and wobbly smile. "But I did."

"You shouldn't have."

"I'm not sorry."

"Lyndie . . ."

She drank in the sensation of his hand holding hers.

He was very familiar to her and yet *this* between them was stunningly new. Like a land they'd never explored.

"I'm not . . ." he spoke haltingly, his voice raspy, ". . . good enough for you."

"Of course you're good enough—"

"No." He inclined his head so that his forehead rested against hers. Their eyes closed, breath intermixing. She could sense his struggle and his despair.

"None of us are perfect," she murmured.

His hands rose to frame her jaw on both sides. "I'm more imperfect than most."

"Not to me."

He groaned, then kissed her with such fiery need and possession that her mind reeled and joy soared.

He walked her backward, easily lifting her onto the sidewalk, stopping when her hips bumped the fence that enclosed the Candy Shoppe. More long and drugging kisses.

She was gasping and laughing when she pulled back so that she could see his face.

He gazed at her for a moment, then swept her off her feet, carrying her much the way he had the day of her spill at the track. Like she had then, she locked an elbow over his shoulder and ran her fingers into his hair. Unlike that day, he cut sizzling glances at her as he walked around the side of the house and up the back staircase. He set her down on the landing and they were kissing again, his hands on her cheeks, into her hair. He hunched his shoulders protectively around her and his tall body blocked her from the world.

When distant thunder rumbled, Jake's head jerked

up and his hands tightened reflexively around her. She watched him sweep the view as if searching for attackers.

Nothing surrounded them but the silent structures of the neighboring Victorians. Jake's attackers hadn't been external for a very long time. They were all internal.

When he fixed his attention on her again, she read conflict in his gorgeous eyes.

Oh dear. "Don't even think about hightailing it out of here."

"I never hightail." He took hold of a lock of her hair, twining it carefully around a finger, then watching as he ran the pads of his fingers down to the end of the strands.

"C—" The thing he was doing with her hair was making her breathless. "Come inside."

"I can't."

"You can."

He flicked an ominous look at her. "You wouldn't say that if you knew what was going on inside my head right now."

Despite how badly she wanted him to come inside so they could kiss longer, the small part of her brain that remained rational knew he had a point. It would be smartest to give them both time to cool down and process things. Rome wasn't built in a day.

He frowned, taking up another section of her hair, treating it as reverently as the first. "This thing between us isn't a good idea."

Such a sweet talker, Jake. So full of flattery. "I disagree. I think it's a very good idea."

"You've disagreed with every single thing I've said tonight."

"That's because you've been wrong every time." Her lips curved.

"I'm afraid that I've been right."

"How about we not worry so much about who's wrong or right? Will you come back tomorrow evening? I'll make you dinner."

He hesitated.

"Jake, this is when you're supposed to say, 'Yes, thanks, Lyndie. I'll show up here tomorrow night for dinner.'"

He freed his fingers from her hair. She lifted her hand so that it met his and their palms were aligned, his bigger hand up against her smaller one, somehow perfectly matched. The moment hung, full of fate and beauty, before Jake broke it by stepping back into a swath of shadow. His thumbs hooked into his pockets. "It's cold. You should go inside, Lyndie. I don't want you to be cold."

"Not until you say, 'Yes, thanks—'"

"Yes, thanks." She could hardly see his face now, he was standing in such a pool of darkness. Even so, the weight of his attention on her felt like the warmth of a fire. "I'll show up here tomorrow night for dinner." He started down the stairs.

Lyndie resisted the urge to lunge forward and grip his shirt to keep him from going. *How* she wanted to launch herself back into his arms for more of the scorching ecstasy of those kisses.

"Go on in, Lyndie." He'd paused near the bottom of the stairs, but he hadn't looked back.

"Okay. I'm going." She scooted into her apartment but leaned back out her door to call, "Good night."

No reply. Either he'd already vanished or didn't feel

it necessary to respond likewise, like most humans did. Strange man. Also, a very hunky man who could kiss like nobody's business.

Lyndie closed herself into her apartment and listened to his truck's engine fade from hearing. Giddy, she went to sit on her bed and covered her mouth with her hands. *Oh my goodness. Oh my goodness!* What had just gone down between them reminded her of trying on a dress in a dressing room and standing in amazement when it fit every inch of your body as perfectly as if it had been made for you. Kissing Jake had been like that for her. Righter than right. So meant-to-be that it felt like . . . she was emotional and thinking melodramatic thoughts . . . but it truly did feel God-ordained.

At the thought, a quiet alarm went off inside of her. Calling what had just happened God-ordained was probably going too far. Kissing Jake had definitely given her that made-to-fit feeling, but if she was being honest with herself, that feeling might have come straight from her own hopes and not from God at all.

She rested her hands in her lap and squeezed the knuckle of each of her fingers, one by one, as if doing so would give her clarity. Up until this moment, she'd been very confident about God's call on her in relation to Jake. She'd known that God wanted her to do what she could to bring Jake back to Him, to life. She'd been doing her best. But along the way, her motivation to do what God had asked her to do had become irrevocably interwoven with her own romantic feelings for Jake. Their romance had taken a step forward tonight, and she wanted to believe that God's plan had taken a step forward, too.

Only . . . that might not be right.

Worry intermixed with her joy, tugging her back down to earth from the happy clouds where she'd been floating. Jake had distanced himself from God, and Lyndie didn't believe that God called His people into romantic relationships with unbelievers. Then again, Jake wasn't *exactly* an unbeliever. He had trusted Christ as a child. She'd known him at the time and had wholehearted confidence in the fact that Jake had been saved. Which meant that his salvation couldn't be revoked. Once God had you in His hand, you couldn't be removed, right? What was that verse?

She located her Bible and after consulting the concordance, paged to John 10:28. She'd highlighted and starred the words, which had been spoken by Jesus Himself. *I give them eternal life, and they shall never perish; no one will snatch them out of my hand.*

That didn't mean that Jake needed God any less in the present. In fact, Jake needed Him desperately. Until Jake got himself right with God, nothing would be right with Jake and thus nothing could be one hundred percent right between them in their relationship.

Even so . . . She had hope that Jake would come to lean on God again.

A little chill of foreboding slid down the back of her neck, because she knew that kind of thinking was dangerous. Women since the beginning of time had bought themselves a lifetime of heartache by falling in love with men they hoped would change one day, men who never changed. She wasn't going to be one of those women, was she? Before Jake, she'd never imagined that she— independent as she was and viewing herself as so secure in her faith—would even toy with the idea of becoming one of those women.

God had ways of humbling a person.

She'd followed God her whole life. She didn't want to break from following Him now or ever. But this situation was murky. She couldn't hear or feel a clear yes or a clear no on dating Jake. And it probably didn't help that she really, really liked Jake. She seriously, he-sets-my-hair-on-fire liked him.

With a frustrated sigh, Lyndie flopped onto her back on her mattress, the bed bouncing slightly.

God *could* change Jake. She had hope in that. Strong hope. Was it faith to place her trust in that, or selfish idiocy?

Faith, she hoped. She was optimistic and not easily swayed when she set her mind to something. And she'd set her mind on Jake. She'd go forward with him, trying her very best not to hang all her dreams on him, not to fall madly in love with him. It was still best to hold a portion of her heart back.

How was he reacting to their kisses at this very moment, and how would he react tomorrow? At no point had she seen even a flash of peace or lightheartedness in him. It could be that he'd flee now—

No. He'd said he'd come for dinner, at least. And so he would. She could stress about the future and about whether or not he'd ever kiss her again. Or she could pray that God would find a way to help Jake deal with all of this, with her. So she'd pray. And replay in her memory every single detail of tonight. And yes . . . maybe she'd stress just a little bit, too.

Because she dearly wanted him to change. And she dearly wanted him to kiss her again.

Amber faced a sudden should-I-hide or should-I-face-this quandary.

In order to raise funds, the Society for the Restoration of Holley had set up a fried chicken Sunday lunch buffet at Holley's athletic fields. Since Jayden would be playing soccer in an hour for the Crazy Cleats, she'd had him change into his soccer gear on the way over from church. She'd planned to knock out a fried chicken lunch followed by his soccer game in just one stop. She hadn't planned on seeing Will McGrath and his two daughters.

Amber and Jayden had just finished filling their plates and been searching for a place to sit when she'd spotted Will and his girls on a navy plaid blanket under a pecan tree.

If it had been Will by himself, Amber would have said a few words, but his daughters? She'd better go with the hide option.

Just as she took Jayden by the hand to lead him in the opposite direction, Will looked over and saw her. He'd been in the middle of saying something, but his words immediately cut off. Curious, his daughters glanced in Amber's direction.

Too late to hide. The only option left: face this. Amber smiled at them as she approached. Mother Teresa had once said, "Let us always meet each other with a smile, for the smile is the beginning of love."

"Hi, Will. How are you doing?"

"Great." Always mannerly, he pushed to his feet. "How are you today, Amber?"

"Doing well, thanks."

"How about you, Jayden?"

Jayden busily stuffed potato chips in his mouth. Amber gave him a nudge. He swallowed and straightened. "I'm doin' good. Thank you, sir."

"Awww," the younger of Will's girls crooned.

"Jayden's soccer team is playing here soon, so we decided to grab lunch before the game." Why was she telling them things they could clearly see for themselves? A combo of nervousness and the need to convince Will that she wasn't stalking him spurred her to keep talking. "I wanted to support the Society for the Restoration of Holley."

"We had the same idea. Taylor's playing softball in a little bit." Sure enough, the smaller of the two girls wore a uniform. She'd swept her hair into a ponytail and tied it with a white ribbon.

Will introduced her to Madison, a high school junior, and Taylor, a freshman. While Amber exchanged greetings and introduced them to Jayden, she tried to look calm and pleasant instead of just tense.

Munch munch munch. Jayden had returned to the

chips. He tugged on her sundress, letting her know he wanted her to finish the boring talking so they could eat.

"Well, we'll let you enjoy your lunch." Amber began to edge away.

"Would you like to join us?" Will was still standing. And yes, he still had the dreamiest bedroom eyes in the ENTIRE WORLD.

"No, no, we don't want to intrude on you guys."

"You're not intruding. We'd like for you to join us." He bent and lifted another navy plaid blanket from behind his cooler. "Here." He settled it onto the ground so that the two blankets overlapped.

Her heart melting—get a grip, Amber, all he did was lay down a blanket—she toed off her high-heeled sandals and lowered onto the fabric. "Thank you." Jayden settled beside her, and she gave his hands a squirt of hand sanitizer.

"Can I get you both something to drink?" Will asked.

"Thank you, but I brought bottled water." She wasn't a very controlling mom, but she tried to avoid giving Jayden sugary drinks. She already had her hands full with his God-given level of hyperactivity.

She and Will spoke politely about the Society for the Restoration of Holley and about the improvements the society had made to the old town square. Amber made every effort to eat very politely. And not to stare impolitely at either Will or his daughters.

In the distance, kids' teams filled the two baseball diamonds and the two soccer fields. The bright spring weather made her want to lift her face to the sun and sigh.

Madison and Taylor said little and checked their smartphones often. They looked enormously alike. Both girls

had straight dark blond hair and had inherited their father's squarish jaw. They were long-legged and pretty.
They'd been raised in a small town just like Amber herself
had been. But she didn't catch any signs of the wildness
she'd flirted with at their ages. Taylor had on softball
stuff and Madison wore a T-shirt and neon Nike shorts
with flip-flops. If Jayden turned out half as wholesome as
Will's daughters appeared to be, she'd be thrilled.

"Look at these little tiny shoes, Maddie," Taylor said,
touching a fingertip to one of Jayden's feet.

"I know. He's a mini. A mini man. Do you mind if I
take your picture, Jayden?"

He set down his chicken leg. "'Kay."

"Sure?"

"Yes, ma'am."

"Awww," both girls said, then assured him that he
could call them Madison and Taylor if he wanted to.
They held up their phones and Jayden immediately put
on the fake smile he wore whenever Amber tried to take
pictures of him. It mostly involved Jayden stretching
his lips as far as they would go and showing his gums.

"You're super cute, Jayden," Madison told him.

"Thank you, ma'am."

"Awww!"

As usual, he was spreading *ma'am* and *sir* on thick,
knowing it would win him positive attention.

Amber glanced at Will and found him watching her
with a half smile. Her stomach did a lift-and-tingle thing.
What if . . . what if she and Will could overlap one day?
The way their blankets were overlapping and joining
their two families right at this moment?

She was getting way, way ahead of herself, but it was

fun to imagine it. The two of them as husband and wife, mother and father. His girls. Her boy. And maybe, Lord willing, one more little baby to share. A big, crazy, blended family with kids spread wildly apart in age. And yet . . . perfect.

So much longing filled Amber that she had to look down and pretend to brush crumbs from the lap of her sundress. She'd never been married. And since she'd left home, her apartment at the Candy Shoppe had been the only place she'd been able to call *hers*. Even that was a stretch, seeing as how she merely rented.

In her worst moments, she felt certain she'd never find a husband or a home of her own. In her best moments, she remembered that she'd found her home in the Lord and needed nothing more to find contentment.

"May I be 'scused?" Jayden asked her.

He'd left his potato salad and green beans untouched, eaten all of his chips and three bites of fried chicken. She nodded. Trying to keep him seated once he'd finished was like trying to pin down a bumblebee. She didn't have the energy. "Throw away your plate and napkin, please."

He did so, then grabbed his soccer ball and ran to an open stretch of lawn. "Mom? Will you play with me?"

God had given Jayden to the wrong mother. He should have been delivered to Mia Hamm instead of a woman so uninterested in sports that she only watched TV during Super Bowl parties when the commercials came on. "I'm not done eating yet, sweetie."

"I'll go kick with him, if you don't mind." Will stood.

"I . . . ah . . . I don't mind at all. If you're sure."

"I'll go, too." Taylor jogged toward Jayden.

Startled, Amber watched them form a triangle and

begin passing the ball. Will looked fit and athletic, naturally graceful. Unlike her, he moved to the ball easily and had no problem aiming and controlling it.

She did believe—no, was really pretty positively sure—that she'd never seen a nicer sight than a handsome fireman and his smiling teenaged daughter kicking a ball with her son. The way to her heart was through her son's soccer ball, apparently.

As if! As if Will McGrath needed another way to her heart. He'd blazed a pretty big trail there already.

She looked over and found Madison studying her.

"Do you play sports?" Amber asked.

"Volleyball."

"Great. And . . . you said you're a junior."

"Mmm-hmm."

"How's that going?"

"Good." Madison ducked her head to peek at something on her phone. "So, yeah. Good."

Amber had no idea what else to say to a girl her age so she took a bite of potato salad and watched Will.

I know you have bigger issues that you're dealing with, God. But if you find the time and if it's in your plan, I'd really like to go on a date with Will.

Just one solitary date would complete Amber's deal with Lyndie. They'd both gone on two dates so far. They each only had one date left. If Lyndie's final date tanked, then Lyndie would most likely return to her anti-social artist's studio. If Amber's final date tanked, then she was planning to interpret it as a "not now" from God and extend her long vacation from the world of dating.

One date with Will to begin with, Lord, would be

*great. More than enough! Don't mean to be greedy. But
if it's in your plan . . .*

One of Jake's yearlings, a bay colt, loped circles around
him inside Whispering Creek's round pen.

After a night mostly spent pacing his loft, he'd been
in a very bad place mentally this morning. He'd needed
his work to keep his mind and hands busy, so he'd spent
the better part of the day at the ranch.

He stopped the colt, then let him go back out, jogging
him in the opposite direction.

For the hundredth time, Jake checked his watch. Lyndie had sent him a text earlier, asking him to arrive for
dinner at her house at seven. It was six thirty. If he was
going to go, he needed to head to his car.

He pushed the heels of his hands against eyes that
ached with exhaustion. Part of him had been counting the seconds until he could see her again. The other
part knew for certain that he shouldn't go to her house
because when he saw her again, he'd kiss her again, and
he'd done more than enough damage already.

Shoving his hands into the pockets of his sleeveless
padded vest, he returned his attention to the colt. He
could use a padded cell at the moment more than a padded vest.

He'd told Lyndie straight out that he wasn't good
enough for her. But she wouldn't see sense. She was
determined to believe that he was better than he was.
Which meant that if one of them was going to be sane
about this, it was going to have to be him. And wasn't

that rich? Him. Who hadn't been sane since the day he'd last ridden in a Humvee through an Iraqi desert.

The colt's groom opened the door to the round pen and gave Jake a questioning look.

"You can take him." Jake chirped and the colt slowed. Patiently, Jake waited until the horse approached him, head down. He fished a piece of carrot from the inside pocket of his vest and fed it to him. Then he issued instructions to the groom, followed them partway down the shed row, and checked his watch again. Six forty.

What good could possibly come out of a relationship with Lyndie? He could only imagine bad endings.

She'd left him once. Back when her family had moved away from Texas. Even as a kid, the grief of losing her had devastated him. If Karen and Mike decided to move Mollie again, Lyndie would go with them. Or Lyndie might date him for a little while, then decide he was boring and flawed. Or she'd take a spill racing Silver Leaf and hurt herself. Or he'd leave for New York just as he did every year when Lone Star closed for the season. And she'd stay here with Mollie.

See? Bad endings.

If they continued down this road and one of those bad endings happened, he feared that it might do him in.

You've been done in ever since she came to Holley. What difference will having dinner with her make at this point? Go see her and take what joy this life has to offer you.

He should go.

No. He shouldn't go. He should return to his loft alone, like he'd done for a thousand nights.

He walked to his truck and drove to Lyndie's. When

he arrived, he climbed the back staircase he'd carried her up less than twenty-four hours before, and stood on the platform where he'd kissed her like he was suffocating and she was air.

He shouldn't be here. His doubts shouted at him to turn back.

"Hey." She pulled the door open before he'd knocked and motioned him inside with her head. In one hand she held a pair of metal kitchen tongs. "Hungry?"

Hungry? He almost laughed a wicked laugh. *Yes.*

"C'mon in." She gave him a light smile and led him into her kitchen. As usual, her dogs went crazy, wagging their tails, jumping up on him. "I'm not that great of a cook," she was saying. "I can follow a recipe if it's simple enough for a monkey to manage. Or I can make tacos. Tonight I'm making tacos." Stopping at the stovetop, she used the tongs to turn two tortillas browning in a skillet of oil.

Light sparkled along the gold hoops of her earrings. In a pale purple shirt and white jeans she looked like everything he wasn't: clean and happy and calm. She'd parted her hair on the side and braided a piece of it before tucking that piece under the rest.

He simply stared, struck silent by her, full of embarrassing emotion. He knew why he'd come tonight even though there had been many reasons not to come. He'd come because he'd sacrifice even his sanity for her. If it came down to it, he'd let her break his heart.

Because he loved her.

No matter how much he'd tried to talk himself out of it, he hadn't been able to stop himself from loving her. He treasured her far more than any of the things he'd spent his life building: money and success and recognition for training Thoroughbreds. None of it meant anything to him compared to her.

"Jake?" She lifted an eyebrow at him.

"Yes?"

"Are you planning on speaking tonight?"

"Yes."

"Okay, good. That's reassuring to hear. Are tacos okay with you?"

"Sure."

She nodded and went back to flipping and bending corn tortillas. "Sit down at the bar and have some guacamole. Can I get you something to drink?"

"I'm good." He took a seat on one of the stools near where she'd placed a bowl of homemade guacamole and a bag of tortilla chips.

Lyndie chatted with him about how she'd spent her day, and he let her voice wash over him like rain. Occasionally, she stopped to dip and eat a chip. She continued to treat him casually, as if what had happened between them last night hadn't changed everything.

He understood her strategy. By playing it cool, she hoped to keep him from freaking out. When she'd been eight, he'd seen her use the same technique on the Stoneleighs' dog. The Stoneleighs had owned land next to the Porters, and Lyndie had, of course, been attached to their dog. Right after the Stoneleighs' dog had surgery, Lyndie had given him sympathy and cuddles. Later, she'd treated him with easy confidence, taking him on therapy walks to the pond and pretending not to notice his sorry limp.

In this situation tonight, he was the Stoneleighs' dog.

Gracefully, she moved the final tortilla from the oil

and turned off the burner. After checking the seasoned ground beef she had going in a pot, she started chopping tomato and lettuce.

"Are we going to talk about the fact that we kissed last night?" he asked.

Instantly, her face rose. She scanned him for a few long moments. Then her forehead creased in confusion. "We kissed last night?"

He smiled.

"You're smiling!" She pointed at him, looking wildly pleased with herself. "You! Are smiling. It's rusty and troubled-looking, but that, right there, is a smile." She set down her knife and came around to him.

He remained on the barstool, his legs braced apart and his boots planted on the floor. He wished he'd changed into something better or, at the very least, shaved this morning. He had on what he'd been working in. He'd left his hat in his truck.

She walked right up to him and interlaced her fingers behind his neck. "You smiled." She beamed at him.

"Yes."

"I didn't mention the kisses because I'm trying not to stress you out."

"I'm not—"

"Please. I haven't seen you or talked to you all day, but I could sense your stress across the miles. I was worried that you might not come tonight."

"I almost didn't."

"I'm glad you did."

He set his hands on her waist. Through her shirt, he could feel the firmness of her skin and the feminine flare of her hips. His desire for her struck to life like a

match to flint. "You're in trouble, Lyndie." He meant
every word. He was trouble, and she'd invited him in.

"I might be," she answered, serious. "Let's just see
what happens, day by day, all right? At this point, there's
just one thing I want from you."

"Which is?"

"To eat dinners with me. You don't eat enough. So
for the next few weeks at least, let's meet somewhere for
dinner. Here, your house, a restaurant, whatever. That's
my one request."

He remembered how she'd fed the Stoneleighs' dog
pieces of cut-up hot dog when she'd been nursing him
back to health. "Bossy."

"Very."

"I don't want you to have to cook for me."

"I'm happy to do it."

"But I should be the one doing things for you."

"No, you don't have to do anything for me. It's enough
just to be with you."

"Lyndie," he whispered roughly. He had not been
enough to save his men all those years ago. He was not
enough for anyone, and not even close to enough for her.

"It's enough," she repeated. Her arms wrapped around
his sides, and she hugged him, laying her cheek against
his chest in a way that tore open his heart.

After a few moments, she brought her face up, just
inches away. Her gaze searched his, and her gentle fingers
slid into the hair at the back of his neck in a caress that
felt like heaven. *She's only touching your neck, Jake.* And
yet his body responded with force, his blood pounding,
his senses rushing.

He'd been living in a dark hole. She was the first light

he'd seen in so long, he'd forgotten what light looked like. It turned out that light looked like Lyndie. To him, she was peace and comfort. And he was selfish and screwed up and he needed her. Heat burned at the backs of his eyes.

He bent his head to hide his feelings and trailed a string of kisses up her neck to below her ear, then along her jaw. She made a soft gasping sound before his lips met hers. He kissed her while time spun out. He could kiss her for hours—

She arched back from him suddenly. "Do you smell that? The meat!" Lightning fast, she dashed into the kitchen and lifted the pot off the burner. She slid him a look full of amused accusation. "You made me burn the taco meat."

"I take full responsibility."

"This is not going to give you a good impression—"

"—I have a very good impression of your kissing—"

"—of my cooking. We're going to have to eat the meat that's on the top. It's not as scorched." She dug into it with a spoon. "The stuff on the bottom is inedible."

Did she know what he usually ate for dinner? Take-out or pre-packaged frozen meals. He'd much rather eat burned meat with her.

They filled their plates and sat side by side at her dining table. During the time they spent eating and talking, something new, like a secret, moved between them. At one point, she crossed her legs and rested the side of her foot against his calf. He found it difficult to concentrate on anything except her foot touching his calf. It was the kind of small thing he often saw Meg and Celia do with Bo and Ty. Except it didn't feel like a small thing to him.

When they were done, they carried their dishes into the kitchen. He moved to open the dishwasher, but she took hold of his hand before he could.

"Leave the dishes." She tugged him into the living room, pausing to light one mellow lamp on the way. "I'm going to run and go get my sketch pad."

"Why?"

"So I can sketch you. You're inspiring me."

He couldn't imagine how.

She chuckled. "You realize, right, that you've mastered the skeptical expression you're giving me? It's very effective. However, you *are* inspiring me, and I want to do a super-quick sketch of you. A super-quick one, if you don't mind. Sit here."

He took a seat on her sofa. By the time she returned from her studio, one of her dogs had already jumped into his lap.

"Down, girl." Lyndie reached over and guided the dog back to the floor. She settled at the end of the sofa, cross-legged and facing him.

"What do you want me to do?" he asked.

She shrugged. "Just relax." Her pencil met paper, and she started drawing.

Both her dogs peered at him, their tails wagging. Her cat studied him from where she sat on the windowsill. Lyndie glanced at him, then down at her paper. He wasn't used to this much attention, and he sure wasn't used to someone drawing him. He couldn't understand why she'd want to. But then, a lot of what went on in Lyndie's head had always been a mystery to him.

He stretched his legs onto her ottoman and extended his hand to her. She smiled and set her free hand in his.

He held it, their fingers interlaced, while she balanced the pad on her thigh and continued drawing with her other hand.

This time, both dogs saw an opportunity to jump up. The same one who'd been in his lap earlier climbed back on. The other one snuggled next to Lyndie.

"It's okay," he murmured before Lyndie could shoo them down again.

The soft sound of pencil scratching against paper filled the space. Contentment he hadn't known since he'd last sat in her apartment with a dog on his lap settled over him. He looked down at the delicate hand he held and took his time exploring every finger, knuckle, every part of her palm and wrist.

Tiredness moved through him. Not the usual anxious tiredness, but a heavy and soft tiredness that didn't carry with it anything to fear. Without letting go of her hand, he relaxed his head against the sofa and closed his eyes.

He knew the exact moment when Lyndie set aside her sketch pad. He opened scratchy eyes halfway.

"I thought you were asleep," she said.

"I am asleep."

She grinned. "You've said that to me once before, Jake Porter."

He opened his arm to her. She immediately moved in next to him, her slight weight against his side, her head resting on his shoulder. He angled his face toward the top of her head. He could feel her hair against his jaw and smell the scent of her shampoo. He pressed her hand against his chest and covered it with his own.

He never wanted to move.

Lyndie began to suspect that Jake really had fallen asleep. At last. The clock on the side table read eight thirty. She waited until it read eight thirty-five, then dared a peek at his face. Yep. Asleep.

Asleep! He couldn't have given her a better gift if he'd given her jewelry or roses.

The man was weary down to his soul. Not just from a long day. Weary from a long eight years. But he'd found enough peace here, with her, to rest, which delighted her. She had a nurturing personality, and until now, she'd only had her sister and her animals to dote on.

Jake needed sleep and food and old-fashioned pampering. She badly wanted to give him all three. The trick would be convincing him to let her.

She noted the tiny details of him she didn't often have the opportunity to study. His stubble. His scar. The crescents of his lashes. The lean contours of his features. His disordered hair. He looked dangerous and scruffy and . . . delicious. A pirate. *Her* pirate.

However, she didn't fully dare to trust the pleasure expanding through every inch of her. She'd been praying over her relationship with Jake, but God's opinion on it had not yet been discernibly clear. She thought she might be doing the right thing with Jake, but there were moments like this one when an uneasy sense of worry twanged within her.

Jake might not make good boyfriend material. He might not. In addition to the fact that he'd shut God out, PTSD was something he'd always live with. No one would ever mistake him for having a sunny disposition.

And he might never be able to shoulder the heavy emotions of a real relationship. So the jury was still out on Jake and on them as a couple.

She stayed next to him on the sofa for thirty minutes. He'd cradled her hand against his chest, and beneath her palm she could feel the rise of his breath, the beat of his heart. She took turns studying his face, then the scuff marks on his boots, then the masculine lines of his body, then his face again.

She had . . . *Jake!* . . . in her apartment.

When she finally eased away, he jerked and slitted open a striking hazel eye.

"You're tired," she whispered.

His hold on her tightened instinctively, telling her that he didn't want her to leave him.

"I'm going to bring you a pillow and a blanket, and you're going to sleep here tonight." She gestured toward the sofa.

"It's okay." The timbre of his voice was sleep-rough. "I'll go back to my place."

The place where he couldn't sleep? "No," she said firmly, planting both hands against him when he looked like he was about to sit upright. "Nope, you're not." She clambered to her feet. "I mean it!" she called over her shoulder as she hurried down the hallway. She took the biggest and softest blanket she owned from her linen closet, then swiped one of the two pillows off her bed.

He watched with sleepy bemusement as she placed the pillow at one end of the sofa and threw the blanket over the other. "Lie down," she instructed. When he moved his boots in the direction she'd indicated, she intercepted them and pulled off one, then the other. She had an extra-long sofa. His frame fit, but barely.

"Vest." She extended a hand.

He shrugged out of it, and she hung it over the back of a chair. She really wanted to say "shirt" and take that from him, too, so that she could check out his upper body. She refrained.

He reclined onto the pillow, tucking one arm behind his head, looking at her as if she were his research project. She unfurled the blanket over him, letting it fall with a breezy murmur.

"You're enjoying this," he observed.

"Shh. Go to sleep, handsome, tired horse trainer."

He gave her a small smile, and like the first time he'd smiled at her earlier, it suffused her with tenderness. She'd been frightened that the boy who'd given her smiles at the age of twelve had lost his ability to smile. But he had not.

In the kitchen she poured him a glass of ice water. She'd meant to pull out a frozen key lime pie after the tacos, but that snuggling thing on the sofa had pretty much caused every other plan to fall out of her head. She'd make sure to feed him dessert after dinner tomorrow.

She set the ice water and two Reese's Peanut Butter Cups on the ottoman within his reach. Hands on hips, she regarded him. "Is there anything else I can get you?"

"Lyndie, I'm not your houseguest."

"You are tonight." She was dying to kiss him again, but there was no telling how much longer that would keep them both awake. "You need sleep. Do you remember what that is?"

"No."

"I'll wake you at five. Will that give you enough time to go home before you're needed at Lone Star?"

He nodded.

"Okay." She paused, not quite able to make herself leave him. "See you in the morning."

She forced her feet to walk to her studio. On the threshold, just before she closed herself in, she glanced back. He was looking directly at her, his eyes glittering with intensity. Oh, have mercy! She was really dying to kiss him. More honestly, she wanted to kiss him, marry him, and take him to bed.

Not so fast, Lyndie.

She closed the door on his image, then stood on the other side in a dreamy daze. She'd come to her studio because she knew she'd need at least forty-five minutes of work to quiet the thoughts chasing themselves around in her brain.

From the front of the apartment, she heard the *thunk* of her deadbolt. She started forward, intending to rush out and stop him from leaving—then remembered that he couldn't have left. The deadbolt locked from the inside.

She'd forgotten all about locking the front door, but he had not. As always, Jake's main concern?

Keeping her safe.

CHAPTER
TWENTY

If tiptoeing had been an Olympic sport, Lyndie would have won gold. She'd managed to slide out of bed and make her way down her hallway with nary a sound. She came to a silent stop near the end of her sofa. This was the third time she'd checked on him since he'd fallen asleep last night. This would also be the final time. Five a.m. would arrive in just three minutes.

Jake slept on his back, his face turned to the side. His expression, often so severe when awake, looked unguarded in sleep. One of his hands gripped the top edge of the blanket, which lay tangled around his hips. The other hand rested on top of Gentleman Tobias, who'd snuggled next to his side and was snoring softly. Empress Felicity had draped herself, belly-up, alongside Jake's shin. And Mrs. Mapleton had her front two paws resting on his ankle. *Defectors*, Lyndie thought, her heart full to bursting.

She couldn't keep Jake in a bubble, even though she wished she could. On this Monday morning, the two of them would fill their usual roles at the track. She could only hope that working alongside her wouldn't throw him for a loop. Goodness knows, he was touchy. She had to tread very carefully with him or she'd scare him away.

Sixty seconds until five. Which gave her one more minute to indulge in staring at him.

She released a sigh, her chest filling with buzzing and tipsy devotion.

When Lyndie arrived at the barn at Lone Star, she went straight to the bulletin board that always contained her instructions for the morning. On it, Jake had listed workout details for the other four horses she exercised but nothing for Silver.

At Silver's stall she found Zoe within, hanging a fresh pail of water on his hook. "Morning."

"Good morning." Zoe smiled.

"I don't have a workout for Silver Leaf on my sheet."

"That's because Jake thinks he's sick."

Concern plummeted through Lyndie. Silver Leaf had come out of his race in excellent form. The vets had checked him afterward, as was standard and required, and declared him completely healthy. "What's wrong?"

"He didn't clean up his feed. And he's running a temperature. More than either of those things, though, I think Jake could tell by looking at him that something's off. The vet's coming by this morning." Zoe gave the horse two pats on his withers, then went to work raking the floor. "I'm not sure . . ."

Whether Silver's contracted chicken pox? Lyndie's

imagination supplied. If Saturn is currently aligned with Neptune?

Lyndie let herself into the enclosure. At first glance, the stallion appeared as placidly regal as always. Yet the more she studied him, the more she could sense what Jake had noticed. The horse's eyes lacked their usual bright intelligence.

Silver rested his head on her shoulder with a little too much heaviness, as if the weight of it taxed him. "You're just getting started," Lyndie murmured, scratching the underside of his cheeks. "Don't go getting sick on me now." Since running to such an overwhelming victory, interest in Silver Leaf had swelled. Lyndie had heard that Meg had fielded several calls from buyers interested in acquiring the horse. Meg, of course, had no intention of selling.

"Is Jake out at the track?" Lyndie made an effort to mention Jake's name casually. It wouldn't do for Zoe to suspect Lyndie's romantic notions toward him at this point.

"No. He got in his truck and left a minute ago."

Lyndie parted from Silver and went about exercising her other horses. Jake did not appear. She followed the plans he'd written out for each of his Thoroughbreds under the oversight of his foreman.

The whole time concern for both Silver and Jake dogged her. Surely Jake hadn't fled the track because he wanted to avoid her. When she'd woken him this morning, they'd shared nothing noteworthy. But then, this morning hadn't been the time for noteworthy interactions. It had been fully dark and her animals had twined around his feet in happy chaos when he'd stood and thanked her and tried to walk to the door. He'd still been three-quarters asleep when he'd left. She shouldn't be concerned. Should she?

She'd just released her final horse to his groom when she saw Dr. Murray, the vet, pull into a parking spot outside their barn. Lyndie poked her head into the break room. "Zoe?"

"Yep?"

"Dr. Murray's here."

Lyndie and Zoe waited in the row outside Silver's stall. At the risk of sounding like a broken record . . . "Is Jake back?" Lyndie asked.

"No, but now that the doctor's arrived, I'm sure he'll be here any second."

Dr. Murray walked toward them down the long shed row, flanked by a college-aged guy who had to be at least six foot six.

"I think I've finally spotted a cute tall guy for you," Lyndie whispered.

"Oh my gosh. He's *so* cute. And he's *so* tall."

Lyndie had nothing but respect for the vet Jake used. A trim woman who wore her gray hair cut short and favored cargo pants and T-shirts, Dr. Murray knew her stuff when it came to Thoroughbreds. The doctor introduced the tall guy as her intern. "Andrew's finishing up his final semester at SMU. He'll be heading to veterinary school in the fall."

"Awesome," Zoe told him. "Will you be going to school close to Dallas?" Her tone all but warbled with hopefulness.

"At Texas A&M in Commerce."

"Oh, I live in Holley. Less than an hour from Commerce."

"Cool." Andrew had brown hair and big dimples and a shy smile. Like Zoe, he had an upper body that bent forward slightly, as if it had grown that way because he'd been forced to lean forward to hear people.

While Dr. Murray examined Silver, Lyndie talked with the two tall people. For the first time since she'd met Zoe, the redhead's posture had straightened to fully upright, from the soles of her lime green boots to the crown of her head.

When Jake strode suddenly into a flush of sunlight at the far end of the barn, Lyndie's heart stuttered. His attention locked on to her, holding as he closed the distance.

Please don't be freaking out over last night. Please be okay with the dynamic between us, both personally and professionally. "Hi." Not the most clever conversational volley.

"Is Dr. Murray with Silver Leaf?" he asked.

"Yep."

"Thanks." He said hello to Zoe, shook hands with Andrew, and moved past Lyndie into the stall. Dr. Murray consulted with him as she continued looking over the horse.

Jake had showered, shaved, and changed since she'd seen him last. His handsomeness blared at her as loudly as a full orchestra. She was stunned that everyone else was able to go about their business in a normal fashion around him.

"Andrew," Dr. Murray called.

Andrew joined the doctor, and the two of them spoke in hushed tones.

Lyndie looked to Jake and found him watching her in such a sober, measuring way that nervousness tightened her lungs.

She mumbled something to Zoe and beelined to the sanctuary of the restroom.

Something was wrong between her and Jake—no, no. Nothing was wrong. Good grief! She couldn't lay expectations on him of any kind. *I just have to take what comes and pray over the rest.* She washed her hands, undid her thick ponytail, and finger-combed it back into a neater ponytail. Then she went to the tack room and polished the bridles belonging to each of her horses—

Jake let himself into the tack room. Every scrap of air seemed to evaporate in the small space.

"What did Dr. Murray say about Silver Leaf?" Very industriously she kept right on polish, polish, polishing away.

"It's a lung infection complicated by a virus."

Lyndie's motion paused. A diagnosis like that could quickly turn dangerous. "He's going to be fine, Jake."

"I know."

"I don't want you to worry."

"I've learned to deal with worry about my horses. I've had to. They get sick now and then."

"Well, he'll be better in no time." She refused to consider the possibility that Silver would be sidelined so soon, after just one race. "Silver's strong. He'll recover quickly—"

Jake turned the lock on the tack room door.

"Um." Lyndie swallowed.

He stepped to her and took her face in his hands. He had a way of circling his upper body, his shoulders and arms and strength, around her. He kissed her like his universe centered on her, and it went right to her head.

He pulled back an inch. "I'm sorry I wasn't here this morning."

"It's okay."

"I had to meet with a horse agent."

"Likely story." She grinned. It was sheer delight to have the freedom to rest her hands on his upper chest. "So. About dinner tonight. I've already made you the only thing I cook well, but I'm willing to try a casserole. Or we could go to a restaurant."

"Do you like barbecue?"

"Yes."

"Taste of Texas at seven? I'm buying."

"No, I'm buying."

"This isn't California. If we go to a restaurant, I'm paying."

She exhaled because she could see he wouldn't budge on the point. "Do they have dessert at Taste of Texas?"

"Cobbler."

"Then bring an appetite for cobbler."

"I don't usually eat dessert."

"I know. But, Jake?"

"Mmm?" He seemed distracted by the sight of his thumb as it smoothed across the skin below her bottom lip.

"You're going to be eating dessert from now on. Like it or not."

"Like it or not?" An ember of humor lit eyes that were usually deadly serious.

"Like it or not."

"I think . . ." His thumb made another pass over her lip. "I'm going to like it."

⌒↙

Around noon the next day, the sound of feminine laughter broke through the barn at Lone Star just as Jake finished a conversation with his foreman. He stepped outdoors to investigate and saw Lyndie standing beneath a tree, wildflowers at her feet. She had Silver Leaf with her, as well as his mom, her mom, and Mollie. Odd. No one had mentioned anything about holding a family reunion at his barn today. He made his way to the group.

Lyndie had finished standing beside him at the track half an hour ago. By now, she should have been on her way back to Holley to spend the afternoon on her art.

"Jake." His mom approached him, arms outstretched. Nancy Porter's hugs were always as energetic as she was.

He hugged his mom back, then greeted Lyndie's mom. "Hi, Karen."

"How are you, Jake?"

"Doing well. Hi, Mollie." They'd settled Mollie into the same special chair they'd used for her on Easter. Her eyes were open, her head angled down and to the side.

"It's fun to see behind the scenes here at the track," Karen said. "Now I'll have a visual of where you and Lyndie work."

"It's been a while since I've visited here, myself," his mom said. "Maybe you can give Karen and me a tour after lunch."

"Lunch?"

His mom bent and lifted a big white sack. "Chicken

tarragon salad sandwiches." She tucked a piece of her hair, dark brown with one gray stripe, behind her ear and smiled.

"We didn't make them ourselves," Karen put in.

"Land sakes!" His mom slapped her thigh. "I certainly couldn't make anything this high-falutin', as Jake well knows."

"Nor me," Karen said. "Lyndie buys frozen enchiladas from the grocery store, and it's all I can do to warm them up."

The two older women looked at each other and laughed. They'd been good friends since before his birth. He could remember them laughing together just this way when he'd been young.

He risked a glance at Lyndie. She returned his attention, a gentle expression of enjoyment on her face. In the past half hour, she'd taken down her hair. She'd also undone a few of the tiny buttons at the top of her pale blue shirt, revealing a V of skin. Completely modest. And yet, *man*, that V of skin . . .

"I brought food for you," his mom said. "Can you join us?"

"I can join you." He remembered how faithfully Lyndie had continued to feed the Stoneleighs' dog after his surgery. "Do you need help getting things set up?"

"Goodness, no. Visit with Mollie."

Karen and his mom pulled out a yellow tablecloth and used it to cover the plastic outdoor table his employees sometimes used for meals or break times.

Lyndie knelt next to Mollie's chair, talking softly, holding Silver's lead rope.

He had a hundred things he needed to get done. He

didn't even know for sure what a chicken tarragon sandwich involved. He probably wouldn't like it. And yet he'd agreed to join them. Because *she* was here.

They'd had a long dinner last night at Taste of Texas, and afterward he'd walked her back to her apartment. It wouldn't have mattered if the barbecue had been terrible or if it had rained on their walk. Lyndie had been there, and she could turn something ordinary into something beautiful. He wished he could spend every minute of his day with her. He wanted to.

When he'd returned to his loft last night, he'd slept better than he had in longer than his memory could reach. After two good nights of sleep in a row, the exhaustion that usually weighed on him like a coat of iron had lifted.

Lyndie drew Silver Leaf near to Mollie's chair. "So this is him, Mols, the horse I've been telling you about. I'd like to introduce you to Silver Leaf."

Mollie's head turned in Lyndie's direction. Her face twitched, as if trying to talk or smile.

"Want to pet him?" Lyndie asked, already taking Mollie's limp hand in her own.

Affection for Lyndie, so sharp it felt almost like pain, scored through Jake. She was amazingly persistent in her efforts to help people and animals. Horses had been his therapy for years, so he understood the powerful effect they could have on humans. Yet it seemed clear to him that nothing could be done to help Mollie more than what medical science and her family's care had already done. Even so, Lyndie had brought her sister here. Mollie was twenty-seven years old, and Lyndie was still trying to do what she could to improve her sister's lot in life.

Silver Leaf whinnied, and Mollie seemed to come to attention in response, lifting her eyebrows a couple of times.

As if he understood exactly what Lyndie expected, the horse stepped forward and carefully lowered his head.

"He's bowing to you, sweetie! Like a king to a queen." Lyndie placed Mollie's hand on Silver Leaf's head. Both Mollie and Silver Leaf seemed to still, the moment stretching.

Jake had had a knot in his gut ever since he'd heard Silver Leaf's diagnosis. He'd been downplaying his worries to Lyndie because he knew she was concerned already and he didn't want to increase her worries.

He'd seen some of his horses come through lung infections and viruses quickly. Others had been taken down by them. He didn't want to think what it would do to Lyndie if this illness took down Silver Leaf.

When Silver Leaf moved away from Mollie, Jake extended his arm for the lead rope. "May I?"

"Thanks." Lyndie passed it over, which freed her to stand beside Mollie and hold her sister's hand.

"You brought Mollie here because you thought Silver Leaf could do her some good. Right?"

She reached back and brought her hair over one shoulder. "Exactly the opposite."

"The opposite?" He furrowed his brow.

"I brought Mollie here because I believe that *she'll* be good for *Silver Leaf*." She gave a tiny shrug. "She has that effect on everyone."

He stared at her, astonished. She thought that Mollie's visit here would heal Silver Leaf? "I don't want you to get your hopes up."

"It'll work," she said with all the confidence in the world. "You'll see."

Jake didn't say anything else because even though he'd turned cynical, he loved her just like she was—a bit of a dreamer, determined, hopeful, and too soft-hearted for her own good.

Lyndie watched the struggle on Jake's face, somewhat entertained by it. Tall, Dark, and Brooding thought her kooky. Fine. She was right about this, as he would soon see.

"Do ya'll have plastic forks and napkins inside somewhere, Lyndie?" Nancy asked.

"Sure. I'll show you." Lyndie led Nancy toward the barn. She'd always liked and admired Jake's mom. Nancy had never met a stranger, and she'd never seen any glass as half empty.

"I have a secret to tell you," Nancy said.

"Oh yeah?" Once they'd entered the barn, they stopped and faced each other.

"You have to promise not to tell my other kids," Nancy said.

"Okay, I promise."

"Jake's always been my favorite."

"Oh." Well . . . how could he not be?

"He was such a wonderful boy, thoughtful and responsible. Smart. *Whooeee*, handsome."

"I agree with you. He's all those things." Were they about to form a Jake fan club? She'd readily become an inaugural member.

"His injuries have been hardest on him, of course.

But his injuries have been hard on John and me, too. His brothers and sister."

"I can imagine."

"I'm glad he's working with you, Lyndie. Karen told me that he's come by their place a few times, that he's started to talk with her."

"I think it's progress."

Nancy took hold of her hands and squeezed. "I know it is." A sheen of moisture came to her eyes. "Thank you, Lyndie."

"He's going to be fine," Lyndie assured her. Had she just said the same thing to Jake yesterday about Silver Leaf? Her intuition that the man's destiny and Silver's destiny were tangled together intensified. "He'll be all right." They both would be.

The next afternoon Lyndie pressed her Jeep's gas pedal hard enough to make the speed limit frown. She didn't like to be late anytime, but especially not for her standing Wednesday afternoon coffee date with Amber.

She'd been absolutely *set* on getting Mollie out to see Silver Leaf again today. Since both her mom and dad were working, and Grandpa Harold hadn't been trusted with a set of car keys since 2008, she'd driven to Holley after work to pick up Mollie, driven her to Lone Star to see Silver, then driven Mollie home again. She'd already logged more than three hours in her car today.

Lyndie needed caffeine. And not just to recover from all the brain-numbing time behind the wheel. She needed it to help her get through the rest of the day. Staying up late for three nights in a row because you were thrilled out of your mind to be dating a handsome man did not make for a solid eight hours of shut-eye.

She arrived at Amber's apartment seven minutes behind schedule. "Sorry I'm late." Harried, she rushed into Amber's kitchen only to find that Amber had the coffee prep—usually Lyndie's domain—well under control.

"Don't worry about it at all. I've got your back." The whipped cream canister made its rasping sound as Amber shot two final mounds onto Jayden's cup of hot chocolate. "You're never late if you get here before the whipped cream melts. If you get here after the whipped cream melts, then we can both agree that you're out of luck." Amber grinned.

Lyndie did the honors with the peppermint sprinkles, expertly dusting the mugs with just the right amount.

Amber carried Jayden's cup outside to him. Lyndie remained behind, leaning her hip against Amber's kitchen counter, letting the warmth of the coffee mug seep into her palms. Through the window she could see Jayden sitting in front of his hero house, sending his army guys on Superman-style flying missions off the roof. Just yesterday she and Jayden had constructed a table and two benches out of Popsicle sticks. They'd made long-range expansion plans for a mini pond behind the house. And—how cute would this be?—a tiny pier. Next time she passed a craft store, she'd stop and pick up some more dollhouse accessories, like fairy-sized buckets and lanterns.

Amber returned to the kitchen and scooped up her mug. "Here's to coffee."

"Here's to friends."

"Long day?"

"Yeah. Silver Leaf is sick."

"Oh no."

Lyndie explained Silver's condition and why his illness had motivated her to drive Mollie to and from Lone Star.

What if she added a Mollie character to her fairy story? The Mollie character could be a still and quiet . . . enchantress? Full of miraculous powers? The blond fairy and the redheaded fairy could take the broken wand to the enchantress to have it fixed so that they could then use it to help the prince.

"More coffee?" Amber asked, holding the coffeepot aloft.

"I will in a minute." In fact, it might be nice to add a yummy drink to the story, too. At the end? They could all celebrate with silver goblets tumbling over with cream and chocolate.

Amber topped off her own mug. She'd combed her glossy hair into a ponytail only two inches in length. With her perfectly applied makeup, scrubs, and curvy body, she looked like the nurse every male between sixteen and ninety-five dreamed of. Lyndie could only guess that Dr. Dean's patient list had grown significantly since Amber had come to work there. "Have any handsome firemen asked you out since we last spoke?"

Amber's shoulders sagged. "No. I saw Will yesterday morning at Cream or Sugar. Every time we talk, I fall for him a little bit more. But still no date invitation, so I'm planning to talk with Celia's Uncle Danny soon to see if he can give me any more advice. The two of us both need one more date." She gave Lyndie a very long and significant look. "Right? Or is there any chance that my upstairs neighbor has already found herself someone to go out with?" A mischievous glint stole into her expression.

"I . . ." Her relationship with Jake felt like a jewel she'd hidden. At the moment it belonged only to her—safe, protected, very fragile.

"Because I happened to see you and a certain cowboy come through the front gate last night after taking your dogs for a walk."

"A certain cowboy and I work together. We've had dinner together a few times. We're friends."

"Friends who hold hands, apparently."

Busted. Lyndie smiled into her coffee and took a few sips, buying time.

"A woman's guess is much more accurate than a man's certainty," Amber said. "Have you heard that one? By Kipling?"

"No, but I like it."

"So, Jake Porter, huh? I thought I sensed some sparks between you two at Easter and at Lone Star the day of Silver Leaf's race. Clearly, his dark and ominous vibe doesn't make you nervous."

"No."

"You like it."

"I like *him*."

"He was your best friend when you were kids."

"Yes."

Amber gave a long-suffering sigh. "I suppose you're going to want to count one of the dinners you've had with him as your final of the three dates."

Lyndie set aside her mug and interlaced her fingers into a begging position. "Yes. Please, please, please."

"Fine." Amber made a sweeping gesture with her free

hand. "I can't believe that you're dating a gorgeous man—
he's frightening, but gorgeous—while I'm going to have to
slog on with the singles scene. That's not very sacrificial
of you, Lyndie." Laughter animated her face.

"I agree. Not very sacrificial of me. How about I give
you my portion of whipped cream next week, and we'll
call it even?"

"And I *really* can't believe," Amber continued, gathering steam, "that three of my friends—first Meg, then
Celia, and now you are all going to marry hunky Porter
brothers."

"What?! Who said anything about marriage? Jake
and I have eaten a couple of dinners together. That's it."

"Was there any kissing involved in these dinners?"

If she didn't answer, her blush would answer for her.
"There was kissing."

"Fabulous kissing?"

"Fabulous kissing."

"Then marriage may follow. From what I've seen,
once the Porter men find someone they like, they don't
mess around."

CHAPTER
TWENTY-ONE

Y ou sure this is a good idea?" Jake asked Lyndie the next night.

She almost laughed at the skepticism in his face. "I'm sure."

"Eating something that comes from a truck?"

"I can't believe that the whole food truck craze has missed you completely, Jake Porter. You live in Texas, not Antarctica. It's high time you ate dinner from a food truck."

"Explain to me again why this is better than eating at a regular restaurant?"

"Because it's fun and you get to sit outside. I like the ambiance out here."

"Ambiance sounds like a California thing." He treated everything remotely Californian with suspicion.

"California does not have a monopoly on ambiance."

Lyndie had her arm through the crook of Jake's and was leaning into the unmovable strength and muscle of his side while they waited for the food truck staff to finish preparing their order. She'd talked him into coming to Holley's largest park, a parcel of land with a creek running across one side, a playground, and a grassy stretch currently occupied by a flag football game.

Four different food trucks pulled up to the park's curb every Thursday evening. Lyndie had been wanting to come and try them out, and tonight's pleasant spring weather had sold her on the idea of a food truck date night.

How amazing. How absolutely, ridiculously wonderful that she suddenly had someone that she loved to go on date nights with.

"After tonight I guess I'll be able to cross food truck off my bucket list," Jake said.

"Food truck isn't a bucket-list item. You have to put things that are more imaginative and harder to achieve on your bucket list."

The front brim of his hat tipped down as he looked at her. The heat in his expression juxtaposed the austerity of his features and scar. "My bucket list is pretty short." He said it as if his bucket list consisted of nothing but her.

The words ran over her like a shiver of delight.

"Porter," a food truck employee called.

Jake picked up their plates, a trio of gourmet sliders for him and a beef tenderloin sandwich for her. Lyndie lifted their glass bottles of Dr Pepper and followed him to a nearby table.

He toyed with her hand while they ate and talked. The sight of his powerful fingers intermixing with hers kept distracting her. She swallowed a bite and paused to stare at their hands, overcome by an insistent tug of desire. She'd begun to suspect that her past non-interest in dating had been God's practical way of saving her for the man He'd picked for her. Because now that Jake had arrived, her non-interest had turned into the most rapt interest imaginable.

"Wh . . . What was I saying?" she asked. "Was I saying something?"

"I don't remember." No smile from him, only fierce concentration. Their food officially forgotten.

She leaned toward him, held his face in her hands, and gave him a light kiss. That she'd somehow earned the ability to kiss him or hold his hand—it awed her every time. Pulling back, she smiled.

"Your food truck idea is starting to grow on me." Tiny, charming lines fanned out from his eyes.

"Good." *Just try not to fall in love with him, Lyndie. Try not to*. Every day it got harder.

A rush of wind snatched her napkin into the air. Before she could react, he was up and retrieving it for her.

Jake had manners. And not the kind of manners that she'd been accustomed to in California. No, he had old-fashioned Southern manners. He stood when she entered a room, opened the door to his truck for her before walking around to his side, and held up her coat so she'd have an easier time putting it on.

"Thank you," she said when he handed her the errant napkin.

"Do you need anything while I'm up?"

See? Manners. "Nope, not a thing. Sit."

He did so, straddling the concrete bench so that he faced her. He leaned over his plate to take a bite of one of his sliders.

She'd succeeded at getting him to eat well at dinnertime, at least. After this, she had a master plan that included a stop for ice cream and then maybe some TV watching at his very bare and sparsely furnished industrial building-turned-loft.

"Is your mom going to bring Mollie out to Lone Star again tomorrow?" he asked.

"Yes. She's already told me that she will." Lyndie's mom loyally supported Lyndie's belief in Mollie's healing power.

"Is there anything I can say to convince you that Silver Leaf's already receiving the best medical care available?"

Jake had gone the traditional route and followed Dr. Murray's prescription, exactly as he should have. "No convincing needed. I agree with you. Silver's getting the best medical care possible. But what Mollie can do for him goes above and beyond all that." She lifted a shoulder. "Healing is her God-given gift."

"I just don't want you to be disappointed if it doesn't work."

"It will work." She picked up a fallen piece of tenderloin and popped it into her mouth. She knew Jake thought her fanciful for repeatedly bringing a woman who couldn't talk to visit a horse who couldn't talk. But Mollie and Silver's communication did not require language. "I haven't totally fallen off my rocker," she stated.

"Just almost totally."

She smiled and stuck out her chin. "Remember my Casanova theory about Silver Leaf? Did that or did that not have merit?"

"Half of me still thinks your Casanova theory was a fluke."

"Oh, how wrong you are. My Casanova theory was genius. And so is my Mollie theory."

He took hold of her hand and brought it up to kiss the back of it.

Happiness buzzed around Lyndie like fireflies.

She'd feared that Jake might not make a good boyfriend. He'd debunked that fear. Tall, Dark, and Brooding had turned out to be a shockingly good boyfriend. Attentive. Generous. And the thing that she really couldn't get over, the thing that made her swoon the most . . . he seemed to think her wonderful.

Now if he'd only get himself straight with God, she could stop fighting this worrisome feeling of fear that came over her in odd moments. Each time doubt struck her, Lyndie had to battle an overwhelming urge to hug Jake to her with all the power and fortitude she possessed.

As if that would make any difference at all, should God decide to rip them apart.

Just try not to fall in love with him, Lyndie. Try not to.

~

On Saturday morning Jake stood in front of Silver Leaf's stall as the dim light of dawn stole into the barn through its doorways and windows.

He'd eaten six dinners now with Lyndie, and he was trying, whenever he remembered Iraq, to force himself to do what Karen had suggested. Instead of shying away from the memories, he'd been working at confronting them. He hoped that Karen knew what she was talking about, hoped that if he could face the IED, then its grip on him would weaken.

He would never again be a completely whole or innocent man. Yet, each day for the last six days, Lyndie
had held his hand and kissed him and smiled at him.
Every day.

Because of that, something bright and calm, like the
light of this new day, had begun to grow within him. He
was starting to feel . . .

Better.

And now there was this.

Jake studied Silver Leaf and the horse studied him.
The stallion had eaten every bit of his food and a good
bit of hay as well. His temperature had vanished.

Silver Leaf raised his head and nickered, his ears
pricked in Jake's direction.

Blackberry, in the stall next door, nickered in answer.

Jake pushed his hands into his pockets, slowly shaking
his head. He could not believe it. He wasn't the only one
who was improving.

Silver Leaf's health had returned. He'd beaten the
infection and virus in less than a week. Another miracle.

He sensed Lyndie's presence before he heard her footsteps. Sure enough, she entered the shed row and walked
toward him in her riding clothes. Of all the strange miracles his world-weary eyes had seen, she was the greatest.

Over the past days, he'd found himself wanting to
tell her that he loved her. But he didn't have the courage to reveal so much of himself. He didn't know how
she felt about him, and until he did, he couldn't begin
to say the words.

Loving her had helped him in many ways. But it had
made life worse for him in one particular way: The more
he loved her and depended on her, the more terrified he

grew of losing her. He couldn't shake the sense that their relationship would not turn out well.

He still worried that she'd move away or that she'd see him for what he was and break up with him. But far more often, he worried that she'd be hurt. His fear for her safety never left him. It only grew colder and larger.

It wasn't normal, this terror he had that she'd injure herself. It had become an obsession.

"Has Silver Leaf improved at all?" Lyndie asked. Since the barn sat empty of everyone but them, she intertwined her fingers with his.

"Yes. As far as I can tell, he's improved a lot."

She slanted a questioning look up at him. "Really?"

"Yes."

"I knew it!" She squeezed his hand, smiling big. "Mollie's magic to the rescue again. Can I say I told you so?"

"You just did."

She laughed. "Jake Porter, this"—she motioned toward the dapple grey Thoroughbred—"is proof that in this life, there is always reason to hope."

"You and your sister healed him, just like you said you would."

She shook her head. "God is the only one who can truly heal. In this case, it seems that He heard my prayers and used Mollie—"

"—and you—"

"—to help the process along. Look at Silver Leaf. Now look at me and tell me that you're beginning to believe that there is a God. A loving God."

He gathered her against his chest. "I'm still not sure about the rest. But I'll gladly look at you any time."

"Where there's God, there's hope," she said. "And

where there's hope, there can be healing. You can't look at Silver Leaf this morning and not see that."

The truth in her words tugged at him. He couldn't argue with her. Nor could he continue writing God off as a myth. If Lyndie's God existed, and Jake had begun to suspect that He did, then Lyndie's God sometimes allowed terrible things to happen to people. But with Lyndie in his arms, he had to admit that her God sometimes brought amazing gifts to people, too. Even to him.

Jake didn't know what to do with this information.

Lyndie arched back just enough to pat the side of his padded vest. She unzipped one of his pockets and pulled out a few pieces of carrot. Her lips twitched with amusement. "You may not have noticed this about me, but I like animals."

"I noticed."

"Turns out that I also like men who like animals."

"Is that so?"

"Especially men who carry carrot slices around in their pockets for horses."

"Does it have to be carrot slices, or would apple slices do just as well?"

"In this instance, carrot is preferred."

"Does it have to be horses? Or would it be fine if this man you're talking about feeds the carrots to longhorns?"

She laughed. "Only a Texan would use a longhorn in that example."

"True."

"In this instance, horses are preferred."

He could read in her brown eyes how much she cared about him. To see that look on her face, for him. . . .

"I'm crazy about you, Lyndie." He tried to smile, but with his scar, it felt crooked and probably looked worse.

She didn't seem to mind because she gripped the lapels of his vest and tugged him down for a kiss.

A week passed during which God allowed Lyndie to indulge her nurturing side. She and Jake continued to eat dinner together every single night. The calendar flipped from April into the warm days of early May. They ate at restaurants. Or ordered in and shared a meal at Jake's loft. Or they sat side by side at Lyndie's antique farm table and ate something she'd attempted to cook. They watched movies and TV and sports together. They talked. A few times, she worked in her studio after dinner, while he sat in the Throne of Dreams, reading. They took her dogs for walks. And once they knelt next to Lyndie's tub to bathe the dogs and ended up getting drenched in the process.

Every night, they kissed, the incredible power of their chemistry causing the very air to snap and their blood to race through their veins at the fated perfection of it all.

Lyndie had never been happier. And she'd never prayed harder for someone's salvation than she prayed for Jake's.

The Friday before their two-week anniversary, they stood at Lone Star's track in an intermittent drizzle. Lyndie brought up the hood of her parka to shield her from the misty rain. If only the hood would keep her hair from frizzing. It wouldn't. The humidity in the air would see to that ably enough on its own.

"Why don't you go in and get warm?" Jake suggested.

His gray sweater skimmed his sculpted arms and torso. "I'm almost done here."

"I don't mind the weather."

He aimed a look at her across his shoulder. "Anyone ever tell you that you have a mind of your own?"

"Nope," she replied with false innocence. "I've never heard that before. Not ever."

He gave her a half smile. "The 'not ever' is laying it on too thick."

"I never lay anything on too thick. Not ever."

They both watched Hank Stephens, Jake's regular jockey, ride by on Firewheel. They'd fitted the horse with blinkers, but even so, Firewheel presented challenges. She and Jake had been discussing the colt's strengths and weaknesses in depth before the latest round of precipitation had arrived.

The sudden sound of Lyndie's cell phone ringing jarred the silence. She fished it from her pocket. "Hi, Mom."

"Hi, honey. Mollie's cold has gotten worse."

The words affected Lyndie like the low and ominous tolling of a bell. They'd noticed Mollie's cold yesterday morning and had been keeping a close eye on it since.

"Your father and I," her mom continued, "just finished checking her in at the hospital." Which meant that Mollie had pneumonia. For as long as Lyndie could remember, she'd lived in fear of that word. *Pneumonia.* It had the power to do terrifying damage to Mollie's poor lungs. At any time, it could steal her sister's life.

"I'll meet you at the hospital in thirty minutes, Mom."

"See you then."

They disconnected. Jake had turned to face her fully.

The line stitching between his brows told her he knew the news wasn't good.

"My parents have taken Mollie to the hospital."

"What's the matter?"

"She has pneumonia." Her words hung in the air. "I need to head to the hospital."

"I'll come with you."

"Jake, no. You have work to do here—"

"Nothing I can't delegate."

Lyndie knew from experience that Mollie's situation would be heavy to deal with. Too heavy for him in his current mental state. She didn't want his kindness toward her to come at the expense of his own improvement.

Implacability marked the line of his jaw. "I'm coming."

CHAPTER

TWENTY-TWO

Jake expected Lyndie's parents to react to his appearance in Mollie's hospital room with polite confusion. They didn't. Mike and Karen welcomed him as if they'd been expecting him, as if he were family.

Lyndie sat on the side of Mollie's bed and picked up her sister's hand. "Hey, Mols. I'm here, sweetheart. I brought Jake with me."

The rest of them stood near the foot of the mattress.

"What's the story?" Lyndie asked her parents.

They talked about liters of oxygen and breathing treatments and Albuterol and other things Jake didn't understand.

The previous times Jake had seen Mollie, there'd been a peacefulness about her. He'd seen her respond in clear ways to her family. At times, it had seemed as if she was listening.

This evening she appeared to be completely unaware of them. Her limbs moved restlessly within her pink pajamas. She'd set her mouth in a sad, pained line, and the sound of her labored breathing rasped through the space.

To see Mollie like this, in this impersonal hospital room, made Jake sick to his stomach. What if she died? Lyndie would be heartbroken. Panic began to close in on him—

A hand squeezed his forearm, and he looked down into Karen's eyes. Her short blond haircut and colorful sweatsuit were as familiar as the look of steady compassion on her face. "God is good, Jake," she said simply.

What? he wanted to growl. *Have you taken a look at your daughter? The daughter who would have been born healthy and full of promise except for a doctor's tragic mistake?*

"God is good all the time," she insisted. "Amen, Mike?"

"Amen," her husband answered.

"It's the truth we've always hung on to," Karen stated.

He didn't know how she could say such things, let alone believe them.

Jake had never been any good at pretense. If he had been, people would have liked him better. In this room with Mollie, all pretense had been stripped back. None of them could maintain any falseness here. Instead of revealing this family's fear, the circumstance revealed that this family—who loved the sick girl on the bed—had chosen to place their whole hearts in God's hands.

"Have either of you eaten lunch?" Lyndie asked her parents.

"Not yet," Mike answered.

"Why don't you head down to the cafeteria and grab something? Jake and I will stay here with Mollie."

"It's not a bad idea, babe," Mike said. "Let's get some food in us."

"All right." Karen slipped her purse strap over her shoulder, then paused. "A word of prayer before we go?"

The next thing Jake knew, he was holding hands with Karen and Mike. Him, the man who didn't hold hands with people other than Lyndie and didn't pray.

"Lord God," Karen said, "you are good. I praise you for your goodness. We place all our burdens on you."

Jake kept his eyes shut and focused on breathing. He grew very aware of his hands and tried not to flinch them, tighten them, or make them too loose.

"Please watch over Mollie," she continued. "Please comfort her and bring her peace. Work through these wonderful nurses and doctors. I pray that you'll heal Mollie's pneumonia as you have so many times before. But most of all, I place my faith in thy will, not my will."

Karen squeezed his hand when the prayer ended. Then she and Mike made their way out.

Lyndie massaged Mollie's forearm.

"Do you . . ." He had a hard time finishing the sentence.

Lyndie glanced at him inquiringly.

"Do you think she could have caught this when she came out to Lone Star?"

She shook her head. "She hasn't been to the track in over a week. She just came down with this yesterday."

He scowled.

"When Mollie gets sick, we try not to beat ourselves up over it or angst about how and where she came into contact with germs," she said gently. "The fact is that we all have lives. We live them. We take Mollie places with us. We're as careful as we can possibly be, but we can't keep her in a bubble."

"When was she in the hospital last?"

"She's had a run of good health. It's been six months or so since she was in the hospital. We were still in California."

"Did she stay in the hospital very long the last time?"

"Five days. When she comes down with pneumonia, she can be in the hospital anywhere from a few days up to two weeks."

He couldn't imagine how her family could stand to see her like this for two weeks in a row. "Will you and your parents stay here with her all day?"

"Yes, and one of us will sleep here. Whenever she's in the hospital, the three of us take shifts so that someone's always here. It's important to us that she has family close."

With Mollie's illness on Lyndie's plate, he didn't want Lyndie having to worry about work, too. "Take tomorrow off."

Her face softened. "That's really nice of you, but I still plan to come to work."

"No. Don't."

Mollie moaned and moved her head from side to side. Lyndie bent near to her sister's ear and soothed her with quietly spoken words.

Didn't Lyndie realize that she could catch pneumonia herself? The possibility sent fear into him even as he told himself that he was overreacting. He had no grounds to protect Lyndie from her own sister, who needed her.

"Tomorrow's Saturday. So if I don't work tomorrow, I won't be back at work until Monday," Lyndie said.

"That's fine. Just—just take care of your own health." Next to Lyndie's well-being, he cared not at all whether Silver Leaf ever won another race.

"I will. Thank you for bringing me here. Really, thank you."

Was he supposed to say "you're welcome" when he'd done nothing?

"My parents will return in a minute. Go back to the track, okay? I don't want your work to pile up because you were kind enough to bring me here." It went unsaid, the fact that they'd shared dinners for a long string of nights. They wouldn't be eating together again tonight.

"What can I do to help?" he asked.

Long seconds passed, painful with the sound of Mollie's wheezing. "Would you mind going by my parents' house tonight around nine and checking on Grandpa Harold?"

"I don't mind."

"If you could just hang out with him until he's ready to turn in, that would be great. It shouldn't take long, he's not a night owl. Oh, and he likes to take a glass of ice water and a newspaper to bed with him."

"Okay."

"Jake?" She extended her free hand to him. For the first time since receiving the phone call about Mollie, he could see a vulnerability in her.

He took her hand immediately and kissed the top of it.

"Thank you," she said.

When Harold answered the door and found Jake standing on the porch, he gave him a long once-over. "Women," the old man stated.

"Sir?"

"Did one of the women put you up to coming here to fuss over me?"

"I'm not planning on fussing."

"Was it Lyndie or Karen?"

"Lyndie."

Shaking his head, Harold led Jake into the living room where he had the Golf Channel playing. Harold sat in his recliner and gestured for Jake to take Mike's recliner. "How's Mollie doing?"

Jake didn't think "terrible" would put Mollie's grandpa at ease. "They've gotten her settled."

"They're all there with her?"

"Yes, sir."

They watched TV side-by-side for thirty minutes straight without exchanging a syllable.

"A few good men," Harold said during a commercial break. "Do you know what I mean?"

"Do you mean the Marine Corps slogan?"

"Yes. There was a captain who was looking for, in other words, trying to enlist a few good men back in 17 . . ."

"1779."

"That's right. What was the captain's name?"

"William Jones."

Harold nodded with satisfaction. "The Marines. They are good men."

"Yes." The faces of the many Marines he'd known flashed through Jake's memory, ending and slowing on the faces of Rob Panzetti, Justin Scott, and Dan Barnes. The remembrance brought the same twist of regret and guilt it always did.

"I like you, Jake." Harold stared at him, spinning the gold wedding band that he wore on his bony finger.

"I like you, too, sir."

"I believe you understand me better than anyone I've met in the past twenty years."

Jake's mouth hitched up in amusement. They were

both former Marines, and they were both set in their ways. They had plenty in common.

"I enjoyed watching your gray Thoroughbred race out there at Lone Star. Good, strong win. Do you think he has what it takes to contend in stakes races?"

"I'm not sure yet." Actually, with Lyndie as his jockey, Jake did believe that Silver Leaf had the potential to compete in stakes. The problem? Lyndie jockeying Silver Leaf would likely kill him before any of them made it that far. Jake had been procrastinating even thinking about another race for Silver Leaf. Bo had not. His brother had come to him a few days ago to strategize Silver's next outing. Bo and Meg had already chosen a race that looked ideal on paper and had every intention of entering Silver Leaf in it. During the meeting, Jake had mostly sat in silence. Because no matter how the race looked on paper, every time he thought about Lyndie riding in it, dread settled over him.

Lyndie was an incredibly talented rider. And she loved riding. Really loved it. The chance to jockey Silver Leaf fulfilled a dream she'd had since childhood.

If she'd had any other dream, he'd have moved heaven and earth to make it come true for her. But this dream . . . This dream endangered her, and he couldn't reconcile himself to that.

"Well, I'm done for the night." Harold's first attempt to push himself out of his recliner failed.

Jake gripped Harold's forearm and helped him up. The older man went into the kitchen and filled a glass with ice and water. "You're welcome to stay and watch more golf."

"Thanks, but I think I'll head home." Jake used the remote to click off the TV. "Good night."

"Night, son." Harold padded down the hallway.

"Sir?" Jake lifted a newspaper off the kitchen table and handed it to him.

A rusty laugh escaped Harold. "They don't think I can get my own newspaper?" He made his way to his bedroom, shaking his head. "Women."

◠◡◠

"There's a very cool event coming up," Uncle Danny told Amber on Monday at Cream or Sugar. "*Very* cool. It's called the Color the World Happy 5K. Great place to meet singles."

Amber paused with a fork full of brown butter cake halfway to her mouth. "A 5K? Are you telling me that I'm going to have to run in order to meet single men?" What was the world coming to? Asking a non-running woman to run seemed like too high a price. She might prefer spinsterhood.

"I've seen the 5K on quite a few of the dating sites. All the meet-up groups are getting teams together. It's for a sweet cause, Amber."

"What cause?"

"Color the World Happy is raising money in support of wildflowers."

"Huh?" She hadn't been aware that wildflowers needed support.

"Each team adopts a color, then all the team members dress in that color. You with me?"

No. No, she was not.

Danny nodded as if she was. "The girls and the dudes all wear costumes and paint their faces or use those fake tattoos on their arms. They run or walk the 5K, then there's a big concert at the finish line."

Amber chewed her cake, her ego cramping at the idea of wearing green face paint while running a 5K with several other team members dressed in green. *God, is this your plan for me? Face paint and stick-on tattoos? More likely, this is your way of telling me to stop. You're letting me know that I'm wrong in thinking that you're ready for me to date, right?*

What sort of men could she possibly hope to meet at the Color the World Happy race? They'd be sporty. Willing to dress in brightly colored costumes. Enthusiastic about the plight of the bluebonnet. "Danny, I have to go on one more date in order to fulfill my three dates in three months agreement with Lyndie."

He nodded at her, commiserating, his skin the color of a walnut.

She would not be discouraged by the fact that Lyndie had found herself a boyfriend. Come hell or high water, she was determined to keep her end of the deal. "Do you think this 5K thing is my best bet?"

"I sure do."

"Well." She set down her fork, resignation stealing over her. "Then I suppose I'm game."

⁂

The elevator binged. Jake exited it and walked down the hospital corridor, his chest tightening the same way it always did when he neared Mollie's hospital room. He hated Mollie's hospital room. He hated it just as much—more—than he'd hated the hospital rooms he'd been trapped in once, long ago. He'd rather be the one suffering than the one watching Lyndie's sister suffer.

Mollie had not improved. Since she'd been admitted five days before, she'd only worsened. For the past three mornings Lyndie had come to work. She'd spent the rest of her time at Mollie's bedside, and some of her nights here, too.

He and Lyndie had shared a couple of rushed dinners, but for the most part, he'd gone back to take-out meals and hours of insomnia inside his loft. And though Lyndie did a good job of covering it, Jake could see the strain on her face.

Whenever he could get away from work, he drove to this suffocating building where fears sank their teeth into him, so he could be near her. She always thanked him for coming and always encouraged him not to stay too long. He didn't know if she wanted him gone because she worried for his sanity or because she needed a break from him or what. He only knew that if Lyndie was here, he wanted to be here, too.

He pushed open Mollie's door, pausing when he saw Karen sitting on one of the two crummy little sofas.

She looked up from the pile of scrapbooking stuff on the coffee table, her face lighting up at the sight of him. "Come on in."

He approached, his attention sweeping the space. No offense to Karen, but if Lyndie wasn't here, which she wasn't, he didn't want to spend any extra time in this room.

Karen lifted her glasses onto the top of her head. "Lyndie should be here any minute. Will you sit down with me until she gets here?"

He hesitated.

"I could use the company," she added.

He let out his breath slowly and sat on the sofa next to the one Karen occupied.

"Your sweet mom visited earlier. She brought all this." Karen motioned to the side table. Snacks, plus a mini coffeemaker and all kinds of coffees and teas covered the surface.

Jake nodded. His mother had never been the type of Christian who sat around expecting others to meet needs. She took care of the needs she saw. "How's Mollie?"

"About the same." Lyndie and her parents talked about Mollie's condition to each other and to the doctors like experts. They talked to him about it in simple terms. "She's sleeping quietly at the moment. I'm relieved about that."

Mollie had an IV going and monitoring machines strapped to her. Her family had tucked her favorite pillow beneath her head and her favorite blanket over her. Mollie's devotional book and two novels rested on her bedside table. Karen had brought in her scrapbooking stuff, Lyndie had brought sketch pads, colored pencils, ink pens. Mike had brought nothing, since all he needed was a remote control and one came with the room. The James family had moved in.

"How are you?" Jake asked, focusing on Karen.

"Doing okay."

Dark circles marked the skin beneath her eyes. She wore no makeup except for shiny pink lip gloss. Her hair looked as wrinkled as her purple shirt. Even so, she seemed at peace. Still. After days of listening to her daughter fighting for breath.

"I'm interested to know how you are," she said. "This has been hard on you, I know."

Jake bristled. "Far more for you guys."

"Can I interest you in some coffee or tea? Something to eat?"

"Plain coffee, please." He might need caffeine for a discussion with Karen.

She filled the pitcher at the sink, then got coffee started. "Do you remember what we discussed the last time we talked? About the things that have helped my clients with PTSD?"

He'd learned to respond to Karen's directness with directness. "Is this when you start psychoanalyzing me and make me want to run out of here?"

"Psychoanalyze—yes. Make you want to run out of here—who knows? Maybe not."

He gave her a dark look.

She chuckled. "I'm hopeless, aren't I? I can't help it! I see you, and I want to talk to you about things that matter. I haven't been to work since we brought Mollie to the hospital, so you're it, the only patient I have at the moment."

"I don't remember signing up to be your patient."

"Quit arguing with me over details in order to avoid the conversation. The last time we talked, I told you that a relationship with God and the practice of remembering the trauma help. Have you tried either?"

"I've been trying to remember."

"And?"

"I don't know."

"Well, don't give up. It's not a quick fix. It's something that's valuable over time. Keep trying. I've noticed that you've improved in the weeks since I first saw you."

The coffee finished, so she poured a cup for him, then

one for herself. "What about the first part? What about God?"

Not enough caffeine in the world for this discussion. Wasn't Karen embarrassed to keep bringing this subject up with him over and over? If so, she didn't look it.

He sipped the coffee, then held it steady on the arm of the sofa. "Not much progress there."

"You know, when God disappoints us, it's natural to want to blame Him and pull away. I tried that myself for a few years after Mollie was born, if you recall. The thing is, rejecting God ends up injuring the person who rejects Him the most."

"I don't think anything I did or didn't do ended up injuring me more than I'd been already."

"Hmm." She tilted her head, seeming to weigh his statement. "And I think that whenever someone distances himself from God, he makes everything a lot worse." A strand of blond hair fell across her forehead near one eye. "It's hard, isn't it? When you've grown up trusting God and trying to live an obedient life, and then you're handed something that breaks your heart? It's crushing."

When he didn't reply, she raised her brows, waiting for him to answer.

Crushing? "Yes." Growing up, he *had* tried to follow where God had led. Right up until God had led his Humvee over an improvised explosive device.

Worse, God had let him live when everyone else had died.

She drank her coffee, studying him kindly. "Terrible things happen to people. But usually there's a lot of good in their lives, too. If you were to put the good and the terrible on a scale, Jake, I'm guessing that the good would outweigh the rest. There are things in your life that you're grateful for, aren't there?"

An image of Lyndie took shape in his mind. They'd been alone in the tack room this morning, and she'd pulled back from hugging him and looked right at him. She'd seen into him, her arms around his sides, her brown eyes glowing.

He was intensely grateful for Lyndie, grateful in a way he'd never been grateful before. Even the ability to feel about her the way that he did was something he'd never expected for himself after the IED. "There are several things I'm grateful for."

"Good."

Karen and Lyndie had been doing their best to bring him around to their point of view. He respected and admired them. He even saw the sense in their arguments in support of faith. Yet, deep within him, something still resisted. Because of Lyndie, he'd only just begun to experience happiness again. She was enough for him right now. She was more than enough. She was everything he needed.

Karen set her cup aside. "Do you want to run from the room?"

"Yes," he answered.

Beneath her answering smile, he saw the steel of certainty. The kind of certainty that no amount of years or trials could shake. "Even if you did run out of here, you'd never be able to run far enough. The God I know is as patient as He is . . ."

"Yes?"

"Unrelenting."

TWENTY-THREE

Mollie had been in the hospital for six nights.

Silver Leaf had a race the day after tomorrow. But as Lyndie watched Jake walk toward her through the early evening darkness, she consciously set thoughts of those things aside in order to focus every bit of her attention on him.

She'd tucked herself into a spot outside the hospital's doors. From here, she had a good view of the crosswalk leading from the parking garage to the building's entrance. Jake hadn't spotted her yet, which gave her an excellent opportunity to stare.

He had on a navy cotton shirt with a pocket over one side of his chest. He'd pushed the sleeves up, revealing muscular forearms. Through the fabric, she could make out the contours of his wide shoulders, his narrow waist and abs. His jeans were as worn-in as his belt and boots. No hat tonight. The darkness of both his shirt and the sky behind him suited the deep brown of his hair and the harsh angles of his face with its distinctive scar.

Though the setting was not romantic—the nearby cars scented the warm air with the smell of exhaust—she couldn't remember when she'd ever seen a more romantic sight in her life. Jake was arriving here at the hospital, again. Even though she knew very well that he hated this hospital, he'd come, just like he had every day since her family had arrived, so that he could be with her. When he left later, he'd run by her parents' house to check on Grandpa Harold. And if he caught Mom at home, he'd ask her if she needed anything.

Tears warbled her vision as he drew closer. She loved him.

Well. For heaven's sake, it was his fault! Jake's actions toward her and Mollie and her family this past week had made it impossible to stay on the "like" side of the line that ran between like and love. How could she have stopped herself from loving him? She couldn't have. She'd tried.

Tiredness had taken its toll on her. Plus, concern over Mollie and worry about what anxiety about Mollie might be doing to Jake had frayed her badly. That didn't explain, though, why she was going so teary and sentimental over him.

She was going teary and sentimental because she was crazy, ridiculously in love with him.

It might not be smart. Probably wasn't. She'd been trying to be cautious and keep some of herself in reserve. Jake had not, after all, gotten himself straight with God. Nor had he articulated his feelings for her. Never once had they even discussed the status of their relationship.

He stepped onto the sidewalk, and she moved forward. "Jake."

At once, as if she'd shouted his name, his vision swung to her and his motion halted. Sparks, their sparks, whirled between them. *Be careful, Lyndie*, her instincts beseeched. *Don't rush him. If you put too much pressure on him, he might break.*

He took her hand, pulled her down the walkway away from the doors, then angled her toward him. "Why are you crying?"

"Crying? Who's crying?" She sniffed and smiled because she, very obviously, was crying.

"Please don't cry."

"It's okay. I'm just thankful."

"Thankful?" he repeated, as if he couldn't understand why she'd cry over a happy emotion.

"I'm thankful for you."

Some of the concern ebbed from his face. "Mollie's condition?"

"The same." The doctors were doing everything they could, but Lyndie feared that the status quo of Mollie's pneumonia could as easily break toward tragedy this time as wellness.

Mollie had already far outlived the number of years the experts had predicted for someone in her condition— a fact that comforted Lyndie not at all. She didn't have six sisters. She had only one. Mollie was integral to her small family of four in the way that four solid corners were integral to a square. "My dad's with her. He's not planning to leave for another hour, so when I got your text saying you were on your way, he shooed me out."

"Good, then I want to take you to dinner."

"You do?"

"Of course I do. Let's go to that pizza place the nurse told us about yesterday. We can walk there from here."

"Perfect." In fact, no dinner invitation had ever sounded more perfect to her. She dashed away the tears that still misted her eyes.

Carefully, Jake ran the tips of his thumbs beneath her eyelashes. "Lyndie, please don't cry. Seriously. Please don't."

"Sometimes I can't help it."

"I understand. I just . . ."

"These are happy tears."

"Still. I really—I can't stand to see you cry."

She stretched up and kissed him. He kissed her back, heart-slaying tenderness traveling between them. When they parted, she couldn't make herself let him go. She hugged him, closing her eyes, letting the comfort of his closeness seep into her and ease her stress for a few bliss-soaked moments.

The whole way to the restaurant, Jake clasped her hand securely in his.

The pizza place turned out to be tiny and somewhat of a hole-in-the-wall. A stretch of bar at the front, which served a bustling number of take-out customers, featured green wine bottles with candles stuffed into their tops and hardened rivulets of wax down their sides. A teen-aged hostess led Jake and Lyndie through a dim interior and sat them at one of only a handful of tables. All the others were occupied.

The electronic candle centered on their table welcomed them with flickering. Its burgundy container matched the burgundy clusters of grapes that hung in intervals above them, where the wall met the ceiling. Both

the plastic grapes and the grapevine that swagged between them looked like they'd been nailed there in 1993.

Lyndie's lips tugged upward insistently as she looked
over the top of her menu at Jake. He was here with her.
She'd desperately missed their nightly dinners together.
Those dinners had been like pearls on a shimmering
golden chain, each one rare and treasured.

Their waitress brought hot breadsticks gleaming with
melted butter. Next came salad, followed by the loaded
pizza they'd ordered to share.

When Jake tried to pick up a slice, the point of his
pizza bent immediately downward and his cheese and
toppings made a bid for freedom.

Laughing, Lyndie slipped a plate underneath just in
time. "The crust is so thin that I think you're supposed
to eat this kind of pizza with a knife and fork."

"Huh?" He lifted the plate from her, one dark eyebrow quirking.

"Give it a try, cowboy." She served herself a slice and
ate a bite off her fork. Melt-in-your-mouth deliciousness.
Tomato, cheese, crust, seasonings, toppings. Her appetite
had mostly been nonexistent since Mollie's hospitaliza-
tion, but this pizza could tempt anyone into binge eating.
"What do you think?"

He tried a bite via fork. "It's not terrible." His eyes
glinted with teasing. He'd have had to be devoid of taste
buds not to notice the amazing status of this pizza.

"Even though you're having to use utensils in order
to eat it?"

"Even so."

"You want to know what's especially excellent about
this dinner?"

"Not my conversational skills, that's for sure."

Laughter bubbled from her. "There's nothing wrong with your conversational skills."

His expression told her he wasn't buying.

"I was going to say that this meal is especially excellent because I'm not going to be required to square dance or participate in icebreakers at a Hibachi restaurant, like I was on the dates Amber organized. Do you remember us discussing it on Easter Sunday? How Amber and I had both agreed to go on three dates in three months—"

"I remember." He leaned back in his chair and lowered his hands to his thighs. Tall, Dark, and Brooding didn't look happy. "I hated that agreement."

"Believe me, I hated it more."

"No, I don't think so."

"I'm the one who had to go on the dates."

"I'm the one who had to hear about it from Bo."

"Oh."

He gave her a challenging look that dared her to keep on claiming her experience had been worse.

"Anyway," she continued, "I've now fulfilled my part of the agreement with Amber thanks to you."

"You're liking this pizza place better than the Hibachi place?" he asked.

"It's the company that's better." He could light her hair on fire with a look. *This* date was the stuff dreams were made of. "I'm enjoying this dinner with you light-years more."

"It's not too dim in here?"

"The lighting is charming."

"I can barely see you."

"You exaggerate."

"The grapes"—he made a motion toward the ceiling—"aren't bothering you?"

"Not at all." She served him and herself another slice of pizza, then dug through her salad for a bite that included both goat cheese and black olive.

"I think I might scratch Silver Leaf from Saturday's race," Jake stated. Just like that, no warning.

Lyndie paused, then slowly straightened her spine. "What?"

"There's no reason to force a race into the schedule right now. I can enter him in another week or two."

Inside, Lyndie's thoughts went into a clamor. *No!* No, no, no. "But we've been preparing him on a timeline so that he'll be at his peak day after tomorrow."

"I'll prepare him again."

"He's healthy now. He's ready. I'm ready."

"I'm not ready," Jake said.

Lyndie had been clinging to the promise of the upcoming race. Amid everything with Mollie this past week, it had represented one shining bit of positivity. "Are you wanting to postpone because of Mollie?"

He scrutinized her for a long moment, his hazel eyes hooded. "Yes."

Lyndie couldn't tell whether he was being a hundred percent truthful with her. "I promise you, Jake, that I won't let what's going on with Mollie affect my ride."

"It's not necessary to get this race in right now, on top of everything else."

"But Bo's been looking ahead. He and Meg have their eye on upcoming races for Silver that will all build on this next one."

"There are always variables." His jaw might as well have been carved from wood.

After days of being able to influence *nothing* with regard to Mollie's health, Lyndie dearly wanted to influence this one thing. She set her elbow on the table and raised her palm toward him. He answered by placing his palm against hers in the way they had. The simple touch, skin to skin, always felt to Lyndie like two parts of the same whole clicking together.

After a moment, he switched the position of their hands, so that he held hers on the surface of the table.

"The race," she said earnestly, honestly, "has given me something to anticipate. It's a . . . a happy counterpoint to everything else right now. I need that."

"I understand." As usual, he gave very little outward evidence of his inner conflict. A slight tensing of his mouth, little more. "I still think we should postpone."

A voice within that sounded like intuition whispered to her that Jake had chosen the better path, that she ran the risk of pushing him too far. She barreled past. She needed this to go her way. "Please don't postpone it. Please let me ride."

His fingers tightened around hers with what felt like urgency. "Are you sure?"

"I'm sure."

A shadow fell across his features.

Twenty-four hours later, Lyndie finished a hallway discussion with one of Mollie's doctors and let herself back into Mollie's hospital room.

She looked to Jake, because like the sight of an island

in a choppy sea, he gave her something fixed and handsome to concentrate on. He'd taken up a position on one
of the loveseats, his boots crossed and propped on the coffee table. His computer sat on his lap. He'd been working while Lyndie spent time reading aloud to Mollie.

She'd tried a couple of times over the past few hours
to convince him to leave the hospital. He'd be up just as
early tomorrow morning for Silver's race as she would
be. He needed sleep, and she couldn't help but think that
he also needed protecting from the sadness of Mollie's
condition.

So far, he'd proven especially stubborn. Bless him,
he'd stayed.

Even before she reached him, he set aside his computer
and opened an arm so that she could slide in beside him.
She rested her head on his upper chest, and he pulled
her in close. As she listened to the thud of his heart,
security coiled around her. That sense of belonging and
safety tempted her to crack open and sob out twenty-
seven years of accumulated anxiety and love and duty
centering around Mollie.

From her earliest conscious memory, Lyndie had
known herself to be the daughter with the health, the
daughter with the luck, the daughter with the expectations, the daughter responsible for the younger, more
vulnerable Mollie. She'd tried to defend Mollie's health.
She'd tried. But God held Mollie's health in His hands,
and Lyndie didn't know if He was going to take her
home this time. The very real possibility that He might
terrified her.

She didn't sob over it. It would put even more pressure
on Jake, when this circumstance already demanded far

more of him than should be required of a brand-new boyfriend. She tucked her knees up and scooted closer.

"You're tired," he said. "Why don't you sleep for a bit?"

She was supposed to be the one nurturing *him*. Lyndie leaned back just enough to look into his face. His eyes had seemed cold to her, once. Now they simmered with so much raw heat that a flush burgeoned across her skin. "I'll go to sleep in a little while, when Mollie's not struggling so much."

"I'm here. I'll stay awake and watch over Mollie for you."

"No. You need to go home yourself and . . ."

She lost her train of thought when he stroked a strand of hair off her temple.

He pressed her head back down against his chest. "You can trust me to wake you up if anything changes. Sleep."

"You don't have to do this for me."

"Yes," he said simply, "I do."

He may as well have saved her from a speeding train or a band of outlaws. Nothing on earth could have endeared him to her more or bolstered her flagging strength quite so much.

From the moment she'd come face-to-face with the adult version of Jake, her expectation had been that God would use her and Mollie and their mom to heal him. But it looked as though God was also using *him* to heal the knotted, injured places in her own heart.

She hadn't seen it until now. How could she have overlooked it? He was an expert at guiding his horses to recovery. The very first time she'd seen him, in fact, that afternoon at Whispering Creek, he'd been checking on the rehabilitation of an injured Thoroughbred.

"I wanted to be the one to help you," she whispered against the soft fabric of his shirt. "But you're the one helping me."

"No, beautiful. I can't help anyone."

His hand, protectively clasping her against him and shielding her from danger, belied his words. Lyndie saw the perfect symmetry of it then. If she and Jake were irrevocably linked together, then of course God had intended them equally for the good of the other. Her for him. Him for her.

Of course He did.

Of course He had, all along.

CHAPTER TWENTY-FOUR

Sickening fury and confusion and despair circled within Jake. It should have been him dead and burned. Not the kid.

He stumbled back. "Panzetti!" he screamed, but he could barely hear his own hoarse voice.

Two of the Marines in his squad ran in his direction. "Make sure someone's called medical," he yelled to them.

They hesitated, nodded, and turned back to follow his order. Jake ran down the road, his attention cutting left and right, searching. He'd couldn't breathe right through the liquid in his lungs. He continued to run. Saw nothing.

Where were Panzetti and Scott? He waded into the brush, heat pouring down one side of his face. He reached up, and his fingers came away dripping with blood. More blood leaked out of him through a gash in his thigh and more from an injury to his right side.

A sound finally penetrated to his brain. Screaming.

Someone was screaming his name. Desperately, he pushed his way through vegetation—

He came upon Justin Scott's body. It lay twisted and unmoving, stomach down. His heart in his throat, Jake put a hand on Scott's shoulder and carefully turned him upright. He uncovered a lake of blood spreading into the dirt. Part of Scott's arms had been blown off and most of his chest. Dead, too.

Dead. The realization sent ice through his arteries, lead through his limbs. Staggering physically and mentally, Jake pressed on. He'd heard screams, screams that hadn't come from Scott. Sweat ran into his eyes. He couldn't get enough air, and he still couldn't find Panzetti.

Rob wouldn't have been thrown this far. Jake moved back toward the wreckage at a different angle. Finally, he spotted movement and sprinted toward it. His legs gave out, pitching him onto the palms of his hands. Disgusted with himself, he forced his body back up and into motion. At last he found his friend.

Jake slid onto his knees beside him, immediately hooking an elbow beneath Rob's shoulder to lend support. Jake saw pain and sorrow and also something like resignation in Panzetti's soot-blackened face.

"I'm glad to see you, brother," Panzetti said.

"Likewise."

"You look like hell." A ghost of a smile moved across Panzetti's face before he winced. He extended his hand, and Jake clasped it.

Jake swept a glance down Panzetti's body. His buddy's uniform was scorched and shredded away in places. His legs . . . his legs were gone from the thighs down. More blood. Too much blood . . .

"I'm not going to make it," Panzetti said.

"Yes. You are. I'm going to tourniquet your legs."

When Jake went to move, Rob jerked him back. "Wait."

Jake paused, frantically trying to think. What could he use for a tourniquet? He'd need—

"An IED got us," Rob said.

Jake nodded. "I swear to you that I was looking for anything out of place." His vehicle had been the first in the convoy. It had been Jake's responsibility to spot any small clue of a buried explosive. "I didn't see anything."

"I know you didn't, man." Rob squeezed his hand to gain Jake's full attention. "I want you to tell my wife something for me."

The chaos in Jake's ears made it hard to hear. He fought to concentrate.

"Tell her that she's the best thing . . . that ever happened to me and that I'm . . . I'm sorry and that I love her."

Tell her yourself, Jake wanted to yell. Instead, he looked his friend full in the face. This was their third tour together. So many years and memories. "I'll tell her."

"Tell my kids that Daddy—" Panzetti choked and coughed. His eyes filled with tears, but he shook his head to clear them, determined to finish. "Tell them that Daddy loves them. That . . . I'll . . . always love them."

"All right."

"Do you think you can remember that, or are you . . . only a pretty face?" Panzetti gave a sad huff of laughter. His breaths had grown shallower, short and quick now.

"I can remember."

"Good."

Jake's peripheral vision registered motion. He looked up to see a CH-46 helicopter racing through the sky. "Medical's coming."

"I'm not feeling . . . so good, man." Rob's eyes closed. "Can you lay me down?"

Jake did so, gently, his hand still gripping Panzetti's. He could feel the strength in his friend's hand lessening. "Medical's coming," Jake repeated. "Almost here. Hang on. I'll get a tourniquet started and they'll get us out of here."

"Don't worry," Rob slurred. "It's okay."

"Panzetti—"

His friend released a long exhale. Then nothing. The life drained from his hand.

No.

The word, the denial, carved through Jake. He felt Rob's wrist for a pulse. No pulse. He rose up, placing his joined palms on Rob's chest to begin chest compressions, counting out loud to focus his mind and his efforts.

A part of him knew it was too late for CPR to help. But he couldn't stop. It wasn't too late. He wouldn't let it be too late—

Jake wrenched awake and upright, sucking in air as if he'd been drowning. Dim light from the bathroom revealed his bed, the window, the dresser.

He cursed and covered his face with his hands, hunching over. His thigh and his side ached the way they had in the dream, phantom pain. Long gone. Sweat rose on his bare skin, and tremors took over control of his body.

It was a nightmare. You're not there anymore. You're at home in Holley. That was eight years ago, Jake. Just a nightmare.

He gripped his skull, trying to feel something, to anchor himself in the present. He'd had the recurring nightmare many, many times over the years. Every time he woke from it he had to face the fact that Rob Panzetti and Justin Scott and Dan Barnes were dead. They were still dead. And he could still do nothing to change it. He *hated* that he couldn't.

Guilt, black and heavy, crept over him.

A memory of Lyndie, in the shed row at Lone Star, slipped into his mind. She smiled at him and pointed at Silver Leaf, who'd recovered from an illness that should have taken him low. *"In this life,"* she'd said to him, *"there is always reason to hope."*

Was there? he thought bitterly. It did not feel that way to him on this particular day, because today was the day she'd race Silver Leaf. He was about to put Lyndie, his only reason to hope, at risk.

Angrily, he slashed the blankets to the side and made his way into the bathroom. The water had only warmed halfway to hot before he stepped under the spray. He stared at the thin white scar on his leg, and then at the one on the side of his abdomen. Both lines were as permanent as the one across his face. He'd wished sometimes that his injuries had been worse. It would have been a better representation of his inner destruction. If he'd suffered brain damage, he'd have lived the rest of his life unaware of what had happened to him. If he'd been in a wheelchair, if his own legs had been taken from him, maybe guilt wouldn't have such power over him.

Jake ducked his head, letting the water drum the cords at the back of his neck. He hadn't had the nightmare since he'd started following Karen's advice to relive the

memories. It didn't take a PhD to know why his nightmare had come back to him tonight. He'd lain in bed for
two hours before falling asleep, watching the red numbers
on his clock, sick with worry about Lyndie's race, before
finally falling asleep around one. It was now four.

After toweling the moisture from his body and hair,
he pulled on a pair of track pants. Then he paused and
rested his palm on top of his dresser, the surface smooth
and cool.

He usually didn't even look in the direction of his
dresser's bottom corner drawer, much less touch it. The
things inside reminded him of the IED, and he'd spent
a long time avoiding reminders.

Today . . . today, though, he *wanted* to be reminded.

Kneeling, he set his hand on the drawer's handle and
took an unsteady breath. Then he pulled it forward.

Anxiety slammed into him. He should slide the drawer
closed again—no. *You need to remember, Jake. You've
told Lyndie that she can ride Silver Leaf today. Stop
hiding. Remember.*

His heart began to knock. A photo of the squad he'd
commanded on that final tour rested on the top of the
stack of items. In the picture, Panzetti grinned at the
camera. Barnes looked like he was trying to impress
everyone with his maturity even though he'd had none.
Scott faced the photographer, easygoing and intelligent.
He remembered each of the other guys in the picture, too.
Their histories, nicknames, personalities. Jake's own face
looked young and soft to him without its scar. He felt
cut off from the man he'd been then, as if it hadn't actually been *him* who'd been captured there in the photo,
but a stranger.

Below the picture lay his dog tags and below them his uniforms. He left the uniforms untouched and rose to sit on the edge of his bed, the photograph next to him and his dog tags in his hands. He frowned at the familiar letters and numbers stamped into his tags.

PORTER
JAKE R. O POS
4343
USMC M
CHRISTIAN

The metal looked worn but not dirty. Someone had cleaned off the soot, sweat, and blood. It almost didn't hit him right, that they looked so clean. They ought to look lousy. But they'd been washed off and shined up. Just like he had. As if exteriors mattered.

The situations he'd lived through with these tags around his neck crowded into his head, bringing back the smells, the temperature, the details of Iraq and Afghanistan. His worry increased, his breath quickening.

For all his success in his former career, these dog tags were a symbol of his greatest failure. Ultimately, Sergeant Jake R. Porter, USMC, CHRISTIAN, hadn't been able to keep his Marines alive. He hadn't brought Panzetti home so that he could be a husband to his wife and a father to his children. Scott had never had the chance to earn a degree in psychology. Barnes hadn't made it back to the girlfriend he'd loved, let alone his nineteenth birthday.

Jake hadn't seen the buried daisy chain of IEDs, so

none of them had made it. What cause did he have to think that Lyndie would make it through today's race?

After what had happened in Iraq, he'd never thought he'd love anything. But her, he loved. He loved her with hard, unrelenting devotion. Loved her far more than anything he'd ever known or known himself capable of.

How had it come to this? Last night, she'd rested against him on the hospital sofa and dozed, his arms around her. She'd been safe. And today he was going to put her up on one of his horses to do something as dangerous as jockeying? Why did she have to love jockeying the way she did? Why hadn't Silver Leaf run for Elizabeth? Why couldn't Lyndie have let this race go? Her sister . . . her poor sister was an inch from death.

His hand fisted around the dog tags, the metal biting into his palm. He was Whispering Creek's trainer. He had the power to sideline Lyndie. His instincts were ringing, telling him to scratch Silver Leaf from the race. He would have done so days ago if he'd had any confidence in his own rationality.

Lyndie was positive that she was the right jockey for Silver Leaf, and Jake's most trusted advisors, Bo and his foreman, agreed. Her performance on the horse had proven her ability. There could be no arguing her skill or her experience.

All week long he'd watched his staff deal with Lyndie. They'd all been excited for her, comfortable with her role as Silver Leaf's jockey. He'd felt just the opposite, which made him doubt whether he could be trusted to make a logical decision where she was concerned.

He didn't think he could.

Was he going to go with his gut and take her off Silver

Leaf? Or was he going to put his faith in Lyndie and in others? The others didn't have fractured minds like he did.

The others also didn't love her like he did.

The others didn't value protecting her above everything else in the world.

～

"How about we go and show these other wannabes what's what, Silver? You game?" Lyndie gave the Thoroughbred an affectionate pat.

"He's game," Zoe answered, bending to adjust the wrapping on one of Silver's back legs.

Lyndie had donned Whispering Creek's silks, her helmet, and the rest of the jockey's uniform. Less than a minute ago, she'd arrived at the saddling paddock to find Zoe and Silver awaiting her, but no Jake. She scanned the setting. "Jake was right behind you, you said?"

"Yep. He'll be here."

Jake's late arrival struck her as odd, but not entirely unusual. Trainers often operated on a tight schedule, with several horses in several races on any given day. "What's the latest with Andrew?" she asked. Zoe and the veterinary intern had been texting each other nonstop and had seen each other a couple of times.

Zoe released a lovelorn sigh. "Everything's going perfectly with Andrew. We're . . ."

Going to French braid each other's hair? Lyndie mused. Dance an Irish jig? "We're?" Lyndie prompted.

"Oh. We're going to see each other this weekend. I volunteered to give him a tour of Whispering Creek

Horses and he said he'd like to, which in my eyes is just about as good as him saying he'd like to marry me."

"Um, sure."

"He's tall, Lyndie."

"I noticed."

"And he has the cutest smile, and he's going to be a veterinarian and—clearly—I love animals so we're—clearly—perfect for each other."

"Clearly. I'm happy for you, Zoe."

"I'm happy for you in advance because I know that you and Silver Leaf here are going to win this race."

Jake strode into view.

Relief and pleasure rolled through Lyndie as she watched him near. "Hey."

Instead of answering, he took hold of her elbow and guided her to the rear corner of the stall. He turned so that his back faced the spectators and shielded her from their view. "You don't have to do this," he said.

"What, wear these silks?" She smiled, deliberately teasing him in hopes of easing his seriousness. "Of course I do. All Whispering Creek jockeys wear them."

"You're not one of Whispering Creek's jockeys."

At his words, her tummy took a downward dip and her smile faltered. Worry spidered its way into her confidence. "Of course I am. I'm Silver Leaf's jockey."

"You're more than that to me."

"And you're more to me than Silver Leaf's trainer. But that doesn't mean we can't be jockey and trainer, too. We *are* jockey and trainer, too."

He crossed his arms, his tall body taut. When people were in pain they did what Jake was doing right at this moment, they drew themselves in tight in order to hold themselves together. She didn't know if he was angry at her for convincing him to let her ride or angry at himself for allowing it. Both, probably. But he'd see. Silver Leaf would win this race.

"Jockeys up!" The paddock judge's voice rang through the space.

Jake's lips flattened. "I mean it, Lyndie. You don't have to ride."

Geez, his pre-race pep talks to his jockeys could use some tweaking. He was supposed to be giving her encouragement and last-minute instructions. She recalled that he'd spent the moments before her previous race this same way, assuring her that she wasn't obligated to do her job. "I don't have to ride," she said, "but I'm going to. I'm prepared for this, and your horse is ready. Just watch. Silver's going to win."

His face went cold and blank. He took a step back when she would have reached out to rest a reassuring hand on his forearm. She could plainly see that he'd shut himself off from her. Gone was the intimacy they'd shared last night.

His reaction caused panic to press in on her. Surely . . . surely he'd get over his anger. She loved him, and she didn't want to do anything to jeopardize their relationship, but he was the one in the wrong here. He was the one acting irrationally. She'd been slated to ride Silver in this race for days. Just like the last time, the race would go off without a hitch, she'd be fine, Silver would excel, and Jake would recover. Their relationship would be fine.

"Jockeys up!" The paddock judge had made his way to their stall. He eyed the two of them impatiently.

Lyndie surveyed Jake, her heart twisting because it felt wrong to leave things undone between them.

He didn't move or speak.

Lyndie walked to Silver. Zoe gave her a leg up.

It's all right, Lyndie. He'll be all right. The spectators lining the walking ring watched them pass. *You can discuss everything that needs discussing with him after the race.* The post parade before the grandstands went by in a blur. *His past has made him overly concerned. That's all.* Except it didn't feel like a small thing. Foreboding sat in her chest, a stark contrast to the cloudless and cheerful blue of the sky.

Almost post time. She'd run out of time with Jake in the saddling paddock, and now she'd run out of time to obsess over him. She had a race to win. She couldn't afford to be distracted. Determinedly, she positioned her goggles.

Once they'd loaded Silver Leaf into the gate, she went into her routine. She ticked off the details she'd memorized and ran through a visualization—

They were off. Exactly as she had the last time, Lyndie let Silver Leaf set his own pace out of the gate while most of the field charged past. Wind whipped against her face. She narrowed her concentration and poured everything she'd ever learned, everything she sensed about Silver Leaf, every drop of her God-given talent into her ride.

Seamlessly, Silver Leaf ran. Perfect fluidity. Astonishing power. The front runners had more distance on them than they had in the previous race, so Lyndie decided to ask Silver to open up his speed earlier than she had the time before. He answered instantaneously.

Down the final stretch, Silver tracked and passed his

competitors mercilessly until only one horse remained in front of them. Lyndie urged Silver to give her a fresh burst of speed, but this time, he didn't respond. She could feel him tiring.

Great horses seemed to know exactly where the wire had been positioned, a fact doubly true of Silver Leaf. The moment he'd passed the wire in second place, he slowed without Lyndie having to offer him direction.

Lyndie's muscles relaxed even as her thoughts started to spin. Had she made a mistake, asking him to sprint as early as she had? It could be that she'd forced Silver out of his preference just enough that she'd caused him to struggle. She may have used all his gas too early.

Or it may be that he'd simply had less gas today. Based on all she knew about Silver and on how the race had unfolded, she'd thought she'd made her move at the perfect time. If Silver had had his usual amount of energy in reserve, they'd have come away with the victory. But he hadn't had the same amount of stamina today, probably because of his recent illness. Sometimes the subtle effects of sickness lingered even after a horse returned to health. Silver probably just needed a few more weeks to regain his best form.

Lyndie stroked Silver's neck. He'd still run a highly impressive race. Second was nothing to sneeze at against a tough field. Everyone who'd bet on Silver to place would still earn money. It's just that . . . Lyndie couldn't help feeling slightly let down. She'd wanted another victory for the horse she loved, trained by the man she loved. In the saddling paddock, she'd told Jake that Silver would win. She hadn't delivered.

She guided the horse toward Zoe, telling herself that

she was being harder on herself than Jake would be. He was a very fair trainer. Her ride had been strong enough to please him, surely.

When he didn't meet her after the race, however, Lyndie's optimism began to crumble. She did her best to converse with Meg and Bo, who were both more than satisfied with Silver's performance and hers.

Zoe escorted Silver to the testing barn. Lyndie did the required post-race weigh-in, then stood alone near the entrance to the jockey's room. She didn't want to go inside and accidentally miss Jake. He might come around the corner at any moment, after all.

Ten minutes passed. Then ten more. She finally had to admit to herself that he wasn't coming. Swallowing her disappointment, she made her way indoors.

The other jockeys and their valets tossed congratulations to her as she passed. Their kind words slid off her without penetrating. "Thanks." She gave them her best imitation of a genuine smile. "Thanks, everyone."

Something was very wrong with Jake, otherwise he would have spoken with her post-race.

She showered and pulled on the clothes she'd packed: an ivory top, hoop earrings, fitted jeans. Then she dried her hair, loaded her tack into her bag, and took off in search of Jake.

She checked the clubhouse and the other public areas first. When she came up empty, she walked to her Jeep. She half-expected that he'd left Lone Star's property. Thus, when she pulled up to their barn on the backstretch, it came as a slight surprise to find his truck in its usual spot.

She parked and sat for a moment, her hands stacked

on top of the steering wheel. Seeing as how he'd remained here at the track, it seemed to her that he could have troubled himself to put in an appearance after the race. For Meg and Bo's sake. For Silver Leaf's. For hers.

She did not understand him. What had kept him from coming? She couldn't imagine what had gone awry in his heart or his head either before the race, when he'd been so grim, or after when he'd deserted her and let her worry herself into a fret over him. Clearly, though, something *had* gone awry. She'd do well to tread carefully. He was wounded—

He was a grown man! His woundedness wasn't going to serve as an excuse for bad behavior for the rest of his life. She scrunched her eyes closed and prayed for God's peace and wisdom. But, honestly, as she let herself into the barn, she did not feel peaceful or wise. She only felt upset and confused and fearful and in need of straight answers.

No one occupied the shed row but a groom, which meant that she'd find Jake in the barn's small office. She went to it and yanked open its door.

CHAPTER
TWENTY-FIVE

Jake sat at the desk. He had his computer, a stack of papers, and the condition book in front of him. He still wore his black Stetson. Beneath it, he leveled a stare at her, his long-lashed hazel eyes every bit as hostile and remote as they'd been when she'd left him at the saddling paddock.

Lyndie stopped just inside the small room's threshold. He was doing *paperwork*? Her frustration mounted. "Silver Leaf placed."

"I know."

"Did you watch the race?"

He nodded, once.

"From where?"

"A TV monitor inside the clubhouse."

"Why didn't you watch with Meg and Bo? Why didn't you meet us after the race?"

He pushed to his feet and took her measure for a long stretch of time that crackled with unspoken emotions. "You're fired." He spoke the two words with deadly finality.

Shock thudded into her. It took her a few moments

to begin to process what he'd said and to find her voice. "What?"

"You're fired."

Fired? She loved and trusted him, and he was firing her? "Why?"

"You made your move too early. You cost Silver Leaf the win today."

Every word pierced her like an arrow. Physical arrows would have been less painful. What—what had happened to his belief in her? Was he going to turn on her because of one small mistake? That he'd even think of doing so felt like a betrayal.

"I've been replaying the race over and over in my mind," she said, her words slightly uneven as she fought for composure. "According to my instincts, I made my move at exactly the right time. It's true, though, that I might have been too early. If I was, I'm very sorry. I wanted a win today as much as anyone."

His expression remained steely.

"Please believe me when I tell you," she went on, "that Silver wasn't at full strength today. He didn't have the same amount of power in reserve that he's had in the past. His illness must have taken more out of him than we realized."

"Enough. We're done here."

She drew tall. "No. We're definitely not done."

"Just go."

Her lungs tightened. Her hands trembled. Anger and indignation swirled within her like fire. She wanted back the man who'd held her in his arms last night and watched over her sister while she'd slept. She didn't understand how he could turn off his kindness like a tap. She'd never

been like that. Her emotions ran deep and true and transparent—

*See him, Lyndie. Take a moment and calm down
enough to really see him.* Everything Jake had shown
her about himself assured her that his emotions ran deep
and true, too. Not transparent. But deep and true. He'd
shut himself away from her, yes. But that didn't have to
mean that his feelings for her had changed.

Color stained Jake's cheeks, making his scar more pale
and vicious. She'd learned to look past all his defenses,
and right now, she could see that there were things he
wasn't telling her. "Today's race isn't the only reason
you're angry, is it?"

He scowled at her with something that almost looked
like rebellion.

Think, Lyndie. He'd been troubled even before she
climbed aboard Silver Leaf. "Are you angry because I
convinced you to run Silver Leaf when you wanted to
scratch him?"

"No."

She didn't wholly believe him. "Does this have anything to do with my sister?" At the pizza place he'd told
her that he didn't want her to ride because of Mollie.

"No."

"Then what? What's changed between last night and
today?"

He was unbending and starkly beautiful, and his eyes
gleamed with that awful haunted coldness again. No!
She couldn't bear the thought of him backsliding. But
she didn't know how to stop it or how to get through
to him. Shake him? Kiss him?

The expression on his face warned her to keep her distance.

"Tell me, Jake. Please." Her voice cracked. The small show of weakness infuriated her. "We can salvage this, I promise you, if you'll only have faith in me."

"I told you everything you need to know when you walked in the door. I'm firing you because you're not a good enough rider. I gave you a try. It didn't work out."

Horrible silence descended. Tears rushed to the backs of her eyes. It crushed her, that he didn't think she was good enough. Him, the person in this industry that she most respected and cared for. "Meg won't let you fire me," she managed to say.

"It's not Meg's decision. In this barn I'm the one who decides. And I've made up my mind."

"She and Bo support me as Silver Leaf's jockey."

"If Meg and Bo have a problem with the way I run things, they can take it up with me."

"Jake," she whispered.

He did not soften. If anything, his body language grew even more defensive.

Why was he doing this? Why would he ruin everything they'd slowly built? She loved him, but she could no longer see any vestige of love in his face for her. *God,* she cried out in her mind. Jake had hurt her and slashed her hopes and on top of all that, he'd made her mad. Spitting mad.

He'd mastered the glare, but he wasn't the only one. She gave him a glare of her own, then slammed the office door behind her.

———

Jake sank onto his desk chair, immediately hunching over and burying his face in his hands. The exchange with

Lyndie had cost him, had drained the strength from his muscles. He hadn't known if he could make it through. If it had gone on one minute longer, he wouldn't have been able to.

Water pushed hard against his eyelids. He tried with all he had to focus on inhaling, exhaling, inhaling. He didn't know which was worse, the grief or the despair.

Why had she come back into his life at all? Why did she have to be so stupidly optimistic? So brave? He didn't want any more good, brave people in his life. The good and the brave ones died.

He'd known since four o'clock this morning that he should scratch Silver Leaf, but he'd convinced himself of his own instability and he'd let her ride.

He'd had to put up a wall between himself and her in his mind, there in the saddling paddock, just to survive. Even so, honest to God, he'd almost lost it inside the clubhouse. He'd stood as far as he could get from the TV during her race, his hand on the handle of a door, almost half-out of the building. In those moments he had *hated* himself for not following his own instincts and taking her out of the race.

She thought he was furious with her. The truth? He was furious with himself.

"Tell me, Jake. Please. We can salvage this, I promise you, if you'll only have faith in me."

He'd wanted to tell her that he was the one who couldn't handle her jockeying, that he'd rather die than let her injure herself on his watch. But he hadn't told her, because he was ashamed and because . . . because part of him had feared that she might actually accept the truth, and him. Her heart was so big and generous that perhaps she'd have loved him anyway.

When it had come down to it just now, he'd been unable to take that chance. It wasn't right, that he should live his life with Lyndie while his men lay rotting in their caskets. He couldn't justify it in his mind. In some sick way, his devastation in this moment felt fair to him. Like he'd evened the score and gotten what he deserved.

He'd told her she wasn't good enough at riding because he'd known it would wound her and end the conversation as quickly as it could be ended. She'd asked Silver Leaf for more speed earlier than she had in his prior race, but today that's exactly what the situation had called for. If she hadn't gone when she did, Silver Leaf would have finished far lower in the ranking. He'd watched every moment of the race, and he'd read Silver Leaf's performance the same way she had. The horse had not had the same amount of speed today. Given that, she'd ridden him perfectly. He didn't care that Silver Leaf had finished second instead of first.

He only cared that his lies had done what he'd meant them to do. They'd broken his relationship with Lyndie permanently. He'd succeeded at that, at least. He'd done an excellent job at cutting himself off from the one thing on earth he treasured most. And if he had to do it over, he'd do the same thing again.

Let Bo or his foreman or his employees or any of the commentators or reporters give him hell about firing her. It didn't matter to him now.

Lyndie was safe. And so long as she was somewhere in the world, protected and whole, then he could find a way to live with himself.

He would not risk her again. Not for any price. Lyndie would never again ride one of his horses, not so long as he had breath in his lungs.

~

Late that night, Will McGrath paced from his living room into his entry room and back. It was 10:52. He knew this because he'd been staring at his watch.

When his oldest, Madison, had turned sixteen and earned her driver's license, he'd set up strict ground rules. One of them: She had a curfew of eleven o'clock on Friday and Saturday nights. Another: She had to keep her cell phone with her so that he could reach her.

She usually came in well before eleven. Sometimes alone, sometimes with a girlfriend or two who'd then spend the night. She always answered her cell the minute he called.

Tonight, he'd first tried calling her at 10:30, just to check on her and make sure she was heading home. She hadn't answered that call or the five he'd placed since then.

Why wouldn't she be answering her phone? She was a sixteen-year-old girl. Her phone was practically glued to her palm. He couldn't think of any reason why she wouldn't be answering it, other than that she'd been in a car wreck.

Just the mental picture of that sent icy fear through him. He'd taught her to drive defensively and given her many, many warnings. She'd proven herself trustworthy every step of the way, so he'd increased her freedom more and more. Even so, she was a very young, very new driver.

It didn't help that as a fireman, he often arrived at the scene of car wrecks. He'd worked hundreds that

had involved teenagers. Some of the worst wrecks rolled
through his mind.

If anything happened to her . . .

Car headlights cut through the living room. He went
to the window and saw her 2008 Volvo coming up the
driveway. Thank God. He exhaled with relief and checked
his watch. 10:58. He'd been pretty close to a heart attack for the past thirty minutes. But in the time it took
Madison to park in the attached garage and let herself
inside, his blood pressure began to lower.

He waited for her in the kitchen.

"Hi, Dad." She set her little purse on the kitchen counter and went to the fridge for one of the pomegranate
Izze sodas he kept stocked for her. "Where's Tay?"

"In her room reading a book. Did your phone run
out of battery?"

"Huh? No." She popped the cap off the bottle and
eyed him with confusion as she took a drink.

He held up his phone. "I've been trying to call."

"Really?" She pulled her phone from her purse. "Wow.
Six times, Dad?"

"Why didn't you answer?"

She did a three-second diagnostic on her phone. "Oh,
no volume. Hannah was playing a game on it earlier. She
must have muted it. Sorry about that."

"I was worried."

"O-kay," she said slowly, giving him a look that said she
thought he was overreacting by a mile. "It wasn't my fault."

"It was, because you didn't make sure your volume
was up when Hannah gave you back your phone."

"Am I in trouble? Because I already said I was sorry."

He ground his teeth together. He wanted to punish her

for making him worry, and at the same time recognized that her most serious crime had been failing to notice that her friend had silenced her phone. With two teen-aged girls in the house, he'd learned to pick his battles. He leaned back against the kitchen counter, bracing his hands against its edge.

Madison stared at him in a way that she rarely did these days, as if really noticing things about him. "It might be time for you to . . . don't be offended, okay?" Whenever she said that, he could bet he'd be offended. "It might be time for you to, um, have a social life of your own."

He lifted his eyebrows and felt his forehead creasing.

"Just sayin'." She shrugged. "I mean, I'm glad you didn't do a lot of dating when Tay and I were younger. It would've been really awkward and gross if you'd brought tons of women around here."

"Mmm-hmm."

"But lately, I've started thinking that it's kind of weird that you *don't* have a girlfriend. I mean, seriously. Why don't you? Mom left when I was like four."

"You want me to go out and get a girlfriend?" He'd been sure they'd hate the idea.

"I think it's time, Daddy," she answered gently, pity in her face. "I'll only be here another year and a half, and Taylor will only be here for three more years. Then what're you going to do?"

"I'll have plenty to do."

"What?" She took another drink of soda. When he didn't reply, she gave him an I-told-you-so expression. "What about that woman at the soccer field the other day? The one with the little boy?"

"Amber?"

"She seemed nice. And you guys like each other."

"Sh—she's too young for me."

"What do you mean? She looked like she was thirty-five or something."

Typical Madison. Everyone over twenty-two looked to her like a washed-up thirty-five-year-old. "I think she's twenty-eight."

"So what if she is? Angelina Jolie and Brad Pitt are twelve years apart in age. Nobody cares. Nobody but you even thinks about stuff like that, Dad."

"I . . ."

She collected her purse and phone and headed toward her bedroom. "Maybe if you were dating Amber"—she didn't bother looking back—"you wouldn't be calling me six times on a Saturday night."

"I'd still be calling you six times on a Saturday night. That's what parents do."

Will stayed in his kitchen, alone, surrounded by the hum of the appliances. Madison had indeed been four when Michelle had left, Taylor only two. Taylor had still been in diapers, for pity's sake. For the first several years it was all Will could do just to try to keep his head above water as a single dad. His girls had needed all he had to give them times ten, so that's what he'd given.

He worked at the fire station and built decks on his off-days while they were in school. For the most part, though, his life had revolved around Madison and Taylor for so long that he found it difficult, standing here alone in his kitchen, to think of himself as anything other than their father.

Madison was right about the fact that they'd both be moving away soon. He'd been investing in college funds for them since the beginning so that he could afford to send them to one of the University of Texas schools. He'd raised them so that they'd be ready to leave him.

He'd planned for their futures.

But not his own.

He looked around at the interior of the house, the same three-bedroom, two-bathroom ranch house that he and Michelle had bought right before Madison's birth. It sat on the edge of town, with horse country behind them and just a few neighbors beside them. He'd always been decent with tools, and he'd renovated the house one project at a time, a bathroom one summer, the kitchen the next, the patio. He was forty years old with a solid house, a solid job, and two almost-grown daughters to show for it.

But what if he was the one in the car wreck a week or a year from now? Would he be completely satisfied with how he'd lived? Life was short, and God only gave you one chance at it. Did he really believe that God had a plan for him—just him, the man—separate from his children? It almost seemed wrong to think that. But the longer Will considered it, the more he began to think that the idea had worth. God wasn't done with him yet.

⌒

Across town, Lyndie was doing some deep thinking of her own. Most of it went along the lines of *How dare he?!* and *I'm going to need more Kleenex.*

She blew her nose, tossed the crumpled tissue in the trash, then pulled another tissue from the box and used it to blot the tears that wouldn't quit trickling down her face. She'd perched on the stool in her studio, her hair in its topknot. Her animals sat on the floor at her feet, staring up at her with agitated concern while she painted as if her life depended on it.

The scene taking shape on her art paper revealed the gloomy prince, his face merciless, his cape billowing. He pointed his finger into the distance, demanding that the fairies and the unicorns leave him to his solitude. The blond fairy had her hands fisted, her face set with belligerence.

In the painting before this one, the prince had slammed the door of his gray castle in the faces of the hopeful fairies. In that one the blond fairy had been crying.

And in the painting before that, the prince had been standing in front of his throne. The blond fairy had been attempting to wave the healing wand over him, but he'd taken it from her and shattered it, despite her pleas.

None of the endings were happy. Her planned story of hope and healing had taken a terrible turn.

He'd had the nerve—*the nerve!*—to tell her she wasn't a good jockey. He didn't have a jockey or an exercise rider who'd done more for his stable than she had for the past two months. And when it came down to it, she believed that Jake knew that.

She couldn't shake the intuition that her ride on Silver Leaf today had been just a small part of his motivation for firing her. He'd had other reasons. But she couldn't begin to comprehend those reasons. When she'd asked him to tell her the truth, he'd refused.

He'd come such a long way. He'd begun to improve. He cared about her, she knew he did!

He never told you he did, Lyndie. He never said the words.

And yet he had told her. He'd told her with his eyes and with his kisses. He'd told her in a way that was both deeper than language and also more reliable. . . . She'd thought. Her mind kept going back over a hundred memories of him, using them as evidence. Jake had cared about her! So why, why, why had he destroyed everything today?

She set her brush aside and braced her hands on her knees, peering at the picture on her easel as if it held the answers she required.

Just ten days ago her sister's health had been stable, she'd had a job riding horses, she'd had Jake. And now it had all fallen through her hands. She didn't know if there was anything she could have done differently that would have kept today from going the way that it had. She'd been second-guessing her actions, wondering if she should have ridden Silver Leaf differently, if she'd pushed Jake too hard or not hard enough.

She'd always believed Jake had a heart of gold underneath his gruffness. But perhaps he didn't. Perhaps she lacked objectivity because she'd adored and admired him so much as a girl. Maybe he'd simply been too deeply wounded to hold up his side of a relationship. Or it could be that the darkness that fought for control of him had gained the upper hand. Maybe the stress of Mollie's illness had been too much. She shouldn't have let him come up to the hospital—

Really, Lyndie? She jerked free another tissue. *He breaks up with you and you're seeking to blame yourself?* She swiped at her eyes and stormed to the window.

She'd actually become one of those women who fell in love with a man she hoped would one day change. From their first kiss onward, she'd understood the dangers of falling for Jake. He was a man who didn't have a relationship with God. A man who hadn't opened up to her about Iraq nor communicated how he felt about her.

It had been her hope and prayer that those things would come in time. That's how she'd rationalized away her misgivings.

"God is good," she said to reassure herself. "God is good." One of the verses she'd memorized came to her like a sigh. *The Lord is trustworthy in all He promises and faithful in all He does. The Lord upholds all who fall and lifts up all who are bowed down.*

She definitely classified as bowed down at this particular moment.

Her phone vibrated to signal an incoming text. She picked it up. Not from Jake. From Teddy, the one who'd taken the purity pledge, asking her if she wanted to go to Bible study with him next week. She set the phone on her desk and returned to staring out the window. Jake, of course, would not deign to text or call her.

He was tall and dark and brooding, and she was over it! She was over the brooding part. *So* over it.

Except . . . she couldn't forget the way he'd carried her in his arms after her spill. Or brought her Reese's. Or the way he'd said *"I'm not good enough for you"* the night they'd kissed. Or all the times he'd checked on her grandpa.

Or all the dozens of other ways . . .

He'd made her love him. She loved the grim, hard-hearted jerk with stunning force, and it felt wretched because he'd made himself impossible to love.

She'd failed at healing the man she'd wanted most to heal. And in the process, he'd ended up wounding her.

CHAPTER TWENTY-SIX

Jayden?" Amber called the next afternoon, coming to a stop just inside his bedroom. She couldn't see him. "Jayden?"

"I'm not here right now."

Amber laughed. "Something tells me you're here."

"What?"

"Your voice."

"Oh." Her son rose into view on the far side of his twin bed.

They'd returned home from church and grabbed a quick lunch, then she'd dressed him in a pair of shorts and a cheap orange T-shirt. If only she were wearing something equally normal for the Color the World Happy 5K. Instead, she'd talked the girls at work into joining her for the 5K and they, of course, all wanted to go big or go home in the costume department. Thanks to Sandra, who handled insurance claims for Dr. Dean, Amber had on orange-and-white striped tights, an orange tutu, an orange T-shirt that read *Not From Concentrate* across the front, white fairy wings, and a fake diamond tiara. She didn't know what the wings and tiara had to do with anything. Yet Sandra had insisted. The 5K had definitely given Amber new insight into Sandra, who'd turned out to be a real bruiser. Also, her outfit kept bringing to mind Frank Sinatra's "Orange is the happiest color" quote, probably because wearing orange for the Color the World Happy *did not* make Amber feel happy.

"Why're you wearing all that, Mom?"

"Because we're doing the 5K today as part of a team. The other ladies on the team wanted to dress like this."

He pulled a face and did back-and-forth motions with his palms. "Not me, not me."

"No, not you. You can count on your mom to spare you from a tiara and a tutu. Listen, we have a few minutes left before we need to leave. How about we go upstairs and check on Lyndie?"

"Okay." Jayden always jumped at the chance to visit Lyndie. Lyndie had animals.

They climbed the Candy Shoppe's exterior staircase, knocked, waited. Lyndie answered the door wearing a huge sweater, leggings, and fuzzy socks with a flower pattern on them.

"Hey there," Amber said. "Still in your pajamas?" It was one fifteen.

"Yep." Her hair looked crazy, and she had Mrs. Mapleton in her arms. "Hi, Jayden."

"Hi, Ms. James. May I play with your dogs?"

"Sure. They'd love that."

Jayden lowered onto his knees and the spaniels danced around him, thrilled to have someone small to fuss over.

"Cute costume," Lyndie said to Amber. "Are you the tooth fairy?"

"Yes. I'm the tooth fairy."

"I didn't realize the tooth fairy was Not From Concentrate." Lyndie attempted a smile, but it didn't quite take. Sadness lurked in her eyes.

"Is everything okay?"

"Everything's okay. Tell me about the costume."

Amber, well aware that everything was not okay with her friend, followed Lyndie into the living area while explaining about the 5K. "Celia's Uncle Danny seems to think I'll have a shot at meeting a man there. As if! Who am I ever going to meet dressed like this?"

"The tooth fairy king?" Lyndie settled onto her sofa, pulled a throw blanket over herself, and placed Mrs. Mapleton on top.

Amber chose a pretty camel-colored chair. When she grew up, she wanted a home that looked like this one did, all serene sand and sky colors. "I got worried when I saw that you hadn't moved your car all day, Lyndie. You usually go to church on Sundays."

Lyndie didn't volunteer any info.

"What're you doing up here watching . . ." The TV screen was frozen on a shot of Keri Russell dressed in old-fashioned clothing.

"Austenland."

"What're you doing up here watching *Austenland* on a Sunday afternoon?"

"Jake fired me."

Amber's jaw sagged. "He fired you! Why?"

"Because he doesn't want me riding Silver Leaf anymore, or any of his horses."

"But why? You're a great jockey."

"Thank you, but Jake disagrees." Lyndie pursed her lips.

"What about your dating relationship?"

"Also over."

"Oh no. I'm so sorry. Really sorry. What can I do?"

"You stopped by to see me. And you've been taking care of my animals for me when I've been up at the hospital." Lyndie reached over to give Amber's hand a squeeze before resettling her cat. "That's more than enough. Thank you. Really, thank you."

"Of course. Listen, why don't you come to the Color the World Happy 5K with Jayden and me? It'll be fun." The last part, the fun part? Pure wishful thinking.

"I'll pass," Lyndie said.

"You, too, might meet a tooth fairy king."

"I'm good here. I have my cat and my dogs and *Austenland*."

"But no humans."

"Which is all right. I need to go up to the hospital soon, anyway."

Amber sighed. "I really thought . . . I mean, when you told me that you and Jake were dating, I was positive that he was the one for you. Maybe there's a chance you'll get back together."

Lyndie brought her hair forward over one shoulder. "He dumped me. And not in a friendly way. In the kind of way that makes me want to kill him."

"Oh." Amber wrinkled her forehead. "Do you want me to slash his tires or something?"

Lyndie's mouth bowed into a weary smile. "No."

"Good, because to be honest with you, I'd be terrified

to slash Jake Porter's tires." Amber stood. "The least I can do is make you some coffee before I go."

"You don't have to do that. I'm not really in the mood—"

"I'm making coffee!"

Jayden continued to play with Lyndie's dogs while Amber quickly fixed one of their signature coffees. She set the concoction on the side table near Lyndie. "The sprinkles are in my kitchen downstairs. Do you want me to run and get them?"

"No, this is perfect. Thank you."

"You're welcome." Amber gave her a hug. "I'll stop by after the 5K."

"I'll be with Mollie at the hospital."

"In that case"—she peeled Jayden away from the dogs—"I'll take Felicity and Tobias for a walk. Also, I'll leave some dinner for you in a cooler outside your door, okay? I want you to have something to eat when you get home."

"You don't need to—"

"I'm supplying dinner!" Amber gave Lyndie a sympathetic wave, then pulled Jayden out the door onto the upper landing.

"Can I go see my hero house?" he asked.

"Just while I pick up my purse and my car keys. Three minutes."

He took off toward the middle of the backyard. As Amber let herself into her downstairs apartment through the back door, she caught the tail end of what sounded like knocking on her front door. Then quiet.

She felt pretty sure that had been an important knock. The kind she wouldn't want to miss. She rushed to the front door and threw it open.

Will McGrath had his back turned and was walking away, already halfway to the Candy Shoppe's gate. Will! *Will.*

"Will?"

He turned, his eyes rounding a little at the sight of her outfit.

This horrible outfit. The man of my dreams is at my door, literally knocking, and I answer wearing an orange tutu. She walked toward him, leaving the front door open so she'd be able to hear Jayden. "I look ridiculous, I know. Jayden and I are doing a 5K today. It's called Color the World Happy and all the participants wear colors. My team is wearing"—she gestured self-consciously to her clothing—"orange."

He smiled, an easy smile full of amusement and kindness. Clear, warm air tinted with sunshine fell around them.

"Had you been knocking for long?" Amber asked.

"Not very long."

"Sorry about that. I was upstairs, hanging out with my friend."

"No problem. I'm glad you're home." He wore a simple gray T-shirt with jeans. His square jaw and those irresistible bedroom eyes were making her go mushy inside.

Will had come. To her house! Did she have any business at all hoping that he might—

"I was wondering if you . . ." Almost uncomfortably, he pushed his hands into the back pockets of his jeans. "If you might like to go out with me sometime."

Happiness went off like a firecracker inside her. She beamed at him. "I'd love to."

He looked genuinely surprised by her answer. As if

he hadn't understood the I'm-interested-in-you signals she'd been trying to give him since the day they'd met.

"I've been worried that I'm too old for you," he said.

His words and the honest apology in his face melted her. Completely melted her. "You're not. The years I've spent being a single mom have aged me like dog years."

He chuckled. "I know the feeling."

"Really," she assured him, "I don't mind your age a bit. I like your age."

"I'm quite a bit older, Amber."

"I like you just the way you are, Will."

"I feel the exact same way about you," he said. "I like you just the way you are."

Mutual attraction connected them together with such force that goose bumps raced down Amber's arms in a shimmering trail. "If you're free, it would be great if you could come to the 5K with Jayden and me."

"Sure. I can come if you'd like me to."

"I'd like for you to." She guided him through the house so that she could scoop up her purse and keys.

It looked like the Color the World Happy, which would count as the third of her three dates, was going to be a *very* happy event for her after all.

For years she'd been trying to convince herself that God really had forgiven her completely for her past mistakes. She'd had doubts and insecurities about it. But she'd also had enough faith to resist temptation and wait on God's timing where men were concerned.

It seemed that God had forgiveness and generosity to spare. He also had a funny sense of timing. Because on the one day that she'd dressed in striped tights and a tiara, Will had shown up to tell her right to her face that he liked her just the way she was.

She probably could have floated outside to round up Jayden, purely on the strength of the delight buzzing through her. The past four years of working on her degree, concentrating on mothering, focusing on building her relationship with God had led her here.

They walked into the backyard, toward the hero house.

"Do I have to run the 5K?" Will asked.

"No."

"Do I have to wear orange?"

"No." She glanced sideways and up at him, her smile full of joy. "Remember? I like you just the way you are."

~

Five days had passed since Jake had broken up with Lyndie. They'd been the worst five days of Jake's life. Which was saying something.

All the light and air and warmth had been sucked out of his world. All of it—gone. Because she was gone.

Sweat ran down him in streams as he worked the seat of his rowing machine forward and backward along its track. At a time of day when most people had finished dinner and were about to turn on prime-time TV, Jake had shut himself into his loft's exercise room. He pumped with his legs, heaving the bar toward his chest. Bent his legs. Extended the bar. Then did it all over again and again. Other than the Led Zeppelin he had playing, he could hear nothing except the machine's rhythmic *wh-oosh wh-oosh*.

Since the day of Silver Leaf's race, he'd been going through the motions like someone who had a body but no soul. The alarm clock still went off each morning, and he still got himself out to the barns at Whispering Creek and Lone Star. In fact, he worked almost all day long, training horses his employees could have trained in the round pen, burying himself in desk work, putting in long hours at Lone Star, overseeing the progress of his recovering horses.

He worked, and he worked out. But he couldn't eat or sleep or think or . . . stand himself.

His T-shirt had plastered to him. His lungs were burning, his muscles were blazing, and he kept going because he actually preferred the physical agony to the agony in his head when left alone with thoughts of Lyndie.

He had horses in Florida. He could go there or he could take some Thoroughbreds to New York earlier than planned. He should leave Holley. It might do him good.

Yet he didn't want to go any more than he wanted to stay. At least here, she was near.

A dull banging noise came from the front of his loft. Jake paused the motion of the rower, panting. More banging. He cursed and went back to rowing. Whoever it was could hang for all he cared. He wasn't in the mood for company.

The banging didn't stop. Finally, Jake lunged from the machine and flicked off the music. He crossed through his kitchen and living room, both mostly dark now that the sun had gone down. Irritated, he pulled open his front door.

His younger sister, Dru, stood in the hallway holding a pistol. Apparently, she'd been using the gun to do the banging.

Dru raised an eyebrow at him as she holstered the gun beneath the black jacket of her suit. "Training for the Olympics?"

"No."

"Then why are you working out so hard? You're already in painfully good shape, Jake. If you ask me, you could use more time watching football and eating Fritos."

He didn't move to let her pass. She slid by him anyway, turning on lights as she made her way to the leather chair near the sofa. She sat on the chair's arm and studied him.

It still surprised him to look at Dru and see a full-grown adult looking back. The Porters had sent a restless, daring, determined eighteen-year-old girl off to the Marines. The Marines had returned a woman. Jake was the third child in their family and she the fourth, but they were ten years apart in age. Until recently, she'd always been a kid to him.

"Mom's worried about you," she stated.

"And?"

"And it's become my problem because she keeps calling me to talk about it." She cocked her head. "Are you holding things together, or do you have a screw loose?"

"I'm holding things together."

"I don't believe you." Among Dru's many faults: Her blue eyes missed nothing, and she could be extremely blunt. "When did you eat last? Have you slept? Have you said more than ten words to anyone lately?"

"Thanks for the fun visit, Dru. But I've got some splinters I need to stick into my fingernails—"

"Plus, this loft is really dark and depressing. And your plan to exercise yourself to death doesn't give the best impression of sanity."

"Giving the impression of sanity isn't my strong suit."

"All that to say, I don't really feel like I can call Mom when I leave here and give her a glowing report."

He'd been ignoring calls from the rest of the Porters for days. They were all concerned. Some, like Meg and Bo, were both concerned and puzzled. Lyndie had warned him that Meg and Bo wouldn't be pleased with him for firing her. They hadn't been. He'd taken Meg's favorite jockey off her favorite horse without an explanation.

Thing was, after what had happened with Lyndie, his life couldn't go any further downhill. He was brutally sorry that he'd hurt Lyndie, that he'd taken jockeying away from her. It wrecked him that he'd lost her and made her hate him. But Lyndie was safe and he was alone, and that was how things should be.

"Hey," Bo said as he and Ty let themselves in.

Jake groaned, anger climbing inside him.

"You're looking sweaty," Ty said.

"Very sweaty," Bo agreed. "Did you just complete an Iron Man?"

"Is this a court-martial?" Jake asked tersely.

"I called them," Dru said, "after the first ten minutes of knocking on your door. I figured I might need them to smooth things over if I had to shoot my way inside."

"Everybody out," Jake said.

"He's grumpy," Dru told Bo and Ty. "He's in love with Lyndie James, but he ruined it somehow and now he's about an inch from a breakdown."

Bo leveled a look on Jake that Jake had become familiar with over their many years of working side by side. The look held both assessment and worry. Jake had always hated it.

"What did you do to ruin it?" Bo asked.

"I don't want to talk about it."

"Ty and I both had ups and downs with our wives before we got married," Bo said. "We get it. The downs are bad."

Jake swung his frown on Ty.

"Don't look at me." Ty shrugged. "I was brought here under false pretenses. Bo told me there'd be donuts."

"That's helpful, Ty," Dru said.

"And all your confrontational crap is making Jake feel better?"

Dru stood, her hands on her hips. Even wearing high heels, Dru was shorter than all three of her brothers. However, she'd been studying martial arts for a decade and could shoot with deadly accuracy. From the age of six onward, she'd been able to hold her own against any of them. She faced Jake directly. "Do you love her?"

None of his siblings could hide their hope as they waited for him to answer.

He wanted to deny it, to say that he didn't love Lyndie.

He'd gotten good at lying. He'd gotten good at lying to himself, even. He'd told himself while he and Lyndie were dating that their relationship had a small chance of turning out well. He'd told himself that he was solid enough to handle his feelings for her, that he could deal with having her jockey for him.

As good as he was at lying, though, he couldn't make himself lie to Bo, Ty, and Dru about his love for her. To do so would be a further betrayal of her, so he remained silent. Even without words, his brothers and sister would be able to read the answer on his face.

What remained of his pride burned. Stupid, hopeless love.

"Go see her," Dru said. "Tell her that you love her and apologize for acting like an idiot."

"In my experience," Bo said, "that actually does tend to work pretty well."

"Mine too," Ty agreed. "Huh. Dru just said something that made sense. Surprising." He aimed a challenging smile on their sister. "I'm not used to hearing anything that makes sense come out of your mouth, Dru."

"God knows I'm even less used to hearing sense out of you, Ty."

Ty glanced toward the kitchen. "Are there any donuts?"

Dru stepped into Jake's line of sight. "Listen, Jake. Every woman I know is scared of you. By some miracle, Lyndie isn't. Which means she's not just brave about horses, she's brave about you. You're not an easy person to care about. Is he, guys?"

"No," Bo and Ty answered in unison.

"Patch things up with her," Dru ordered.

"You can't go on like this," Bo said.

"I can," Jake insisted, though nothing within him believed it.

"Lyndie's good for you." Ty crossed his arms and gave Jake a look that told him he thought he was a fool for having broken up with her. "Because of her, you were doing better these past few months than I've seen you do in a long time. You don't want to go back to living without her, do you?"

No.

"Whatever's broken between you," Dru said, "can be fixed."

"Not when I'm the broken thing," Jake said.

Quiet met his answer.

"Even you can be fixed," Bo said, holding Jake's gaze.

Jake started to shake his head.

"Get on your knees in front of God," Bo said. "See what happens. You might not have the power to fix yourself, but He can fix anything. Even you. Even your relationship with Lyndie."

God was the last thing Jake wanted brought into this discussion. He crossed to his door and held it open. "I appreciate the lecture. Now everybody out."

"Always the gracious host." Ty clapped him on the shoulder as he passed.

Dru gave him the evil eye and exited.

Bo paused, looking troubled. "Jake—"

"Please go."

Bo had mercy on him and left. Except it didn't feel like mercy when Jake turned back to his apartment, which echoed with emptiness, loneliness, and that vacuum of light and air and warmth. All of it, gone.

Because she was gone.

Past midnight that night, Jake came to a stop at the foot of Mollie's hospital bed.

When he'd arrived at the hospital's parking garage, both Karen's and Mike's cars had been there. He'd waited in his truck, knowing that Mike most often took the late shift with Mollie. Sure enough, Karen had eventually gone, exactly as Jake had hoped. Mike could be counted on to fall asleep, and Jake hadn't wanted an audience.

He'd waited thirty minutes and entered the hospital in ways that would have made hospital security unhappy.

Mollie's room lay in semi-darkness. As Jake had expected, Mike was sleeping. He'd stretched out on the reclining chair next to Mollie's bed, his face turned toward his daughter as if begging her to get well.

Jake could tell that Mollie still hadn't improved. He could hardly stand to listen to her tortured breath. Thirteen days. How could Mollie's weak body have battled pneumonia so long? Like him, something was eating away at her from the inside. And like him, she was losing.

"You might not have the power to fix yourself, but He can fix anything. Even you," Bo had said to him earlier. Jake hadn't been able to get the words out of his head. Part of him wanted to believe Bo. And that's why he'd come here, because he'd known that Mollie would prove Bo wrong.

God could *not* fix everything. He hadn't fixed Mollie. He hadn't even cured her pneumonia.

Someone, Karen or Lyndie probably, had dressed Mollie in a pair of pale yellow pajamas. Her dark blond hair had been neatly combed into a small ponytail. Her eyebrows were drawn down in what looked like worry. Her mouth hung ajar, her eyes closed. She moaned quietly.

Jake cut his attention to Mike, but the small sound hadn't caused Mike to stir.

Mollie moved her head, then seemed to calm when her cheek came up against her pillow from home.

Jake stood, unmoving, compassion cutting a path inside him like a river cutting its way down a mountainside.

He couldn't imagine the life she'd led. He remembered what she'd been like as a child, and in all this time, her situation hadn't changed. She was still trapped in a body that didn't move like his did, that suffered frequent seizures. She had no sight. What went on in her head? He didn't know, wasn't sure what she might think or feel, because she couldn't speak. Mollie was twenty-seven years old and totally reliant on her family.

Lyndie thought, or wanted to think, that Mollie had abilities to heal. But the woman in the bed in front of him was frail and sick. She had no magic.

You didn't heal Silver Leaf, Mollie. You couldn't have. And, unfortunately, there's no one here to heal you. Who's going to heal you, Mollie?

The reply stole into his mind like intuition. **I am.**

His brow knit.

I am.

A chill bolted down Jake's spine. Mike and Mollie continued to sleep. Mollie's IV dripped steadily. He was the only one awake in the room. Except, it didn't feel that way any longer. He didn't feel alone.

Resentments, deep and old, stirred within Jake. *Your world*, he wanted to yell, *is unfair and screwed up*. He'd never been able to make his peace with the lack of justice God allowed. Mollie had done nothing wrong, nothing to deserve the life she'd received.

And you, Jake? What do you deserve?

He deserved hell. Death. Jake had always had a strong sense of right and wrong.

Standing at the foot of Mollie's bed, he saw exactly what he'd come to see. He saw Mollie, innocent. Yet she'd not been given a healthy body or a future. He saw himself, guilty. Yet he did have a healthy body and a future. They had not been given what they each deserved.

Deserve meant something to Jake. But God did not operate based on what or who was deserving.

See? Jake cried out within his mind. Unfair. Wrong. He couldn't accept it.

Even so, he knew what Lyndie and Karen would say. They'd say that the fact that God did not give what was deserved was cause to praise Him. Instead of giving what was deserved, they'd say, God offered something far better. Grace.

Was grace better? He didn't see how. And he definitely didn't see how God could offer grace to him.

Silently, he exited the room. He'd go home, he'd try to get some sleep and go on about his life—only he didn't have Lyndie anymore, and without her, he hated his life. His exhaustion and disgust and misery were catching up to him. He didn't know how much further he could carry them.

He rounded a corner into a short hallway that ended with elevators on one side and a door leading to a stairwell on the other. His arms and legs began to shake. He stumbled slightly and had to catch himself by bracing a hand against the wall.

Lyndie. His heart broke at the thought of her. When they'd been together, he'd hoped she was enough to make him better. But even she had not been. And now she was gone. And God was using her absence to show him that no human person could ever be equal to his flaws. God was using Lyndie's absence to take him to rock bottom.

"No," Jake whispered, still fighting. He didn't want

what God offered. God's perfection and holiness only made Jake feel all the blacker.

He opened the door to the stairwell. Cement stairs led up and down from the landing. Industrial lighting hung above.

He'd go home—

No, he wouldn't. Couldn't. His legs were giving out. He managed to get his back up against the wall, then lowered into a sitting position. He planted his elbows on his upraised knees and bent his head. He struggled to hold himself together, but it was no use. He couldn't do it anymore. He couldn't shoulder all his fears and sorrows for one more step. He'd come to the very end of himself.

Jake had turned from God long ago. But not so long that he didn't remember what he'd once been taught. The punishment that he should have received, they'd told him, Jesus had received in his place. And in so doing, He'd paid Jake's ransom and set him free.

It had been easier to believe that when he'd thought of himself as a good person. Harder to believe that now, when regrets pressed down on him like dirt on a buried coffin.

I'm messed up, God.

But I'm perfect.

I'm a failure.

I am not.

I'm filled with darkness.

I am the light.

He only had brokenness to offer—and very little faith. But he directed what faith he had toward accepting that

Jesus' death could pay for his mistakes. "Forgive me," he whispered, so quietly the sound barely reached his ears.

And then he let everything else fall. His unbearable guilt. The blame he'd put on himself. His self-hatred. His endless fear for Lyndie's safety. His fury toward God. His outrage that he had lived when his men had died. His wounds.

Jake worked to bring it all up and in turn to release it all.

In answer he could almost . . . almost *feel* God's readiness to take his burdens from him.

Gradually, Jake's shaking stilled. His stomach unknotted. His tiredness began to pull back. For the first time since the day of the IED, he felt as though his past had been lifted from him.

Slowly, like mist moving into a valley, peace began to come over him. Thin strands at first, then more and more. It had been so long since he'd experienced the stillness of true inner peace that he began to sob. Silent sobs without tears racked his chest.

He didn't know how God might help him. He'd been changed the day that Panzetti, Barnes, and Scott had died. He'd never be who he'd been before. He'd carry scars and fight PTSD and struggle. But maybe . . . maybe God *could* help him.

His battered hope gathered itself and began to rise.

chapter TWENTY-SEVEN

The very next night, Lyndie sighed as she came from sleep into drowsy semi-consciousness. She pried her eyes open a millimeter and saw the surroundings of Mollie's hospital room. It was her turn to sleep in the chair next to her sister's bed through the night. The room's darkness assured her that dawn would be a long time coming.

She'd been dreaming about Jake. *Oh, Jake*. She closed her eyes and willed herself to return to the dream. In it, he'd loved her. They'd been standing side by side at the track at Lone Star, and his lovely horses had been galloping by, their manes and tails rippling. She'd been telling him in great detail about a new story idea that included a cast of friendly giants fighting to retain their kingdom of plums against an army of ogres bent on making plum jam. He'd been teasing her and smiling, and there'd been the most wonderful look of tenderness in his eyes. . . .

She didn't want reality. She wanted more of *that*. So she tried to grasp the dream back. Only . . . something tickled at her brain. Something that wanted her notice.

She let her hearing stretch out and extend. She heard

nothing. No wheezing. She sprang upward as her attention swung to Mollie. Her sister slept comfortably, her chest rising and falling smoothly. The machines that watched over Mollie had not let down their guard. The quiet wasn't a bad sign. It was a good one.

Relief poured through Lyndie from head to toe. Praise God! Praise God, praise God, praise God. Mollie had turned the corner toward recovery.

Smiling tearfully, Lyndie placed a hand on Mollie's shoulder and prayed over her, thanking the God who'd healed her sister yet again.

You are good, God. Which would have been true even if He'd taken Mollie to heaven. Just as true if He'd returned Jake to her. She desperately wanted Him to return Jake to her. He hadn't. But He had spared Mollie's life. Lyndie would have more time with the sweetest person she knew, her one and only sister. More time to love her and read to her and care for her. She and her mom and her dad would still have their Mollie.

Praise you, God! Thank you. You are good.

⁓

Lyndie arranged the flowers she'd just bought while craning her neck to listen to her mom's voice coming from the phone wedged between her ear and her shoulder. "Uh-huh." Her mom was explaining how hard it had been to part from one of the nurses on Mollie's wing. The nurse, who had a husband with sleep apnea and a son with ADHD, had forged a deep friendship with Lyndie's mother.

Lyndie added two stems of hydrangea to the glass bowl on her antique farm table.

More than two days had passed since she'd first noticed Mollie's improvement, and today the James family had brought Mollie home. Once they'd gotten Mollie tucked in her own bed, bathed in sunshine and the sounds of her outdoor birdfeeder, Lyndie had hit the grocery store in order to restock both her parents' shelves and her own. While there, she'd splurged on a large bouquet of pink roses, white hydrangea, lavender stock, and yellow tulips.

The flowers had seemed like a good way to celebrate Mollie's homecoming, and a semi-decent way to brighten an apartment—and heart—that had been shrouded in gray ever since Jake had broken up with her.

Grandpa Harold had taken to asking Lyndie about Jake every time she saw him. Grandpa missed Jake. So did her parents. Had Mollie a voice, Lyndie was quite certain she, too, would be inquiring as to Jake's whereabouts. Even her dogs and cat had been giving her questioning looks.

She wanted to tell them all that Jake had acted like a colossal jerk to her. She hadn't, though, because she couldn't convince herself that he *was* a colossal jerk underneath that spiky exterior. Her foolish heart kept expecting him to call or come by to check on her and Mollie.

Three different trainers, all of whom had horses currently racing at Lone Star, had contacted her and asked if she'd be interested in riding for them. She wasn't interested as of yet. Her heart needed more time to put away her hopes for Jake and Silver Leaf before she'd be able to consider a position with another stable. The income from her books gave her the financial freedom to wait for a little while before she'd need to make a decision.

"Have you seen the weather report?" Karen now asked.

"Nope."

"Big storms are coming."

"Really?" Lyndie adjusted one of the roses.

"There's a tornado warning over Holley for the next three hours, until 7 p.m. Do you want to drive back over to our house?"

"No, that's okay. I can't leave the animals here alone." Storms tended to set them on edge.

"I'd feel better if you were here with us. You're welcome to bring the animals."

"Mom, it's fine. Texans overreact to the weather." Several spring storms had barreled over them in the past months. Each time, the local weathermen seemed to enjoy superseding network programming to show radar diagrams and talk at length about sustained wind speeds. The worst thing Lyndie had seen so far? A few good old-fashioned downpours accompanied by lightning displays.

"If you're sure . . ."

"I am."

"Okay. Talk to you later, honey."

They disconnected, and Lyndie glanced out the nearest window. The afternoon sky spread outward, a faintly overcast dove gray. Not a speck of rain in sight.

How bad could the weather get?

***

Around six o'clock, Jake's head came up at the sound of a siren. Every kid raised in north Texas recognized the whine of a tornado siren when they heard it.

He'd just finished pulling on jeans after a workout and shower. Tugging a shirt over his head, he walked into his living room to flip on the TV. Jake always paid attention to forecasts, because weather could impact his horses. This morning he'd noticed the possibility of storms. He and Bo had gone back over their preparedness plans with their employees this afternoon before leaving the barns. He hadn't worried about the weather since.

He stood in his living room in his bare feet, watching the news coverage, while anxiety for Lyndie gathered in his chest. He'd lived through too many tornado seasons to count. He knew a dangerous storm front when he saw one. Twisters had been spotted on the ground in counties to the south and west. Within the next forty-five minutes, the front would take aim at Holley.

Where was Lyndie taking shelter?

He'd given up the right to know that information. He could call her—no. He shouldn't.

He paced and texted Bo about the horses. *I'm already on it*, Bo responded. *They're being taken care of. Just stay inside and stay safe.*

Jake continued to pace, watching the ominous weather coverage out of the corner of his eye, holding his phone in his hand. Over the past few days he'd been trying to get his head sorted out. His prayer in the hospital stairwell had changed him in a fundamental way. He wasn't cured or even half as normal as he wished he were. But guilt no longer had him in its fist, and for him, that was big.

He'd been working to accept the radical idea of grace. It wasn't easy for him. It required a big mental shift and the changing of thought patterns that had become old habit. But slowly, he was coming around.

His faith and his prayers might be weak, but Lyndie's God was not. He wanted to tell her she'd been right about that. She'd be pleased about that piece of their situation, he knew. It was all the other pieces of their breakup that held him back.

He wouldn't let her ride for him again. That hadn't changed and wouldn't change. Which meant that he was the guy who'd stolen her dream from her. She'd ridden Silver Leaf beautifully, and it could be that she might have ridden him straight to the top of horse racing, if it hadn't been for Jake.

The sirens fell silent.

The trainers in California hadn't seen her potential and hadn't given her the chance she'd needed. He'd seen her potential, but he, too, had stripped the opportunity from her. It made him sick to his stomach when he thought about it. And yet he would not risk her.

He couldn't.

She might not be able to forgive him for that. He wouldn't blame her if she couldn't. Nor did he expect her to forgive him for the cutting things he'd said to her the day he'd fired her. Over the past months she'd been nothing but kind, decent, and loyal to him. And in return, he'd shoved her away.

He wanted to see her again, and he definitely wanted to apologize. Of those two things he'd grown sure. But before he spoke with her, he needed more time to figure out how to ask for her forgiveness and also how and if he could bring himself to trust her with the details of his past and the details of his mental illness.

The siren sounded again, growing louder and quieter as it spun.

He needed more time before he saw Lyndie, but he wasn't going to get more time. The storm was closing in on them, and he couldn't stand not knowing where she was and that she was safe.

He shouldn't call her. But even before he finished the thought, his finger punched in her number. He listened to her phone ring. It went to voice mail. He waited a few more minutes. The weatherman reported that another tornado had touched down. His urgency grew. He called again. And again.

He stuffed his phone into his back pocket as he went for his keys. Why wasn't she answering her phone? Probably because it was him calling. Chances were, she was at her parents' house or at the hospital. She was probably fine.

He jerked on socks and boots, not stopping to grab a jacket or his hat, too worried to do anything but run for his truck. Before the worst hit, he'd confirm for himself that she wasn't home alone, then return to his loft.

Low ashy clouds raced above him as he drove, darkening what was left of the day's light. The sirens cut off, then came back on again. The people on the radio advised taking shelter. Wind rocked his truck.

He saw exactly what he'd hoped not to see when he pulled up in front of Lyndie's building. Lights blazed from the second floor, Lyndie's floor. He rushed from his truck, the first fat raindrops blowing sideways into him. A third of the way up the exterior staircase, he spotted her in the middle of her backyard.

She was in *the middle of the backyard*. Outside and unprotected, hunched over something on the ground. Terrified, he turned and took the stairs two at a time on his way down.

When he'd neared to within a few feet of her, her face

angled sharply toward him. He came to a stop beside her, his heart thudding fast.

Lyndie stared at him with confusion and distrust. The hostility in her expression knocked into him, filling him with regret.

In her arms she held things that looked like they belonged in a dollhouse. Tiny chairs, a ladder, a table. The wind tossed her hair around the shoulders of the black sweatshirt she wore.

"What are you doing here?" she asked.

He hadn't seen her in days and days. He struggled to adjust to the reality of her again. Her nearness. Her dislike of him. His crippling love for her. "I came because I wanted to make sure you were okay."

The rain increased.

He knelt, bringing him closer to her level. Wetness soaked into his jeans.

"You fired me," she said. "Remember?"

"Yes."

"Whether or not I'm okay isn't your concern anymore."

Her words hurt him. Him, who'd been an expert at using sharp words to keep people, including her, away. "Tornados are headed this way."

"I'm aware of that. I'm almost done. Once I have everything, I'll head inside."

"I need to get you inside now."

Her brown eyes snapped with anger. "You don't get your way at this house. Here, I'm the one who decides."

She'd turned one of the things he'd said to her at Lone Star back on him. He set his teeth and fought his growing desperation.

She gathered up more items. "I can't let anything happen to Jayden's hero house. It means a lot to him. He and Amber are at Will's. They aren't here to bring it inside."

Thunder boomed in the distance. Jake considered picking her up and carrying her to her apartment. He cared nothing for Jayden's playhouse in relation to her safety, but the determined tilt of her chin told him that Lyndie cared.

This little house meant something to her, so he pulled up the hem of his shirt and quickly moved everything into it that he could. "Now?" he gritted out.

"There's still . . ." She leaned across him, indicating more pieces he hadn't seen.

He loaded up the rest. Twisters were bearing down on them, and he was saving a dollhouse.

Once they'd gotten it all, they ran for the staircase, both of them bent against a sudden stinging downpour that did its best to drench them. They burst into her apartment. Her dogs watched them with frightened eyes as they unloaded everything onto the dining room table. A pile of tiny stuff had been placed there already, evidence that she'd made other trips.

The TV played weather coverage, the sound of it mostly overpowered by the noise of the rain and wind.

"I tried to call you," he said.

Her hair was completely saturated. Moisture slicked the clean and lovely angles of her face. Mud marked her jeans and riding boots. "I must have been outside, getting the stuff from the hero house."

A series of barks came from outdoors.

Lyndie went to one of the windows. She looked out at her backyard for a moment, then moved toward the door.

Jake planted his palm against the door to keep it closed. "You're not going back out there."

"I am. My neighbor's golden retriever is outside."

"And?"

"He must have gotten loose. I'll run out and bring him back inside with me."

"Your neighbor's dog will take care of himself."

"There's still enough time for me to go out there and get him."

"No, there isn't."

"There's enough." The dismay in her expression undid him. "I can't let anything happen to him."

He remembered all the times she'd pleaded with him as a girl to save an animal. He'd never been able to say no to her then, either. "I'll go and get the dog."

Lightning flashed and in the split second after, the electricity cut out. The TV silenced. The apartment fell dim.

"Do you have candles?" he asked.

"Yes."

"Stay inside and light them."

"Jake—"

He shouldered through the door and back into the storm, searching through the chaos of the weather for the dog. To the south, the clouds had gone dark gray and uneven at the bottom. Lightning flashed almost horizontally there, several strikes at a time. Thunder rolled again and again, approaching.

He couldn't see the retriever—

Lyndie streaked down the stairs in his direction.

"Stay inside!" he yelled, motioning her back.

She sprinted to him, one arm up and shielding her head. "He doesn't know you." She had to shout to be heard. "He won't come to you."

Furious, frightened for her, Jake hauled her up and

over his shoulder. His patience for reasoning with her and her stubborn bravery had passed. He carried her back upstairs, ignoring the muffled sound of her voice. His men had died under his command. He *was not* going to let the same thing happen to her.

When he had her back in her apartment, he set her on her feet. They were both breathing hard, facing off against each other with their hands fisted. The two candles she'd lit and placed on the bar shed muted light.

She whipped wet hair out of her eyes. "He won't come to you!"

"I'll get him," Jake growled. "You're going to have to trust me."

"Trust you?" Her eyes blazed.

"Are you going to stay inside or not?"

She pulled her head back. The sirens began again.

"What'll it be?" he demanded.

"I . . . I'll stay inside."

As he moved to leave, she took a step forward. "Jake, wait." She darted a look outside. "I don't know if I want you to go now. We might have run out of time."

At this point, there was no way he was leaving the lousy dog out there to get impaled by a flying piece of wood. "I'll get him. And I'll be right back."

Lyndie stood at her window and watched Jake disappear beneath the cover of the swaying trees. She'd made a bad decision. She shouldn't have let him go just now. She hadn't intended for him to go at all! She'd intended to go herself.

The weather had turned fierce and terrible. The eerie

black clouds weren't moving in one direction like they usually did but had begun to form a huge circle.

Lyndie chewed the inside of her lip. Why had Jake come here, in the middle of this storm, after days of silence?

He'd said he'd come to make sure she was okay, the same way he'd always made sure she was okay when they were kids and since she'd been working for him. Regardless of whether or not he loved her, it seemed as though he couldn't stop himself from protecting her. It was built into him.

Shivering from cold and fear, she scoured the view for a sign of him. It had seemed worthwhile to rescue Max, her neighbor's sweet dog, when it had been her hide at risk. But Jake's hide? Too high a price. Maybe she should go out and bring him in—only she'd told him she wouldn't.

He rushed from beneath the trees, carrying Max. A relieved exhale wrenched from her.

Jake's jeans had turned as dark as the shirt he wore. His face was set in relentless, determined lines. And Lyndie was positively certain that even if a tornado had been upon him and he'd had to lasso the dog, he'd have brought the animal back for her.

He was not and never had been a colossal jerk. Her wild emotions didn't know which way to spin, toward tears of love for him or tears of angry frustration because he'd broken her heart.

She wrestled the door open, then slammed and bolted it behind him. He set Max down. The retriever shot into the living room, leaving muddy tracks in his wake. He hid under an armchair, his tail between his legs, trembling. Mrs. Mapleton meowed at the bad-mannered houseguest, and Lyndie's dogs blinked nervously at her from where they sat beside her sofa.

The remains of Jayden's hero house rested on her table, uprooted, a reminder of what could happen to things that had been carefully built, when forsaken to the wind.

It took effort to make herself meet Jake's gaze. When she did, she felt the clash of it all the way to her toes. The hazel depths of his eyes, rimmed by wet lashes, glowed with emotion. Water slicked his dark hair. The power of his blunt handsomeness, slashed by his scar, had never been so obvious.

Her mouth went dry. She was sorry she'd sent him into the thunderstorm and grateful to him for helping her rescue the hero house and Max. At the same time, the painful memory of what had happened between them the last time they'd seen each other hung in the air, destructive. "Thank you for getting the dog."

He didn't respond. His chest was hitching in and out, and he was no doubt trying to organize a blistering lecture on tornado safety.

She didn't want a lecture. She wanted honest answers from him. Did she have the guts to deal with him head-on?

She had a great many faults. But a lack of guts had never been one. "Ever since I moved back from California," she said slowly, distinctly, "I've been trying to pull the truth from you, Jake. I haven't succeeded. But I think the time has come for us to be honest with each other. Even if it ends up hurting me, I *need* for you to tell me the truth now."

His forehead furrowed.

She gathered her courage. "Do you care about me?"

Sheets of rain drummed the roof. "Yes."

"Then why did you ruin what we had?"

"I . . ."

She gave him time to finish. He didn't. "Was it because of how I jockeyed Silver Leaf?"

"No. It was never about that. I lied."

Her adrenaline began to race. He was finally opening up to her. "Then why did you take me off Silver Leaf?"

He appeared to be wrestling internally with whether to trust her with all of it.

Trust me, she wanted to beg—

"I took you off Silver Leaf because I can't stand to put you in danger. I can't do it. It overwhelms me with fear, and I can't . . . I can't risk your safety." His face looked anguished. "Not for any reason. I'll lose it if I have to."

Lyndie's sympathy swelled. "Why didn't you tell me?"

"I'm not proud of it. And also I . . ." His lips set.

"Yes?"

"I worried that you might understand."

"Which would have been a bad thing because . . . ?"

"Because then I would have had a chance at happiness."

Comprehension dawned. It had been his fear for her and his survivor's guilt that had sabotaged him—*them*.

"You love riding," he said. "I hope you can forgive me for taking it from you and for the things I said to you at Lone Star. I won't blame you if you can't."

What she'd learned from her life with Mollie was proving true with Jake, also. Loving someone wasn't about their perfection. It was about coming to accept every part of them, their good qualities and their weaknesses and flaws—looking on everything they were and loving it all.

As she looked on everything Jake was, right down to his center, she loved him.

She closed the space between them. "You're right. I love riding. But is it worth more to me than you? If I have to choose between it and your sense of peace, then *I choose you*."

"Lyndie," he rasped. He studied her as if trying to find enough hope within himself to put faith in her words. His hands remained at his sides.

"I think I've made a mistake with you, Jake." She took fierce hold of his rain-soaked shirt, intent on keeping him right where he was, on making him hear her. "I didn't tell you exactly how I felt about you because I didn't want to scare you or rush you. But now I see that I was wrong, that maybe I should have made myself very plain from the beginning."

She felt his big body brace, as if preparing for bad news.

"Given a choice between my riding and your sense of peace," she repeated, "I choose you. Do you understand me? Am I being plain enough?" Tears piled up on her lashes.

"Yes."

"I choose you because I love you. Just so that there can be absolutely no doubt or worry about it in your mind from this day on, I love you."

His face revealed heartbreaking uncertainty. "You love me?"

"I love you."

"I'm not—" His voice broke. "I'm not . . . whole. I'm afraid I never will be."

"None of us is whole. Only God is."

Tenderness filled his gaze. "I love you, Lyndie."

"Then what more could a girl ask, Jake Porter?" She

smiled shakily. "You're something better than perfect. You're mine. We'll trust God with our shortcomings."

He dug his hands into her hair and took her mouth in a kiss of such spiraling adoration and passion that Lyndie felt her tears tumbling down her cheeks. He walked her backward while they kissed, finally settling her against the smooth hallway wall and kissing her like he was never going to stop.

When he lifted his head, they stared at each other, breathless. In the candlelight, his eyes glittered with his dedication to her. "I'm sorry that I took jockeying from you," he said.

She set a hand on his uninjured cheek, marveling over him. He loved her! He *loved* her. "Whispering Creek has a lot of horses, and not all of them are in training. When I feel like taking out a horse, I'll take out one of those. I don't have to ride on a racetrack to enjoy it."

"It was your dream."

"It was one of my dreams. You're giving me reasons to dream new dreams." She interlaced her fingers behind his neck, feeling muscles there. Jake loved her! He'd said it in a way that could not be mistaken. "I'll go to Elizabeth and tell her we've decided that she'll be Silver's jockey from now on. I'll show her how to win him over." She could see how it would be, and though the sacrifice stung, she wasn't sorry. "It'll take Elizabeth time, but for Silver Leaf, she'll be willing to put in the time. And she'll be excellent. She is excellent. They'll win together, and you and Bo and Meg will have your champion horse."

"Lyndie," he whispered. "I don't care about having a champion horse so long as I have you."

"Even so, you'll see what'll happen. You'll have me and your champion horse, too."

He caught an escaping tear on his thumb, wiping it away with incredible softness. "Will you come to the track and train horses with me?"

"Of course I will." Standing next to him at the rail had been the best part of her day.

"When my horses go to New York, they'll go without me."

"You'll stay in Holley?"

"Yes, because you can't leave Mollie."

"No. I can't."

"And I can't leave you."

She sniffed, used the back of a hand to dash away the last of her tears, and returned her hands to behind his neck. "Speaking of Mollie, I want you to know that she's improved. We brought her home today."

"That's very good news."

"Very."

He gave her a small and crooked smile.

"Did . . ." Her brows lowered as sudden suspicion twined through her. "Did you go see Mollie this past week?"

"Just once."

"And God used her to help you, didn't He?"

"God helped me. I don't know if He used Mollie."

"Of course He did! He always uses Mollie to heal." She laughed, then found herself getting choked up all over again. "You're different. And it's because God changed you." She could see it in him. She could sense it. Jake had finally made his way back to the God who loved him and had never stopped pursuing him.

Jake's fear for her safety, she knew, stemmed from his mistaken belief that her protection rested on his shoulders. One day, he'd see that it didn't. In time, she believed that Jake could learn to trust the God who was able, the God who was good, with it all. If God had the power to overcome Jake's darkness and return Jake to Himself, then He had the power to accomplish still more. In time.

In her mind she saw a picture taking shape. The once gloomy prince stood in the center of the page, with beams of sun pouring down on him from heaven. And not just upon him. The sun was also inside of him, illuminating. He'd swept the grinning blond fairy into his arms. The unicorns and the red-haired fairy circled them, applauding while roses fell from the sky.

"I guess," Jake said, "the roof of this building isn't going to get ripped off by a tornado."

The lightning and thunder had bowled past them. She could hear their fury receding into the distance. "I guess not. It looks like you and I aren't going to get blown away this time."

"*You* blow me away." Seriousness overtook his features. "I love you, Lyndie. I'll always love you. As long as there's an earth and a sun," he promised. "Longer. I will love you."

She rose on her toes to kiss him again, elation singing through every fiber of her. She could sense the awe-inspiring generosity of God's blessing. God had made a way for her to return to Jake and him to her.

Jake. The best friend of her childhood. Her defender. The one she would defend.

Her future.

EPILOGUE

He felt Rob's wrist for a pulse. No pulse. He rose up, placing his joined palms on Rob's chest to begin chest compressions, counting out loud to focus his mind and his efforts.

A part of him knew it was too late for CPR to help. But he couldn't stop. It wasn't too late. He wouldn't let it be too late.

Panzetti and Scott and Barnes were his men. He'd picked them all to ride in his Humvee today. This couldn't be happening. He was responsible for these men—*my God . . . his men*. Their safety depended on him and he wanted to go back in time and let all of them—any of them—live and him die. He hadn't seen the IEDs. He'd overlooked something.

He continued CPR, devastated, wild inside, as the chopper lowered. Whipping wind and the roar of the blades pounded him. He was a shattered man who shouldn't be alive, and all he could think while the blood dripped from the wound on his face onto Panzetti's torso was: *no. No! No, no, no—*

"Jake." A hand gripped his shoulder, calm and reassuring. "Wake up. You're having a nightmare, my love."

Lyndie. Though his heart was racing and confused panic beat against him from the inside, her presence instantly began to settle him.

The warmth and softness of her body stretched alongside him in their bed. He opened his eyes to see her in the semi-darkness, raised up on one elbow, looking down at him. Strands of her hair trailed onto his bare chest. The scent of a waterfall, fresh and peaceful, filled his senses. Her scent.

Hoarsely, he whispered her name.

"Yes, I'm here."

Here. He was no longer left to deal with his memories alone, thank God. He pulled her against him, holding her with fierce, possessive power and rolling them both onto their sides. She clung to him, her slender arms surprisingly strong.

In the six months leading up to their wedding and in the two months since, he'd only had the nightmare a handful of times. It was losing its power over him, slowly letting go.

Jake could just make out her features in the dim glow of the nightlight she always left on for him. Their bedroom, here on the second story of the building she called the Candy Shoppe, surrounded them. Antique windows, blankets, snoring animals.

"Are you all right?" She stroked her fingers over his cheek and into the hair above his ear.

He nodded, even though he wasn't yet. The scene in Iraq still had its hooks in him, but he didn't want to say so and worry her.

"Liar." She spoke the word gently.

He'd told her every detail of the things he'd seen and experienced on his tours.

"It wasn't your fault, Jake." She assured him of this every time he faced a setback, like now. Did she know that her words flowed into him like light? "God had a reason for sparing your life. He has plans for you and a future."

"With you."

"With me. A love like ours only comes along once in a hundred years, you know." She smiled.

"Once in a thousand. I love you, Lyndie. I love you so much." Fervently, he clasped her to him and kissed her.

He loved her. He loved her with single-minded commitment as deep as the ocean. As powerful as the tide.

"For I know the plans I have for you,"
declares the Lord,
"plans to prosper you and not to harm you,
plans to give you hope and a future."

—Jeremiah 29:11

QUESTIONS
FOR CONVERSATION

1. Lyndie and Jake were childhood friends. Did you have someone you'd consider to be your childhood "best friend"? Do you still have clear memories of that person? Do you still feel fondly toward them? Still keep in touch?

2. *A Love Like Ours* begins with a prologue that gives the reader a glimpse into Jake and Lyndie's childhood. What did that glimpse add to the story and why do you think Becky Wade included it in the novel?

3. This novel is the third in a four-book series about the Porter family. Do you enjoy reading series? What are some of the things you most appreciate about them in general or about the Porter Family series in particular?

4. Jake is a quintessential brooding hero. How did you feel toward Jake? Why do you think this hero type has had such enduring popularity?

5. According to statistics from the Department of Veterans Affairs, 11-20% of veterans who served in Operations Iraqi Freedom and Enduring Freedom have PTSD in a given year. Civilians who've endured a trauma are also at risk. Have you been personally affected or known someone who's been affected by PTSD?

6. Thoroughbred horse racing plays a large role in the plot of A *Love Like Ours*. Becky Wade loved horses as a child but never owned one of her own. She enjoyed "owning" Silver Leaf while writing this story. What did/didn't you like about the horse-related plotline? Did you learn anything about horse racing that you didn't know before?

7. How do you think God used Lyndie's history with Mollie to prepare Lyndie for a relationship with Jake?

8. The theme of this book is "finding hope." Jake tries to make Lyndie the source of his hope, but he soon discovers that even his powerful love for her isn't enough to redeem him. Why do you think we're so susceptible to looking for hope in sources apart from God?

9. Those of you who read the first two books in the Porter Family series might remember Amber Richardson's appearance in *Undeniably Yours*. In *A Love Like Ours* Amber wrestles with waiting on God's timing instead of giving in to the temptation to force her own timing. Has waiting on God's timing ever been difficult for you?

10. After Lyndie and Jake's first kiss, Lyndie struggles with her feelings for Jake because she knows he's an unbeliever and that her hopes of him changing in the future might prove futile. Have you or your family members ever struggled with this dilemma?

11. What scenes from the book stick out most in your memory?

12. How did you feel about Lyndie's decision at the end of the novel to give up her dream of jockeying Silver Leaf? What did her sacrifice prove about her character?

Becky Wade is a native of California who attended Baylor University, met and married a Texan, and moved to Dallas. She published historical romances for the general market, then put her career on hold for several years to care for her children. When God called her back to writing, Becky knew He meant for her to turn her attention to Christian fiction. Her humorous, heart-pounding contemporary romance novels have won the Carol Award, the INSPY Award, and the Inspirational Reader's Choice Award for Romance. Becky lives in Dallas, Texas, with her husband and three children.

To find out more about Becky and her books,
visit www.beckywade.com.

More from Becky Wade

Visit beckywade.com for a full list of her books.

Genealogist Nora Bradford has decided that focusing on her work is far safer than romance. But when a former Navy Seal hires her to find his birth mother, their connection is undeniable. The trouble is they seem to have met the right person at the worst possible time.

True to You
BRADFORD SISTERS ROMANCE

Burned out on work and disappointed in dating relationships, Kate Donovan decides to take a break from both to help restore her grandmother's home. But when she encounters the former hockey star hired to do the renovations, Kate discovers her heart may have other plans.

My Stubborn Heart

If you enjoyed *A Love Like Ours*, you may also like . . .

Nurse practitioner Mia Robinson is done with dating. Instead, she's focused on caring for her teenage sister, Lucy—who, it turns out, is pregnant and plans to marry her boyfriend. Mia is determined to stop the wedding, but she's in for a surprise when she meets the best man.

The Two of Us by Victoria Bylin
victoriabylin.com

On a visit home to Maple Valley, Iowa, political speechwriter Logan Walker meets intriguing reporter Amelia Bentley. She wants his help on a story, and he wants to get to know her better. Their attraction is mutual, but what will happen when he tells her the real reason he's returned?

Like Never Before by Melissa Tagg
melissatagg.com

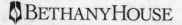